THE THIEF OF TIME

John Boyne

BLACK SWAN

TRANSWORLD PUBLISHERS
61–63 Uxbridge Road, London W5 5SA
A Random House Group Company
www.rbooks.co.uk

THE THIEF OF TIME
A BLACK SWAN BOOK: 9780552776158

First published in Great Britain
in 2000 by Weidenfeld & Nicolson
Black Swan export edition published 2010
Black Swan edition published 2011

Addresses for Random House Group Ltd companies outside the UK
can be found at: www.randomhouse.co.uk
The Random House Group Ltd Reg. No. 954009

The Random House Group Limited supports The Forest Stewardship
Council (FSC), the leading international forest certification organisation.
All our titles that are printed on Greenpeace approved FSC certified
paper carry the FSC logo. Our paper procurement policy can be
found at www.rbooks.co.uk/environment

Typeset in 11/14pt Giovanni Book by
Kestrel Data, Exeter, Devon.
Printed in the UK by
CPI Cox & Wyman, Reading, RG1 8EX.

2 4 6 8 10 9 7 5 3 1

Mixed Sources
Product group from well-managed
forests and other controlled sources
www.fsc.org Cert no. TT-COC-2139
© 1996 Forest Stewardship Council
FSC

Acclaim for *The Boy in the Striped Pyjamas*:

'A small wonder of a book. A particular historical moment, one that cannot be told too often'
Guardian

'Simply written and highly memorable. There are no monstrosities on the page but the true horror is all the more potent for being implicit'
Ireland on Sunday

'The Holocaust as a subject insists on respect, precludes criticism, prefers silence. One thing is clear: this book will not go gently into any good night'
Observer

'An extraordinary tale of friendship and the horrors of war. Raw literary talent at its best'
Irish Independent

'Full of shocking juxtapositions and leads to a horrifying denouement . . . this is a deeply affecting novel'
Sunday Times

'A book that lingers in the mind for quite some time. A subtle, calculatedly simple and ultimately moving story'
Irish Times

'It's a great book, energetic, vivid, and amazing in the scope of its appeal. In the space of three days it had been read, and loved, by everybody in my house. The dog felt left out'
Roddy Doyle

'Stays ahead of its readers before delivering its killer-punch final pages'
Independent

By John Boyne

Novels
The Thief of Time
The Congress of Rough Riders
Crippen
Next of Kin
Mutiny on the Bounty
The House of Special Purpose

Novels for Younger Readers
The Boy in the Striped Pyjamas
Noah Barleywater Runs Away

Novellas
The Second Child
The Dare

*For my parents
and in memory of Michael*

Acknowledgements

For their advice and encouragement, thanks to: Seán and Helen Boyne, Carol and Rory Lynch, Paul Boyne, Sinéad Boyne, Lily and Tessie Canavan; Anne Griffin, Gareth Quill, Gary O'Neill, Katherine Gallagher, John Gorman, Kevin Manning, Michele Birch, Linda Miller, Noel Murphy and Paula Comerford; Simon Trewin and Neil Taylor.

Chapter 1

A Beginning

I don't die. I just get older and older and older.

To look at me today, you would most likely suggest that I am a man approaching fifty years of age. I stand at precisely six feet and one half inch in height – a perfectly reasonable stance for any man, you will agree. My weight fluctuates between 190 and 220 pounds – again, not unusual, although I am forced to admit that the number tends to swing from the lower to the higher range gradually as the year progresses, for I make it a standard exercise to go on a crash diet every January and do not allow myself to return to any form of gluttonous excess until after the month of August, when the chills set in and I find myself in need of a little gentle padding. I have been fortunate in that my hair – once thick and dark and blessed with a slight wave – has resisted the temptation to fall out altogether and instead has simply thinned slightly across the top and turned a rather attractive shade of grey. My skin is tanned and, while I will admit to a few small lines beneath my eyes, only the harshest of critics would suggest that I have wrinkles. Throughout the years, there have been those – both men and women – who have indicated that I am an attractive man, possessed of a crisp sexual allure.

The suggestion, however, regarding my age – that I am perhaps not quite fifty years old – would flatter me immensely. For it is many years now since I have been able to say in all honesty that I have only seen half a century. This is simply the age, or at least the visual representation of an age, at which I have been stuck for a large proportion of my 256 years of life. I am an old man. I may seem young – relatively speaking – and not physically dissimilar to a large proportion of men born while Truman was in the White House, but I am far from any flush of normal youth. It has long been my belief that looks are the most deceptive of all human traits and I am pleased to stand as proof positive of my own theory.

I was born in Paris in 1743, during the Bourbon dynasty, when Louis XV was on the throne and the city was still relatively peaceful. Obviously, I recall very little of the political times, but I do have some early memories of my parents, Jean and Marie Zéla. We were reasonably well off, despite the fact that France was then immersed in a series of financial crises; the country appeared to be living in the shadow of our frequent small wars which drained the cities of both their natural resources and the men who might help excavate them.

My father died when I was four, but not on a battle-field. He worked as a transcriber for a famous dramatist of the time whose name I could offer, but as he and his works have since been completely forgotten, it would mean nothing to you. I have decided, for the most part, to keep the unknown names out of this memoir in order to prevent myself from having to present a cast list at the start – you can meet an awful lot of people in 256 years, you know. He was murdered on his way home from the theatre late one night by – who knows? A sharp object to the back of the neck threw him to the ground and a blade across the throat saw him off. His killer was never caught; random acts of violence were as common then as they are today and justice as arbitrary. But the dramatist himself had been a kind man and he had allocated my mother a pension, and so for her remaining years we never went hungry.

My mother, Marie, lived until 1758, by which time she had married again to one of the actors in the theatre company where my father had worked, a Philippe DuMarqué, who had delusions of grandeur and claimed to have once performed before Pope Benedict XIV in Rome, a claim which on one occasion was mocked by my mother, resulting in a severe beating from her charming husband. The marriage, while unhappy and stained with a recurring theme of violence, did however result in a son, a half-brother for me, named Tomas, which has since become a family name. Indeed, Tomas's great-great-great-great-great-great-great-grandson Tommy lives only a few miles away from me now, in central London, and we meet regularly for dinner, when I invariably 'loan' him money to pay off the debts he accrues from his extravagant and ambitious lifestyle, not to mention his – to speak plainly – pharmaceutical bills.

This same lad is only twenty-two years old and I very much doubt if he will live to see twenty-three. His nose is practically on fire from the amount of cocaine that he has inserted into it over the past eight years – it's constantly twitching, like the nose of a housewife witch – and his eyes wear a permanently glazed and giddy expression. When we dine together, always at my expense, he is prone to bouts of either nervous energy or severe depression. I've seen him hysterical and catatonic and am unsure which state I prefer. He laughs suddenly, for no apparent reason, and always disappears shortly after I have loaned him some more money when pressing business whisks him away. I would attempt to seek help for him but his lineage has always been troublesome and, as you shall see, every one of his ancestors has met with an unhappy ending so there is little point. I am long past the age when I will try to interfere in any of their lives. They don't appreciate my help anyway. I feel that I shouldn't grow too attached to any of these boys because the Tomases, the Thomases, the Thoms, the Toms and the Tommys invariably die young and there's always another one waiting around the corner to bother me. Indeed, only last week Tommy informed me that he has 'knocked up', as he so charmingly puts it, his current girlfriend, so I can only assume from experience that his own days are now numbered. It's midsummer now and the child is due around Christmas time; he has provided an heir to the DuMarqué line and, like the mate of a black widow spider, has thus outlived his usefulness.

I might add at this point that it was not until around the end of the eighteenth century, at which time I was reaching fifty years old anyway, that I stopped the physical act of ageing. Until then I was a man like any other, although I always took a particular pride in my appearance – atypical of the times – and made sure to keep both my body and mind healthy, something which in itself wasn't to become fashionable for another hundred and fifty years or so. In fact, I seem to recall noticing, some time around 1793 or 1794, that my physical appearance was remaining intact, something

14

which pleased me at the time, not least because to live to that age was practically unheard of in the late eighteenth century. By about 1810, it was frightening to me as by rights I should have looked like a man approaching seventy and by 1843, the hundredth anniversary of my birth, I knew that something unusual was occurring. By then I was learning to live with it. I have never sought medical advice on my condition as my motto has long been 'why tempt fate?' And I am not one of these long-living fictional characters who prays for death as a release from the captivity of eternal life; not for me the endless whining and wailing of the undead. After all, I am perfectly happy. I lead a constructive existence. I contribute to the world in which I live. And perhaps my life will not be eternal anyway. Just because I am 256 does not necessarily mean that I will survive to 257. Although I suspect I will.

But I am moving ahead of myself now by the best part of two and a half centuries so allow me to return for a moment, if I may, to my stepfather Philippe who outlived my mother only owing to the fact that he beat her one too many times and she collapsed in a heap on the floor one evening with blood emerging from her mouth and her left ear and never rose again. I was fifteen years old at the time and having seen to it that she got a decent burial and Philippe had been tried and executed for his crime, I left Paris with the infant Tomas to seek my fortune.

And it was as a fifteen-year-old boy, travelling from Calais to Dover with my half-brother in tow, that I met Dominique Sauvet, my first true love and quite possibly the girl against whom none of my subsequent nineteen wives or nine hundred lovers could ever quite compare.

Chapter 2

Meeting Dominique

I have often heard it stated that one never forgets one's first love; the novelty of the emotions alone should be enough to ensure a long-lasting memory in all but the hardest of hearts. But, while this should not be too unusual for the average man who takes maybe a dozen lovers in a lifetime, along with a wife or two, it is a little more difficult for someone who has lived as long as I have. I dare say that I have forgotten the names and identities of hundreds of women with whom I have enjoyed liaisons – on a good day, I can actually recall only about fourteen or fifteen of my wives – but Dominique Sauvet is fixed in my memory like a landmark of when I left my childhood behind to begin a new life.

The boat from Calais to Dover was crowded and dirty and it was difficult to escape the stale, miserable stench of urine, perspiration and dead fish. Nevertheless, I was exuberant from having seen my stepfather executed a few days earlier. From the safety of a small crowd, I had willed him to look in my direction as he placed his head upon the block and he did, for a brief moment, and while our eyes met I feared that in his terror he did not recognize me. Although it chilled me, I was glad he was going to die. Throughout the centuries, though, I have not forgotten the image of the axe falling upon his neck, the sudden slice and the groan of the people, intermingled with a cheer and the sound of a young man vomiting. I remember once, when I was aged around 115, hearing Charles Dickens read from a novel of his which contained a guillotine scene and being forced to stand up and walk out, so disconcerting was the memory of that day a century earlier, so chilling the recollection of my stepfather smiling at me before his life ended, although the guillotine itself would not be introduced until the Revolution began, some thirty-odd years later, I recall the novelist pinning me with a chilly glance as I left, thinking perhaps that I objected to his work or found it dull, something which was impossible.

I chose England as our new home because it was an island, unconnected to France in any way, and I liked the idea of being in a place which was independent and entire unto itself. It was not a long journey and I spent much of it tending to the five-year-old Tomas, who was ill and kept attempting to throw up what was no longer in his stomach over the side of ship. I brought my brother to the railings and sat him down with the wind blowing in his face, hoping that the fresh air might help him somewhat and it was then that I noticed Dominique Sauvet, who was standing only a few feet away from us, her thick dark hair blowing backwards and picking up the light as she stared back towards France, towards the memories of her own troubles.

She caught me staring and stared back briefly before turning away. A moment later, she looked at me again and I blushed and fell in love and picked up Tomas, who instantly started to scream again in pain.

17

'Be quiet!' I urged him. 'Hush!' I did not want it to appear that I was incapable of looking after the child, yet I was also loath to allow him to wander around aimlessly, crying and screaming and urinating at will, like some of the other children on the boat.

'I have some fresh water,' said Dominique, approaching us and touching me on the shoulder lightly, her thin pale fingers glancing off that part of my skin which was revealed by the long tear in my cheap shirt, making my whole body burst into a flame of excitement. 'Perhaps that would calm him down a little?'

'Thank you, but he'll be fine,' I answered nervously, afraid to talk with this vision of beauty, simultaneously cursing my own ineptitude. I was just a boy and unable to pretend otherwise.

'Really, I don't need it,' she continued. 'It won't be long before we arrive anyway.' She sat down and I turned around slowly, watching as her hand slid down the front of her dress and then emerged with a small, thin bottle of clear water. 'I have kept it hidden,' she explained. 'I was afraid someone might try to steal it.'

I smiled and accepted the proffered bottle, watching her now as I unscrewed the cap and handed it to Tomas, who drank a little of it gratefully. Peace was restored to him and I sighed in relief.

'Thank you,' I said. 'You are very kind.'

'I made sure to carry some provisions with me when we left Calais,' she said, 'just in case. Where are your parents anyway? Shouldn't they be taking charge of the boy?'

'They lie six feet underground in a Parisian graveyard,' I told her. 'One murdered by her husband, one murdered by thieves.'

'I'm sorry,' she said. 'Then you are like me. Travelling alone.'

'I have my brother.'

'Of course. What's your name anyway?'

I extended a hand towards her and felt mature, like an adult, as I did so, as if the very act of shaking hands asserted my independence. 'Matthieu,' I replied. 'Matthieu Zéla. And this belching creature is my brother, Tomas.'

'Dominique Sauvet,' she said, ignoring my hand and giving us both a light peck on the cheek which stirred me even more. 'Pleased to meet you,' she added.

Our relationship began at that moment and developed later that night in a tiny room in a Dover hostel where we three took refuge. Dominique was four years older than me at nineteen and naturally had a little more experience in romantic matters than I had. We lay in the bed together, holding each other for warmth, and tense with our desires. Eventually, her hand slid down beneath the thin, moth-eaten sheet that barely covered us and roamed around my chest and below, until we kissed and allowed ourselves to become consumed with our passion.

When we woke the next morning, I was filled with fear for what had happened. I looked at her body beside me, the sheets covering her enough to hide her modesty but none the less causing me to feel a rush of desire once again, and was afraid that she would wake up and regret our behaviour of the night before. Indeed, when her eyes eventually opened, there was an awkwardness at first as she covered herself even further with the single sheet – thus revealing more of my own body to her which caused me no end of embarrassment – until finally she relented and pulled me to her once again with a sigh.

We spent that day walking around Dover with Tomas in tow, looking to the world no doubt as if we were husband and wife and Tomas our son. I was filled with joy, sure that this was as perfect a life as I could ever possibly have. I wanted the day to carry on for ever and yet I also wanted it to pass by quickly, that we might return to our bedroom as soon as possible.

But that night I had a shock. Dominique told me to sleep on the floor with Tomas and, when I protested, she said that if I did not then she would give me the bed and sleep on the floor herself, at which point I relented. I wanted to ask her what was wrong, why she was suddenly rejecting me like this, but could not find the words. I thought she would think me stupid, infantile, a baby, if I demanded more from her than she wanted to give, and was determined not to have her despise me. Already I was thinking that I wanted to take care of her, to be with her for ever, but I have no doubt now that she was thinking that I was only fifteen years of age and that, if she was to have any real future in the world, it was unlikely that it would be with me. She was holding out for something better.

A mistake, as it turned out.

Chapter 3

January 1999

I live in a pleasant, south-facing apartment in Piccadilly, London. It is the basement flat of a four-storey house. The upper part of the property is lived in by a former minister in Mrs Thatcher's cabinet whose attempts to secure a place in the Lords were given short shrift by her successor Mr Major – whom he despised for an incident at the Treasury some years before – and who has since wound up in the less prestigious but far more financially rewarding world of satellite broadcasting. As a major shareholder in the corporation which employs my upstairs neighbour, I take an interest in his career and was partly responsible for his being granted a thrice weekly political chat-show, which has recently been performing badly in the ratings, owing to the general perception of him as a has-been. Although I find the public's belief that anyone from the previous decade is a has-been completely absurd – surely my own longevity is testament to that – I suspect that the man's career is coming to an end and I regret it, for he is a pleasant enough man with a taste for fine things, in which respect we are quite similar. He has been kind enough to invite me into his home on a number of occasions and I once dined off a rather fine piece of mid-nineteenth-century

Hungarian dishware which I could have sworn I saw being made in Tatabánya while I was honeymooning with, if I remember correctly, Jane Dealey (1830–1866, *m.* 1863). Lovely girl. Fine features. Awful end.

I could afford to live in the same luxury as my broadcasting friend but really can't be bothered. Right now, simplicity suits me. I've lived rough and I've lived well. I've slept on streets and collapsed drunk in palaces, a felonious vagrant or vomiting fool. I'll most likely do both again. I took the apartment in 1992 and have been here ever since. I've made it quite the home. There is a small vestibule as you enter the front door, leading into a tiny hallway which opens out into the living room – sunken by a step – with a beautiful set of bay windows. Here, I keep my books, my recordings, my piano and my pipes. Scattered around the rest of the apartment is a bedroom, a bathroom and a small guest room which is only ever used by my many times removed nephew Tommy, who calls around to see me from time to time, whenever he needs cash.

Financially, I have been fortunate in life. I can't quite put my finger on how I made my money but there's an awful lot of it there. Most of it has grown without my realizing it. To make the leap from the Dover boat to my position today there are certainly many jobs and positions which I have taken but I think I have been lucky in that I always kept my money as money, never stocks, never shares, never insurance policies or pensions. (Life insurance is a waste of money as far as I am concerned.) I had a friend – Denton Irving – who lost a bundle in the Wall Street crash in the early part of this century. One of those chaps who threw himself from his office window out of a sense of failure. Foolish chap; personalizing something which the whole country went through. It was hardly his fault. Even as he jumped he could surely see half of New York's Old Money standing in their hotel windows, contemplating their own ends. Actually, he even failed at that. He misjudged the distance and ended up with a broken leg, a smashed arm and a couple of fractured ribs in the middle of the Avenue of the Americas, screaming in agony for about ten seconds before a tram came around the corner at speed and finished him off. He got what he wanted, I suppose.

I have always spent money too, believing that there's precious little point in having the stuff if you don't use it to make yourself comfortable. I have no offspring so there's no one to leave it to in the unlikely event of my death – except for the current Tommy, of course – and, even if there were, I rather feel a person should make his or her own way without any outside help.

I never criticize the times either. I know a couple of young chaps of about seventy or eighty who complain about the world that they're living in and the changes which constantly take place in it. I speak to them every so often in my club and I find their disdain for Today a little ridiculous. They refuse to have so-called modern contraptions in their homes, feigning a lack of comprehension whenever a telephone rings or someone asks them for their fax number. Nonsensical. The telephone predates them, for heaven's sake. I say take whatever the age offers you. That's what living is all about. Personally, I think the late twentieth century has been perfectly all right. A little dull at times, perhaps, although I did become momentarily obsessed with the American space programme during the 1960s, but it'll do for now; I've known worse. You should have tried things a century earlier. End of the nineteenth. I have about two memories of a twenty-year period back then, things were so dull. And one of those is simply of a bad back complaint that kept me in bed for six months.

In mid-January, Tommy phoned me and invited me to dinner for the fourth time in three weeks. I hadn't laid eyes on him since before Christmas and had so far managed to put him off. But I knew that any further delay would induce him to come around late at night, and whenever he did that he would end up staying over – something I discouraged. Overnight guests are fine the night before, when there's a drink to be taken and a conversation to be had, but in the morning there's always an awkwardness when you are wishing they would just go home and let you get on with your routine. He's not my favourite of the Thomases, certainly not a patch on his great-great-great-grandfather, but he's not the worst either. There's a certain charming arrogance to the lad, a mixture of self-confidence, *naïveté* and recklessness which attracts me. At twenty-two, he's a twenty-first-century boy if ever I saw one. If he can simply make it that far.

We met in a West End restaurant which was a little busier than I had hoped. The problem with being seen in public with Tommy is that it's impossible to spend any private time with him whatsoever. From the minute he walks into a room until the minute he walks out, everyone is staring and whispering and casting furtive glances at him. His celebrity both intimidates and hypnotizes people in equal parts and I have the dubious thrill of being caught up in it all. Last Tuesday night was no different. He arrived late and almost collapsed through the door, smiling as he came towards me in a dark Versace suit with a dark shirt and dark tie to match, looking like something from a funeral parlour or an Italian-American Mafia film. His hair was cut jagged just above the shoulder and he sported a two-day stubble. He fell into the seat, grinning at me and licking his lips, oblivious to the silence that had fallen on the restaurant. Thrice weekly appearances in the living rooms of the nation, not to mention the omnibus repeats at the weekend, have made my nephew into something of a celebrity. And the consistency of that celebrity has made him immune to its accompanying irritations.

Tommy, like so many of the Thomases before him, is a handsome boy and as he matures (physically) he only becomes more attractive to people. He has been in his television programme for eight years now, ever since he was fourteen, and has moved from being a teenage sensation, to a magazine cover boy, to a twenty-two-year-old national treasure. He has enjoyed two number one singles (although his album failed to make the top ten) and even spent six months in a production of *Aladdin* in the West End where there was widespread screaming whenever he appeared in his waistcoat, pantaloons and precious little else. He is fond of recounting how he was voted 'most shaggable boy' four years running in some teen magazine, a title that chills me but delights him. He knows the television business inside out. He's not really an actor, he's a star.

His screen persona is that of a good hearted angel, not too blessed in the brains department, to whom nothing good ever happens. Since his first appearance in the programme in the early nineties, his character has appeared to find no reason whatsoever to leave a one mile radius of London. I'm not even sure he knows that any other world exists. He has grown up there, gone to school there, and now works there. He has had several girlfriends, two wives, enjoyed an affair with his sister and an unconsummated romance with another boy – quite controversial at the time – was briefly being considered by an important football club before leukaemia laid him low, had a great love for the ballet which he was obliged to keep secret, flirted with drink, drugs and athletics, and has done God only knows how many other things in his illustrious career. Any other boy would be dead by now with all the exertions that have come his way. Tommy – or 'Sam Cutler' as the nation better knows him – lives on and always comes back for more. He has, for want of a better word, pluck. Apparently this endears him to grandmothers, mothers and daughters alike, not to mention quite a few young men who copy his mannerisms and catchphrases with gay abandon.

'You look ill,' I told him as we ate, glancing briefly at his pale, blotchy skin and the red rings hovering beneath his eyes. 'And can we *please* just eat in peace?' I begged a hovering waitress who was holding a notebook and pen expectantly as she stared at her hero with barely disguised lust.

'It's the make-up, Uncle Matt,' said Tommy. 'You have no idea what it does to my skin. I used it at first because you need a little for the cameras, but then it affected my skin so badly that I needed even more to look any way normal. Now I look like Zsa Zsa Gabor on screen and Andy Warhol off.'

'Your nose is inflamed,' I observed. 'You take too many drugs. You'll burn a hole in it one of these days. Just a suggestion, but perhaps you should try injecting rather than inhaling?'

'I don't do drugs,' he shrugged, his voice perfectly

even, as if he felt it was simply the socially correct thing to do – *denying* it, I mean – while being completely aware that neither of us believed him for a moment.

'It's not that I'm *opposed* to it, you understand,' I said, dabbing at my lips with a napkin. I was hardly in a position to lecture him. After all, I was an opium fiend at the turn of the century and I survived it. Lord, what I went through with that though. 'It's just that the drugs that you take will kill you. Unless you take them right, that is.'

'Unless I what?' He looked at me, baffled, grasping a hand around the base of his wine glass and rotating it slowly.

'The problem with today's young people,' I said, 'isn't that they do things which are bad for them, as so much of the media likes to think. It's that they don't do these things right. You're all so intent on getting off your heads on drugs that you don't think about the fact that you could overdose and, to put it plainly, die. You drink until your liver explodes. You smoke until your lungs collapse beneath the rot. You create diseases which threaten to wipe you out. Have fun, by all means. Be debauched, it's your duty. But be wise about it. All things in excess, but just know how to cope with them, that's all I ask.'

'I don't do drugs, Uncle Matt,' he repeated, his voice firm but unconvincing.

'Then why do you want to borrow money from me?'

'Who says I do?'

'Why else would you be here?'

'The pleasure of your company?'

I laughed. It was a nice thought, if nothing else. I enjoyed the way he stuck to convention. 'You're so famous,' I observed, mystified by the very idea. 'And yet you're paid so little. I don't understand that. Why is it exactly? Explain it to me.'

'It's a catch-22,' said Tommy. 'There's a standard rate for what I do, and it's not very high. I can't leave because I'm typecast now and would never get another job – unless I went into production or something, which is exactly what I should do because I know this industry from the top down. I've seen every kind of scam pulled and every kind of deal ruined. That's what I want to look towards when I get older. Eight years playing some gormless *fuck* on some stupid TV show doesn't exactly lead to a Martin Scorsese movie, you know. For Christ's sake, I'm lucky if I get offered the chance to press the button on the National Lottery more than once a year. You know I was supposed to do that a couple of months ago but they bumped me?'

'Yes, you mentioned.'

'And for Madonna of all people. *Madonna!* For Christ's sake, how am I supposed to compete with that? And I work for the fucking BBC, she doesn't. You'd think they'd show a little bit of loyalty. But the lifestyle I lead to perpetuate my success demands a certain level of solvency. I can't win. I'm like a hamster on a wheel. I'd take on some advertising, do a little modelling perhaps, but it's in my contract that I'm not allowed to promote any products while still working on the show. Otherwise I swear I'd be a capitalist *whore* right now. I'd advertise everything from aftershave to tampons if I could.'

I shrugged. It made sense, I suppose. 'I can let you have a couple of thousand,' I said. 'But I'd rather pay off some of your bills for you than just give you cash outright. You don't have men after you by any chance, do you?'

'Men. Women. Anything with a pulse follows me

28

down the street,' he said with a cocky smile. 'I got my teeth bleached last week, by the way,' he added as a *non sequitur*, pulling back his lips to show me a melon slice of snow-white teeth. 'They look good, don't they?'

'*Men*,' I repeated. 'Don't play stupid with me. Save it for your show.'

'What kind of men? What do you mean?'

'You know exactly what I mean, Tommy. Loan sharks. Dealers. Men of dubious character.' I leaned forward and stared him in the eye. 'Do you owe people money?' I demanded. 'Is that what you're worried about? I've seen men laid low by such people. Ancestors of yours, for example.'

He sat back and his tongue skirted around the inside of his mouth slowly. I could see it pushing his left cheek out slightly as he watched me. 'I could do with a couple of grand,' he said. 'If you've got it to spare. I'm sorting myself out, you know.'

'Oh, I'm sure you are.'

'It's all going to come together for me.'

'I hope it does,' I said dismissively, standing up and adjusting my tie slightly as I made to leave. 'I have your account details at home. I'll post the money for you tomorrow. When can I expect to hear from you next? A couple of weeks? Will you have spent it all by then?'

He smiled at me and sat back with a shrug. I touched him lightly on the shoulder as I said goodbye, admiring the silk in his shirt, which couldn't have come cheap. He has a taste for clothes, the current Tommy. When he dies, the tabloids will have a field day with him.

Chapter 4

Living with Dominique

Dominique, Tomas and I stayed in Dover for the best part of a year. I perfected my English and learned to speak with only a trace of an accent, which I could turn on or off at will. I became a professional pickpocket, wandering the streets from six in the morning until late at night relieving people of their wallets and pocketbooks. I became quite good at it. No one ever felt my hand slip inside the long sleeves of their overcoats, my fingers quickly locating a valuable, a watch, some coins and swallowing them up quickly, but from time to time I misjudged the streets and some civic-minded individual would spot me and raise an alarm. A chase would ensue – often an enjoyable one – and I almost always won, as I was sixteen years old then and in peak condition. The three of us lived well from my dubious endeavours and rented a small room at the back of a public house which was not too dirty or rat-infested. There were two beds in the room, one for Dominique and one for Tomas and me. In the six months since we had first met, we had never enjoyed a repeat of that first night. And Dominique's feelings towards me had become increasingly fraternal. I would lay awake at night, listening to the sounds of her breathing, and

30

sometimes I would crawl over to her bed slowly and feel that night-tinged breath on my face. I would watch her as she slept, racked with the desire to share her bed again.

Dominique observed a slightly distant maternal feeling towards Tomas, taking care of him while I went out to steal, but relinquishing him to me immediately upon my return, almost as if she was simply a childminder, employed to look after the infant and accepting my payment for her work at the end of each day. Tomas was a quiet child, most of the time, and didn't cause much trouble to either of us and, on those rare occasions when we would all spend the evening in our room together, he tended to fall asleep early, allowing us to sit up and talk late into the night, Dominique telling me about her plans for the future, while my mind was always set on seducing her once again. Or allowing her to seduce me, whichever would come first.

'We should leave Dover,' she said to me one night, as it came close to being a full twelve months since we had first arrived. 'We've been here far too long.'

'I like it here,' I said. 'We have enough to get us through every day. We eat well enough, don't we?'

'I don't want to eat "well enough",' she said in frustration. 'I want to eat *well*. I want to *live* well. We'll never get that here. There's no future for us here. We have to move on.'

'But where would we go?' I asked. I could travel all the way from France to England, but once settled I couldn't imagine a world outside of our small room and my kaleidoscope streets. I was happy there.

'We can't survive on your pick-pocketing for ever, Matthieu. I can't, anyway.'

I thought about it and stared at the floor. 'You want

31

to return to France?' I asked and she shook her head quickly.

'I'll never return to France,' she said. 'Never.' She hadn't told me much at that time about why she had left the country of her birth, but I knew that it had something to do with her father, who drank. She was never the kind of girl who opened up very much. It always amazed me that in the few short years that we knew each other, she was never as honest with me as she was on the very first day that we had met. For Dominique, unlike most people I have known in my life, with familiarity grew distance. 'We could go to the country,' she suggested. 'I could find work there.'

'Doing what?'

'In a house, maybe. I've spoken to people about it. There's always openings for servants in houses. I could do that for a while. Make a little money. Save it up. Maybe start my own business somewhere.'

I laughed. 'Don't be ridiculous,' I said. 'How could you do that? You're a girl.' The very idea was outrageous.

'I could do it,' she insisted. 'I'm not sitting in this stinking hole for ever, Matthieu. I don't want to grow old and *die* here. And I don't intend to spend the rest of my life on my knees washing someone else's floors either. I'm willing to give up a few years of my life in order to make something for myself. For us, if you like.'

I thought about it but wasn't sure. I liked Dover. I got a perverse thrill from my life of petty crime. I had even found ways to amuse myself without Dominique's knowledge. I had fallen in with a gang of street boys who led similar lives to my own, indulging in various crimes in order to feed ourselves. Ranging in age from six to eighteen or nineteen, some lived on street corners, finding a place to call their own and collapsing in it every night beneath whatever they could find to keep them warm. Their young bodies had built up an immunity against the cold and disease and they remain among the healthiest people I have ever known in 256 years. Some banded together and shared rooms, sometimes eight or nine to an area no bigger than a prison cell. Some were kept in finer rooms by older men who took a portion of their earnings, molesting them when they felt like it, a knife to the throat, an arm around the ribcage, a grasping mouth around the smooth-skinned neck.

Together we planned more elaborate crimes, often involving no financial reward for ourselves but simply as exciting ways to pass our afternoons, for we were young and given to reckless endeavour. Stealing hansoms, rolling barrels of beer away from cellars, tormenting harmless old ladies; these were all part of a normal day for me and my kind. As my earnings began to grow, I realized that I could keep a portion for myself without telling Dominique and this money went into my developing sexual freedom. I tried not to return to any particular prostitute more than once but it was difficult for me to make sure of that for, whenever I was in some hovel, naked and pressed deep into the body of a girl whose stench of sweat and grime was too easily located beneath the nauseous spray of cheap perfume, it was only Dominique's face that I could see, her almond shaped eyes, her small brown nose, her slim body with the slight scar above her left shoulder where I longed to run my tongue once again. For me, all these girls were Dominique, and for them I was simply a few shillings' worth of boredom. It was a fine life. I was young.

There were girls from the street as well, girls who did not guard their virtue with the same determination as Dominique was now guarding hers. These girls, often the sisters or cousins of my fellow criminals – more often than not, criminals themselves – would capture my mind for a week, sometimes two, but our union would lead to disinterest on my part afterwards and they would quickly move on to the next lad. In the end I either paid for it or went without, for at least with the passing over of money I could pretend that my partner was the one I wanted the most.

It was always bound to happen that I would be caught. The night that sealed our fate in Dover was a dark October evening in 1760. I was standing on a quiet street corner opposite the Law Courts watching for a likely victim to emerge. I saw him – a tall, elderly gentleman, with a black hat and a fine, oak stick – pause briefly as he stood on the street, patting his overcoat to check for his wallet, locating it and moving on with a reassuring smile. I pulled my cap down over my face, looked around me for any spotters, and followed him slowly through the streets.

My footsteps fell in automatic timing with his, my arms hanging loosely by my sides as his own did so that he would not hear me approaching behind him. I reached my hand into his pocket and my fingers clasped around a thick leather wallet within, which I eased out without losing a step. As my hand emerged, I rotated and began to walk off in the opposite direction at a steady pace, my footsteps still in perfect time, ready to return home for the evening, when I heard a voice cry out behind me.

I spun around to see the old man standing in the street, staring in bewilderment at a middle-aged man who was running in my direction, his arms waving in the air as he bore down upon me. I stared too in surprise, unsure what he was after, when I remembered the wallet and realized that he must have spotted me and decided to fulfil some ridiculous sense of civic responsibility. I turned on my heel and ran, cursing my luck but not for a moment believing that I could fail to outrun this giant of a man, whose paunch alone would surely slow him down. I sped on, my long legs leaping across the cobblestones as I tried to make out the direction in which I could make my escape. I wanted to get towards the market square, where I knew there were five separate lanes leading in different directions, each of which gave off on to laneways of their own. There were always crowds there and I would be lost within their number with no difficulty, being, as I was, dressed like every other street boy. But it was dark that night and in my confusion I lost my sense of direction and after a few moments I knew that I had gone wrong and began to worry. The man was gaining on me, shouting for me to stop – which was an unlikely outcome – but as I glanced over my shoulder briefly I could see the determination in his face and worse, the stick in his hand, and felt for the first time a real sense of fear. I saw two laneways ahead off what I thought might be Castle Street, one running left and one running right, chose the latter and was dismayed to find the street growing narrower and narrower ahead of me until a sinking feeling inside confirmed that a wall stood before me, a dead end, too tall to climb, too solid to break through. I turned and stood as the man turned into the street, himself stopping and gasping for breath as he realized that I was cornered.

There was still a chance. I was sixteen. I was strong and fit. He was forty if he was a day. He was lucky to still be alive. If I could simply steer around him quickly before he could grab me, I could continue running as long as I had to. He was almost out of breath while I could have run on for another ten minutes yet without breaking into a sweat, let alone having to slow down. The trick was to get past him.

We stood staring at each other and he cursed at me, calling me a thieving swine, a money grabbing knave to whom he would teach a thing or two when he caught me. I waited until he was as close to the left hand side of the street as I thought he would go, before running right with a shout, determined to outflank him, but he lunged in that direction at the same moment and we collided, me falling to the ground with the weight of him, he falling on top of me with a gasp. I tried to stand up but his reactions were quicker than mine and with one hand he pinned my neck to the ground as his other felt through my pockets for the old man's wallet. Taking it, he put it inside his own and, as I struggled beneath him, he let his stick crash down on my face, blinding me for a moment, the sound of my breaking nose crashing across my head, the taste of blood and mucus in my throat, a sharp white light exploding before my eyes. He rose and my hands went to my face to ease the pain and he let loose with that stick on the rest of me, until I was rolled in a messy ball in the corner of the street, my mouth a mixture of blood and phlegm, my body a separate entity to my mind, my ribs kicked and beaten, my jaw swollen and bruised. I could feel a trickle of blood at my scalp and I know not how long I lay there curled up within myself, before I realized that he had gone and that I could gather myself together and get up.

It was hours before I found my way home, blinded as I was by the blood in my eyes, and, as I pushed open the door, Dominique screamed as she saw me. Tomas burst into tears and hid under the bedclothes. Dominique pulled out a bucket of tepid water and stripped me of my clothes as she tended to my wounds, my body in such pain that I had not even the energy to be excited by her attending to me. I slept for three days and when I woke, clean but battered, aching with pain, she told me that my pick-pocketing days were over for good.

'Say goodbye to Dover, Matthieu,' she said as I opened my one good eye. 'We're leaving the minute you can get out of that bed.'

I was too weak to argue with her and by the time I had recovered my health – several weeks later – our plans had already been determined.

Chapter 5

Constance & The Movie Star

The most short-lived of my marriages occurred in 1921 and, despite its brevity, it is one that I look back upon with a great deal of fondness – Constance was certainly my second-favourite wife of this century. I had moved back to America just after the war, seeking a complete release from all my associations with the hospital, the Foreign Office and the awful Beatrice, widow of my then recently deceased nephew Thomas. I boarded an ocean liner and set sail for the States, enjoying the pleasant and revitalizing few weeks of sunshine and romance which the transatlantic crossing afforded me. I landed in New York and found that to my dismay the city was still obsessed by European affairs and hungry for more information about such matters as Versailles and the Kaiser. Strangers would hear my accent in a local saloon and immediately attempt to engage me in conversation. Had I ever met the King, they would ask? Is it true what they say about him? What news of France? What were the trenches actually like? Really, one of the greatest achievements of this modern age of global television networks is that complete strangers no longer need to ask for the most mundane of information. For that alone, we should be grateful to modern technology.

Irritated by this constant intrusion into my life, and feeling a little lost in the city without friends or employment, I decided to spend one afternoon at a local theatre, watching the newsreels and some of the new kinescopes. The theatre I chose was really no more than a small room with a high ceiling, capable of fitting about twenty-five people in some discomfort, and it was half full as I took my seat in the centre of a row towards the back, as far away from the local *hoipolloi* as possible. The seats were hard and wooden and the place smelled of a startling mix of perspiration and alcohol, but it was dark and it was private so I stayed where I was, knowing that I would grow immune to the unpleasant scents of the populace soon enough. The newsreels began and they were the same old nonsense I had seen a thousand times in real life – war, appeasement, universal suffrage – but the moving pictures amused me. I saw *Easy Street* and *The Cure*, both of which featured Charlie Chaplin, and the crowd groaned when each began – evidently they had seen them before, many times, and were looking for new entertainment already – but almost immediately, they started to laugh along at the fairly slapstick affairs that they were watching. As the projectionist changed the reels in the middle of each feature, I found myself growing restless, anxious to see more, intrigued by the flickering black and white images before me, my mind finally released from the events of recent years, if only for an afternoon. I stayed and watched the same show several times over and by the time I left the theatre – by which time it was dark outside and my throat was dry and in need of liquid refreshment – I had made up my mind.

I would go to Hollywood and work in pictures.

* * *

It was a three-day train journey across the country but it afforded me an opportunity to plan my assault on what I had already perceived would be a fast-growing art form. There would be money to be made in it – already the newspapers were starting to carry features on the enormous riches and playboy lifestyles of Keaton, Sennett, Fairbanks and others. Their tanned visages, so different from their pale, often impoverished *alter egos* that we saw fooling around on screen, shone out from the front pages of the dailies as they pranced about in tennis gear on the lawns of some lavish estate, or in black tie at the latest birthday party for Mary Pickford, Mabel Normand or Edna Purviance. It would not be hard to find a route into this society, I assumed, as I was wealthy and handsome and a recently demobbed Frenchman to boot. With such credentials, how could I fail? Already I had phoned ahead to a real estate agency and rented a house in Beverly Hills for six months and knew that simply by attending a few select parties I could meet all the right people and perhaps spend a year or two enjoying myself. The war was behind me; I needed entertainment. And where better to go in order to find it than the emerging wonderland that was Hollywood, California?

But I was also interested in the idea of working within the industry, at a production level of course, as I am no actor. My first thought was that I should involve myself with the financing of motion pictures, or possibly their distribution, which was still in the process of evolving and creating a network efficiency. While stuck in my railway carriage during those three hot days, I read an interview with Chaplin who at the time was working at First National, and while he came across as a man obsessed with his work, an artist who wanted nothing more than to produce feature after feature after feature without breaking for so much as a weekend in the sun, I felt that there was some hidden meaning in his carefully phrased comments about his relationship with FN. It was a decent place to work, he seemed to be suggesting, but there was no overall control for the artist. He wanted to own the place, he said, or at least run his own studio. In the meantime I believed I could be of some use to him and wrote him a letter suggesting a meeting, implying that I wanted to invest in the motion-picture industry and saw him as its most reliable asset. If my money was to go anywhere, I pointed out, I wanted to take his advice on where I should put it. Perhaps, I suggested, I should even invest it in Chaplin himself.

To my great delight, he telephoned me one evening while I was sitting at home alone, bored with my own company, weary of solitaire, and invited me to lunch the next day at his house, an offer which I gladly accepted. And it was there that I met Constance Delaney.

At the time, Chaplin was living in a rented house only a few streets away from my own. He had just come through a messy divorce with Mildred Harris and the papers had only recently let the scandal die away. He was not the man I expected, so used was I to seeing his tramp incarnation on the screen and in photographs, and when I was led out to the pool area and saw a short, handsome man sitting alone reading Sinclair Lewis, I wondered at first whether he was simply an acquaintance or a family friend of the film star. I had heard that Chaplin's brother Sydney also worked in Hollywood and wondered whether it might not be him. Of course, once he rose and came towards me, his face broad with a white-toothed smile,

I knew immediately who he was but somehow failed to engage that strange sensation one develops upon meeting a person one has only previously seen on a cinema screen, enlarged beyond all reality, a sequence of lines and dots bouncing across canvas. As we talked, I examined his face for elements of the familiar screen persona but the constant smile, the bare upper lip, the hand ruffling through the curly, unhatted hair, was a far cry from the *alter ego* I knew so well and I was left amazed at his ability to transform himself so utterly. He was aged thirty-one then and looked twenty-three. I was 177 and looked like a respectable, wealthy man in my late forties. While there were many aspects to his character that distinguished him from other men, there was one that brought him directly into line with the countrymen of the nation in which he chose to live. He wanted only to speak of the war.

'How much fighting did you see?' he asked me, sitting back in his chair in a pose of relaxation while his eyes flickered with fascination at all times, bouncing from my face, to the trees behind, to the house beyond, to the sky above. 'Was it as bad as the papers reported?'

'I saw some,' I offered reluctantly. 'It wasn't pleasant. I managed to avoid the trenches, except for one brief miserable period. I sat a lot of it out in an encampment in Bordeaux.'

'Doing what?'

'I cracked codes,' I said, shrugging gently, 'intelligence work mostly.'

He laughed. 'That's where you made your money?' he asked me, looking towards the pool and shaking his head as if he had the mark of me now, in a line, in the briefest of sentences. 'Lot of money to be made in war, I expect.'

'I inherited my money,' I said, lying but resenting his implication. 'Believe me, I had no wish to profit from the experience of the last few years. It has been ... unpleasant,' I muttered, understating the experience somewhat.

'Wanted to go myself, you know,' he said quickly, and I noticed how his London accent was being carefully suffused with a nasal American twang. Only the odd word slipped out to betray his origins. Later, I learned that he had taken weekly voice lessons from a speech therapist to improve his American accent, a strange concept for a silent movie star. 'The boys at the top suggested I would be better off here though.'

'I'm sure you were,' I said, not meaning to sound sarcastic as I gestured towards the lavish surroundings with my hand and sipped my margarita, mixed with a little too much lime I thought, but cold and refreshing on the throat nevertheless. 'It's magnificent.'

'I mean working,' he said tetchily. 'Making movies, you know. Sent them all over the world. Free of charge to servicemen when it costs a fortune for any distributor to buy them off the studio. I think the army wanted to have something to show the troops on off days to help improve morale. You might say I earned my medals as chief morale officer for the British Army,' he added with a smile.

It was odd, I thought. In four years I had never seen any movies at all except when I was on leave in a city and paid for them myself. Nor could I remember an awful lot of 'off days' for the servicemen. I tried to change the subject but it was too valuable for him as source material.

'Thought of making a movie about the war, you

43

know,' he said. 'Afraid of trivializing it though. What do you think?'

'I expect there is a lot that has yet to be said about it. It might take a hundred years to get to the heart of the matter.'

'Yes, but we're not going to be here in a hundred years, are we?'

'You probably won't, no.'

'And so we have to start somewhere, yes?' he asked, leaning forward and smiling so widely now that I was afraid his cheeks would crack. 'It's something I'm thinking of anyway,' he said eventually, leaning back and waving his hand dismissively. 'Maybe I'll do it. Maybe not. There is so much time and so many ideas and I am still so young. I am a lucky man, Mr Zéla.'

'Matthieu, please.'

'And I expect you would like to get lucky too, am I right?'

At that moment I saw a movement behind him and two young girls emerged from the house, wearing what I took to be the latest style in bathing wear and hats to cover their hair. They wore swimming goggles across their eyes and all in all they were so covered up as to be laughable. They strode past us without a word, although the first girl, the shorter – in black – laid a hand gently on Chaplin's shoulder as she passed him. For his part, he ignored them except to stroke his shoulder gently after her touch and stare directly into my eyes with possibly the most disturbing smile I had ever seen until then, a smile of such collusion and manipulation that it made me shudder. I heard a splash behind me and the kinetic silence of two swimmers lost beneath the surface, gliding smoothly to the other side of the pool. Chaplin brought his drink to his mouth and took a long swallow, licking his lips in appreciation afterwards.

'There are a lot of advantages to being in this industry at this time, Mr Zéla. Matthieu. A lot of . . . joyful things can come to a wise investor.' He leaned forward and the smile finally vanished now as he took my hand. 'But make no mistake,' he added. 'Timing is everything. And the time is *now*!'

We dined in Chaplin's kitchen that evening, the four of us, eating toasted sandwiches which he made himself and drinking cocktails afterwards in the lounge. The help had been dismissed for the evening and it seemed that our host enjoyed taking control of the kitchen and the fully stocked frigidaire before him, for he spent an awful lot of time judging exactly the right ingredients for the rather simple sandwiches that he was preparing.

Constance Delaney was the older of the two sisters by four years and the evening that we met was three full weeks before her twenty-second birthday. Although I am not usually attracted to extremely young women – my ideal partner (at least since I myself turned forty) has tended to be in the thirty to forty age group – Constance had my attention from the moment she stepped out of the pool and took off her goggles and cap to reveal a black bobbed hairstyle which was quite the style then and the most beautiful eyes I had seen in a century. They were wide, with ovals of chocolate brown swimming in the centre, and when she looked to the side without turning her head, the sheets of white ice which flowed in to take their place transfixed me. She had changed into trousers and a linen shirt – an unusual enough outfit for a woman then – although her younger sister Amelia, who was by Chaplin's side all through the evening and I dare say the night afterwards, was the more obviously feminine of the two, her baby doll dress being only one of the presents with which I later learned her brief romance with celebrity had enriched her.

'What did you do in London, Mr Zéla?' asked Constance, biting into the olive from her Martini as I protested that she must call me by my given name or we could not be friends. 'Before the war, I mean?'

'I lived a lot before the war,' I admitted. 'But it's the strangest thing. These last four years seem to have taken me over so enormously that the past before it fades away like a childhood memory. People remind me of events that took place around the turn of the century and I can hardly remember them. It's almost as if they all took place in a different life. Does that seem strange to you?'

'Not at all. I only have the news reports to go on, of course, but it seems to have been . . .' She searched for the right word and my heart was held by her as I watched her think, knowing that she wanted to find the exact phrase or say nothing at all. She was aware of the effect of that time on those who were part of it.

'Beyond anything that I could comprehend,' she settled on eventually with a shrug. 'Silly of me to try to think up words for such a terrible thing. Here. In California, of all places.'

'That's why I never use any,' said Chaplin, laughing loudly as he poured more drinks, even for Amelia who had barely touched hers. 'Movies are just for the imagination, you see. Not for real life. The silence makes the mind work better. It may be that—'

'Then why do you use so much of that infernal music?'

asked Constance quickly, cutting off his monologue. Chaplin stared at her. 'I mean honestly, Charlie,' she added with a laugh, 'I love your little films as much as anyone but do we really need those awful piano rags that accompany them? Whenever I go, I curse myself for forgetting to bring some cotton wool along for my ears. Remind me, Mr Zéla,' she added, touching my knee gently, 'the next time that *you* take me to a movie theatre.'

'He told you to call him Matthieu,' said Chaplin indignantly, his voice raised a decibel or two above everyone else's. 'And you need that music to reflect the characters and the plots. Fast for action, dirges for misery. You know it exactly. You can sense mood. The music conjures up the emotions as valuably as the performances or the direction. Without the music—'

'Charlie is a wonderful composer,' said Amelia quietly and Chaplin barely missed a beat.

'Kind of you to say, my dear,' he said, his voice so much louder and overpowering than hers that she all but disappeared beneath it. 'But my movies are an all round creation. Writing, directing, acting, composing. It's all part of something which I create out of my own mind. That's why I've had such trouble in the past, trying to wrest control over what I do. Without control, Matthieu, over *everything*, there is nothing at all. You wouldn't ask Booth Tarkington to write a novel and have someone else give him the chapter titles, now would you?'

'No, but you might ask someone to design the lettering on the cover,' said Constance and I couldn't help but smile. It occurred to me how much she disliked her sister's lover and how incapable he was of responding to her barbs, as if he was unaccustomed to women who did not want anything from him. Amelia may have been besotted with the man but it was clear that Constance was in charge and could whisk her away at any time.

'If it was *my* book, I'd design it myself,' said Chaplin, looking towards me with a smile as he sought to edge her away from the conversation and maintain an alliance with me against her, a foolish plan of complicity against a woman of Constance's humour.

'Oh, good heavens!' she cried then and I jumped as she let out a roar of laughter that echoed around the room. 'Don't tell me you *draw* too!'

I continued to see Constance on a daily basis after that and it was she who convinced me not to invest in Chaplin, whose knowledge of his craft had impressed me almost as much as his self-obsession had bored me.

'I've heard him talking about his plans before,' she told me. 'When he gets very drunk, that is, and starts in on his Alexander the Great philosophy. Conquer the world before you're thirty and all that. Too late for him, of course. I dare say he will one day start out on his own, but any investors he brings in will get milked dry. Charlie isn't interested in anyone who isn't as famous as he is, you see. Celebrity is the only thing that interests him. I'm sure a psychologist could make something of it, you know. He'll take every cent you own and he may even make you a lot of money in return but you'll have no control over what he does with it. You'll simply be a glorified bank, Matthieu. Chaplin's Savings and Loan, that's all.'

To my relief, Charlie didn't ask me to invest in his ideas anyway, although I dare say he would have accepted any offers I might have made. We continued to be friends during that year, but it was a slightly distant friendship, linked as it was through Amelia, whom Constance refused to let out of her sight for very long.

'The man's a lech,' she told me. 'It's one young thing after another. I'm amazed he's kept up with her this long. I want to be there when he throws her aside though. She'll be eighteen soon and he'll want to be rid of her then.'

My feelings for Constance had grown considerably, to the point where I believed I had fallen in love with her. For her part, she linked her romantic life exclusively to me but showed no great interest in mutual declarations of affection. Passionate cries of 'I love you' from me would most often be followed by an 'Aren't you sweet?' or a 'How kind of you to say' from her. It wasn't that she was cold – indeed, she could be extremely affectionate in showing delight at my arrival to take her to dinner or to a show – it was simply that she was suspicious of amorous declarations or any form of public affection. I started to spend most nights at her apartment and considered giving up my house, which was far too large for my needs anyway, in order to move in with her but she urged me to hold on to it, just in case.

'I don't want to feel that we're married already,' she told me, 'like there's no turning back. Knowing you still have your own house gives me a sense of security.'

I had thought of that too and considered asking her to marry me but I had been down that road so many times already with such mixed success that I was loath to see another union go awry, another friendship destroyed. We spoke of our pasts to each other in some detail, although I made sure not to go back further than about 1900 to begin my romantic life. I have always found it best not to bore people with the details of my ageing process as I suspect that their interest in me would be superseded by their interest in it.

'I've never been married,' I lied to her. 'There was only one girl I ever really wanted to marry but it didn't work out.'

'Throw you over for another Joe?' she asked me and I shook my head.

'She died,' I said. 'There was . . . some trouble. We were both very young. It was a long time ago.'

'I'm sorry,' said Constance, looking away, unsure whether I wanted consolation or whether she was even the right person to give it or not. 'What was her name?'

'Dominique,' I said quietly. 'It doesn't matter. I don't like to talk about her. Let's—'

'And there's been no one else? You've never been in love since?'

I laughed. 'Oh, there've been others, of course,' I said. 'I've lost track of the number of people I've become involved with, and there've been one or two of course that I've developed strong feelings for, feelings that could rival those I had for Dominique. You, for example.'

She nodded and lit another cigarette, looking away as she breathed the smoke out through her nose. I stared at her but her eyes refused to meet mine. 'How about you?' I asked her eventually, in order to break the silence. 'When am I going to hear all about your wonderful past?'

'I thought that a gentleman didn't want to end up with a woman with a past,' she said with a smile. 'Isn't that what all the young ladies are taught? To keep themselves pure and virginal for their husbands?'

'Believe me, I'm in no position to talk,' I acknowledged

50

with a smile. 'You've no idea how far back my past goes.'

'I've never really got involved with people,' she told me hesitantly. 'After my parents died, I was left to look after Amelia and I've spent the last few years doing exactly that. I knew a few people here and of course there was this place which was left to us, so it seemed like as good an idea as any to stay on. Then Amelia met Charlie and I seem to have been playing the role of chaperone ever since. Sometimes I fear that, at twenty-two, my best is already behind me. I feel like one of those maiden aunts in those novels that Amelia's always reading. You know the ones, a young girl goes off to Italy and has her corsets loosened by some Roman god while her prim and proper chaperone stands a few feet behind and goes tut-tut-tut.'

'You're no maiden aunt,' I said deliberately. 'You're about the most—'

'Please, no gratuitous flattery,' she said quickly, stubbing her half smoked cigarette out in the ashtray as she stood up and walked over to the window. 'I don't have any problems with my self-esteem, thank you.'

'Do you like California?' I asked her after a long pause. A plan was starting to form in my mind, to take her away from the state and these drab people who were already beginning to bore me. Everywhere I looked, people were obsessed only with celebrity, with moving pictures, with a handful of big names and how you could get to stand close to one at a party.

'What's not to like?' she asked indifferently. 'I have everything I need here. Friends, a place to live, you . . .' she conceded.

'How about we take a trip?' I asked her. 'We could go on a cruise. The Caribbean perhaps.'

'Sounds wonderful. Would I get to wear what I wanted and put on no make-up whatsoever? *Read*, rather than *watch*?'

'If you wanted,' I laughed. 'How about it? We could go tomorrow, you know. Or ten minutes from now.'

For a moment, she looked as if she was about to agree but then her face grew dark and her shoulders sagged and I knew it wouldn't be on. In a moment, her whole body represented the word 'disappointment'. 'There's Amelia,' she said. 'I can't leave her.'

'She's old enough to look after herself,' I protested. 'And she has Charlie, after all.'

'Two statements, Matthieu,' she said coldly, 'which you know to be patently untrue.'

'Look, Constance,' I said, standing up and taking her by the shoulders, 'you can't live your life looking out for your sister. You said as much yourself a moment ago, that you were afraid your best years might be behind you. Don't let that happen, Constance. Why, you were younger than Amelia when you were left to look after her yourself!'

'Yes, and look what a terrible job I did! Almost eighteen years old and the plaything of some rich movie star twice her age who'll throw her over in a flash the moment it suits him.'

'You don't know that.'

'I do.'

'Maybe he loves her.'

'*I* love her, Matthieu, can't you realize that? *I* love her and I refuse to leave her to her own devices until I am sure that she can stand on her own two feet. It may not be that long. Once they break, it will be hard for her but she'll come through it a stronger person. If she can survive that, she'll survive anything. Believe me, I know.'

52

A long silence followed as her words came slowly towards me and developed a life of their own within my mind. I turned to look at her and sat down slowly as she faced me, her body trying to hold its strength together as she fought to hold back her fear of my reaction.

'You and Charlie . . . ?' I asked, shaking my head. Such a union hadn't occurred to me for even a moment. 'When . . . ? When was this? Was it recently? Since you've known me?'

'Oh, Lord no, it was years ago,' she said, pouring herself another drink. 'Well about two years ago anyway if that's the same thing. I met him at some party. I was a fan, I was bewitched by him. Didn't care that he was married. Everyone knew he hated Mildred anyway. Foolish to say he seduced me because he didn't. I wanted him just as badly. And he was very kind to me, I have to give him that. When we were together, he couldn't do enough for me. He's actually a wonderful boyfriend, you know. It was just the . . . the manner of parting which hurt.'

I looked at her and raised my eyebrows quizzically. 'Go on,' I urged her.

'It's ridiculous really,' she laughed, wiping a tear from her eye. 'And I don't come out of it looking particularly attractive.'

'Tell me anyway,' I insisted. She shrugged wearily, as if none of it mattered any more in her romantic exhaustions.

'We were at a party at Doug and Mary's. It was a birthday party, and I was standing in a corner talking with some small time actor from Essanay who'd played roles in *The Bank* and *A Night In The Show*, I think. Charlie had fallen out with him over something – God knows what, something trivial no doubt – and hadn't brought him over to Mutual with him when he switched studios. Anyway, this kid had fallen on difficult times since then and was asking me to help him out, to get him back in Charlie's good books or whatever, and I was doing everything I could to get rid of him because if there was one thing I could never stand it was people assuming that, because Charlie and I were a couple, I could get them roles in his films. I decided to bring him over to speak to Charlie, leave them together to sort it all out and go talk to someone interesting instead. I found him out by the pool talking with Leopold Godowsky, the concert pianist who I knew Charlie admired enormously, and reintroduced him to this boy, who he shook warmly by the hand and allowed to join in the conversation. He seemed perfectly happy to have him there. I said I was returning inside to the party and Godowsky said that he would join me. I didn't think anything of it and we simply stood inside and chatted for a few minutes. I told him I had heard him play once in Boston, when I was a child – my father was an enormous fan. He was flattered that I remembered the performance and told me some story about an overweight soprano who drank snake juice to improve her voice, which made me laugh. And that was all there was to it as far as I was concerned. Afterwards, as we drove home, Charlie said nothing at all to me and I could tell that he was angry about something but I was feeling tired and didn't want to humour him by asking what it was so I pretended to fall asleep until we got there, at which time I went inside and up to bed. I didn't want to return home to Amelia that night, hoping that whatever quarrel he had with me would have blown over by the morning.'

She was shaking as she told the story, avoiding my

eyes, and I wanted to go over and hold her but decided to stay where I was, not wishing to interrupt her telling of this story, something which I suspected she had never done before, not even to Amelia.

'Anyway,' she continued, 'I got into bed and tried to fall asleep as I waited for Charlie to appear, which he did after about fifteen minutes.

'"Get up," he said in a firm voice as he came into the room and slammed the door behind him. "Get up and go."

'"What?" I asked, pretending that he'd just woken me up. "What's wrong, Charlie?" I asked him.

'He leaned over the bed, pressed his hands down on my shoulders so they would bruise and said very clearly, each phrase precisely enunciated: "Get up. Get dressed. Get out."

'When I started to ask him why, what I had done wrong, he packed a few things for me, cursed me for bringing that boy out to the pool when he was talking to Godowsky. "The man is maybe the greatest pianist in the world," he roared, his arms flailing around dramatically. "And you inflict some unemployed actor on me just so you can whisk him away to flirt with him in another room? Not enough for you, am I?"

'"I never—" I began, but he wouldn't let me finish. He was purple with rage, as if I had orchestrated the whole scene myself when all I had done was try to rid myself of a bore and not interfere with Charlie's business. Anyway, the scene grew terrible and at four o'clock in the morning I found myself out in the street attempting to call a cab. He didn't speak to me for months, but I called him constantly. I was in love, you see. I wrote to him, turned up at the studio, sent him telegrams, but he ignored everything. I was in absolute despair.

Then, one afternoon, while having lunch in the city with Amelia, I saw him enter the restaurant with a couple of his cronies. He saw me and grew a little pale as he tried to get away before I could spot him because he has always hated public scenes and could see one coming now. I determined not to approach him. Then he saw my sister, who was staring at him with wide eyes and within a few minutes the room and the world were spinning on me. He joined us for lunch, he spent the day with us, and never once referred to anything that had happened between us over the previous few months, acting as if we were simply good friends who liked nothing more than to run into each other every so often and catch up on the latest society gossip. When he and Amelia became more serious, I refused to disappear. It was my way of staying close to Charlie, you see. The fact is, Matthieu, I've been very dishonest about all of this right from the start.'

I nodded and felt sick. All this time she had been deceiving me? It seemed outrageous. I was sure she had been falling in love with me.

'Then I met you,' she added after a moment. 'And everything changed.'

'How so?' I asked.

'Do you remember that day you came to see Charlie at his home and the four of us stayed up all night together, drinking Martinis and Highballs?' I nodded. 'Well, I'd been there before, you see,' she continued. 'I'd seen rich men come through that house on more than one occasion and they were all looking for a little piece of him, hoping to receive a little of his reflected glory. You didn't. You seemed suspicious of him. You didn't laugh at his jokes too loudly. You didn't even seem to like him very much.'

56

'You're wrong,' I said honestly. 'I did like him. I enjoyed his self-confidence. I hadn't seen that in some time. I found it very refreshing, to be honest.'

'Really?' She seemed surprised. 'Well, regardless. You didn't fawn on him. I admired that. For the first time, I thought that I could see past him. To another man. I began to conceive of having nothing more to do with him and that was when you and I began to see each other and I realized that I didn't love him any more, that I didn't even need him. That I loved you.'

My heart jumped and I came towards her and took her hand. 'You do love me?' I asked.

'Oh yes,' she said, almost apologetically.

'So why stay here then? If you feel nothing more for him now, why stay here? Why insist on spending time around him?'

Her voice grew cold and she spoke her next sentence with conviction. 'Because what he did to me, he will do to Amelia. I survived it, she might not. And I need to be here for her when it happens. Can you understand that, Matthieu? Does that make any sense at all?'

I paused and stared at her. A thin line of perspiration had broken out along her upper lip. Her eyes were tired and her hair hung loosely around her neck and needed washing. She was more beautiful than I could ever remember her being.

We were married on a Saturday afternoon in October in a small chapel on the eastern side of the Hollywood Hills. Eighty people were in attendance, mostly socialite friends of ours from the circles in which we moved, a lot of studio people, a few newspaper columnists, a couple of writers. We were famous for being famous and adored for being adorable and everyone wanted to celebrate our celebrity with us. We were Matthieu and Constance, Matt and Connie, celebrity couple, socialite darlings, the talk of the town. Doug had sprained his ankle in a tennis match and arrived on crutches, supported as usual by Mary, and received an awful lot of attention for someone with such a minor wound. William Allan Thompson was there, and, as it had been rumoured that Warren Harding was about to appoint him Secretary of Defense, he represented another centre of attention. (In the end, he lost the job when a scandal involving a bordello erupted and the Senate vetoed his appointment; he lost heavily in gambling thereafter and killed himself in 1931, on the day F.D.R., his mortal enemy, was elected president for the first time.) My young nephew Tom arrived from Milwaukee where he was living with his wife Annette and I was pleased to reacquaint myself with the lad, even if I did find him a little churlish. He seemed more interested in trying to spot movie stars than in telling me of his life and career plans and I was a little surprised that he had failed to bring his bride to meet me. When I challenged him on it, he said that she was newly pregnant and that the thought of a trip – any trip – made her ill from morning to night. If I didn't want a scene at my wedding, he said, it was for the best that he leave her at home. Charlie and Amelia arrived arm in arm, the former grinning away as usual with the smile that now served no purpose other than to infuriate me, the latter looking red eyed and dazed, barely even acknowledging me when I reached down to kiss her cheek. She appeared drained, as if life with Charlie had all but vanquished her, and I didn't hold out much hope for their future happiness together, or hers on her own.

The ceremony was simple and quick; Constance and

I exchanged vows, we were pronounced husband and wife and the whole wedding party repaired to a large marquee which had been erected outside a building a few hundred feet away where a dinner was to be served, followed by dancing and revelry. Constance wore a simple, figure hugging dress of pale ivory, a lace veil covering her perfect face, offering only whispers of her features to me as we stood at the altar. Afterwards, when she removed it, her smile was perfect and joyful, her happiness absolute. Even when Charlie kissed his congratulations, she was smiling, making no unpleasant associations which could spoil our day. He was simply another guest whom she could barely even see, so intent were we on staring at each other.

Speeches were made. Doug called me a 'lucky son of a gun', Charlie wondered aloud why he had never proposed himself – then made the audience laugh by saying it was because he realized he had not been attracted to me and so it would never have worked out. Even Constance and I found him amusing and I felt a warmth for my fellow man which had not been present for a good sixty or seventy years. We danced late into the evening, Constance performing a perfect tango with a young Spanish waiter which was one of the highlights of the evening. The young lad – who couldn't have been more than about seventeen – appeared flushed with pride at his success on the dance floor and his tan deepened by several shades when his dancing partner kissed his lips hard at the end. The day had been perfect and, in retrospect, trouble was almost inevitable.

Constance had gone to change clothes – we were leaving for an overnight express train which would bring us to Florida, where we intended beginning a three month honeymoon cruise. I stood alone in the corner of the marquee, nursing a banana milk shake, having decided not to drink too much alcohol on such a special day. A friend of mine, a banker named Alex Tremsil, came up to wish me well and we were speaking animatedly of wives and responsibilities and suchlike when I noticed Charlie strolling around outside with a young girl, the daughter (I believed) of one of the Richmonds. She was about sixteen years old and bore a striking resemblance to Amelia, so striking that at first I wasn't sure whether it was her or not. But then I looked around and saw my new sister-in-law helping herself to something off the fruit trolley and saw her waver slightly as she sat down to eat, the result of one too many glasses of champagne, I thought. I was afraid of what might happen if she saw the scene being enacted outside and wished that Constance would hurry up so that we might leave soon. It wasn't that I didn't care about Amelia – I did, she was an extremely pleasant, if troubled girl – but I cared about my new wife more and, hang it, our own happiness together. I didn't want our lives to be run by Constance's refusal to allow her sister to make her own mistakes and live with their consequences.

I kept one eye on the chapel where my wife was changing and was shocked to see Amelia coming towards me and the view to the outside. Charlie and the girl were now engaged in a little mutual flirtation, and it was plain to see his hand caressing her cheek as she laughed at his jokes. Amelia froze when she saw it too and dropped her glass which landed softly on the grass beside her. She ran out to Charlie and, pulling her hands back to her side as she approached them, pushed the girl over with such force that the poor thing went rolling down the side of the hill a little, muddying her pale yellow dress. If it hadn't been so ludicrous, I would have laughed. Charlie looked down at the girl and helped her up, saying something to Amelia which made her run towards him and throw her arms around his legs, a gesture which embarrassed me so much that I turned away. Before long, all our guests could hear the commotion and Charlie strolled inside, his ubiquitous smile a little forced now, as Amelia followed him in, alternating between cursing at him for a cheat and announcing how much she loved him. When she stopped, he turned and looked at her and the entire wedding party, everyone from the cheap seats to the circle to the stalls, fell silent, waiting for his response.

'Amelia,' he said, his voice holding steady and cutting through the room, 'go away now, you silly girl. You bore me.'

I looked past him and saw Constance standing in the distance, also looking on in horror as Amelia turned on her heels and ran towards the cars which lined the side of the hills.

'Amelia!' called Constance and I ran towards her.

'Leave it,' I shouted. 'Let her calm down. Let her be alone.'

'You saw what he did to her,' she cried. 'I can't leave her when she's in this condition. I have to go after her. She could injure herself.'

'Let *me* go then,' I said, not releasing her arm, but she pulled away and charged after her sister instead. I turned back to the party and shrugged indifferently at my guests, as if it had just been a minor disagreement, glared at Charlie who, to his credit, stared at the ground in shame and went quickly towards the bar.

Later, I discovered that Constance had managed to clamber into the car whose ignition Amelia was turning on and that the young girl drove erratically down the mountain at top speed. The two of them were observed shouting and trying to take the wheel from each other, before the car careered off the hillside, did a double flip, landed head first on the road beneath where my nephew Tom was standing talking to a teenage starlet and promptly exploded.

We had been married for the best part of three hours.

Chapter 6

February–March 1999

It was late at night – past twelve o'clock, by which time I am usually fast asleep – when I had a moment of epiphany.

It started earlier in the evening when I was alone in my apartment. I was listening to *The Ring of the Nibelung* and was on my third night of it, playing *Siegfried*, eating some pâté on toast and enjoying a bottle of red wine.

It had been a troublesome day. I visit the offices of our satellite broadcasting corporation every Monday, when I attend a meeting of the major shareholders, have lunch with the managing director and generally fuss around the building a little, seeing if I can think up any ideas to improve our ratings, boost profits, increase our consumer base. It tends to be a pleasant enough experience, although I couldn't bear to do it more than once a week and have no idea how people with jobs actually manage to survive. It seems like terrible drudgery to spend one's entire life working, leaving only the weekends free for relaxation, at which time one is probably too busy recovering from the excesses of the week to enjoy oneself anyway. Not for me, I'm afraid.

On this day, however, there were some problems to

be sorted out. It seemed that our lead anchor for the six o'clock news – a Ms Tara Morrison – had been made a serious offer by the BBC and she was considering accepting the position which they were dangling before her like a noose. Ms Morrison is one of our prime assets and we could scarcely afford to lose her. She has led our advertising campaign with gusto, her face and (I'm embarrassed to admit) her body have adorned billboards, buses and the walls of tube stations for the past twelve months and her considerable physical appeal has been held responsible for our increased market share of almost three per cent within the same time period. She gives interviews to the glossy magazines on the subject of the female orgasm, appears as a contestant on television quiz shows, specializing in her PhD-calibre knowledge of the Cretaceous period, and even brought out a book last Christmas, detailing how one can combine relationships, motherhood and a career, entitled *Tara Says: You Can Have It All!* That's her catchphrase. *Tara Says:*. It seems that everybody says it now.

We already pay her a ridiculous amount of money and James Hocknell, the managing director of our station, implied to us at the board meeting that he wasn't sure that was what was behind her desire to leave.

'It's all about exposure, gents,' said James, who personifies a certain type of Fleet Street journalist turned television mogul. He's all pinstriped suits, pastel shirts with white collars, rings, the sides of his hair combed over the balding centre. His face is permanently red and he wipes his nose with the back of his hand, but for all that we'd be lost without him. We employ him for his talents, not his beauty. We don't expect him to be a guest model in any designer's spring collection. His control over his employees is absolute, his ability at his job unquestioned, his commitment unparalleled. In the business it's known that he's screwed half the women and screwed-over half the men. The lack of a conscience has taken him to the top. And he knows this industry better than I or my two fellow investors do. We are businessmen, he's in television, that's the difference. 'Tart wants to be seen on the BBC, it's as simple as that.' Tart is James's nickname for Tara, one which he is always sure to use very discreetly. 'Childhood dream or something, she says. It's got nothing to do with the money she's being offered, which I can tell you, gents, is not that much different to the money we shell out on her as it is. She just wants fame, that's all. She's addicted to it. Says she even wants to have a go at investigative documentary stuff, as if the powers-that-be over there would ever let her do any of that. Chances are they'll have her fronting *Top of the Pops* in about a fortnight's time and five minutes after that she'll be in the tabloids for shagging some poncey boy band member just out of short trousers. I hear there's soon to be a spot opening up as co-host of *Tomorrow's World* though. Big money there, gents. University circuit's crying out for them too.'

'Well, we can't lose her, James, you realize that,' said P.W., the ageing world famous record producer who invested his life savings into this business and lives in constant fear of losing the lot, which is unlikely. 'She's about the only big name we have.'

'There's Billy Boy Davis,' said Alan, another investor, old money. He's almost eighty and it's well known that he has pancreatic cancer, although he never speaks of it to anyone, not even his closest friends. I did hear a rumour that he was waiting for an offer from Oprah

Winfrey, but that's unconfirmed. 'We still have The Kid.'

'No one's interested in him,' countered P.W. 'His heyday was twenty years ago. He's been put out to pasture here, commentating on second rate sporting events and trying to forget that the entire country knows that he likes to dress up in a nappy and have his bottom spanked by sixth-formers. And why does he still insist on being called "The Kid" anyway? He's fucking fifty, if he's a day. He's a joke, for God's sake.'

'He's still a big name.'

'I've got a name for him,' said P.W. 'Wanker.'

The animosity between P.W. and Alan continues week after week and dates back to a derogatory comment the latter made about the former in an unauthorized biography (which he himself wrote) ten years ago. Although they attempt to keep relations on a strictly professional and polite basis, it is obvious to all that they cannot stand each other. Every week at the meeting one of them waits for the other to make some comment and then jumps in, trying to discredit the other fellow.

'What Billy Boy is or isn't doesn't matter right now, gentlemen,' I said, placing my hands on the table in an attempt to stop their petty bickering. 'I imagine what matters is that Ms Morrison wants to leave us for pastures new and we would prefer it if she didn't go. Isn't that it in a nutshell?' There was a grudging round of head nodding, and Yes, Matthieus. 'In which case, our question is a simple one: how do we persuade her to stay?'

'Tart says there's nothing we can offer her,' said James, and I leaned back in my chair and shook my head.

'Tara says a lot of things,' I countered. 'Tara's made a virtual career out of saying things. What Tara is actually saying is that we haven't made her the *right* offer yet. Believe me, that's what she's saying right now, only none of you are listening. You surprise me, James.'

James, P.W. and Alan looked at each other blankly and only James started to smile. 'All right then, Mattie,' he said – a diminutive that always sends a shiver down me in recollection of an old friend, two hundred years dead – 'what do you suggest?'

'I suggest I take Ms Morrison out to lunch with me today and find out exactly what it is that she's after. Then I shall attempt to give it to her. It's as simple as that.'

'I know what I'd like to give her, gents,' said James with a laugh.

Ms Morrison – 'Tara Says:' – and I had lunch together in a small Italian restaurant in Soho. It's a pleasant, family run place, and one to which I often take business acquaintances if I'm trying to get something out of them. I know the owner and she always takes time to come out and talk to me when I dine there.

'How are you and yours?' she asked, true to form as we were seated in a quiet booth away from the door. 'Keeping well, are they?'

'We're all perfectly well, thank you, Gloria,' I said, despite the fact that me and mine consists solely of Tommy and I. 'And you?' The pleasantries continued for a few minutes. Tara took the opportunity to visit the ladies' room and came back looking refreshed, lipstick subtly applied, a scent of perfume mingling with the crostini. She walked between the tables as if the centre aisle was a catwalk in Milan, the waiting staff store buyers, our fellow diners photographers. Her hair, a professional blonde bob, simple and easy to control, is one of her most recognizable features, and her beauty stems much from the fact that her face is perfectly symmetrical, each feature reproduced perfectly through recognition of a central line. One can only stare at her and marvel. She'd be perfect if one could only find a flaw.

'So, Matthieu,' she said, taking a sip of wine gingerly, careful not to leave a lipstick trace along the rim of her glass, 'are we going to make small talk for a while or get straight down to business?'

I laughed. 'I simply wanted to enjoy a pleasant lunch with you, Tara,' I said, feigning offence. 'I gather we may not be seeing you around the office quite so much in the future and I want to enjoy your company in the daytime while I still can. You might have told me you were fielding offers, you know,' I added, a hurt tone – entirely natural – creeping into my voice.

'I had to keep it quiet,' she said. 'I'm sorry, I wanted to tell you, but I wasn't sure what was going to happen. Anyway, it's not as if I went out there *looking* for work. The Beeb came to me, I swear it. They've made me a very generous offer and I do have my future to consider.'

'I know exactly the size of the offer they've made you and, in all fairness, it's not that much more generous than what you have already. You really should hold out for more from them. They will pay it, you know.'

'Do you think so?'

'Oh, I know so, believe me. They could up their offer by a good . . . ten per cent, I imagine, without so much as breaking a sweat. Maybe more. You're a valuable commodity. I hear you could be offered *Live & Kicking*.'

'But you won't be able to go that far,' she said, ignoring the dig. 'I know what the budgets are like, remember.'

'I have no intentions of even attempting to go that high,' I said, twirling a little pasta around on my fork.

'I don't intend getting into an auction for you, my dear. You're not cattle. Anyway, you're under contract to me as it is. And there's not an awful lot you can do about that, is there?'

'For another eight weeks, Matthieu, that's all. You know that and so do they.'

'So in eight weeks' time, we'll negotiate. Until then, let's not talk of dismissals or resignations or reassignments or anything so distasteful. And, for heaven's sake, let's keep the press out of it this time, can we?'

Tara looked at me and put her cutlery down. 'You're just going to let me go,' she stated matter-of-factly, 'after all we've been through together.'

'I'm not *letting* you do anything, Ms Morrison,' I protested. 'I'm inviting you to see your contract through and at the end of that time, if you wish to leave us for a better offer, then you must follow what you believe to be the correct course of action for you and your career. Some would call me a generous employer, you know.'

'Must you talk like that all the time,' she muttered, staring at the table in disgust.

'Talk like what?' I protested.

'Like a fucking lawyer. Like someone who's afraid that I'm recording every word you say so that I can use it in a lawsuit six months down the line. Can't you speak to me in a normal tone of voice? I thought we meant something to each other.'

I sighed and looked out of the window, unsure whether I wanted to be dragged down this well worn road once again. 'Tara,' I said eventually, leaning forward and taking her tiny hand within my own, 'for all I know you may very well be recording this conversation. It's not as if you have a very good track record of honesty with me, now is it?'

69

*   *   *

I suppose at this point I should point out a few things about my relationship with Ms Tara Morrison. Approximately a year before, we attended an awards ceremony together – well, not so much together as part of a group representing our station. Tara was accompanied by her then boyfriend, an underwear model for Tommy Hilfiger, while I had booked a professional escort – nothing sexual, purely accompaniment – for the evening as I was between relationships at the time and really had no desire to begin a new one with anyone. Considering that I hit puberty over 240 years ago, it can't come as too much of a surprise to learn that I grow weary of the endless round of dating, breaking up, dating, marrying, dating, divorcing, dating, widowing, etc. Every few decades I need a little time alone.

On the night in question Tara had a disagreement with her model friend – something about him actually being a homosexual, I believe, which was bound to throw a spanner into the works – and she accepted my offer of a lift home. After driving my escort back to her own house, we stopped off for a drink at my club and talked well into the night, mostly about her ambitions, which were plenteous, and her commitment to journalism and our television station, which she called 'the future of broadcasting in Britain', something even I didn't believe. She cited a number of responsible role models and I admired her grasp of the history of her profession, her awareness of how the professional and the sleaze raker can co-exist in one industry, and how it can be difficult at times to differentiate between the two. I remember a particularly interesting dialogue we had on the subject of the public interest. Afterwards we returned to my apartment, where we said goodnight to each other and slept in the same bed without so much as kissing, an unusual but appealing arrangement at the time.

The next morning, I cooked breakfast and invited her back for dinner, which in the end we skipped in favour of a return to bed, where rather a lot more happened than had taken place the previous night. After that we continued our relationship for some months in an extremely discreet fashion – I told no one and to the best of my knowledge neither did she. I was fond of her, I trusted her and I made a mistake.

She was intrigued by the fact that Tommy DuMarqué was my nephew. (I didn't tell her that it was actually his great-great-great-great-great-great-grandfather who was my nephew; such information seemed surplus to requirements.) She'd been watching his programme for years and had apparently had a crush on him since he'd first turned up on television in his teenage years. When I first revealed the relationship between us, she went quite red, as if I had caught her doing something she shouldn't, and almost choked on some cantaloupe. She begged me to introduce her to him and I did, one fairly pleasant evening the previous summer, when she practically tore his trousers off in front of me. He wasn't at all interested – he was in a volatile relationship with his screen grandmother at the time and she was apparently a jealous lover – and I think he found her a little silly, although to be fair to her she had had a little too much to drink that night and alcohol does bring out the schoolgirl in her. She called him the next day and invited him out for a drink; he declined. So she faxed him and invited him to dinner; he passed. Then she sent him an e-mail with her address and the promise that if he came around 'NOW', he would find the front door open and her lying naked on a Persian rug before an open fire, and that a bottle of champagne was chilling in an ice box even as she typed. This time he laughed and phoned me up to tell me what my girlfriend was up to. I was disappointed but not surprised and took his place on the date, arriving at her apartment to find her in exactly the position she had described. She looked surprised to see me but recovered well and tried to pretend that she had thought I might call around and wanted to surprise me. I told her that she was lying, that I didn't mind particularly, but that it was all over between us now and it would be best if we returned to a strictly professional relationship.

The following Sunday, she wrote an article in a prominent Sunday newspaper – 'Tara Says: Just Say No!' – claiming to have recently been involved in a relationship with a famous soap star (unnamed, but the description made it obvious to whom she was referring). She alleged that their sexual activities had bordered on the illegal and that she had enjoyed acting out all of this young man's fantasies and forcing him to act out hers. She chose to end their affair, she said, only when he tried to drag her into his world of alcohol, heroin and cocaine abuse. 'I saw the look in his eyes as he offered me the silver spoon and Bunsen burner of disgrace', she wrote hysterically, 'and knew that I could never be the woman he wanted me to be. A woman who was as much of a mess as he was. A woman who would do anything for that next fix, sell myself on the streets perhaps, rob old ladies, push drugs on to babies, a worthless nothing. I took one look at him and shook my head. "Tara says: You're dumped," I told him.'

Tommy – the innocent party in all of this, although everything she imagines about his private life is no doubt true – was summoned into the offices of his executive producer on the Monday morning after publication where he was informed that had Ms Morrison actually named him he would have been fired immediately. As she hadn't, and as they couldn't prove that it was him she was referring to, he was to consider himself on an official warning. He had a responsibility to his fans he was told, the young girls who dreamed of marrying him, the teenage boys who were following his battle with testicular cancer with dread. They acknowledged that he was far and away the most popular character on the show, but said they would have no qualms about involving him in a car crash, or having him shot, or giving him AIDS if he stepped out of line again.

'You mean my character, of course,' said Tommy. 'You'd do those things to my character.'

'Yes, whatever,' they muttered.

The incident had preceded a particularly bad couple of months in Tommy's life, where the tabloids were hounding him at night to see what he was digesting, inhaling, swallowing, smoking or injecting, whom he was kissing, touching, fondling, molesting or screwing, and exacerbating the problems which he had already developed through the lifestyle they had forced upon him in order to help their circulation. Although I expected nothing more from one of the Thomases, I was less than happy with Ms Morrison for her part in his troubles and made my feelings clear to her at a stormy meeting a few days later. I'm not one to lose my temper, but by God it got the better of me that day. Since then, we had kept a distance from each other and, far from being concerned about her departure for pastures new, I was pleased by the idea. With us, she was a big fish in a small pond. We had made her a star. A small-time, small-screen star, granted, but a star none the less. She would find life a lot more difficult with Auntie.

And so, at home that night, eating my pâté, listening to my Wagner, drinking my wine, I wanted nothing more than to relax and put the events of that day out of my mind. It would be a full seven days before I had to return to the station and until that time they were under the strictest of instructions not to contact me, except in the most dire of emergencies. It was with some surprise then that I heard my buzzer ring and, as I went to the front door, I said a silent prayer that it was just an electrical fault on the wire and that no one would be out there.

My nephew stood outside, a hand running through his dark hair as he waited for me to answer.

'Tommy,' I said in surprise. 'It's very late. I was—'

'I have to talk to you, Uncle Matt,' he said, pushing me out of the way and coming inside. I closed the door with a sigh as he led the way back to the living room, instinctively heading for the room where I kept the alcohol. 'You said you were going to give me the money,' he shouted, his voice breaking with nervousness and for a moment I believed he was going to cry. 'You promised me the—'

'Tommy, will you please sit down and relax. I forgot. I'm sorry. I was supposed to post it to you, wasn't I? It went right out of my mind.'

'You are going to give it to me, aren't you?' he begged, grabbing my shoulders and it was all I could do to prevent myself from pushing him back on to the sofa in frustration. 'Because if you don't give it to me, Uncle Matt, they're going to—'

'I'll write you a cheque right now,' I said quickly,

74

pulling away from him and going behind my desk in the corner. 'Honestly, it was a simple mistake, Tommy. There's hardly any need to come around here in the middle of the night disturbing my peace, is there? How much did we say anyway? A thousand, was it?'

'Two thousand,' he said quickly and I could see by the firelight how much he was perspiring. 'We said two thousand, Uncle Matt. You promised me two—'

'Oh, for heaven's sake, I'll write you three. Is that better? Three thousand pounds, all right?'

He nodded and buried his face in his hands quickly, leaving it there for a moment before looking back up with a smile on his face. 'I'm . . . I'm sorry about this,' he said.

'It's quite all right.'

'I hate to ask but . . . There's just so many *bills* right now.'

'I'm sure there are. Electricity, gas, council tax.'

'Council tax, yeah,' said Tommy, nodding, as if that was as good an excuse as any.

I ripped out the cheque and handed it to him. He examined it closely before putting it in his wallet. 'Relax,' I said, sitting down opposite him and pouring him a glass of wine which he took eagerly. 'I've signed it.'

'Thanks,' he muttered. 'I should go though. I'm expected.'

'Stay a few minutes,' I said, not wishing to know who expected him, or for what. 'Tell me, how much of that money is already spent?'

'Spent?'

'How much do you owe to people, and I don't mean British Telecom or the gas board. How much has to be divided out when the banks open tomorrow?'

He hesitated. 'All of it,' he said. 'But that's it then. I'm through with the stuff.'

I leaned forward. 'What is it exactly that you *do*, Tommy?' I asked, truly intrigued.

'You know what I do, Uncle Matt. I'm an actor.'

'No, no. I mean what is it that you do when you're not on set? What kind of trouble have you got yourself involved in?'

He laughed and shook his head violently and I could tell that he wanted to leave, now that he had his money. 'No trouble,' he said. 'I've just made a few bad investments, that's all. This will clear them and then I'll be home free. I'll pay you back, I promise.'

'No, you won't,' I said in a matter of fact voice. 'But it doesn't matter, I'm not concerned about a few thousand pounds. I'm just afraid for you, that's all.'

'You are not.'

'I am,' I protested. 'Remember, I was there when your father met his end. And his father too.' I stopped at that generation.

'Look, Uncle Matt, you couldn't save their lives and you're not going to save mine, all right? Just let me alone to get on with my life. I'll sort myself out.'

'I'm not in the saving business, Tommy. I'm not a priest, I'm an investor in a satellite broadcasting station. I just hate seeing somebody die young, that's all. I find the whole concept ridiculous.'

He stood up and pounded around the room, looking at me from time to time and opening his mouth to speak every so often without actually saying a word. 'I'm not – going – to die,' he enunciated carefully, his two index fingers held close together as he pointed them towards the ceiling. 'You hear me? I'm not – going – to die.'

'Oh, of course you are,' I said, dismissing what he had said with a wave of my hand. 'You've obviously got bad men after you. It's only a matter of time. I've seen it all before.'

'Fuck you!'

'That's enough!' I shouted. 'I abhor bad language and won't have it in my apartment. Remember that the next time you come looking for money.'

Tommy shook his head and made for the door. 'Look,' he said quietly, his voice speeding up in his anxiety for us to part on good terms. He didn't know when he might need me again. 'I appreciate this. I really do. Maybe I'll be able to help you out some day. We'll get together next week, OK? We'll do lunch. Somewhere quiet where every fucker in the place isn't staring at me and wondering whether I really have testicular cancer or not, all right? Sorry. Everyone. I promise. Thanks, OK?'

I shrugged and watched him leave before returning to my armchair with a sigh, this time with a large brandy nestling between my hands for comfort. And that was when my moment of epiphany hit. I'm 256 years old and I've sat back and watched nine of the Thomases die and done nothing at all to prevent any of these tragedies. I've helped them out when they've needed assistance but accepted their fate as predestined. Something which I cannot help alter in any way. So I have lived all this time. And one by one they've died. And most of them have been nice enough people, troubled yes, but worthy of help. Worthy of *my* help. Worthy of a life. And here was another one in trouble. Another Thomas ready to meet his end and I'd still be here afterwards, waiting for the next one to be born. Watching out for his time. When he gets into trouble, meets the girl, gets

77

her pregnant and gets himself killed. I thought: *this can't go on.*

The epiphany was this: I would do something I should have done a long time ago – I would save one of the Thomases. Specifically, I would save Tommy.

Chapter 7

Travelling with Dominique

We left Dover – Dominique, Tomas and I – on a mid-afternoon in September, when the city's colours remained in a state of gloom from morning 'til night and it seemed, some days, that the sky forgot to brighten up at all. I was much recovered from my recent beating and, in the weeks since it had robbed me of a portion of my dignity, I had grown even more daring in my escapades, as if I already knew that survival itself would turn out to be my forte. I escaped my sickbed on a Monday morning and after that it was a full week before we were ready to move on; considering we had little or no belongings to call our own, I cannot quite recall or understand the reason for our delay. Still, it did not make me unhappy for I took that time to bid farewell to the friends that I had made on the streets, the empty boys like myself who stole for food or to pass the time, the homeless children whose larceny provided them with the only regular job in the city, and the urchins who looked through me when I spoke to them and didn't understand the concept of leaving the only world they had ever known. I visited three of my favourite prostitutes on three consecutive nights and felt sad as I paid my goodbyes to them, for they had been my only source of comfort throughout my despairing longing for Dominique. As they nurtured my adolescent longings for an hour at a time, and a few shillings a turn, I would picture her face on the pillow beneath my own, and call out her name, closing my eyes and dreaming that she was there. At times, I wasn't sure that our single night of lovemaking had even taken place or whether it was simply a hallucination that my illness had conjured up for me, but looking at her made me disavow this idea, for it was clear that there was a spark between us, however dull on her part, but one that had once been lit none the less.

Tomas seemed unconcerned about the move, as long as we were with him. By now, he was almost seven and he was a bright, energetic child, always wanting to be set loose on his own to explore the streets, but eager none the less to report back to us – his surrogate parents – on his actions whenever he would return. I was not so keen on allowing him to be left to his own devices in Dover but Dominique seemed less concerned. My brush with violence had made me more aware of the dangers on the streets and I was afraid for my brother, who I knew could too easily become involved with the same types as I myself had. I would have defended them to anyone, had the question concerned my own safety, but when it came to Tomas I didn't trust them an inch.

'He's six years old,' Dominique told me. 'There's boys out there younger than him earning money to feed their own families. What harm can he come to, Matthieu?'

'There's plenty of harm out there,' I protested. 'Look at the trouble I got into and I'm ten years older than him and able to look after myself. Do you want that happening to—'

'You went looking for it. You try so many dangerous

moves that it was only a matter of time before your thieving caught up with you. Tomas isn't like that. He doesn't steal. He just wants to explore, that's all.'

'Explore *what*?' I asked, confused by her explanations. 'What exactly is there out there to explore? The streets are just full of dirt, that's all. The gutters are filled with rats. There's nothing for him to find out there except people who will hurt him.'

She shrugged but continued to permit him to disappear for hours on end on his own. My concerns were genuine but I had a tendency to bow to her decisions, despite the fact that he was my brother and not hers. For she was older than me, and seemed more worldly, and held me completely in her thrall. Her dominance was complete but also maternal and sweet, her control over my life absolute and something not just desired by her, but by me also. At times, when we were alone together, she would allow me to sit close to her, laying my head upon her shoulder before the small fire, my face gradually sinking deeper and deeper towards her breasts until she would sit suddenly erect and claim that it was time for bed – for our separate beds. Although the chances of our union seemed more than remote, the night never came when I did not imagine that it could finally happen again.

We decided to travel to London where we believed our fortunes would lie. It was a long walk – almost eighty miles – from Dover to the capital but it was not unknown at that time for people to travel large distances by foot. The passage of time has made what was once not only possible but also commonplace now seem beyond all human endurance. Although it was late in the year, the weather was not inclement and there were always places to set up small camps for an evening. We had saved a little money – or rather Dominique had, through a careful hoarding of small change and a little laundry work she had been doing by day – and knew that in an emergency we could rent a small room for the night in an inn or farmhouse along the way. However, we knew that we had to be sparing for we would also need money for food, although I still planned to do a lot of stealing as we travelled, and hoped even to have a little left over to see us make a good start in London upon our arrival.

Leaving our small room that Monday morning delivered a curiously melancholy sensation to me. Although I had lived in the same house in Paris for fifteen years, I had never felt any great attachment to it and had never once looked back upon it or thought about it with any degree of homesickness from the day I had left. And yet, after only one year, there was a tear in my eye as I pulled the door shut for the last time in our Dover hovel, glancing at the two small beds, the shabby table, the chairs by the fire with the broken legs, our home. I turned to look at Dominique, to give her one last smile in this place, but she was already walking away, reaching down to slap some dust off the back of Tomas's pants, never turning around, never looking back. I shrugged and pulled the door behind me, leaving the room within in darkness, awaiting its next unfortunate occupants.

I was concerned about my boots. They were a dark black pair with fine lacings, a size too big, which I had stolen a few nights earlier from a young gentleman who had foolishly left them outside his room in The Traveller's Retreat, a small hostel near the harbour. I was in the habit of entering that place by its back door late at night and foraging around the hallways when the occupants had all gone to bed. It was not unusual to find a shirt or a pair of trousers outside the doors in the low, cramped corridors, left there by some gentlemen who thought they were still back in London or Paris and who expected to find their clothing neatly ironed and waiting for them in the morning. The things they left there were almost always impossible to sell but they made good clothes for my small family and cost me nothing, not even the smallest pang of conscience.

The boots were worn down a little at the soles, however, and I didn't much like the idea of walking to London in my bare feet. Already I could feel the gravel below my left foot pressing in as I moved along, and knew from experience that they had no more than a mile of comfort left in them before I would begin to develop blisters or cuts. Dominique had a similar pair but wore a fine pair of stockings between the leather and her skin that I had taken from a washing line three miles south the day before my beating, and I had found a brand new pair for Tomas only the previous day. He appeared almost as uncomfortable as I was as he broke them in and whined so often that they were cutting his feet that eventually Dominique took a hanky from her pocket and stuffed it around his toes to prevent any more friction. I would have preferred it if she'd wrapped it around his mouth, but nevertheless it kept him quiet, briefly.

I estimated that we would make it to London in about five days if we were left alone to walk; less if we managed to find some form of transport along the way, which I doubted as the chances were limited for a young man and woman, together with a small child, growing dirtier and more malodorous as the days progressed.

But even a week was reasonable to us all and, as Dominique pointed out, seemed a small price to pay to escape Dover and the relentless life of drudgery that inevitably lay in store for us there. A week, she insisted, would see us to rights.

We were fortunate that first day, however, to catch the attention of a young farmer who was travelling in a cart from Dover to Canterbury, and who spotted us along the side of the road, attending to my feet. We had only travelled about six miles but it was at this point that I had begun to give up all hope for the boots and considered walking in bare feet and taking my chances. I was sitting on a milestone, examining my toes which had grown red with pain, as Dominique squatted in the grass behind me and Tomas lay on the ground to my right, one hand over his eyes, sighing with dramatic exhaustion when I heard the cart approaching.

'You may as well stop that, you know,' I told Tomas. 'We have to continue until we get there and no amount of whingeing or complaining is going to change that, all right?'

'But it's so *far*!' he cried, almost in tears. 'How soon will we be there?'

'It might be a week yet,' I muttered stupidly, exaggerating the time even though I knew it would set him off even worse, but I was hot and in pain and nervous about how I was going to make it much further myself. The last thing I needed was this child complaining when Dominique was sure to drive us on relentlessly towards London. I sympathized with him only too well for I was only seventeen and no better than a child myself. There were times – like then – when I too wanted to lie down on the ground and stamp my feet and throw a tantrum and let someone else take control of things for a change but I couldn't, for only one of us could play that role successfully. 'So just you get your mind accustomed to it, Tomas, and you'll be the better for it,' I added gloomily.

'A *week*,' he cried, adding almost immediately, 'how long is that?'

'A week is—' I began to tell him just how long it could be when I heard the sound of the cart coming towards us on the road. A few had passed us by already and I had attempted to flag them down with no success. Generally the occupant would either lash out at me with his whip or simply curse at me to get off the roads, as if we were creating some sort of terrible obstacle. If those trap-drivers could only see Piccadilly at five o'clock on an evening today they would know how well they had it and wouldn't have been so quick to give way to their tempers. I glanced at the cart as it approached and was pleased to see that it had only one occupant but still didn't hold out too much hope as I thrust my hand in the air and called out to the young man who came towards me.

'Halloa! Sir!' I cried. 'Do you have room for us in your cart?'

I stood back as he approached, expecting the whip to appear or for him simply to try to run me over at any moment and was surprised to see him pull up on the reins and shout to his horse to stand easy.

'Looking for a lift, are ye?' he asked, coming to a halt beside me as Tomas looked up in desperate hope and Dominique emerged from the grass adjusting her skirts, staring at our benefactor suspiciously.

'There's three of us, if that's not too many,' I said, putting on my most polite voice as I watched him glance briefly from one of us to the other, hoping that deference on my part would give way to compassion on his. 'But we don't have much to carry. Just one bag, that's all,' I added, lifting my small hold-all from the grass. 'We can't pay you, unfortunately, but we would be much obliged.'

'Well, you may as well step on then,' he said with a smile. 'Can't leave ye out here on a hot afternoon like this now, can I?' His voice was rich with a country strain that I didn't recognize, his words inflected with merriment and humour. 'Just three of ye, ye say? Why, that 'un's only a mite.' He nodded towards Tomas, who was scrambling vigorously into the cart, as if he feared the young man might change his mind at any moment and leave us behind. 'More like two and a half.'

'My brother,' I explained, stepping up beside him as Dominique got into the back quietly with Tomas. 'Six years old.' I sat back and for a moment, before we even set off, wished we could simply stay in this horse and trap for ever, there on that road, the future a drama yet to begin, the simple past not played out as yet. It was the final reassurance that we were leaving Dover for ever for in a moment our chauffeur would crack his whip, let out a cry to the horse and we would jerk into movement. It was a quiet moment of gratitude and apprehension for me and I have never quite forgotten it. To my surprise I felt a lump in my throat as we started to move with generous speed along the road.

'That's a queer accent you've got there,' said the farmer after a few moments. 'Where is it you said you're from?'

'We're coming from Dover but we hail originally from France. Paris, in fact. Do you know it?'

'I know *of* it,' he said with a smile and I couldn't help but smile back at him. He was young – no more than about twenty-five – but had the face of a teenage boy. His cheeks were bright and clean as if they had never known the cut of a razor and his blond hair flopped merrily over his forehead. He was dressed with little expense, although it was clear from the cart and the condition of his horse that he was not poor. 'I never been much out of the country,' he added. 'Come up to Dover to see some supplies on to merchant vessels regular like. Maybe I seen you there and didn't know it.'

'Perhaps,' I said.

'That your missus?' he whispered quietly, his head flicking back towards Dominique as he winked at me. 'You're a lucky thing to have a woman like her, ain't you? She'd keep ye busy through the night.'

'I'm his sister,' said Dominique coldly, her head coming between us as she leaned forward to hear our conversation. 'That's all. How far are you going anyway?' I looked back at her in surprise. To claim to be my sister was one thing. To appear unfriendly and sullen was another and could easily get us thrown off this wagon and back on to the road in a heartbeat, something my feet did not desire for a moment.

'I'm only going as far as Canterbury for the night,' said the young man. 'I can take you there but I'll be stopping to sleep when I reaches it and I turns off the road towards Bramling after that. If you want to continue to London then you're best getting out there and seeing what luck you can find along the road after that. There's an old barn I know there where I tends to sleep. It'll be dark by then and you're best off staying there with me and moving on in the morning. Or walk on in the dark but I don't know the roads from there so you'd need to be on your guard.'

Dominique nodded as if she was giving her approval to these plans and lay back in the cart. Furlong – he introduced himself to me a moment later – said nothing more for a time and appeared content to slow down the horse a little and stare ahead. He took some chewing tobacco from his pocket and bit off a chunk. He went to put it back in his pocket before hesitating and offering me some, which I accepted a little nervously. It was a delicacy I had never tasted before but did not want to appear so rude as to decline. I bit down on the chewy mound and took off a lump equal in size to the one he had taken himself. It tasted foul – like a mouthful of burnt, spiced fruit, only more bitter on the tongue – and I wondered how he could chew it with such relish, not to mention noise. As I rolled it around my mouth it released a liquid poisonous taste whose odour seemed to take a hold of the passageways up to my nostrils and constrict them suddenly. I felt a tightening in my throat and for a moment I could not breathe. I gasped and could hear the catch, knowing my voice was, for now at least, vanished.

'Not often I get company on these roads,' Furlong was saying. 'My father sends me once a month to do this trip. We're suppliers, you see. We run a farm but we sends some of our dairy food to the continent. It doesn't earn us much, if you want to know the truth, but it helps my father's claims to being an international man of business. That's how he styles himself in our village, you see.' I nodded and gave a slight cough, spitting the foul mucus into my hand and letting it drop over the side of the cart as we drove on. I looked back and saw Dominique watching me, an eyebrow raised in amusement. My face was purple from the experience and I swallowed several times to rid myself of the tobacco's taste and wished for a pitcher of cold water with which to wash it away. 'There's often people along this road, of course,' he said. 'But I don't likes taking single men. You don't know where you'll end up with some of them. Rob you blind, they would. Slit your throat for a few pounds. That's why I carries this.' He reached to the side of the cart and extracted a long knife, perhaps twelve inches in length, with a serrated edge. He touched it with the tip of a finger and I winced, expecting blood to appear in a sudden spurt. 'That's sharp, that is,' he said. 'I makes sure to sharpen it on a leather before I leave each month. For self-protection, you understand.'

'Right,' I said, unsure what answer he was looking for here.

'But when I saw you there, you and your missus and your little boy, I—'

'My sister and brother,' I corrected him, continuing the deception.

'I thought I'd stop and lend a hand,' he continued, ignoring me. 'Seemed like a good idea anyway. Helps make the time go a little quicker.'

'We're very grateful,' I said, feeling a sudden rush of warmth for this young man and his lonely monthly trips from Bramling to Dover and back. 'My boots were beginning to hurt me and Tomas was beginning to whine.'

'Not much I can do about the boots,' he said, peering ahead at the deserted road as the light grew a little more dim. 'But, as for the child, I should expect a sound thrashing at the starts of any complaining would put an end to that sort of thing.'

I looked across at him, expecting to see him smiling at his joke, but it was no joke and I was pleased that my half-brother had fallen asleep almost immediately after getting into the cart, for if he had not I could only have guessed what his behaviour might have been or what it might have resulted in for all of us.

'Are you married then, Mr Furlong?' I said after another extended period of silence during which time I had thrashed around in my mind for conversation topics. For a man who was looking for company, he seemed content simply to sit beside me and stare at the road ahead, as if the presence of some other human beings in the cart with him was company enough. Furlong laughed.

'Not married yet,' he said. 'But I hopes to be shortly.'

'A sweetheart?'

He blushed scarlet and I was taken aback by his modesty, a characteristic I had come across in few people. 'I am,' he said slowly, in the manner of a courtly gentleman, 'under something of a commitment to a young lady of my parish although an actual arrangement for nuptials has yet to be made.'

I grinned. 'Well, good luck to you,' I said.

'Thank 'ee.'

'When do you think your arrangements will be made then?'

He paused and the smile seemed to fade slightly. 'Someday soon,' he said. 'There has been a . . .' – he searched for the right word – 'a complication. But I expect it will be solved soon enough.'

'All romances are complicated,' I said cheerily, seventeen years old, once loved, and behaving for all my worth like a man of the world. 'I expect their resolutions make the complications all the more worthwhile in the end.'

'Aye, I expect so,' he said. He opened and closed his mouth several times and I guessed he was trying to tell me something but was unsure of how to begin or whether he even wanted to discuss it or not. I said nothing and stared ahead, closing my eyes for a moment to relax myself, when I heard his voice again, louder now, and without any of its previous good humour. 'I known Jane – that's her name, you see, Jane – I known her a good eight year now and we've been under something of an understanding to each other, you see. Sometimes I takes her for walks and sometimes I visit her of an afternoon and bring her a fancy something which she always takes with great pleasure. We made a haystack once, in the summer, two year back. Six feet high, it was. Taller than me.' I nodded and looked at him. In profile, his head was nodding and I could see a glisten in his eyes as he spoke of her.

'Sounds like quite the courtship,' I said in order to appear agreeable.

'It has been,' he agreed heartily. 'No question that it has been. She's a very able girl, you see.' I nodded, although I hadn't the faintest idea what he meant by that phrase. 'Now she's trying to distance herself from some army fellow who's come through. Made himself a little forward with her and I know that she don't like him much but can't find the way to tell him to leave her alone. With him fighting for king and country and all that. And just passing through. He can't stay long.'

'Nuisance,' I muttered.

'Takes her for walks every afternoon,' he continued, ignoring me as if I wasn't in the cart at all. 'Down by the river once, I heard. Visits her and likes to sing with piano, if you can believe it, the nance. You'll not find me singing at her, sir. Not a bit of it. Needs to pack his bags and get on with himself, that's what I think. Stop bothering her. She's too polite, though, you see.

Too polite to tell him to be on his way. Humours him. Goes for her walks with him. Listens to his pretty voice. Makes him tea and listens to his talk of adventures in Scotland, if you please. Some might say, unkind folk, that she's leading the poor blighter on, but I say he should just pack his bags and go, that's all. It's her and me who are under a commitment.'

His face was quite red now and his hands shook as he held the reins. I nodded but said nothing, seeing only too well the situation which was taking place in Bramling. I felt sorry for him but my mind was else-where already. I was thinking about the morning, about how we would still have a long way to travel after our sleep. About London. The night grew around us and we all fell silent. I thought of my prostitutes in Dover and drifted away with happy thoughts of them, wishing I could be there at that moment with a few pennies in my pocket to spend, and would have happily closed my eyes to dream of our encounters had not the horse come to an abrupt stop with Furlong's cry and we all four sat up suddenly. We had arrived at our resting place for the night.

It was a small barn but we all fitted in comfortably. It smelled of cattle although there were none to be seen now. 'They milk them here, during the day, one by one,' said Furlong. 'There's a farm a mile up the road there. They bring the cows to the field to graze and in here to milk 'em. That's what you're smelling. The milk.'

He had a small basket of food but it was enough only to feed himself with a little left over. I declined his offer to share, feeling it would be rude to deprive him of his meal after he had driven us so far for so many hours, but Dominique ate a leg of chicken which he forced on her, and Tomas would have greedily eaten the lot if she had not insisted that she share her portion with him. I watched as they ate, my mouth salivating, still resonant with the taste of the chewing tobacco, but claimed I felt ill from the motion of the cart so as not to appear the martyr. We talked for a little more time, the four of us, and Dominique grew animated now, asking him many questions about his village and the activities of – as she put it – the surrounding ten square miles, as if she was considering changing our London plans now that we had a horse and cart to take us elsewhere. It sounded a pleasant enough place but then I was not too concerned with our final destination, so sure was I that I could make a go of our lives anywhere, as long as we were together. It grew darker in the barn as our candle burned out but in its flicker her smile, as she told some tale of a show she had once seen in Paris where the girls had worn no underwear and the men had been tied to their seats in order to avoid a riot, made me long to hold her, to take her in my arms and feel my body become one with hers. My mind swam with the madness of my desire for her and I wondered whether I could get through an evening without wanting to kiss her. I questioned our friendship, whether it was simply based on my desire to touch her, to be touched by her, and found that I no longer heard a word of her conversation as I simply stared at her face and body and allowed my head to be filled with visions of the two of us together. I longed to tell her how I felt but the words were not to be found. My mouth opened and closed and despite Tomas and despite Furlong I found myself close to falling on top of her as the room would swim in darkness around us and there would be just us, just the two of us, just Dominique and Matthieu. No one else.

'Matthieu,' said Dominique, pushing me gently on the arm and snapping me out of my daze. 'You look as if you are about to collapse with exhaustion.'

I smiled and looked around the group, blinking several times as I tried to focus on them. Tomas was already curled up asleep in a corner, his jacket taken off and thrown carelessly across his body. Furlong was watching Dominique as she stepped outside the barn for a few moments and walked not so far away that we could not hear her pissing in the grass, a sound which embarrassed me as we sat there in silence. When Furlong and I went outside upon her return to do similar, I tried to move further away but he stopped short and I was obliged to stand alongside him as he talked.

'You're a lucky lad to have a sister like that,' he said, laughing. 'She's something for the eyes, ain't she? And those stories she tells, saucy girl. Why, she must have suitors all the way from here to Paris and back.'

Something in the tone of his voice offended me and I looked across at him sharply as he shook himself dry. 'She keeps to herself and to Tomas and I,' I said gruffly. 'We still have a distance to travel and we have no time for suitors or anything of that sort.' I decided immediately that we would continue on to London in the morning and nowhere else.

'I meant no harm,' said Furlong as we stepped back inside and settled ourselves in the remaining two corners of the barn for a night's sleep. 'Some things just cry out to be said, that's all,' he whispered in my ear as he left me, his breath stinking now from the chicken he had brought with him. 'Like some deeds just cry out for the doing, am I right?'

*　　*　　*

Sleep came quickly to me for I had not managed to get a moment to myself the whole day long, and the distance we had covered, along with the groaning of my empty stomach, brought me to the point where my whole body wanted to be finished with this day for good.

I dreamed first of Paris and of my mother and of a time when I was a child when she had made me hold the end of a huge, colourful rug while she beat it soundly with a carpet-beater. The dust which rose off it had made me cough and had gone down my throat, producing tears, much like the tobacco had done earlier on. Paris gave way to another city, an unknown one, where a man led me by the hand through a bazaar and handed me a candle which he lit with a golden lighter. And here is a light that only you can see, he told me in mid-conversation. As it burned, the marketplace surrendered to a horse fair, where men shouted to outbid each other, and a fight ensued. A man rushed towards me, his fist pulled back, his whole face grim with determined anger, and as he made to hit me I jerked back into consciousness, my legs stabbing into the air and for a moment I knew not where I was.

It was still dark – despite all I had dreamed, it was perhaps no more than fifteen minutes after I had gone to sleep – but I was freezing with the cold and my stomach pained me. I heard a thumping sound from the other side of the barn and hoped that it would lull me back to sleep quickly. It was joined by a throaty breathing and a muffled complaint, the sound of a mouth trying to scream while a hand holds it tight. I sat and listened as full consciousness returned to me and then jumped, in sudden recognition, as I looked around, my eyes trying to grow accustomed to the blackness. There was Tomas, shifting slightly in his sleep, a finger in his mouth, emitting a sigh of contentment. And there was an empty corner, which Furlong had left. And there was a struggle opposite me and the picture of a man above a woman, still clothed but with a hand missing, a hand working its way between them somewhere to undo clothing, to break through. I threw myself at him and he gasped but recovered quickly, a hand lashing out to hit me which sent me sprawling across the barn in a daze. He was strong and powerful, much more than I had ever imagined, and I lay there struggling to pull myself back into action. I heard Dominique shout in agony and then her cry became muffled again as he whispered to her and sent his hand beneath her dress once again. I stood up, my hands in my hair, knowing not what to do, aware that another attempt on my part to pull him off could lead to my death and possibly hers and Tomas' too. Instead, I ran outside the barn into the cold night, where the moon threw a thin prism of light on to the cart, which I threw myself at before running back inside, back behind Furlong who by the relaxed motions of his hand and his release of Dominique's mouth appeared to be getting closer to his intention. He lifted himself off her slightly, positioned his body back a little and was about to fall inside her when my hands came down, and the sharp serrated edge of the knife he had shown me earlier slid, as if through melting butter, between his powerful shoulder blades. His body drew a deep intake of breath – hollow and animal-like – as he jerked upwards, his shoulders bouncing backwards to relieve the pain as his hands grasped aimlessly in the air. I jumped back towards the wall of the barn, knowing that this was it, that I had only one chance to finish Furlong off and that chance was already behind me and if I had not succeeded we would all pay the price within minutes. Dominique scrambled out from beneath him and also plastered herself to the opposite wall as he slowly stood and spun around, staring at us with wide, disbelieving eyes, before swaying and falling backwards, the knife making a wretched sound as it pushed up inside his body – even the handle – a few more inches.

There was silence for some minutes before Dominique and I came shivering towards his corpse, looking down on the mouth which was leaking a thin line of blood and staring up at us in a finished rage. My body shook and, without meaning to, I vomited on him, my empty stomach somehow finding something new for me to deliver upon his face, covering those awful eyes for good. I stood back up in horror and looked towards Dominique.

'I'm sorry,' I said, idiotically.

Chapter 8

The Opera House

I received an extraordinary letter some weeks before my 104th birthday in 1847, which saw me leave my then home in Paris – where I had returned for a couple of years after a brief spell in the Scandinavian countries – and travel to Rome, a city I had never ventured into before. I was going through a particularly peaceful time in my life. Carla had finally died of the consumption, ridding me of the plague which our torturously enduring marriage had created for me. My nephew Thomas (IV) had joined me in my lodgings a few weeks after her funeral – a happy affair at which I got drunk on brandy and sang the praises of Thackeray's *Vanity Fair*, which was being published in monthly editions at the time – and I had agreed to let him stay on afterwards as his apprenticeship as a stagehand with a local theatre paid him very little and the hovel he was renting was unfit for human habitation. He was not an unpleasant lad to have around; at nineteen years old he was the first of the Thomases to have blond hair, a characteristic he had inherited from his mother's side of the family. He would sometimes bring friends home late at night to discuss the latest plays. They would help themselves to my supply of liquor and, although I could tell that he was more than popular with one or two of the actresses who came by, it seemed to me that the young men used him more for the wealth of his acquaintance than the pleasure of his company.

I had been gainfully employed myself for several years as an administrator of local government funding. There had been a plan to erect some new theatres in the environs of the city and I was responsible for selecting suitable locations and producing reasonable costings and timeframes for their construction. Only two of my eight detailed proposals were ever actually constructed, but they were popular successes both of them, and my name was being spoken of in society with great admiration. I was living a profligate lifestyle and socializing most evenings, my single status allowing me once again to mingle with the ladies of the city without any hint of a scandal.

Somehow news of my Parisian administrative abilities reached Rome, and I was invited to accept a new position as administrator of the arts within that city. The original letter, which was sent by a high-ranking official in their local government, was vague and hinted of enormous plans for the future while making few concrete statements about the nature of those schemes. However I was intrigued by the proposal – not to mention the amount of money which was on offer, not just for budgeting purposes but also for my own salary – and wanting to leave Paris anyway, I decided that I would accept. I spoke to Thomas one evening and made it clear that, while he was perfectly entitled to stay in Paris on his own, he was also welcome to come with me to Rome. The fact that he would be obliged to find suitable lodgings after my departure for Italy probably swung his decision – and sealed for him the natural fate of his ancestry – and he decided to pack up his few belongings and join me on my voyage.

Unlike the first time I had left Paris, some ninety years before, I was now a man of some success and wealth and hired a private coach to take us on the five day trip from capital to capital. It was money well spent, for the alternatives to such private travel were too hideous even to contemplate, but the journey itself was none the less miserable, involving bad weather, bumpy roads and a rude, arrogant driver who appeared to resent the fact that he was employed to drive anyone anywhere. By the time we arrived in Rome, I was ready to swear that I would make the city my home for ever – even if I should live to be a thousand – as I could not bear the idea of another journey as awful as that one had been.

An apartment had been rented for us in the heart of the city and we travelled there directly. I was pleased to see that it had been furnished with some taste and was delighted by the view that my bedroom gave over a picturesque market square, one not dissimilar to the haunt of my Dover youth, where I had robbed from stall to stall and from person to person in my necessary attempts to feed myself and my family.

'I have never known such heat,' said Thomas, collapsing in a wicker chair in the living room. 'I thought Paris was hot in the summer, but this . . . This is intolerable.'

'Well, what choice do we have?' I asked with a shrug, unwilling to be quite as negative as him so early into our Roman life, particularly if the object of criticism was something as uncontrollable as the weather. 'We cannot dictate the climate. You spend too much time indoors as it is and are as white as chalk. A little sun will be good for your complexion.'

'That's the fashion, Uncle Matthieu,' he said child-ishly. 'Honestly, don't you know anything?'

'What is the fashion in Paris may not be the fashion in Rome,' I told him. 'Go out. Discover the city. See the people. Find *work*,' I urged him.

'I will, I will.'

'We're here now and there are many opportunities to be had and I can't be expected to support you for ever.'

'We've just *got* here! We've just walked in the *door*!'

'Well, walk out of it again. Find *work*,' I repeated with a smile. I wasn't trying to irritate him – I was fond of the lad after all – but I did not want to see him sitting in our apartment day after day, relying on me to bring him his dinner and his ale, watching as his youth and beauty passed him by. Sometimes I think I have been too generous with the Thomases. Maybe if I had been a little less charitable, a little less willing to be the person who caught them whenever they fell over, at least one of them might have made it past their mid-twenties. 'Discover the joys of self-reliance,' I begged him, seven years after Emerson.

The following day, I ventured towards the central offices of the local government agency to meet Signor Alfredo Carlati, the gentleman who had written to me in Paris and had invited me to bring to Italy whatever expertise to which I could lay claim. With some difficulty I located the building in which Signor Carlati was based and was a little nervous to find that it was a somewhat dilapidated structure on the less prosperous side of central Rome. The door on the ground floor was hanging wide open – something to do with the fact that the upper hinge which might have held it in place had no screws attached on one side – and as I stepped inside

I could distinctly hear, from an office to my right, the sound of a man and woman screaming at each other in what was to me an almost untranslatable babble. Naturally I am fluent in French, but my Italian was poor and it was to be some months before I felt confident. The natural inclination of the natives to speak at high speed did not help matters either. I stepped closer to the door and looked for any sign as to what the office might contain before placing an ear against the wood and listening to the din from within. Whatever was taking place inside, it appeared that the woman was getting the better of the argument for, while she continued to shriek and scream at what can only have been a rate of one hundred words per minute, the man's tone had shrunk audibly and all he could manage was a defeated 'Si' whenever she paused for breath. Her voice grew clearer and clearer as she shouted until I realized that she had obviously approached the door from the inside and was now standing directly on the other side, only a few feet away from me. I jumped back as she swung it open and her screaming stopped in mid-sentence as she saw me there, smiling inanely at her.

'Excuse me,' I said quickly.

'Who are you?' she asked, reaching down and scratching herself in a most unladylike way as I held my hat humbly before her. 'Are you Ricardo?'

'I am not,' I admitted.

'Petro then?'

I shrugged and looked over her shoulder towards her companion, who was small and round with dark hair greased to his head from a sharp centre parting, and who scurried towards me excitedly as I acknowledged his existence.

'Cara, please,' he said, pushing her slightly aside as

102

he came into the doorway, and it surprised me a little how she deferred to him now that there was a stranger present. She shrunk back a few steps in her bright red dress and allowed him to do the talking. 'How may I help you?' he asked, his face sporting a broad smile, delighted no doubt that someone had appeared who had stopped the shrieking woman from continuing with her tirade against him.

'I'm sorry to intrude—' I began, before he cut me off by waving his arms in the air dramatically.

'No intrusion!' he shouted, clapping them together now. 'We are delighted to see you. You are Ricardo of course.'

'Neither Ricardo nor Petro,' I admitted with a shrug of my shoulders. 'I am looking for—'

'You are sent by one of them then,' he asked and I shook my head.

'I am new to the city,' I replied. 'I'm looking for the offices of a Signor Alfredo Carlati. Are you him?' I hoped he was not.

'There is no Carlati here,' he said dismissively, the smile leaving his face completely now that I was neither Ricardo nor Petro, his missing associates. 'You are wrong.'

'But this is the address, surely,' I said, extending my letter to him and he glanced at it briefly before pointing towards the stairs.

'Those offices are the next flight up. I know no Carlati but he may well be up there.'

'Thank you,' I said, edging away as he closed the door sharply and the woman took up her screaming chorus once again from within. Already, I disliked Rome.

The next floor up had a brass plaque outside the door with the word Officialdom inscribed on it beside a neat, silver bell, which I pulled once as I smoothed my hair with my left hand. This time, a tall, thin man, with grey hair and a beak for a nose, opened the door and stared at me with nothing short of pure distress on his face. The effort which it took for him to say 'Can I help you?' seemed almost too much for a moment and I feared that he would collapse under the strain of speaking.

'Signor Carlati?' I inquired, forcing my voice to be at its most polite and sincere.

'That is me,' he sighed, his eyes filling with tears as he stroked his temples.

'I am Matthieu Zéla,' I said. 'We have communicated through letter regarding—'

'Why, Signor Zéla,' he said, his face lighting up now as he clasped my arms and hugged me to his body, kissing first my left cheek and then my right, and then my left again with his dry, chapped lips, 'of course it is you. I am so pleased you are here.'

'You were difficult to locate,' I said, stepping inside as he ushered me through to his office. 'I didn't expect such—' I wanted to say 'squalor' but settled instead on the phrase 'an informal setting'.

'You mean you expected a lavish government building, replete with servants and wine and beautiful music being played by a string orchestra chained together in one corner?' he asked bitterly.

'Well, no,' I began. 'That's not—'

'For all that the world appears to think of us, Signor Zéla, Rome is not a wealthy city. What funds the government has within its control to disperse it chooses not to waste on ridiculous ornamentation for its public servants. Most of the government buildings are currently situated in small dwellings such as this one around the city. It is not perfect but our minds are more concentrated on our work than on our surroundings.'

'Quite so,' I said, feeling suitably humbled by the philanthropy of his sentiment. 'I meant no offence, you understand.'

'You will have a glass of wine?' he inquired, clearly ready to move on from his diatribe as I settled in an easy chair opposite his desk, where a Tower of Pisa in paperwork stood ominously before me. I indicated that I would have whatever he was having and he poured me a glass with a shaky hand, more than a few dropfuls landing on the tray upon which the bottle stood. I accepted the glass with a smile and he sat opposite me, putting his glasses on and off as he peered at me, clearly unsure whether he liked what he saw or not.

'Strange,' he said eventually, settling back with a shake of his head. 'I expected someone older.'

'I'm older than I look,' I admitted.

'From what I heard of your work, you sounded like a most distinguished man.' I moved to protest but he shook his hand in the air dismissively. 'I don't mean that in an offensive way,' he said. 'I just meant that your reputation suggested a man who had spent a lifetime learning about the arts. How old are you anyway, forty? Forty-one?'

'I wish,' I said with a smile. 'But I've crammed a lot of experience into my life, I promise you that.'

'I think you should know,' said Signor Carlati, 'that it was not my idea to invite you to Rome.'

'Right . . .' I said slowly, nodding my head.

'Personally I am of the belief that the administration of the arts within Italy should be undertaken by Italians and that the disbursement of government funding within Rome should be overseen by a Roman.'

'Such as yourself?' I asked politely.

'Actually, I am from Geneva,' he said, sitting up straight and pulling his jacket down slightly.

'Not even Italian then?'

'That does not mean I cannot believe in a principle. I would feel the same way about a foreigner making government decisions within my own country as I feel about this one. Have you read Borsieri?'

I shook my head. 'Not really,' I said. 'Maybe a little here and there, nothing substantial.'

'Borsieri suggests that the Italians should put aside their own artistic bents and look to the literature and artistic creations of other nations and adapt them for this country.'

'I'm not sure that's exactly it,' I said doubtfully, considering that Carlati was simplifying Borsieri's statements significantly.

'He seeks to make us a nation of translators, Signor Zéla,' continued Carlati with a look of pure disbelief. 'Italy. The country which produced Michelangelo, Leonardo, the great Renaissance writers and artists. He seeks that we should put aside all our national characteristics and look to simply import ideas from the rest of the world. Madame de Staël too,' he added, spitting on the floor as he said her name, an action which made me jump back in surprise. '*L'Avventure Letterarie di un Giorno*,' he shouted. 'You, signor, are the natural embodiment of that piece. That is why you are here. To deprive us of our culture and introduce your own. It is part of a continuing process to denigrate the Italian and rid him of his self-confidence and natural talents. Rome is to be a little Paris.'

I thought about it for a moment and wondered whether I should point out the obvious flaw in his argument. He was, after all, a perfect embodiment of that which he disapproved of. He was Swiss, not Italian. His argument – while theoretically debatable – did not merit such passion on his part, as the enforcement of his convictions would surely have led him back across the Alps and into a career in clock-making or conducting the local chapter of the Swiss Yodelling Society. I considered pointing this out to him in ungentlemanly language but decided against it. He did not like me. We had just met but he did not like me, of that I was sure.

'I would be keen to find out more about my responsibilities,' I said eventually, hoping to move the conversation on a little. 'The duties you mentioned in your letter, while fascinating, remain a little vague. I suspect there is a lot more that you can tell me about them. For instance, to whom do I report? Who will offer me instruction? Whose plans am I here to fulfil?'

Signor Carlati sat back in his chair and smiled bitterly at me, his fingertips creating a temple before his nose. He waited before answering and watched for my amazed expression as he told me who had desired my appointment to the Roman government and from whom I could expect to receive my instructions.

'You are here,' he said clearly, 'under the direct will and desire of *Il Papa* himself. You are to meet with him tomorrow afternoon in his apartments in the Vatican. It seems that your reputation has spread even to his ears. How very fortunate for you.'

He took me so much by surprise that I burst out laughing, a reaction which I can assume only from his disgusted expression he considered to be typical of an ignorant French immigrant such as myself.

*   *   *

Sabella Donato was thirty-two years old when I met her. She had dark brown hair, pulled back fiercely from the sides of her head into a bunch behind, and wide, green eyes, which were her most captivating feature. She had a habit of looking at you from their corners, her face turned slightly to one side as she observed your every movement, and was widely considered to be one of the three most beautiful women in Rome at that time. Her skin was not quite so dark as those Italians who worked out of doors all the time, and she exuded an air of worldliness, of European mystique, despite the fact that she had grown up the daughter of a fisherman in Sicily.

She was introduced to me at a reception given by the Comte de Jorvé and his wife, where their daughter Isobel was to sing a selection from *Tancredi*. I had met the Comte a few weeks earlier at one of the many official lunches I had to attend in my new role and had been drawn to him immediately. A round faced fellow whose whole body betrayed a love of fine food and wine, he had come to speak to me about the opera house which he had heard I was designing.

'It's true then, isn't it, Signor Zéla? It is to be the finest opera house in Italy, I believe. Set to rival La Scala?'

'I don't know where you are receiving your information from, Comte,' I replied with a smile, swirling a glass of port in my hand. 'As you know, no announcement has yet been made as to where the major funds are to be distributed.'

'Come, come, signor. All of Rome knows that His Holiness is intending for it to be built. His obsession with outclassing Lombardy dates back to before his elevation, you know. Some say he sees his relationship with you as resonant of that between Leonardo and—'

'Really, Comte,' I said, amused but flattered. 'That is ridiculous. I am a mere civil servant, that is all. Even if we were planning an opera house, I would not be the designer, merely the man who sees that all the funds are dispersed in a sensible manner. The artistic creations I am bound to leave to other, more talented people than myself.'

He laughed some more and poked my ribs with a chubby index finger. 'I can't get you to let loose any secrets then?' he asked, his face growing purple with curiosity as I shook my head.

'Afraid not,' I replied. Of course, it was not long afterwards that the announcement *was* made and from then on I was fair game for anyone in the city to corner with their ideas of how the building should be constructed, how large the stage should be, how deep the pit, the very design for the drop curtains. But it was the Comte whose views I listened to the most at the time, for we became friends quickly and I learned that I could trust him to keep our conversations to himself. I was only sorry that his daughter was not a better singer, for I had hoped to be able to repay my debt of friendship to him by offering some assistance to Isobel, who was twenty-five, plain, unmarried and without a future.

'She's dreadful, isn't she?' asked Sabella, approaching me for the first time just as Isobel finished her third excerpt and we were finally allowed to disperse for some much needed refreshments.

'With training, there is some hope,' I muttered charitably, immediately attracted to the smiling vision beside me, but unwilling to be disloyal to my friend simply in order to ingratiate myself with a woman. 'She handled the second movement skilfully, I thought.'

'She sounded like she needed to have a movement

herself,' said Sabella lightly, picking up a cracker and inspecting its burden suspiciously before popping it inside her mouth. 'But she's a lovely girl all the same. I spoke to her earlier and she told me not to expect much from her singing.' I smiled. 'Sabella Donate,' she said after a moment and extended a gloved hand towards me. I took it and kissed it gently, the satin warm beneath my lips.

'Matthieu Zéla,' I said, bowing a little as I stood back up.

'The great arts administrator,' she replied with an intake of breath, looking me up and down as if she had been waiting to meet me all day. 'So much is expected of you, signor. The city is talking of your plans day and night. I hear there is to be an opera house somewhere in our future.'

'Nothing has been confirmed as yet,' I muttered.

'It will be good for the city,' she said, ignoring my half-denial, 'although your friend the Comte should not expect his daughter to be singing there on opening night. She is more likely to end up gracing one of the many boxes in the audience.'

'And you, Madame Donate,' I began.

'Sabella, please.'

'You will be singing if such a great achievement was to come into place? Your reputation precedes even my own, you know. I hear it sometimes gets its own invitation to parties.'

She laughed. 'I don't come cheap, you know,' she said. 'Are you sure you could afford me?'

'The Holy Father has a very large purse.'

'Which he keeps very tight control over, I believe.' I opened my hands a little to indicate that I had no comment on that matter and she laughed. 'You are very discreet, Signor Zéla,' she said. 'That's an admirable trait in a man these days. I think I would like to know you better. All I ever hear are rumours and, while such things do have an unpleasant habit of being true, it is foolish to rely upon them.'

'And I you,' I said, 'although the stories I have heard concern your talent and beauty, both of which are undeniable. I know not what you have heard of me.'

'Charm is not everything,' she answered, looking suddenly irritated. 'Do you know, wherever I go, from morning till night, people flatter me? Or try to anyway. They tell me how my voice is God's own instrument, how my beauty is incomparable, how this, how that, how everything in the world is wonderful because of my presence in it. They think this will make me happy. They think it will make me like them. Do you think it works?'

'I doubt it,' I said. 'A confident person knows their own talents and doesn't need to have them reinforced by being assured that they are there. And you seem to me confident already.'

'So how would you seek to flatter me then? What would you do to impress me?'

I shrugged lightly. 'I don't try to impress people, Sabella,' I said. 'That's not in my nature. The older I get, the less interested I am in being popular. I don't wish to be actively disliked, you understand, I just find that I don't care so much about the opinions of others. My own opinion is what matters. That I respect myself. Which I do.'

'So you wouldn't try to impress me at all?' she asked, smiling, flirting with me as we stood there. I felt powerfully drawn to her and wanted to take her somewhere we could talk in private, but grew weary of this slightly forced repartee, the language of two people who are trying to make a good impression on each other, something which despite my assertions to the contrary I was clearly attempting to do.

'I think I would point out your flaws,' I said, moving away slightly and putting my glass down on a table. 'I'd tell you where your voice lets you down, why your beauty will some day fade, and why none of it really matters a jot. I'd talk about the things that other people never talk about.'

'If you were trying to impress me, you mean.'

'Exactly.'

'Well, then, I look forward to hearing about all my flaws,' she said, stepping away now and looking back with a smile, 'when you feel brave enough to point them out to me.'

I watched her disappear back into the crowd and would have followed her immediately had not Isobel begun another movement with a surprisingly flawless B flat which forced me to stay where I was out of respect for the best part of fifteen minutes, by which time the famous singer and beauty had already disappeared.

All this talk of opera houses related back to the afternoon following my stormy meeting with Signor Carlati. By the time I gratefully left his shabby office that day he had given me instructions on how to conduct myself throughout my appointment with Giovanni Maria Mastai-Feretti, the Vicar of Rome, Pope Pius IX, my new employer.

We were to meet in his private apartments in the Vatican at 3 p.m. and I admit that I was somewhat nervous as I made my way through the stately, historical palace, guided at every step by a nervous, priestly secretary who informed me on at least seven occasions that I was to address the Pope as 'Your Holiness' at all times, and never interrupt him when he was speaking, as it gave him a migraine and he would become irritable. I was also not to contradict anything that the Holy Father said, nor was I to offer any alternatives which were particularly contrary to the requirements which he would make of me. It seemed that conversation was frowned upon by the Holy See.

I had made it my business to find out a little about this Pope in the twenty-four hours at my disposal between interviews. At a mere fifty-six years of age – a child in comparison to my 104 – he had been in office only for a couple of years at the time. His personality confused me as I read through various newspaper articles about him, for they were all quite contradictory in what they believed to be his true persona. Some considered him a dangerous liberal whose opinions on freeing political prisoners and allowing laymen into his council of ministers could spell a dangerous end to the authority of the Papacy in Italy. Others viewed him as potentially the most powerful force for change within the country, able to unite the old left and right factions into a union of accord, opening up the press for discussion and setting about writing constitutions for the Papal States. For a man so close to the start of his reign, he appeared to have mastered the art of the true politician in that no one, neither friend nor enemy, seemed able to define his true beliefs or plans for either himself or the country.

The room into which I was ushered was smaller than I expected and the walls were furnished with books, long religious tracts, enormous histories, some biographies, poetry, even a little of the new fiction. It was Pius's private study, I was told, the room to which he went when he wanted to relax a little, unburden himself from his duties for a time. I was privileged, the nervous priest told me, that I was being invited to meet with him there for it meant that our meeting would be somewhat informal, even enjoyable, and that I would perhaps see a less official side to the Pope than others did.

He entered from a side door with, surprisingly, a bottle of red wine in one hand. Had he not been walking in a perfectly straight line, I would have suspected drunkenness.

'Your Holiness,' I said, bowing slightly, unsure for all that I had been told whether that was in fact the correct etiquette. 'It's a pleasure to meet you.'

'Sit down, please, Signor Zéla,' he sighed as if I had already exhausted his patience, indicating one of the seats by the window. 'You will take a glass of wine with me of course.' I was unsure whether this was a statement of fact or a request so I merely smiled and inclined my head a little to one side. He barely noticed anyway and poured the wine slowly into two glasses, turning the rim as he finished pouring like a waiter might. The notion crossed my mind that he might have been a waiter in his youth before he had settled on his vocation. He was a little shorter than me, about five foot eleven, with a large round head and the thinnest eyebrows and lips I had ever seen on a grown man. From beneath his skull-cap, a peak of dark hair pointed forward in an ironic display of diabolism and I couldn't help but observe from his upper neck that he must have cut himself shaving that morning, a human inaccuracy that one might never have expected of the Supreme

Pontiff; his infallibility obviously did not extend to a steady hand.

We made some idle chatter regarding my trip to Rome, my lodgings, and I told a few lies about my early life, getting the basic facts right but loosening up the chronology a little. The last thing I wanted was for him to summon forth a conclave of cardinals to declare me a modern day miracle. We talked of the arts – he cited *The Beggar's Opera* in music, *Reflections on the Revolution in France* in literature, *The Hay Wain* in painting and *The Count of Monte Cristo* in fiction, claiming to have read the latter five times since its publication a few years earlier.

'Have you read it, Signor Zéla?' he asked me and I shook my head.

'Not as yet, I'm afraid. I haven't a great deal of time for fiction these days. I liked the days of the pure imagination, rather than the social commentary. So many of these novelists seem to want to preach rather than to entertain. I don't care for that so much. I like a good story.'

'*The Count of Monte Cristo* is an adventure story,' he said, laughing. 'The kind of book one wanted to read as a child but which had not been written as yet. I will give you a copy before you leave and perhaps you will let me know what you think of it.'

I indicated that I would be glad to but inside felt a little aggrieved that I would be obliged to plough through five hundred pages of Dumas when I would prefer to be acquainting myself with the city. He asked me whether I was alone and I spoke briefly of Thomas, suggesting that I hoped to find suitable employment for the time that we remained in Rome, however long that may be.

'And how long would you like to stay?' he asked me, a thin smile spreading across his face.

'As long as is necessary, I expect,' I said. 'I'm not entirely sure of the commission which you have for me. Perhaps you—'

'There are many things which I would like to do as Pope,' he announced, addressing me suddenly as if I were a college of cardinals. 'You have probably read of some of the reforms I am being accused of undertaking. I will doubtless be drawn into this war with Austria at some point and I do not relish the political reverberations of that. But I also want to create something to be proud of. Here in Rome. Something which the everyday Roman can come to and enjoy and celebrate. Something that will make the city feel alive again and vibrant. People become happier in a city which has some sort of central focus. Have you ever been to Milan or Naples, Signor Zéla?'

'Neither,' I admitted.

'In Milan there is the great opera house La Scala. In Naples there is San Carlo. Even little Venice has La Fenice. I want to build an opera house in the city of Rome which will rival these fine buildings and bring a little culture back to the city. And that, Signor Zéla, is why I have brought you here.'

I nodded slowly and took a long sip from my wine glass. 'I'm no architect,' I said eventually.

'You are an administrator,' he said, pointing at me. 'I have heard of the work you undertook in Paris. I have heard people speak very highly of you. I have friends in all the cities of Europe and beyond and they tell me many things. Here in Rome I have a certain amount of funding at my disposal and, as I have neither the time nor the talent to find the best artists and architects in Italy, I thought of you. You will undertake this commission for me and you will, of course, be handsomely rewarded for it.'

'How handsomely?' I inquired with a smile. He may have been the Pope but I was still young then and had a living to earn. He mentioned a sum which was more than generous and indicated that I would receive half at the start of the project and the rest in increments throughout a proposed three year building plan.

'So,' he said eventually with a smile, 'does this meet with your approval? Will you agree to undertake the construction of an opera house in Rome for me? What do you say, Signor Zéla? The choice is yours.'

What could I say? I had already been told that I could never turn this man down. I shrugged my shoulders and smiled at him. '*Accepto*,' I said.

Throughout that summer my romance with Sabella blossomed. We attended parties together, the theatre, salon functions. We were written up in a court reporter and all interest was continually directed towards Sabella, who had appeared in Roman society out of nowhere with a beauty and a talent that was envied by all and a past known by no one. We became lovers as the city sweltered to summer and the young men began discreetly to leave the city for the Italian war with Austria, from which Pius was holding himself aloof. There was talk of insurrection, of the Pope himself being turned out of his city, and the commentators were divided on whether he should become involved – and by default involve the Papal See – or not.

I myself cared not. I had no taste for war during those decades and wanted nothing more at that point than to enjoy Rome, Sabella and the commission I had been granted. I had grown instantly wealthy when I agreed to build the opera house and, although I made sure to live well within my means, I found that those means could from time to time turn to the lavish.

Sabella delighted in my company and lost few opportunities to tell me how much she was in love with me. Within a short time of our first encounter she was telling me that I was the love of her life, the only true love she had known since her girlhood, and that she had fallen in love with me that first afternoon at the home of the Comte de Jorvé and his tone-deaf daughter.

'When I was seventeen,' she told me, 'I began a liaison with a young farmer in Naples. He was no more than a boy, maybe eighteen or nineteen years old. We were in love for a brief time but he soon became engaged to another and broke my heart. I left our village shortly afterwards but have never forgotten him. Our affair was brief – maybe four weeks out of my entire lifetime – but the impression that it left lingers. I thought I would never recover from it.'

'I have known such a romance,' I said but declined to discuss it.

'It was after this that I found that I could sing and began to use my voice to make a little money along the coast. Every song led to another and I was soon becoming employed because of it and found that I had the ability to make a living with this instrument. Somehow I ended up in Rome. With you.'

For my part, I was fond of her but not so in love as she. And yet, shortly afterwards, almost by chance, we married. She claimed to have become Catholic after she had joined me for a meeting with the Pope, and said thereafter that she did not want to sleep with me any more without the tenets of marriage. I was unsure at first – marriage had not been working well for me those past fifty years or so – and I considered breaking off the attachment, but any such suggestion drove her into a hysteria which I could not control. These sudden and inexplicable bursts of anger contrasted with the deep affection she displayed towards me in our quieter moments, and in the end I agreed that we should wed. Unlike some of my other marriages, we opted for a simple ceremony in a small chapel, with only Thomas and his new lover, a dark haired girl called Marita, as witnesses.

We did not honeymoon but returned instead to our apartment, where she surrendered herself to me as if we had never before known intimacy. Thomas had moved out and become engaged to Marita, although he claimed it would be a long engagement as he was not yet ready for marriage, and we were alone together at last. For a brief period anyway. Once again, through no fault of my own, I was a married man.

After an initial competition phase, I hired a man named Girno to design the opera house and he brought me some plans in the summer of 1848. They were rough sketches of what appeared to be an enormous amphitheatre with a huge stage set at the front. The ground held eighty-two rows of seating, fronted by the orchestra, and on either side there were four levels of boxes – seventy-two in all – each of which could hold up to eight people in comfort, or a dozen without. Where the curtains were to meet was the seal of Pope Pius IX, which I took to be a little sycophantic and requested that he think up a different idea, suggesting a representation of the twin founders of the city, Romulus and Remus, on either curtain, separated during the performance and joined before and after. Girno was an intelligent man and excited to be involved in such a lavish production, even if it was at an early stage and even if it was destined to come to nothing.

The revolutions had been growing in ardour throughout the year, from shortly before our arrival in the city, and I studied the newspapers carefully every morning for news of any political unrest. It was on one such morning, while enjoying a coffee in a small café near St Peter's Square, that I read how the four main Italian leaders – Ferdinand II, Leopold of Tuscany, Charles Albert and Pius IX – had each issued constitutions in an act of appeasement and in order to prevent further rioting after the Palermo revolution in January had caused such trouble. These disturbances continued around the country with the mainly conservative governments being attacked by the more radical elements of each separate society. The Italian reporters were typically verbose as they described how Charles Albert declared war on Austria from Lombardy. Immediately the country was devastated by the Pope's decision not to side with his countryman, a move which might have 'unified' Italy against a common enemy. Rather, he denounced the war, a move which strengthened the Austrian position and led to Lombardy's eventual defeat, for which he would then receive the blame.

'It is not that I am opposed to Lombardy's views,' the Pope told me at one of our regular meetings at the time. We had become confidants of a type and it was not unusual for him to discuss such matters with me. 'On the contrary I am privately concerned about Austria's imperial threats, although I consider them of less danger to Rome than to anywhere else. But what is most important is that I, as Pope, do not side with a nationalist leader in a matter which could potentially lead to the destruction of the Italian nation states as we know them.'

'You are opposed to unification then?' I asked, somewhat surprised.

'I am opposed to the idea of central government. Italy is a large country, once all our states are joined together. And if that was to happen we would become nothing more than elements in a greater whole and who knows who would be in charge of Italy then or what it might become.'

'A powerful country, perhaps,' I suggested, at which he roared with laughter.

'How little you know of Italy,' he said. 'What you see before you is a country whose very organs are ruled by men who see themselves as the natural offspring of Romulus and Remus. Each one of these so-called nationalist leaders looks towards a unified country of which they themselves are king. Some even suggest that *I* should be king,' he added thoughtfully.

'Which you don't want,' I stated flatly, watching his reaction closely – a shrug, a wave of the hand, a dismissive gesture, a change of tack.

'I will hold Rome independent,' he said, tapping each word out on the side of his armchair with his index finger. 'That is what is of importance to me here. I will not allow her to be destroyed by the vain and wholly impossible concept of political unity. We have been here too long to see her brought to her knees by the Italians themselves, let alone the Austrian invaders.' By 'we', I assumed he meant the long line of pontiffs to which his own name had recently been added.

'I don't follow your reasoning,' I continued, irritated

by his arrogance and forgetting all that I had been instructed on my very first visit to the Vatican. 'If you consider—'

'Enough of this!' he roared, standing up and allowing his face to grow purple with rage as he moved towards the window. 'You get on with building my opera house and allow me to run my city as I see fit.'

'I meant no offence,' I said after a long pause, standing up and walking towards the door. He didn't turn around to see me or to say goodbye and my last view of him was of a huddled man leaning towards a narrow window over St Peter's Square, watching as the people – *his* people – busied themselves for the storm to come.

The events of 11 and 12 November 1848 remain somewhat incredible to me, even now from a distance of some 151 years. Sabella returned home early in the afternoon, clearly agitated and unable to answer even my most simple questions.

'My dear,' I said, rising and going over to embrace her. Her body was rigid against my own and as I stood back to look at her I was amazed by how pale she appeared. 'Sabella, you look like you've seen a ghost. What's the matter?'

'Nothing,' she answered quickly, stepping back and pinching her own cheeks to invite a little colour to reappear. 'I can't stay here right now. I have to go out again. I'll be back later.'

'But where are you going?' I asked. 'You can't go out in this state.'

'I'm fine, Matthieu, honestly. I just need to find my—' There was a sudden rap on the door and she jumped back in fright. 'Oh, my God,' she said. 'Don't answer it!'

'Don't answer it? Why ever not? It's probably only Thomas, come to—'

'Leave it, Matthieu. It's trouble, that's all.'

But it was too late. I had opened the door and standing before me was a middle aged man in the uniform of a Piedmontese officer. He had a broad moustache above his lip, which seemed to curl back in towards his mouth as he looked me up and down.

'Can I help you, sir?' I asked politely.

'You have already helped yourself,' he replied, stepping inside quickly, one hand hovering dangerously above the sword buried within his side scabbard, 'to that which is not yours.'

I looked across at Sabella who was rocking back and forth on a seat by the window, moaning audibly. 'Who are you?' I asked baffled.

'Who am I? Who are *you*, sir?'

'Matthieu Zéla,' I replied. 'And this is my home so I'll thank you not to make demands in it.'

'And that woman,' he said quickly, pointing roughly at Sabella, 'I'd say lady but that's not the right word for her. Who is she, then, might I ask?'

'That's my wife,' I answered, growing annoyed now. 'And I'll thank you to treat her with respect please!'

'Ha!' he laughed. 'Here's a riddle for you then. How can she be your wife when she is already married to me, eh? Can you answer that? In your fine clothes,' he added as a *non sequitur*.

'Married to you?' I asked baffled. 'Don't be ridiculous. She—'

I could continue this scene and play it out, phrase by phrase, admission by admission, to its logical conclusion but it is the stuff of farce. Suffice to say that my so-called wife, Sabella Donato, had omitted to

123

inform me that at the time of our nuptials she already had a husband, this dolt whose name was Marco Lanzoni. They had got married some ten years earlier, shortly before her rise to fame, and he had joined the army almost immediately after the wedding in order to make enough money for them to live comfortably in the future. When he returned to his hometown she had vanished, taking with her most of his belongings which she had sold to finance her early adventures throughout Italy. It had taken him this long to track her down to Rome and now he was here to claim her back. The one thing he hadn't counted on was a second husband. A fiery chap, he demanded satisfaction and immediately challenged me to a duel the following morning, which I was forced to accept or bear the brand of cowardice. After he left, a troubling scene took place between my 'wife' and leading to many tears and recriminations. Our farcical wedding had taken place because she had placed herself in a state of self-delusion regarding her earlier alliance. And now there was a chance that I would pay the ultimate price for it. Time could not wither me, but Lanzoni's sword certainly could.

In the meantime, word came to me via Thomas that the cowardly Pius IX, terrified of a Roman invasion which could cost him either his position or his life, or possibly both, had quit Rome for Gaeta, south of Naples – where he was eventually to stay in exile for several years – thus depriving me of both my income and my employment. All plans to build an opera house in Rome were shelved due to a sudden lack of funding and I found myself, temporarily at least, unwed and unemployed. This change in my fortunes caused me to question the sanity of taking part in the proposed duel. After all, there was nothing holding me in Italy. I could have easily fled the city and never had to encounter Lanzoni again, and I will admit that a part of me wanted to follow this course of action. However, it would have been a dishonourable act and even if my character were to remain unblemished I would have always remembered that I had run away from a fight. Therefore, almost despite myself, I resolved to stay and accept Lanzoni's challenge.

The following morning was misty and as I stood in a private courtyard with Sabella in hysterics by the wall and Thomas acting as my second I felt incredibly miserable and was convinced that my life was finally coming to an end.

'It's ridiculous, isn't it?' I said to my nephew who stood holding my coat with a look of utter distress on his face. 'I don't know this man, I meant him no harm by marrying his wife, and I look set to die for my sins because of it. Why can't a man duel with a woman, eh? Can you tell me that? It's hardly my argument.'

'You're not going to die, Uncle Matthieu,' said Thomas, and for a moment I was afraid that he was going to start crying. 'You can win, you know. You may be a lot older than him but physically you have ten years on him. He is full of rage, you couldn't care less. His passions are stronger.'

I shook my head, experiencing a rare moment of self doubt. 'Maybe it's for the best,' I said, taking off my jacket and waistcoat and examining the blade that I held in my hand. 'I can't go on living for ever, after all. Despite all signs to the contrary.'

'You can't die either. You have too much to live for.'

'Such as?' If I was going, I wasn't going to go without a little sympathy.

'There's me for one thing,' said Thomas. 'And there's Marita. Our unborn child too.'

I stared at him in surprise. A hundred years later I would have screamed at him for his carelessness but, for now, I could only feel joy. 'Your child,' I said in some surprise, not seeing him as anything more than a child himself. 'When did all this happen?'

'Just recently. We only found out two days ago. So you see you cannot die. We need you.'

I nodded and experienced a rush of previously unfelt strength. 'You are right, my boy,' I said. 'He can't beat me. None of this has anything to do with me. Come on then, sir,' I called across the courtyard. 'Let us begin.'

We crossed swords back and forth across that courtyard for no more than four minutes, but it felt like days were passing us by as we danced from side to side. I could hear Sabella's cries but ignored them – I had decided that no matter what happened, our relationship was over. I saw Thomas urging me on from the side, wincing whenever Lanzoni's blade stung my arm or snagged my cheek. Eventually, with a great sweeping movement of one hand, I disarmed my adversary and pinned him to the ground. The tip of my sword pressed in upon his Adam's apple and he stared up at me with beseeching eyes, begging for mercy, pleading for his life. I was furious that things had got this far and was close to pressing it in all the way and finishing the man off.

'This has nothing to do with me!' I roared. 'It's not my fault she was married!'

I toyed with the handle of the blade some more but eventually let him up and walked away. I strolled back towards Thomas, attempting to calm myself as I walked, pleased that I had overcome the certain blood-lust that exists inside all of us and allowed myself to feel compassion instead. I stepped ahead of my nephew and he turned to put my coat on my back.

'You see, Thomas,' I began happily, 'there are times in a man's life when—'

A great rush of feet came towards me from behind and, as I turned, my nephew did too, only too late to allow him to step out of the way and his unhappy body stood there, an upright corpse, as Lanzoni ran towards him, blade outstretched, ready to run one or both of us through. Within seconds both were dead, one by my sword, one by Lanzoni's.

There was silence in the courtyard and I merely glanced at my sometime wife who sat crying on the kerb now before bringing my nephew's body back to his pregnant mistress. After we buried him, I left Italy and vowed never to return. Not if I lived to be a thousand.

Chapter 9

April 1999

The phone rang in the middle of the night and I immediately feared the worst. My eyes sprang open to utter darkness with an image of Tommy emblazoned on my mind. What I saw was a picture of my nephew, dead in a gutter somewhere in Soho, with his own eyes staring blindly upwards towards the sky, terrified by his last sight before death, his mouth open, his arms draped at improper angles from his torso, a trickle of blood creeping slowly away from him and escaping his body through his left ear as he grew colder and more rigid by the minute. Another death, another nephew, another boy I had failed to save. I answered the phone and the worst was confirmed. There had indeed been a death – why else would one be disturbed in the middle of the night – but it had not been Tommy's.

'Matthieu?' said a voice, shocked and nervous at the other end. Not a police officer, I knew immediately, for there was panic in the tone. A sense of frightened urgency. I recognized the voice but couldn't place it, as if the added resonance of fear changed it so slightly as to make it seem more distant to my memory.

'Yes. Who is this?'

'It's P.W., Matthieu.' My record producing friend and

fellow investor at our satellite broadcasting station. 'I've got the most shocking news. I don't know how to tell you this.' He paused as he struggled to find the three simple words. 'James is dead.'

I sat up and shook my head in amazement. I've seen a lot of deaths in my time, some natural, some a little less so, but they never fail to surprise me when they take place. There's a part of me that simply can't fathom why other people's bodies let them down so much when my own is so incredibly faithful to me. 'Good Lord,' I said after a moment, not quite sure how I should react or what response he was looking for. 'How did it happen?'

'It's a little difficult to go into over the phone, Matthieu. Could you come over here?'

'Over where? What hospital are you in?'

'I'm not in a hospital, neither is James. We're in his house. We need some . . . help.'

My eyes narrowed; he wasn't making any sense. 'James is dead and you're in his *house*?' I asked. 'Well, have you called a doctor, the police even? Maybe he isn't dead at all. Maybe he's just—'

'Matthieu, he's dead. Believe me. You have to come over here. Please. I don't ask much of you, but—' He started to ramble on about how long we had known each other, how much I meant to him, the kind of nonsense a man comes out with when he's either about to get married, been drinking too much or finds himself in a state of bankruptcy. I held the phone away from my ear and reached over to pick up my bedside clock, which registered 03:18. I sighed and shook my head violently to shake off the sleep, running a hand through my hair and licking my dry lips as I did so. My mouth felt dry and the bed was warm and inviting. P.W.

129

was still talking on the other end of the phone though and sounded as if he could go on for ever so eventually I was forced to interrupt.

'I'll be there in thirty minutes,' I said. 'And for God's sake, you'd better not do anything until I *do* get there, all right?'

'Oh, thank God. Thank *you*, Matthieu. I don't know how I'm going to—'

I hung up.

I first met James Hocknell a couple of years before at a dinner at the Guildhall. We were there to celebrate the life of some worthy who had spent his entire career in the newspaper business and had recently made a small fortune from his autobiography, mostly because in it he hinted at relationships between prominent politicians of the previous forty years and some close female relations of the present Queen, some savoury, some not quite so much. Like so many men who are well versed in the libel laws of the country, however, he made sure never to mention a situation when an innuendo would do just as well, and never quoted an actual source other than to use the time honoured phrase 'friends of . . . told me . . .'. I was seated at a table with the Foreign Secretary and his wife, a young actress who had just been nominated for an Academy Award and her middle-aged boyfriend – a well known figure in the racing world – a couple of young Honourables who were talking about a supermodel's drug habit, and my own partner at the time, whose name I completely forget right now but who I recall had short dark hair, large lips and was a Lloyd's name.

I was standing at the bar ordering drinks when I first laid eyes on James. He had just turned fifty then and

130

was the editor of a tabloid newspaper, having left an assistant editor's job at a reputable broadsheet a few years before. Circulation figures were down since he had taken over, mostly due to his decision to axe the bare breast from the inner pages of the rag, and he bore the look of a man who feared that the entire room was conspiring against him, when all that they were actually doing was ignoring him and allowing him to get on with his drinking in peace. Although I had never spoken to him before, I approached him and told him that I thought his work on *The Times*, particularly on a political scandal that had surfaced in the late eighties, had been admirable. I mentioned a *Newsweek* article he had once written on de Klerk, which had impressed me for its even handed ability to condemn without appearing to take a side, a rare talent in a commentator. He seemed pleased by my familiarity with his work and was keen to discuss it further.

'What about now, then?' he asked, frowning slightly as he accepted my offer of a small brandy. 'Don't think what I'm doing now is up to much, do you?'

I shrugged. 'I'm sure it's excellent,' I said, perhaps in too much of a patronizing manner for my own good. 'Only I never get as much time to read the papers as I wish. Otherwise I'd have a better grasp of the current *œuvre*, I suppose.'

'Oh, yes?' he asked. 'What is it you do then?' I thought about it. It was a tough question. At the time I wasn't doing anything much. Just relaxing. Enjoying life. Not a bad way to spend a decade or two.

'I'm one of the idle rich,' I said with a smile. 'The kind of person you probably despise.'

'Not at all. I've had ambitions to join that class myself for half my life.'

'Any luck?'

'Not a lot.'

He opened his mouth and waved his hand expansively over the mass of people who were milling around the hall, air-kissing each other with gusto, shaking each other's hands, exuding wealth and privilege from every open orifice and puckered pore. Large breasts, small diamonds, older men, younger women. There were a lot of dinner jackets and small black dresses on display. As I squinted, the room appeared to be a collection of black and white dots, rushing to and from each other with alarming speed; for a moment I was taken back to images from some of Charlie's old films. James appeared to be on the verge of saying something impressive about the other guests, *les mots justes* that would have summed up this ridiculous bunch and their general inanity, but an appropriate phrase escaped him on this occasion and eventually he just shook his head in defeat instead. 'I'm a little drunk,' he mentioned, which made me laugh as he said it with the slightly self-congratulatory air of a schoolboy caught in an illicit embrace with a girl from the upper sixth. I introduced myself to him then and he shook my hand firmly, attracting the barmaid's attention with an arrogant click of his fingers.

'Do you know what I hate about the rich?' he asked me and I shook my head. 'It's the fact that you only meet them when they're out like this, parading their glamour around for all to see, and they're always so damn happy too. Have you ever seen any section of society who smiles as much as the rich? Of course they *are* rich, hence the name, so that would probably explain it . . .' He trailed off there, lost in the obvious nature of his remarks.

132

'Even the rich have their worries,' I said quietly. 'It's not a bed of roses for anyone, I expect.'

'Are you rich?' he asked me.

'Very.'

'And are you happy?'

'Well, I'm satisfied.'

'Listen, let me tell you something about money,' he said, leaning forward and tapping me on the shoulder. 'I've been in this game for thirty years and I don't have a penny to call my own. Not a single fucking penny. I'm living from hand to mouth, from paycheque to paycheque. I've got a nice house, sure!' he shouted. 'But I've got three ex-wives to support and every fucking one of them has at least one kid that I have to shell out for as well. My money's not my own, Mattie—'

'It's Matthieu.'

'It goes into my account on payday and it's taken out a few hours later, siphoned off to those blood-sucking leeches whom I had the misfortune to marry. Never again, I tell you. There's not another woman on this planet who will ever get me to marry them now. Not one. Are you married?'

'I have been,' I said.

'Widowed? Divorced? Separated?'

'Let's just say I've run the gamut.'

'Then you know what I'm talking about. Every fucking one of them. Blood-sucking leeches. I can barely afford to feed myself three square meals some days and they're all out there living the life of fucking Riley. I ask you. Is that right?' I made to answer but he cut me off. 'Listen,' he continued, as if I had a choice now that he was on to what I would later realize to be his favourite topic. 'When I was a boy starting out in this game, back when I was in my early twenties, that's how I lived but

133

it seemed all right then because my future was ahead of me. I never had a penny back then either and come the end of the month I was eating cheese and crackers night after night with a cup of weak tea and calling it dinner. But I never minded then because I knew I was going to go far in this business and that, when I did, I'd make a fortune. I saw it coming, and it came too, I just never expected that I'd have to give the whole fucking lot of it away, that's all.'

Around the time of meeting James, I was growing weary of my idle lifestyle and looking for a new investment. I hadn't worked since leaving California with Stina in the fifties after the whole Buddy Rickles business and, while my bank balance was more than healthy and my annual income could have comfortably supported the annual expenses of, say, Manchester, I was growing a little restless with my own company and needed some excitement to be injected back into my life. I had attended that dinner at the Guildhall on the advice of a banker friend who was advising me on some of the avenues that I might take in order to re-enter the commercial world. He had already introduced me to P.W. and Alan, who had expressed an interest in setting up a satellite broadcasting station and the idea had appealed to me. My previous experience in television had been on the production side and, although it had ended in blacklisted disaster, I had enjoyed my time there and was attracted to the idea of a more hands-off managerial role, such as Rusty Wilson had enjoyed during my days at the Peacock. The concept of *satellite* broadcasting was one entirely of the age and that has always been a strong factor in influencing my decisions to become involved in a venture. However, neither of them had ever taken charge of a large business before and I was sure that I didn't actually want to *run* the thing myself, just take an interest in it. After consulting with my fellow investors, I decided to approach James over a terrible dinner at San Paolo's.

'Here's the thing, James,' I said afterwards as the four of us sat with brandy and cigars in leather chairs by the log fire in the bar outside. 'We have a little proposition for you.'

'I thought you might, gents,' he responded with a wide smile, settling back in his chair and stuffing the cigar between his mouth, like a movie star about to make a multi-million dollar deal. 'Didn't think you were bringing me here just to watch me stuff me face and scratch me arse.'

Alan shuddered and I coughed away a laugh. 'The three of us,' I began, indicating P.W., Alan and myself, 'are planning a little business venture which we think you might be interested in joining us on.'

'I've no money,' he said quickly, interjecting with his favourite topic before I could cut him off. 'There's no point looking at me for money because those blood-sucking—'

'Hold on, James,' I said, raising a hand in the air to silence him. 'Just listen to the offer first, that's all I ask. We're not looking for money.'

'I've put my life savings into this business,' said P.W. nervously and I glared at him as I don't like to lose my momentum in a conversation, particularly when I am trying to get something out of it. 'So we have to make it work,' he continued before seeing my expression and shutting up.

'We're planning a little business venture,' I repeated, my voice raised a little higher now to avoid interruption. 'The funding is in place, we've already started recruiting

135

in fact. It's a satellite broadcasting station. Mostly news and lifestyle shows, a few imported TV dramas from the States. The quality ones. Subscription based, of course. What we're looking for is a managing director. Someone to run the day to day operations, bring a little expertise to the business, make the decisions on the shop floor, so to speak. We all intend to be fairly hands off, although not entirely asleep you understand, and we need someone we can rely on and who understands the media world as it's run today. Someone who can make the station work. In short, James, we'd like you to do the job.'

I sat back with a fairly satisfied smile, pleased with the simplicity of my explanation and the way that his face appeared to be betraying more eagerness by the moment, particularly at the words 'managing director', 'make the decisions' and 'we all intend to be fairly hands off'. There was silence for a few moments before he sat forward in his chair, smiled widely and took the cigar out of his mouth.

'Gents,' he said, his eyes positively lit up with excitement, 'let's talk numbers.'

As things turned out, the numbers, when suitably tweaked, proved satisfactory to all concerned, as did a previously unexpected demand for a five per cent share in pre-tax profits, something which I was glad to give him in lieu of annual bonuses for an initial three year period, and within a month he was showing up for work before the early-morning cleaners and leaving after the late-night janitors. Over the course of the following two years, he made momentous decisions for the station, some of which I approved of, some of which made me a little uneasy, all of which proved correct my decision to employ him in the first place. He brought in a solid team of anchors and reporters, most notably Ms Tara Morrison who owes him a lot, and rearranged the schedules constantly to provide natural leads in and out of carefully planned programming. Market share grew considerably, and we all made money. Together, we became a success.

Alongside our business accomplishments, James and I became good friends. We were very different types of men but we respected each other and enjoyed each other's company. We argued across the boardroom table but always with a healthy regard for the other's opinion and the success of the station. We met once a month, alone, for a meal and drinks where the rule was that we did not mention anything to do with the station but spoke instead of politics, history and art. Our lives. (Of course, he was a little bit more honest with me about his life than I ever was with him about mine, but such is the way of all good relationships; one has to be a little economical with the truth, particularly when there is absolutely nothing to be gained by revealing all.) He worked reasonably well with P.W. and Alan, although they were not close, and it was this very fact which confused me as I took a taxi to James's home that early March morning, through a drizzly London mist. What on earth was P.W. doing there and what circumstances had led to James's death? I would have feared the worst, but had no idea whatsoever what 'the worst' might be. As I paid the driver and stepped outside the cab, I paused for a moment on the street outside, which was quiet and deserted. The lights in almost all the houses were off but there were five streetlights shining brightly. James's house was in darkness, except for the bay windows in the front room, where heavy curtains were drawn, a thin light breaking through where they did not quite meet. I took a deep breath and ran up the steps to ring the doorbell.

Two days later, with the exhausting events of the previous forty-eight hours behind me, I sat down behind my desk and dialled the unfamiliar number carefully. The connection seemed to take for ever and it rang for quite some time before being answered with a shout by what sounded like a young Cockney woman with pins in her mouth.

'Twelve!' she shouted into the phone and I raised an eyebrow in surprise. Had I rung the right number? Was 'twelve' her name? Was she some sort of robotic answering device? 'Set twelve!' she shouted now.

'Set twelve!' I repeated loudly, for some unknown reason, making it more of a command than anything else.

'Set twelve!' the voice said again. 'Who is this?'

'I'm sorry,' I said quickly, gathering myself together as I realized that she meant 'set' as a noun, not a verb. 'I was hoping to speak to Tommy DuMarqué please.'

'Who is this?' she asked again, more suspiciously this time. 'How did you get this number?'

'He gave it to me, of course,' I said, surprised by the aggression in her tone. 'How else would I—'

'This isn't some stalker, is it?' she asked and my mouth fell open. I didn't know what to say. 'Or a *journalist*.' She spat out the word with the distaste of someone who knew they would never read their own name in a newspaper. 'Tommy's filming at the moment,' she added then, her tone a little less suspicious now as if she was suddenly afraid of just who I might actually be and whether I had any involvement in the continuation of her employment. 'He won't be finished for another

138

– oh no, hold on. There he is. I'm not sure if he's busy though. Who can I say is calling?'

'Tell him it's his Uncle Matthieu,' I said, suddenly feeling exhausted again. 'If it's not too much trouble, that is.' The phone slammed down on a table and I heard a whispering in the background and Tommy's voice rising, saying, 'It's all right, honestly,' and then, 'Five minutes, OK?' in a louder voice before he picked it up.

'Uncle Matt?' he asked and I sighed with relief.

'At last,' I said. 'That was a most unpleasant girl. Who was she?'

'Just some runner. Don't worry about it. Thinks she's the director or something. God knows. This is the private number after all.'

'Well, whatever. I just wanted to phone you to say thanks, that's all. For what you did the other night. It was much appreciated.'

Tommy laughed as if it had been nothing at all, as if that kind of thing happened to him all the time, something which worried me. 'No sweat,' he said. 'Listen, you've helped me out often enough, right? Glad to be able to give a little bit back.'

'I must admit to feeling a few pangs of conscience,' I said. 'You don't think it was a little immoral what we did, do you?'

'I don't believe in shit like that,' he said nonchalantly. He paused and I said nothing, waiting for him to fill in the silence. I wanted him to reassure me, to tell me that my actions were proper and accountable. I've lived a long time and, while I may not have ever been a saint, I like to think that I've never deliberately hurt anyone since Dominique, particularly not my friends. 'The way I see it is that the guy was dead anyway, all we did was fix it. There's nothing that you or I or any of those creepy friends of yours could have done to make him any better or any worse. You got dragged into something that was nothing to do with you, that's all. You need to pick your friends better, Uncle Matt.'

'I wouldn't exactly call them friends,' I pointed out.

'Don't let your conscience get to you,' he said. '*You* didn't kill him.'

'No, I suppose not.'

'So just relax. It's behind us now. We sorted a situation, that's all. Let's move on, OK?' He sounded like a character in his television show. I nodded but still didn't feel completely happy about the way things had worked out.

'Thanks, Tommy,' I said eventually, realizing we had nothing more to say on the matter, that if it needed further consideration then I would have to do it on my own. 'We'll speak soon, yes?'

'I hope so. The testicular cancer is in remission now, you'll be glad to hear. I'm getting the all clear from the doctors later on today. So it looks like I'm not going to be looking for work any time soon, which is just as well as the *last* thing I need right now is more cashflow problems.'

'The *what*?' I asked, sitting up in surprise. 'What testicular—? Oh,' I said quickly, laughing as I collapsed back in the seat again. 'What's his name's, you mean.'

'Sam's.'

'You have to stop thinking that you *are* your character, you know.'

'Why? The rest of the country thinks I am. Some old bag attacked me in Tesco's yesterday and said it was my own fault for screwing around with Tina behind Carl's back. She said it was God's revenge on my balls.'

140

'God's revenge, yes,' I said with a sigh. 'I have no idea who any of these people are, you understand. I must start actually *watching* your programme.'

'I wouldn't bother,' he replied, as if he was responding to a journalist's question with a pre-prepared statement. 'Sure, there's a certain element of gritty inner city realism that reflects and transposes the breakdown of the traditional family circle in London, the historical shared memory that is, into a contemporary desire for singular pleasures and personal gratification, and as such there are universal themes to be explored, but the writing's shit and the acting's rushed and repetitive on a quotidian basis due to the lack of rehearsal time and production directives for as few takes as possible. Everyone knows that.'

I paused for a long, long time, blinking away my surprise. '*What?*' I asked eventually, unsure that that sentence had just come out of my drug-taking party-going nephew's mouth. '*What did you just say?*'

'Forget about it. It's just TV,' he said, laughing loudly. 'It's just *fiction*. It's all makey-up.' He paused and waited for me to say something further but I had nothing else to add. What could I possibly add to that? 'Later, Uncle Matt,' he said eventually to the silence, laughing as he hung up. I held the receiver in my hand for a few moments, listening to the dial tone before setting it back in place and closing my eyes to remember. There was no doubt about it, for once one of the Thomases had helped *me* out. And it made a pleasant change.

P.W. opened the door and grabbed me by the shoulders dramatically. His hair, which he grows long on one side of his head before combing it all the way across his pate to the other ear, was hanging askew, like a curtain falling just beneath his left ear. It was most unattractive. He wore a pale blue shirt with dark half-moons of perspiration looming beneath the armpits and he was in stockinged feet. 'Thank God,' he said in a harried tone, pulling me inside and closing the door behind me quickly. 'I don't know how this happened,' he began. 'We were just . . . we were . . . we were . . .'

'Calm down,' I said, stepping back as an overpowering smell of liquor hit me. 'My God, man. How much have you drunk tonight?'

'A lot,' he said. 'Too much. But I'm sober now, I swear it.'

And he was too. He looked to be the most sober man in the country, although his face was pale and he was shivering slightly. I moved towards the door which led to the living room and, as my hand reached for the knob, he placed his own on top of mine, forcing me to stay where I was for a moment. I looked at him. 'Before you go in there,' he said quickly, 'I want you to know that it wasn't my fault. I *swear* it wasn't my fault.'

I nodded and felt a sudden rush of fear, mingled with panic. I was genuinely afraid of what horrors I might find on the other side of the door. In the end, while the actual result was as bad as I had feared, the scene itself was unremarkable. James was sitting on the floor, his back to the sofa, fully clothed, his legs slightly parted with a large glass of Scotch sitting between them. His arms lay palm upwards by his side. His eyes were open and he was staring at the opposite wall. Although I knew instantly that he was indeed dead, my eyes immediately darted to the other side of the room, to see whom he was looking at. Over there, in semi-darkness, huddled up on an armchair with another glass of Scotch for company was a young girl of no more than eighteen years of age. She was shivering violently and hugged her entire body to herself as she stared back at James, their eyes locked together as if they were engaged in some ridiculous contest. 'Get me a blanket,' I said quickly to P.W., who stood hovering behind me nervously, waiting for my reaction. 'In fact you'd better get me two.' He disappeared and reappeared a moment later with two heavy blankets, one of which I laid over James's body. The moment I did this, the girl snapped back to life, looking at me with wide eyes. I came towards her with the other blanket and she shrank back, her whole body attempting to press itself back into the seat in panic.

'It's all right,' I said quietly, holding one hand in the air in a gesture of friendship. 'It's just to keep you warm, that's all. I'm here to help.'

'It wasn't me,' she said quickly. 'It's nothing to do with me. He said he could handle it, that's all. Said he'd done it before.' She was surprisingly well spoken for a girl who was obviously a teenage prostitute. Her inflections were those of the private school, her manner that of the educated, the rich. James's type of girl, no doubt. She had a pretty face and wore little make-up, although her eyes were circled with mascara too richly applied, which was running a little now in the heat of the room.

'How old are you?' I asked quietly, kneeling before her as I tucked the blanket into the chair.

'Fifteen,' she said quickly, answering me with the polite speed and honesty that she might direct towards a tutor or parent.

'Oh, for Christ's sake,' I said, spinning around and staring at P.W. in disgust. 'What the fuck have you two been doing here?' It's not my way to curse but her answer had stung me. 'What the *fuck* has gone on here tonight?'

'I'm sorry, Matthieu,' said P.W., his mouth busy chewing his fingernails, his face streaming tears. 'We didn't know. She said she was older. She said—'

A spark of light caught my eye and I looked at the ground where a silver teaspoon lay, its centre slightly brown, a tiny bubble blinking at the lip. I picked it up and stared at it for a moment before dropping it to the ground. 'Jesus fucking Christ,' I said again, marching over to James's body and pulling back the blanket. The girl screamed as I pulled up his shirt sleeve and saw the hypodermic syringe nestled securely in a vein, its lever pushed in, its load emptied. 'What was in here?' I asked. 'What did he use?'

'It was her!' cried P.W. petulantly. 'She brought it over here. She said it would make it better.'

'That's a damned lie,' screamed the girl. 'You said you wanted me to bring it. You said you needed it to have a good time. You gave me the fucking *money* for it, you bastard!'

P.W. started to move towards her in a fury but I stopped him and pushed him back on to the sofa, where he narrowly avoided landing on James's body. 'Sit down!' I said firmly, feeling as if I was breaking up a playground fight between a couple of children and not trying to stop a middle-aged man from slapping a girl forty years his junior. 'Now tell me what happened.'

There was silence for a few moments as I waited for one of them to speak. Eventually, P.W. shrugged and looked up at me apologetically. 'It was just supposed to be a bit of fun,' he said. 'That's all. We were out for a few drinks. It got a bit rowdy. You know how he liked a drink. Made everyone else drink as much as him. We were getting a taxi. That's when we saw her, that little tart over there.'

'Fuck off!' she screamed.

'James went up to her, asked her did she fancy a bit, you know, and she said all right and—'

'And that's a lie too!' she roared and I spun round and stared at her furiously, at which she sat back in the seat quickly with a whimper and looked like she might never speak again in this world.

'Go on,' I said to P.W., turning back to him. 'Tell me it as it happened. The *truth* now.'

'Well, we got back here,' he said, 'and we were all set for it, you know. I was going to go first and then let James have a go. He said he'd been having a bit of trouble recently. With the old todger, you know. Said he needed something to help him get it up. Asked her what she had and that's when she produced the heroin.'

'But that would knock him out altogether!' I said in protest, turning back to look at her. 'What were you thinking of?'

'Don't you dare shout at me,' she cried. 'It's not my fault. You think I wanted that fat bastard banging away on top of me? I told him what I had, he said he wanted heroin, I asked him had he used it before and he swore he had so I gave it to him. I didn't care as long as I got paid. I'm not his fucking *mother*, you know.'

'Look at him!' I roared. 'He's dead, for Christ's sake.'

'He stuck the needle in,' said P.W., 'and then he just started shaking all over. His mouth was dribbling and he had some sort of fit. Collapsed on the floor and a minute later he stopped moving altogether. That's when I picked him up and set him against the couch. It was no one's fault really. No one can blame either of us. He did it to himself.'

'Jesus, P.W.,' I said, staring at him. 'You've hired a prostitute. And she's fucking *under age* at that. You've got drugs here. Hard drugs. And a dead body. There's not a single legal thing in any of those sentences.'

He buried his head in his hands and started to cry some more. I looked across at the girl who was watching him with disgust and who, for some reason, had taken a nail file from her pocket and was sawing away at her nails with some speed. 'I'm going,' she said when I looked at her. 'It's got nothing to do with me.'

'Sit down,' I said. 'No one's going anywhere. Not 'til I decide what to do for the best. Nobody moves from this room until I say they can. And I don't want to hear a sound, all right?'

I went out into the hall, like the parent of two small children caught talking to each other late at night, and closed the door behind me firmly. I even considered locking it but the key was on the other side. I sat down on the stairs and thought about the situation as it had presented itself to me. I could just walk away, I thought. I could open the front door, go down the stairs and go home. Leave them to it. It's nothing to do with me, after all. Sure, a taxi driver had taken me here and my fingerprints would be all over the place by now, not least on the hypodermic syringe, but I had a good story. I could explain it away, surely. And whatever happened to those two in there; well it was hardly *my* problem, was it? *I could just walk away.*

And yet I didn't. The risk was too big. Life imprisonment could be an awfully long time. I thought about it; I was not an expert on contemporary drug-taking, where one goes to get them, how they are used, the things they result in. I needed someone who knew about such things. I took out my pocket diary and leafed through it for the number, which I dialled from the hall phone. I breathed in deeply and hoped I was doing the right thing.

Tommy arrived twenty minutes later, dressed once again completely in black, but this time with the addition of a dark woollen cap on his head. I knew no one who could be as much an expert on drugs as my nephew. He had surely tried everything that was available to man or beast and had seen situations like this one develop before. He would know how to handle it. He listened to the story and shook his head.

'You're already involved,' he said. 'And there's not an awful lot you can do about it now. That fucker should never have phoned you in the first place or you just shouldn't have come. Now you're here you have to solve the problem.'

'Look,' I said, having been thinking about it while he was *en route*. 'He took the drug himself, yes? And it's not uncommon for that to happen and for people to die of it. All we need to do is find somewhere to leave him that will make it look as if he did it to himself. I mean, he *did* do it to himself of course, but we have to show that beyond a shadow of a doubt. He's in a stressful job, these things happen all the time. You've no idea how many people I've seen kill themselves through the pressures of work. I saw one do it before my very eyes once,' I added, thinking of Denton Irving, my Wall Street friend.

'His office,' said Tommy, clapping his hands together in excitement. 'You've got a key. We bring him back to his office, prop him up in the chair behind his desk, and you go in first thing in the morning and find him sitting there. You call the police. No one will think anything of it. They'll think it was his own fault.'

'That's good,' I said, nodding. 'And those two in there?'

As I spoke, the door opened and the girl came out. Tommy spun around so that she couldn't see him but it was too late and her face creased up in surprise. 'Sam?' she asked slowly. 'You're—'

'Back inside!' I roared at her and she jumped and screamed. 'You get back inside and sit down until I tell you to do otherwise. Or we call the police right now, your choice.' She ran back inside immediately and closed the door. Tommy turned back and looked at me in anger.

'You see?' he cried in despair.

We did everything as Tommy had suggested. We loaded James's body into his car and drove him to the office where I 'discovered' him the next morning. The girl was gone by the time I got back and P.W. was acting as if nothing untoward had ever happened. It was the headline story in all the papers the next day: 'TV BOSS OD'S IN OFFICE', 'SATELLITE EXEC IN DRUGS DEATH'. It ran right into pages five and six of the tabloids where the anticipated loss of Ms Tara Morrison to the BBC was cited as one of the possible reasons for the increased stress that James Hocknell had been feeling in recent times. Tara herself did a 'Tara Says: Just Say No' piece on her former boss in which she praised his talent wildly and despaired – 'I despair, readers' – for the way the country was turning. I ran through the arranged story with the police a number of times and they believed every word of it, fortunately. Within a week, death had been declared 'by misadventure' and our former managing director was laid to rest with only about twenty people in attendance at his funeral. Notable by his absence was P.W., who was down with flu.

I reaffirmed my commitment to saving Tommy's own life after this event; if there had ever been any doubt about it before, it was gone now. I would not see him reach this kind of end. I would not let him disappear off the face of the earth like James had, or like so many of Tommy's ancestors had before him. He had come to my assistance, I would come to his.

The guy was dead anyway, all we did was fix it. Despite Tommy's attempts to salve my conscience, I could not help but feel a twinge of guilt over what had happened. The crime had not been mine, but the cover-up had and I prayed that there would be no further questions to answer on the subject.

Chapter 10

Sticking with Dominique

We argued over whether we should continue with Furlong's horse and cart or not and in the end it took Tomas to make up our minds for us. To my dismay, Dominique wanted to drive it all the way to London. She was drained by the events of the previous twenty-four hours, and could hardly bear the idea of walking for another three days in order to reach the capital and so the transportation seemed heaven sent to her. For my part, I maintained that it would only draw attention to us, that, if anyone came looking for the young farmer and recognized his vehicle, it would surely land us all in trouble. Certainly, we were not intending to continue in the direction in which he had been headed, but nevertheless there was always the chance that we might come across a relative or acquaintance at some point and it just wasn't worth the risk. Eventually, Tomas's constant whining about the fact that he didn't want to walk any further made Dominique throw her lot in with mine – in order to spite him, I think – and we sent the horse back down the road which would eventually lead him home to Bramling. Without his driver.

We had got no sleep the night before but agreed to walk on for a few more hours before settling down for a rest as we both wanted to be as far away from that dreadful place as possible. After I had killed Furlong, we had taken his body outside and into a clump of trees a few yards beyond the barn. I wanted to bury him, but we had nothing with which to dig, so it would have proved an impossible exercise. Dominique suggested hiding him in the undergrowth, taking his money and making it look as if he had been robbed along the road. That way, she said, there was little chance that we would ever be discovered and we could simply continue with our original plan, to go towards London and to start our lives afresh as if none of this had ever taken place. Although I had been right to kill him – for he would have surely succeeded with his designs on Dominique had I not – there seemed little chance that our adventures would have a happy conclusion if we reported the events of the previous night to the authorities. We were still very young and naturally afraid of the constabulary; there was a chance that we could be separated, all three of us, if a trial ensued. The deed was already done, there was no way that we could alter the events that had taken place; it was for the best that we simply moved on and disclaimed all knowledge of the man from then on.

Having wiped the vomit from his face, we rolled Furlong over on to his stomach and took a small bag of money from his pocket, enough perhaps to help us for an extra few days if necessary. Dominique dropped two guineas a few yards away from his corpse to make it look as if, in the nervous excitement of theft and murder, the villains had carelessly lost some of their reward. We tore his clothes a little and ripped his jacket at the back. Finally, Dominique suggested one final touch.

'You can't be serious,' I said, growing cold at the idea.

'We have to, Matthieu,' she said. 'Think about it. It's not likely that any thief would simply stab him once in the back and rob him. There has to have been a struggle. He was a big man after all. It has to appear as if he tried to stave them off.' Without warning, she lifted her right foot off the ground and drove it into Furlong's ribcage with a ferocity that chilled me. I heard the crack within his body and then she repeated the gesture, this time to the side of his face which lay exposed on the grass. 'Where's the knife?' she asked, looking across at me and I feared that I would vomit again, although my stomach was well and truly empty by now and showed no signs of being refilled at any time soon.

'The knife?' I asked. 'What do you need the knife for? He's already dead.'

She caught the sparkle of the blade beneath my jacket and reached for it quickly. I stepped back as she plunged it into his back several times, before lifting his head off the ground slightly and tearing his throat from ear to ear. There was a deep slicing sound and a whistling release of air that sounded like no natural sound that could be produced. 'There,' she said, standing back up and running her hand along her jaw roughly. 'That ought to do it. Now we'd better get moving. Oh, don't look so horrified,' she added, seeing my expression, my pale features grown whiter than usual. 'We have to survive, don't we? Do you want us to end up at the end of a rope? Remember who started all this, Matthieu. It wasn't you and it wasn't me. It was him.'

I nodded but said nothing and started to walk back towards the barn where we had instructed Tomas to stay while we disposed of the body. He had woken up while we dragged the corpse outside, but his head was full of sleep and it only took Dominique smoothing his hair away from his forehead to send him back to unconsciousness again. He was breathing heavily when I went inside and I lay down close to him, pleased to feel the warmth of his body against my own. My whole being was exhausted and shivering and I longed for sleep. I heard Dominique enter the barn and close the door behind her. She toyed with the fire for a few moments but it had gone out long ago and was giving off no more warmth and it was too late now to relight it. I closed my eyes and pretended to be asleep, going so far as to begin a light snoring to fool her. I didn't want to talk any more, I didn't want to discuss what had happened. Truth to tell, I felt like bursting into tears, despite the fact that I still believed that I had acted correctly, at least up to the point where I had killed him.

She walked around to the other side of me and picked Tomas up gently, carrying him over to the other side of the barn where she lay him down with a mass of straw beneath his head. He muttered something unintelligible before becoming silent and she came over and lay down in the warm spot beside me where he had lain a few moments before. I could feel her breath on my face and before long the fingers of her left hand were stroking my cheeks, causing me to grow excited, despite the fact that – for once – a sexual encounter with Dominique was the furthest thing from my thoughts. To my embarrassment, I could hear the thick fabric of my trousers pressing outwards as she continued to stroke me and I tried to keep my eyes shut, so convinced was I that she would stop her attentions to me if she thought that I was awake and gaining any pleasure from it. I struggled with the urges of my body and eventually I could hold back no longer, opening my eyes and allowing her to pull me towards her. She took control of me, loosening my trousers and guiding me into her, where I lay rigid for a few moments before beginning that rhythmic movement she had taught me once before on my first night in England, and which I had repeated on countless occasions with the prostitutes and street girls of Dover in the ensuing year. As I grew closer towards a climax, my lips ached for hers but she pushed my face aside whenever I tried to kiss her, never once allowing our mouths to connect. Soon, it was over and I collapsed back on the hay, one arm pressed flat across my face as I wondered how long it would be before we made love again – fifteen minutes or another year. She slid down between my legs and kissed me there before drying me with a little straw and re-tying my trousers. Then she turned her back on me and without a word went directly off to sleep.

I tried to speak to her of these events as we walked along the road that morning, Tomas keeping up the pace a steady ten feet behind us and muttering to himself as he went. He was growing taller, I noticed, and his thin body was starting to fill out a little; for a moment I felt a surge of almost paternal pride towards him and worried about the day that he would no longer be under my guardianship. It was a warm morning and I wanted to take off my shirt but felt embarrassed to appear half naked before Dominique in the daytime, when my body might not take on the Adonis-like appearance that I could at least pretend to have at night, in the dark, when we were alone. Instead, I allowed myself to grow warmer and warmer, feeling a trail of perspiration sticking my clothing to my back as we walked. I looked across at her from time to time as I spoke, but she was staring directly ahead all the time, never so much as turning her face to glance at me.

'He didn't hurt you, did he?' I asked eventually, my voice quiet and patient as I stepped closer to her. 'Furlong, I mean. He didn't hurt you at all?'

'Not really,' she muttered after a pause. 'He hadn't even got started to be honest. If he hurt me at all it was when he was holding me down beneath him. He grabbed my wrists a little, my throat. I feel a little sore this morning, that's all. He was heavier than he looked.'

I nodded. 'So what are we . . . ?' I began, unsure how to phrase it. 'What are we going to do about this? Later, I mean. When we get to London.'

'Do about what?'

'About you and me.'

She shrugged. 'What you and me?' she asked innocently and I frowned at her, refusing to answer her, forcing her to continue instead. 'Nothing,' she said eventually. 'There's no chance that anyone is going to discover it was you who killed him. It'll probably be days before he's found and, even when he is, who's going to—'

'No,' I cried in frustration. 'I mean *you* and *me*,' I repeated with emphasis.

'Oh. You and me. You mean . . .' She trailed off as she thought about it and for a moment it seemed to me that she had completely forgotten about our lovemaking the night before. No, I thought. You can't do this to me again. 'I think it's best if we stick to the story,' she added. 'That we're sister and brother. I think there's more chance that we'll find somewhere together, the three of us I mean, if we stick to that story.'

'But we're *not* sister and brother,' I pointed out. 'Not at all. Sisters and brothers don't—'

155

'We're as near as.'

'No, we're *not* as near as,' I cried in frustration. 'If we were as near as sister and brother then why would we have done what we did last night? What we did the night we first came to England?'

'That was more than a year ago!'

'That's not the point, Dominique. Those are not the actions of a sister and brother!'

She sighed and shook her head. 'Oh, Matthieu,' she said, as if we had gone through this conversation a hundred times already, even though we had never spoken of these matters even once. 'You and I . . . we're not supposed to be together. You have to understand that.'

'Why aren't we? We're happy together. We rely on each other. And I love you after all.'

'Don't be ridiculous,' she said angrily. 'I'm just the only girl you've ever felt anything for other than pure and simple lust, that's all. And so you translate this into love. But that's *not* love. It's just comfort. Familiarity.'

'How do you know it's not? Last night, what we did, that meant more to me than—'

'Matthieu, I don't want to discuss this, all right? What happened happened but it won't be happening again. You have to accept that I don't see you like that. It's not what I want from you. It might be what you want from me and I'm sorry about that but it's not going to continue. In fact it's *never* going to happen again.'

I stopped talking and started walking slightly ahead of her, cutting her with my silence. I grew weary of having her in my mind, of feeling that my life revolved around the question of whether we would or would not be together. For a moment, I hated her and wished that we had never met; that Tomas and I had stood on the

156

other side of that boat from Calais to Dover on that fateful day and stayed there, never talking to this girl who had held dominion over my emotions for more than a year now. I needed her to love me or not to exist at all and I hated her for the fact that she could not do either. And yet, despite it all, I could not even imagine a world that she was not part of. I could barely remember my life before she had entered it.

'There are things about me that you don't know,' she said eventually, catching up with me and linking my arm, her voice soft and warm about my shoulder. 'You must remember that I lived for nineteen years in Paris before we met; you lived there almost as long. Surely there are many things that went on there that *you* have yet to tell *me*.'

'I've told you everything,' I protested and she laughed.

'That's ridiculous,' she said. 'You've never said much to me about your parents. You've told me how they died but that's about all. You've never tried to tell me how they made you feel, how it felt to be left alone, what it feels like to be in charge of Tomas. You go along with the plans that I make and you don't tell me what *you* want out of life. You're as closed up as I am. You keep everything in. You don't offer me any more knowledge of yourself than I do to you. All you want is physicality, nothing else. I can't offer you that. The fact is I had a life before we met as well. You left Paris for a reason – well, so did I. And you can't force me to fall in love with you too when you don't even know what my reasons were.'

'Then *tell* me your reasons,' I shouted. 'Tell me why you left. Tell me what you're running away from and maybe I'll tell you some of my secrets too.'

'I left because I had nothing there. No family, no

future. I wanted more. I wanted to start again. But believe me, in my own way, I do love you, but it *is* the love of a sister for a brother, that's all. And it's not going to change. Not any time soon anyway.'

I pulled my arm away from her and with a look of contempt dropped back to see how Tomas was feeling. At that moment I saw him as my only real family, my only true friend.

Dominique had asked about my life in Paris before I had met her and she was right on one count – I *had* never spoken to her about my past in any great detail. This was mostly owing to the fact that I had tried to put my old Parisian life behind me from the moment Tomas and I had stepped on board the boat from Calais; when I thought about Dominique and me, it was always with an eye to the future, to the life that we could share together some day. And yet, as close as we doubtless were, it was true that we had in fact shared very little of our separate histories with each other and it seemed like it was finally time to change that.

I had only a slight recollection of my father, Jean, whose throat was cut by a murderer when I was four years old. I remembered him as being a tall man with a grey-tinted beard but, when I once mentioned this fact to my mother, she shook her head and said she could not remember him ever growing a beard and insisted that I was mixing him up with someone else, some stranger who might have passed through our house once and whose image had remained with me. This revelation disappointed me as it was the only memory that I had of my father – or *thought* that I had – and I was sorry to know that it was a false one. Still, I know that he was respected and well liked, for there were many people in my first fifteen years of life in Paris who told me that they had known him and liked him and were sorry for his loss.

My mother, Marie, met her second husband in the same theatre where her first had been employed for so many years. She was there to meet the dramatist for whom my father had worked and who had so generously granted her a pension after his death. Every month she would call around to his office at the theatre on the pretext of taking tea with him and they would chat amiably for an hour or so together. As she would leave, he would silently pop a small bag of money into her pocket, which would subsidize our existence for the next thirty days; I don't know how we could have possibly survived without it, as we were constantly short of money anyway. It was on one of these occasions, while leaving the theatre, that she had the misfortune to meet Philippe DuMarqué for the first time. She had stepped outside on to the street and was about to begin her walk home when a small boy ran past her and grabbed at the bag she was carrying. She lost her balance and fell to the ground, letting out a scream as the thief disappeared down a side street with whatever possessions she had on her at the time, plus her monthly pension. The boy – whom I was virtually to become myself when I went to Dover some years later – was apprehended by Philippe as he made his getaway and it was rumoured afterwards that he actually broke the child's arm as punishment for his theft, a severe penalty to pay for so petty a crime. Philippe returned the bag to my mother, who was greatly upset by the incident, and then offered to walk her home. Exactly what happened from then on I am not so clear upon but it seemed that he became a regular visitor to our house from that day onwards and he would call around at all hours of the day and night.

At first he was polite and charming and would entertain me with a ball or some card-trick that he had perfected. He was a fine mimic and would satirize our neighbours perfectly in order to amuse me. Our relationship was almost friendly on those occasions but his moods could alter without warning. Whenever I discovered him sitting alone at our kitchen table in the morning, nursing his regular hangover, I knew better than to approach him. He was a handsome man in his early twenties whose face appeared to have been chiselled out of granite. His cheekbones were pronounced and he had the most perfect eyebrows I have ever seen on a man, two perfect arches of deep black over his ocean-blue eyes. He wore his hair shoulder length and would often tie it into a ponytail behind his head, a fashion at the time. His looks have travelled down through the centuries, his genes reproducing an image of himself in all of his line. Although there have of course been differences and alterations made through the influx of the female side, even the present Tommy has a look which is unmistakably Philippe's and he has the ability sometimes to look at me in a way which sends a chill through me, a shiver of unpleasant memory, of centuries-old distaste. Of all the DuMarqués, Philippe – their progenitor – has been my least favourite one. The only one whose death actually pleased me.

I wasn't present at their wedding and didn't even know that it had taken place until I realized that my new stepfather had moved all his belongings into the house and was staying with us every night. My mother explained that I had to treat him with respect, as I would my natural father, and not anger him for he was under too much pressure to deal with the idle rantings of children. I don't know exactly what kind of actor he was – I never actually saw him perform in any serious production – but he couldn't have been too talented as all the parts that he played were small and he would even take the position of understudy from time to time. This frustrated him, of course, and he started to grow moody around the house, generating an atmosphere of tension which scared me. It delighted me whenever he would disappear from our lives, sometimes for days at a time.

Shortly after their marriage, Tomas was born and Philippe made only rare appearances for a time, mostly to eat or sleep, and this pleased me. My half-brother was a noisy baby and frustrated all of us with his screaming for food and then refusing to eat it when it was offered to him. My stepfather ignored the child most of the time, as he did me, and continued with his obsessional quest to become a success in the theatre, but it seemed as if he was destined to be always frustrated as the parts he coveted were given to other actors whom he despised. Then one day he announced his decision to become a writer.

'A writer?' asked my mother, looking at him in some surprise for she could probably not remember him so much as reading a book, let alone wanting to write one. 'What kind of a writer?'

'I could write a play,' he said enthusiastically. 'Think about it. How many plays have I performed in since I was a child? I know the way they are constructed, I know what works in the theatre and what doesn't. I know what makes good dialogue and what sounds false. Have you any idea how much money some of these dramatists are making? The theatres are full every night, Marie.'

My mother was unsure but relentlessly encouraging and thereafter he would sit at home every evening at our table with paper and a quill pen and scratch away noisily for hours on end, looking up at the ceiling from time to time for inspiration before charging through a few pages of writing. I watched him in awe, always waiting for that moment when an idea would hit and he would race to realize it on paper. Eventually, one night a month later, he was finished. He lavishly wrote 'The End' across the bottom of one page, underlined it and signed his name with a flourish, before standing up with an enormous grin and taking my mother in his arms, twirling her around the room until she shouted that she would throw up if he didn't put her down immediately. He told us both to sit down and he would read it to us and so he did. For almost two hours we sat silently side by side as he paced in front of us, reading the play in a variety of voices, adding in the stage directions as he went, his face contorted with pride, anger, hilarity, depending on the scene. Acting out every word as if his very life depended on it.

I can't remember the title of Philippe's play, but it concerned a rich nobleman in Paris in the mid-1600s. His wife had gone mad and killed herself and he had married another, but found her unfaithful with a rich landlord in the city. He tortured her until she went mad and killed herself, at which time he realized that he had loved her all along, at which point he went mad and killed *himself*. And that was it. That was the end. There wasn't anything more to it than that, just a lot of people going mad all the time. And killing themselves. The final scene presented a stageful of corpses and a character who had previously not appeared at all entering stage left to speak a resolution in sonnet form. It was not a good play but we applauded at the end of it in order to make ourselves agreeable and my mother talked of all the things we would buy when we were rich, even though we both knew that the chances of our making our fortune from Philippe's masterpiece were beyond slim.

The following day, he took the play to the theatre and showed it to the owner who read it carefully before telling the actor that he should stick to the understudying and leave the words to someone else. Furious, Philippe stormed out – after knocking the man over and breaking his nose – and tried several more theatres over the following week before accepting that no one was willing to produce his play or, after his behaviour after each rejection, even employ him any more. Within a week, he had lost not only his ambition to become a writer but also the chance of ever working in the theatre again. He was probably the only playwright who was so bad that he wasn't even allowed to act any more.

Following this disappointment, he took to staying at home and drinking. My mother was taking in laundry at the time and still accepting her pension money, but most of this was swallowed up by her husband who became violent as that year progressed, towards both her and me, a violence which eventually led to the wicked afternoon when he beat my mother so badly that she never rose again. When it became clear that she was dead, he sat at the kitchen table and prepared a little bread and cheese, apparently oblivious to her corpse on the ground beside him. I ran to fetch help, my tears and growing hysteria making it difficult for anyone to understand me, but eventually I returned with a gendarme who raised the alarm to others and Philippe was arrested. I had expected him to be gone by the time I returned home but he was seated in exactly the same position in which I had left him, staring at the table in apparent boredom. He was tried for his crime, showed little or no remorse for his actions, was executed, and that was when Tomas and I left the city for England.

There are many stories from those days which I had never told Dominique, stories which were just as unpleasant as that one, and I had failed to speak of them because I did not want to remind myself of my early life if I did not have to. I didn't want her to think that I was being secretive, merely private, an important distinction I felt. As we walked along the road that day, however, I told her that story and she listened quietly, offering no comment or story of her own in response. Eventually, I had no choice but to ask her outright whether anything similar had ever happened to her, but she ignored my question and pointed instead to an inn which was appearing over the horizon, perhaps half an hour's walk away, where she suggested we go to rest and find some cheap food. We walked the remainder of the way in silence as my mind drifted from memories of my parents to wondering what secrets Dominique stored inside her head.

We had eaten little over the previous day so we decided to treat ourselves to a decent meal which might last us throughout the next twenty-four hours and raise our spirits as well. It was a pleasant enough inn on a quiet corner of the road, raucous with the noise of music and laughter, eating and drinking, and we were fortunate to find the end of one small table near the fire at which to rest and eat our food. I sat opposite Dominique, with Tomas by my side, and to his left and opposite were a middle-aged man and his wife, reasonably well dressed, eating food which was piled dangerously high on their plates like towers. They were noisy eaters and stopped only briefly as we sat down to look at us with suspicious glances before returning to their meals. We ate in silence for a while, glad to be putting something into our stomachs at last. I was proud of Tomas who, for all his unhappiness with the long walk, had not complained too much about the lack of food so far.

'Perhaps we should not go as far as London,' said Dominique eventually, breaking the long silence between us. 'There are other places after all. We could find a small village or—'

'It depends what we're looking for, doesn't it?' I said. 'Our best chance of work is within a large house, servants or some such position.'

'Not with Tomas,' she pointed out. 'No one will take us on with a six-year-old child.' Tomas looked across at her suspiciously as if he was concerned that she might be trying to get rid of him, which she never would have done. 'I just think we might have more luck getting jobs in a busy village or town.'

'You don't want to go to London,' said the man beside Tomas, effortlessly entering into the conversation as if he had been part of it all along. 'London's an 'eartless place. Absolutely 'eartless.' We looked at him blankly and continued to talk among ourselves.

'We can continue along the road,' I said after a decent interval but in a quieter voice now, ignoring him completely, 'and, if we come across a place that seems pleasant, we can stop for as long as we choose. We don't have to make any decisions right away.'

The man gave out a loud belch, followed by an extra-ordinary fart, and the sigh he followed it up with gave testament to the pleasure they had both afforded him. 'Mr Amberton,' said his wife, tapping him on the hand casually, more as an instinctive gesture than an offended one, 'you mind your manners now.'

'It's natural, lad,' he said, looking across at me. 'You don't mind hearing a little from the natural bodily functions, do you?' I stared at him and wasn't quite sure whether the question was rhetorical or not. He was a man of about forty-five, rather obese, with a shaved head and a two-day stubble that flickered around his ugly features like dirt. His teeth were yellow and he displayed them prominently. As he looked at me, he wiped his nose with the back of his hand, and then inspected it carefully before smiling at me and offering the same hand in my direction. 'Joseph Amberton,' he said cheerfully and when he smiled I was afforded a view of those miserable teeth within that filthy mouth. 'At your service,' he added. 'So tell me, lad, you never answered my question; you don't mind hearing a little from the natural bodily functions, do you?'

'Not at all, sir,' I said, afraid of what might happen if I answered in a way which displeased him for the idea of being jumped upon by a man possessed of quite so much blubber terrified me. He was like a demon hybrid of man and whale. You could have skinned him for oil or raised a signal from his movements. 'It's perfectly all right.'

'And you, missy,' he said, looking at Dominique. 'You don't want to go to London, mark me now. It's only rotten things go on down there. I should know.'

'You're right there, Mr Amberton,' said his wife, turning now to look at us, a woman equally rotund, but with apple cheeks and a pleasant smile. 'Mr Amberton and I spent the early years of our marriage in London,' she explained. 'We courted there, married there, lived there, worked there. And it was there that he had his accident, you see. That's what drove us out of the place.'

'Aye, it was,' said Mr Amberton, collapsing savagely into a lamb chop. 'And that did it for me in that department, I don't mind telling you. Thankfully, Mrs Amberton stood by me all the same and hasn't moved on to some other chap, which she could have done 'cos she's still an 'andsome woman.'

I thought it unlikely, regardless of what his injury might be, that Mrs Amberton would find another chap of similar girth either to accommodate or satisfy her, but smiled acquiescence none the less before looking across at Dominique with a shrug. 'We could—' I began, before they interrupted us once more.

'Do you know Cageley?' Mrs Amberton asked and I shook my head. 'That's where we live,' she explained. 'Right busy place it is too. Plenty of work to be found there. We could bring you that direction if you wanted. Be travelling back there later on tonight. We don't mind, do we, Mr Amberton? Be pleased of the company, to tell you the truth.'

'How far is it?' asked Dominique, newly suspicious of generous offers after our encounter of the previous day; the last thing I wanted too was more blood on my hands. Mrs Amberton told us that it was about an hour's drive in their cart, that we would be there by nightfall, and we nervously agreed to accompany them. 'If nothing else,' Dominique whispered quietly to me, 'it will get us a further distance along the way. We don't have to stay there if we don't want to.' I nodded. I did what I was told.

The evening grew dark as we drove along the bumpy road. Unusually, Mrs Amberton drove the cart and insisted on having Dominique sit up front with her, while her husband, Tomas and I stayed in the back. Once again, Tomas took advantage of his youth and fell straight to sleep, forcing me to sit up and talk with the hideously flatulent Mr Amberton who took great pleasure from the shots he took from a flagon of whiskey every few minutes, following each one with a disgusting orchestra of coughing, phlegm and spittle.

'So what is it you do?' I asked him eventually, in an attempt at conversation.

'I'm a schoolteacher,' he told me. 'I teach about forty little brats in the village. Mrs Amberton here's a cook.'

'Right,' I said, nodding. 'Any children of your own?'

'Oh, no,' he said, laughing loudly, as if the very idea was ridiculous. 'On account of my accident in London, that is. I can't get 'im up, you see,' he whispered with a grin. I blinked in surprise at the openness of the confession. 'Happened when I was helping with the building of some new houses in the city. Had an accident with a large piece of piping. Put me out of the game for ever it seems. Maybe it'll come back to me some day, but I doubt it after all this time. Never much cared for it anyway to tell you the truth. Mrs Amberton don't seem to mind either. There's other ways to satisfy a woman, you see, as you'll learn yourself some day, lad.'

'Uh-huh,' I nodded and closed my eyes, sure that I did not want to hear any more of his private business.

'Unless you and . . .' He nodded towards Dominique and rolled his eyes lasciviously, his tongue bobbing out of his mouth in a disgusting fashion. 'Are you two—?'

'She's my sister,' I said, cutting him off before he could even get started. 'That's all. My sister.'

'Oh, I do apologize, lad,' he said with a laugh. 'Never insult a man's mother, his sister or his horse, that's what I always says.' I nodded and for a moment fell suddenly asleep before being jolted back into consciousness as Mrs Amberton drove us into the village of Cageley. We had arrived.

Chapter 11

The Games

In November 1892, at the tender age of 149, I once again passed through my home city of Paris, on this occasion accompanied by my wife Céline de Fredi Zéla. We were in fact travelling from our home in Brussels to spend a few weeks in Madrid and decided on a whim to stop off in the French capital to visit Céline's brother, who was due to give a lecture at the Sorbonne during that week. At the time, Céline and I had been married for three years and things were not going well. I feared that it might be the first occasion when I would actually end up divorcing a spouse (or being divorced by one) – a process with which I have never been enamoured – and our holiday was intended as one final effort to save our union.

We had met in Brussels in 1888, where I was living comfortably off the proceeds of an operetta I had written and produced for the Belgian stage. It was entitled *The Necessary Murder*, and although it does not appear to have lasted the test of time – I was recently surprised to find a brief mention of it in an academic text concerning little-known European operas of the late nineteenth century, but have never heard anyone refer to it outside of that – it was something of a popular success at the time. The second most important opera critic of the time, Karpuil – who was an ignorant drunk most of the time but could write beautifully – described it as the 'sublime reflection of a generous talent towards a disturbing subject matter', although I must admit that the *leading* critic was not quite so generous in his praise. He considered it transient and derivative; in retrospect, his perceptiveness probably explains his premiership. Céline was a guest at the opening night, and sat in a box with her older brother Pierre, Baron de Coubertin, and some of their friends. She sought me out after the show and complimented me on the performance, singling out a libretto in the second act, performed by a young girl to her lover, for particular praise.

'I found the whole thing quite chilling,' she said, her brown eyes darting back and forth at the cast as they ran around behind us in a state of post-show excitement. The atmosphere behind a stage always excites those who are not used to the theatre. 'The music is so beautiful and yet these two young people have just committed a terrible crime. Taking the two together makes the whole thing seem quite chilling, but surprisingly moving none the less.'

'A necessary crime, however,' I pointed out, 'as the title suggests. The boy is forced to kill the man to prevent the attack on his beloved. Otherwise, the consequences would have been—'

'Oh, certainly,' she said quickly. 'I understood that perfectly. But it's the manner in which they dispose of the body and then simply continue on their way that disturbed me. It made me wonder what end would lie in store for them. I knew from that moment that it would all end in tragedy. As if the cover-up necessitated a balancing end for one or both of them. It was a sad story.'

I nodded slowly and considered inviting her to join some friends and me for dinner after the show. Although I am not a man who thrives on the praise of others, it was my first (my only) great success in the theatre and, for a brief time, I became intoxicated with the idea of myself as a talented artist. Little did I realize then that my true calling was not to be a creator but rather to be a benevolent patron of the arts; in truth, I was born in the wrong century. Had I lived a few hundred years earlier, I would no doubt have challenged Lorenzo de Medici for his position. I was not immediately attracted to Céline – at the time, the Belgian style was to wear the hair pulled back harshly from the face and hanging in strands at the side, and it drew attention to her forehead which protruded slightly – but I found her company more and more intoxicating as the evening wore on. She had an intelligent grasp of many subjects in which I myself was interested. We had both discovered Conan Doyle's *A Study in Scarlet*, which had only recently been published as the first of the Sherlock Holmes stories, and had each read it over and over again, waiting with anticipation for the next tale to appear. When she returned home that night, we said as one that we would like to meet again and within about eight months we had married and settled down in a townhouse in the heart of the city.

For a time we were happy, but I must admit to damaging our marriage when I entered into a misguided alliance with a young actress – a girl whom I hardly cared for at all, truth to tell – and Céline discovered my infidelity. For several weeks she could not bring herself to talk to me, and when she eventually did it was some time before we could even hold a conversation without her bursting into tears after a few moments. I had truly hurt her and was sorry for it. I discovered, during our months of trouble, that I had been a fool for behaving in such a manner for it was clear that Céline loved me and our life together and, until that point, we had been getting along pretty well. As I was an old hand at both relationships and marriage by then, I should have known a good thing when I saw one, but I admit that I am not a man who has always learned from his mistakes.

Eventually, we tried to patch up our differences and to return to our former state of happy wedlock, agreeing not to discuss the matter again, but it was clear that the affair still hung over us like a rain cloud. Even as we continued with our day to day lives, never daring to discuss it, it seemed that our every conversation was tinged with an awareness of that of which we did not dare speak. Céline became distracted, I became unhappy, as a couple we found that our intimacy had been damaged by my actions and the whole relationship seemed almost irreparable, which saddened me. I had never been in a situation before where I had behaved badly, been completely forgiven for my actions, and yet left absolutely aware that what had taken place had scarred our union too deeply ever to be mended. I could find no way to atone for my crime.

'Perhaps,' I suggested one afternoon over a quiet game of fantan, 'we could think about children.' It was a foolish suggestion, designed to wed us closer together even as I knew that we should be drifting apart.

Céline looked at me in some surprise and placed two spades over my heart before shaking her head. 'Perhaps,'

173

she echoed, 'we should consider a small holiday to-gether instead.'

And so it was set. Without saying it in so many words, it became clear that this holiday would be our last attempt to keep our marriage together without any hidden enmity or hurt feelings. We chose Madrid as our destination and it was Céline who suggested meeting her brother for a few days in Paris as we travelled, a decision which was to define a period of my life during the early 1890s and bring me into contact with the final, most extraordinary event of the nineteenth century.

I first met my brother-in-law on the same night that I had met Céline in 1888 but, through the rigours of distance and a lack of familial intimacy, we had not maintained a close relationship in the intervening years. Although quite wealthy from his inherited title of Baron de Coubertin, Pierre worked for the French government, taking on various projects which inter-ested him, more often than not those of an aesthetic nature, designed to improve the cultural life of a nation as opposed to the financial health of the civil purse. His relationship with his sister was distant but cordial and on the evening we arrived in Paris – 24 November 1892 – they had not actually laid eyes on each other in some eighteen months. Céline had written several letters to her brother, telling him of the life that we were leading in Brussels, the continued success of *The Necessary Murder* and the stunning failure of its successor *The Cigar Box*, which put an end to my creative desires once and for all. The previous Christmas we had received a card from him with a short note wishing us well and informing us that he was very happy and busy in France and, outside of that, we knew nothing of him or his work. However, as we would be staying in Paris for a few days, an arrangement was made to meet for dinner and it was during that meal that he informed us of the great plans that he was then setting in place.

A middle-aged man by now, Pierre wore his dark, wiry moustache long at the sides, its ends teased into a fine twist that stood out from his face, much like Salvador Dali would do during the mid-twentieth century. He was quite tall at six foot two, but lean and strong, due to the physical regimen he had been religiously following.

'Every morning,' he told me over an indifferent sole as we dined in an expensive restaurant where all the waiters appeared to know his name and acknowledge his presence with some deference, 'I rise at half past five exactly and plunge myself immediately into a cold bath, which revitalizes me and prepares me for the morning's activities. I do one hundred push-ups, one hundred sit-ups, and various other muscle toning exercises before cycling my bicycle for fifteen miles around the city. Upon my return, I take a long hot bath to ease any muscle strain, finish my ablutions, and by nine o'clock I am ready to start my work for the day. I cannot begin to explain how much better each day is when one has followed a schedule like that. And what of you, sir?' he asked me. 'What physical activities do you prefer?'

I considered a polite answer over the obvious one but it took me a moment to decide. 'I have been known to play a game of tennis,' I offered eventually. 'I've been told that my backhand is passable but my serving is an embarrassment to behold. Team sports have never quite been my thing, I have to admit. I've always preferred to test my own abilities, either alone or competing singularly against others. Athletics, fencing, swimming, that kind of thing.'

Once begun on his pet subject, there was no stopping him. As I would later learn, he could speak for hours about the benefits of a good sporting life, the advantages not just to oneself but to society as a whole that energetic activities of a competitive nature could provide. I found his passion both entertaining and unusual, for it was a side of life that I had never taken much interest in myself. Although generally fit, having been blessed with a good constitution and surely the most reliable body in the history of mankind, I have never found it necessary to adopt a regimen of my own. Indeed, the only exercise I constantly receive is walking, for I have owned a car only once in my life and even then couldn't get the hang of the thing, and find public transport generally disturbing.

We chatted briefly about Céline and our trip to Madrid, not detailing the dalliances which had caused this necessary effort at marital unity, before he grew weary of the subject and began to appear preoccupied over the brandy. When we asked him whether anything was the matter, he explained that he was due to give an important lecture at the Sorbonne the following day, and he was worried about it.

'It's the culmination of the last few years of my life,' he said, putting down his cigar briefly and allowing his hands to become animated as he talked. 'I have an idea which I want to put to the people at the lecture tomorrow and, depending on the response which I receive, I believe I will be undertaking the most extraordinary project of my life.'

I looked at him with some interest. 'Well, can you tell it to us now?' I asked. 'Or is it to be kept secret until tomorrow afternoon? Remember, we will be halfway to Madrid by then and may never hear of it otherwise.'

'Oh, you'll hear of it, Matthieu,' he said quickly. 'I have no doubts on that score. Assuming others believe it to be as good an idea as I do. You see—' He leaned forward on the table and Céline and I did likewise, forming a conspiratorial troika which seemed appropriate to the moment. 'A couple of years ago, one of our government departments commissioned me to study various physical culture methods, with a view to the reintroduction of a sporting curriculum to our schools. It was not a difficult task but it was one which intrigued me, fascinated as I was by the different methods for health preservation practised by different countries around the globe. Upon its conclusion my research had led me around Europe where I met various different people whose ideas were almost at one with my own and which eventually brought me to the point I arrive at tomorrow. To this lecture. You have heard, of course, of the Olympic Games?'

I looked at Céline, who clearly had not, and shrugged my shoulders non-committally. 'I know a little about them,' I offered cautiously, for my knowledge of their history and ideals was slight. 'They took place in ancient Greece, am I right? Around AD 100 or 200?'

'Close,' he said with a smile. 'Actually, they began around 800 BC, so you're only about a thousand years off. And they only came to a definitive end around the close of the fourth century, when Theodosius I, who was the Roman Emperor at the time, issued a decree prohibiting their taking place.' His eyes grew animated as he began his delivery of a stream of names and dates clearly etched into his consciousness. 'Of course, the Olympiad has not been entirely forgotten in the fourteen hundred years since,' he said eventually, his erudition shining through and eclipsing both our ignorance and our presence at the table. 'You will of course know the references to the games throughout Pindar.' I did not, but took his word for it. 'And there have been others who have been discussing a contemporary form of late. I met a man in England, a Dr William Penny Brooks – you may have heard of him – who founded the Much Wenlock Olympic Society which generated a little interest here and there but nobody was interested in funding it, it seems. And there have been others, of course. Muths, Curtius, Zappas in Greece. But they have not been international projects and that is where their failing has come about. And this is what I intend to speak of at the Sorbonne tomorrow afternoon. I intend to propose a modern-day Olympiad, with international participation and funding, which can be seen not only as a triumph of personal excellence and sporting achievement, but which can also help to reunify the countries in the world and provide a source for positive collaboration. Matthieu, Céline,' – here he positively glowed with the excitement of his convictions – 'I intend to bring back the Olympic Games.'

The marriage failed. We were not long in Madrid before it became clear that we would be unable to get past the matter of my indiscretion and Céline and I – amicably but with regret – decided to part. It grieved me to see the end come to this marriage, which I had finally decided was one to which I wished to devote if not my, then at least the rest of Céline's life, and I cursed myself for my apparent inability to remain faithful to one woman or to maintain a healthy, successful relationship. I begged for another chance but her disappointment in me was as obvious as her sense of betrayal. When we parted, I became disconsolate and drifted from Spain to Egypt where I invested for a time in a project aimed at building low-cost housing around Alexandria, a rare departure from the artistic world for me. I made a lot of money in my time there for the city was prosperous and in need of more dwellings and when I sold my share of the buildings, I made a profit of almost two million drachma, a fortune at the time. The kind of money one could live off for ever if one was careful with it.

Although it was to be three years after our dinner together before I again met Baron de Coubertin, I had followed his continuing story in the newspapers with some interest. The initial lecture at the Sorbonne had met with a positive response from his audience, although it was barely reported in the media, but eventually I heard that he had travelled to America with Céline by his side to meet with representatives of the Ivy League universities, among others, to stir interest in a modern Games. It seemed that she had taken on the position of his secretary and had become almost as involved in his work as he was himself. He returned to the Sorbonne in 1894 where the definitive decision to hold the Games was made, with representatives from twelve countries in attendance, and he himself was appointed secretary-general, under the presidency of a Greek man named Demetrius Vikelas.

'I wanted to hold off the Games until 1900,' he told me some years later. 'I thought it would make sense to see in the new century with a new Olympiad, but I was outvoted, eleven to one. Most of the delegates from the individual countries, having got the bit between their teeth, were pushing for quicker action. Of course, I had been planning this for years. I didn't want to rush into

179

it without due preparatory time. Not after devoting so much of my life to the endeavour anyway.'

He had also favoured holding the Games in Paris, but Vikelas overruled him and insisted that they be held in Athens where the Games had originally taken place. It was agreed that they should be held every four years and the date for the first of the modern era was set for April of 1896. Elaborate plans immediately got underway.

Visiting Paris again, I was attending a reception to welcome the flautist Juré back home from his triumphant American tour when I saw Pierre locked in conversation with a couple of acquaintances of mine outside on the lawn. Going out to join them, I extended a hand to Pierre, who shook it warmly as if we were old friends.

'I don't believe we've met, sir,' he said, however, introducing himself to me as if for the first time. 'Pierre de Fredi.'

I laughed, a little embarrassed and surprised that he did not remember our one-time familial relationship. 'Indeed we have,' I replied. 'Do you not recall a dinner we had in Paris a few years ago, on the night before your first lecture to the Sorbonne?' He looked a little unsure and stroked his moustache nervously. 'I was with your sister,' I added.

'My sister?'

'Céline,' I reminded him. 'We were . . . well, we were married at the time, I was your brother-in-law. I still am, I suppose, as we have never divorced.'

He clapped his hands together suddenly, a slight affectation I observed in him from time to time, before grasping my shoulders tightly. 'Of course,' he shouted, his face breaking into a broad grin. 'Then you must be

Mr Zéla, that's it, isn't it?' His uncertainty testified to me the fact that Céline did not speak of me often.

'Matthieu,' I insisted. 'Please.'

'Indeed, indeed,' he said, nodding slowly, his face growing reflective as he looked at me and took me aside gently. 'Actually, I remember that night quite well. I believe I told you both about my plans for the Games, am I right?'

'You did,' I acknowledged, remembering his enthusiasm with pleasure. 'And I must admit that at the time, while intrigued by your ideas, I thought they were a little too far-fetched to be realized. I never believed you could bring things as far as you have. I've followed your adventures quite avidly in the newspapers, you know. You are to be congratulated for your work.'

'Have you really?' he asked, laughing. 'Have you indeed? Well it's kind of you to take an—'

'And what of Céline?' I asked quickly. 'You see her often, I presume.'

He shrugged his shoulders almost imperceptibly before answering. 'She is based in Paris at the moment, with me. She became rather interested in the idea of the Games and I must admit has become indispensable to me now. Her advice and encouragement, not to mention her skill as a hostess, are worth a great deal to me. We have become true siblings in a way we were not for so many years. You hurt her quite badly, you know, Mr Zéla,' he added a little haughtily.

'Matthieu,' I repeated. 'And I realize that, I assure you. I miss her greatly, Pierre. Might I ask is she involved with anyone else right now?'

He breathed in deeply and looked around, unsure what to say for the best. 'She is devoted to her work and to me. To *our* work, I should say,' he explained eventually. 'Whatever happened in the past . . . well, I do not believe she thinks about it too often these days. She has moved on. She does not, however, consort with young men if that is what you are getting at. She is still a married woman, after all.'

I nodded and wondered whether I would be quite so civil to someone who had treated my sister in so cavalier a manner as I had his. I felt it would be inappropriate, however, to continue to talk about her behind her back and so complimented him once more upon his success, the only thing outside of Céline that I felt we could discuss with any enthusiasm. Again, it was like lighting a Christmas tree in a darkened room. His face bobbed up, his eyes shone, his cheeks grew slightly red and he immediately forgot the awkward moment we had just gone through.

'I must admit,' he told me, 'that there were many times when I did not believe myself that we could actually do it. And now, it seems, the Games are almost upon us. Only another seventeen months to go.'

'And are you prepared?' I asked. He opened his mouth to say something, thought better of it, and looked around the garden nervously. 'Let us go inside,' he suggested. 'Let us find a quiet corner somewhere we can talk. Perhaps you might be able to advise me on some matters. You are quite the businessman, are you not?'

'I've made a little money over the years,' I admitted.

'Good, good,' he said quickly. 'Then perhaps you will know where I can turn to on a certain matter. Come now. Let us go inside.' And with that he took me by the arm and led me inside the reception area to a room upstairs where we sat by a log fire and he told me of the difficulties he was facing and I explained a way that I might yet be able to help him.

A week later I returned to Egypt to close off my final business transactions there, and watched the papers anxiously for any fresh news on the Olympics. Incredibly, it seemed that the decision had been made to hold the Games in Athens without so much as consulting the Greek government, who had precious little money to spare on something so potentially frivolous as an Olympiad. Because of this, the Hungarian government had stepped in and offered to host the inaugural games themselves, with the condition that a top ranking Budapest official be given a position of authority alongside Vikelas. Any such move would of course have involved the removal of Pierre from the proceedings, the very idea of which devastated him.

'This is exactly the reason I wanted to wait until 1900,' he told me that evening at Juré's party in Paris as we became gradually more and more drunk on wine; his mood was tense but he was trying not to believe that the worst could in fact happen. 'We aren't ready. Athens isn't ready. Budapest *certainly* isn't ready. If we only had a few more years to prepare we could make everything perfect. As things stand, I can see this whole dream just vanishing into thin air.'

I saw this as my opportunity to make amends with Céline for the unhappiness I had caused her in her life. If she heard that I had helped her brother fulfil his ambition, perhaps she could then forgive me for the unhappiness I had caused her in her own life. I did not expect a reconciliation – nor was I sure that I even desired one – but I felt then as now that I must pay my debts and not cause hurt to people unnecessarily. I had damaged my wife; now I had an opportunity to help her brother. It seemed only right that I should do so.

Pierre arranged a meeting between the two of us and Crown Prince Constantine, who had already set up various committees aimed at generating funds for the Games and we discussed different plans for making sure that they stayed in Athens. Afterwards, I travelled to Egypt once again and arranged an appointment with Georges Averoff, one of the most important businessmen in the country. He was a well-known benefactor to various Greek causes, having paid for the building of the Athens Polytechnic, the military academy and the juvenile prisons among other places of common good. I had met him many times over the course of the previous few years and, while it was well known that he had the means to support a project such as this, we had not enjoyed a good relationship during my time there. I had made the error in judgement of giving an interview to a local newspaper regarding building plans within the city and had been critical of some of Averoff's holdings. Although we were both engaged in very similar projects, he was a much wealthier man than I – in interest alone he earned an annual income which came to about half of my capital. I was in poor form at the time and had foolishly felt threatened by the constant signs of 'Averoff' throughout Alexandria and elsewhere, where I wanted to see the name 'Zéla'. I felt personally affronted that I myself was not afforded the respect and admiration of the populace which flowed so easily towards the great entrepreneur. And so I had made light of some of his buildings, going so far as to call his trademark high windows and rococo finishes a blight on a great city, a pock-mark on the face of modern Alexandria. I said more than that too but it was all childish stuff and unworthy of me. One of Averoff's people came to see me shortly afterwards and told me that while they were not going to take any action against me at that time, Averoff would appreciate it if I never spoke his name to a media body again, and I was so embarrassed by the way that the newspaper had portrayed me as a shallow, childish simpleton that I complied immediately. So, naturally, I was not particularly looking forward to meeting with him, cap in hand, and asking for help.

We met in his office on a Saturday morning in mid-1895. He sat behind a large mahogany desk and came out to shake my hand warmly when I arrived, which surprised me. His grey hair had turned completely white since I had last seen him and I couldn't help but think that he looked a little like the American writer Mark Twain.

'Matthieu,' he said, guiding me to a comfortable sofa, across from which he sat in an armchair. 'It's good to see you again. How long has it been?'

'A year or so,' I said nervously, wondering whether I should apologize immediately for my previous behaviour or simply pretend that it had never taken place. A man in his position, with his responsibilities, was surely too busy to remember every single slight, every word which was said against him, I reassured myself, eventually deciding to let it go. 'At the Krakov party, if I remember correctly.'

'Ah, yes,' he said. 'Terrible thing that happened there, wasn't it?' (Petr Krakov, a government minister, had been shot dead only a few weeks earlier on the street outside his house. No one had yet claimed responsibility, but there was talk of underground involvement, which surprised everyone, for this was not a city of violence.)

'Awful,' I said, nodding my head piously. 'Who knows

185

what kind of business he was involved in? A most unhappy end.'

'Well, let's not speculate,' he said quickly, as if he
knew only too well. 'The truth will out sooner or later.
Idle gossip will get us nowhere.' I looked at him and
wondered whether this was a dig or not but decided
against, for the moment anyway. His desk was littered
with framed photographs and I asked whether I might
take a look at them. He assented with a smile and a
wave of his hand.

'That is my wife, Dolores,' he said, indicating a
smiling woman who was ageing gracefully by his side.
Her features were fine and I could tell that she must
have been a great beauty in her youth, and perhaps
the kind of woman who becomes completely stunning
when she reaches her natural middle age. 'And those
are my children. And some of their wives and children.'
There were a lot of them and I could see a glowing pride
in his face as he showed them to me, which I envied. He
lived a similar life to me, Georges Averoff; we were both
entrepreneurs, we had both made a lot of money, we
were both intelligent businessmen, and yet somehow
this aspect of life had escaped me. I wondered how it was
that after so many failed marriages and relationships I
had yet to father a child or begin a happy family such
as he had. Perhaps it was true; perhaps there really was
only one woman for every man and I had already lost
her. Not that I could have ever hoped to have kept her.

'So,' he said with a smile as we sat back down across
from each other, 'what did you want to see me about?'

I explained the events of the past few months with
Georges, telling him about Pierre's brilliant plans and
how they looked increasingly likely to be spurned. I
showed him the letter from Crown Prince Constantine,

urging him to help us, and repeated the series of disasters which had led to the possibility of a Hungarian Games. I appealed to his sense of patriotism, stressing how important the Games would be for Greece but, in truth, I did not have to speak for long for he almost immediately gave in.

'Of course I will help,' he insisted, opening his arms wide. 'This is a great thing which is taking place. I will do everything I can. But tell me, Matthieu, why are you so concerned? You are not Greek, are you?'

'I'm French.'

'Yes, I thought as much. So why are you going to so much trouble to help the Greeks and de Coubertin anyway? It seems curious to me.'

I looked at the floor for a moment, wondering whether I should explain the truth to him or not. 'Some years ago,' I said eventually, 'I married the sister of Pierre de Fredi. We are still married, to tell you the truth. And I treated her . . .' I searched for an appropriate word, '. . . badly. I spoiled what could have been a wonderful relationship and hurt her. I do not like hurting people, Georges. I am trying to make amends.'

He nodded slowly. 'I see,' he said. 'And are you trying to win her back?'

'I don't think so,' I said. 'That wasn't my original plan anyway. I simply wanted to help her in some way. Although we have, of course, been thrown together a little in this matter once again and there are some feelings which have resurfaced. When we came back into contact again, she did me a great service. I have a nephew, Thom, who has not had an easy life. His father died in violent circumstances when he was a baby and his mother took to the bottle. He came to visit me when he was released from prison earlier this year for a minor

187

offence and he was in desperate need of some stability. Céline very kindly agreed to give my nephew a job in her offices, helping with the administrative duties, and it has come as a godsend to him as he needed money and something to do. For some reason, the boy refuses to have anything to do with me or accept anything from me but she has been an angel to him because of our old acquaintanceship. I think that I—' I stopped short suddenly, hearing what I was saying. 'I'm sorry,' I said quickly. 'You don't want to hear any of this. I'm sorry to make myself sound so ridiculous.'

He shrugged and gave a gentle laugh. 'On the contrary, Matthieu,' he said. 'It is interesting to meet a man with a conscience. Unusual, even. Where did you come across it exactly?' I looked at him in some amusement, unsure whether he was poking fun at me or not, no doubt thinking about the dispute we had had in the past. I suddenly respected him enormously and decided to tell him the truth.

'I killed someone once,' I said. 'The only woman I ever really loved. And after that I swore I would never hurt anyone again. The conscience, as you put it, developed from there.'

Averoff donated almost a million drachmas to the Olympic fund which was put towards the reconstruction of the Panathenaen Stadium, where the Games were to be held. The stadium had been built in 330 BC but had gradually disintegrated and ended up being completely covered up for several centuries. The Crown Prince erected a statue to Averoff outside, created by the famous sculptor Vroutos, as a mark of gratitude for his patriotism and generosity, and this was unveiled on the eve of the first day of the Games, 5 April 1896.

I was excited by the ease with which I had persuaded Averoff to help us. I had envisioned many months of careful discussion and planning, months which would have led us ever closer to the prospect of a Budapest takeover, and the fact that I could return within the week was seen as a great victory. Pierre got to keep his job, the Games were held in Athens, and I could make amends with Céline.

'So,' she said shortly after my return. 'You were good for something after all. Have you seen how happy Pierre is? It would have killed him if we had lost the Games.'

'It was the least I could do,' I said. 'I owed you, after all.'

'You did, that's true.'

'Perhaps—' I began, wondering whether I should wait for a more romantic setting to introduce the topic of a reconciliation but deciding against. I have always been a firm believer in grasping the moment. 'Perhaps we could—'

'Before you say anything,' said Céline quickly, looking slightly nervous as she interrupted me, 'I think it's high time that we began to sort out our marital arrangements.'

'But that's fantastic,' I said. 'I was thinking the exact same thing.'

'I think we should divorce,' she said firmly.

'We should *what*?'

'Divorce, Matthieu. We haven't been together in several years, after all. It's time to move on, don't you agree?'

I looked at her, stunned. 'But what about all I've done for your brother?' I exclaimed. 'I've devoted so much of my energy to helping him, to getting the Games for Athens. I've been a true friend to him during my time

189

here. What about all the money I raised from Averoff?'

'Well, you can marry my brother if you feel so strongly about him,' she said quickly. 'I *need* a divorce, Matthieu,' she said. 'I've . . . I've fallen in love with another and we wish to marry.'

I couldn't believe my ears. My pride was hurt. 'Well, can't you wait awhile?' I begged. 'See whether either of these relationships work out before deciding to—'

'Matthieu, I *need* to marry this man. Soon. It's imperative.'

I frowned, wondering what she could mean by this, before my mouth fell open and I looked her up and down. 'You're with child?' I asked and she blushed, nodding quickly. 'Good God,' I said, amazed, as it was the last thing I would have expected from her. 'And who's the father, might I ask?'

'I think it's for the best if you don't.'

'I believe I have the right!' I shouted, mortally offended by the idea of my wife being impregnated by another. 'I shall kill whoever it is!'

'*Why?*' she screamed. 'You cheated on me, we split up, that was three years ago. I chose to move on. I've fallen in love. Can't you understand that?'

Over her shoulder I spied a portrait on her desk, a gilt-framed picture of her with a handsome, dark haired young man, smiling happily, their arms wrapped around each other. I walked towards it and picked it up, my face draining of blood as I realized who I was looking at. 'It can't be . . .' I said and she shrugged.

'I'm sorry, Matthieu,' she said. 'We became very close, that's all. We fell in love.'

'Obviously. I don't know what to say to you, Céline. You shall have your divorce, of course.' I put the picture down and left the room. Shortly afterwards, our decree

190

came through. Seven months later, I heard that she had given birth to a baby boy, and six months after that I saw my nephew's name listed in the dead of the Boer War for he was a British subject, and had been enlisted into the army, and wondered whether she would be able to cope once again with life on her own. I would have got in touch but by then my life had led me in a completely different and unexpected direction and, anyway, sometimes one has to leave the past where it belongs.

Chapter 12

May–June 1999

Things changed at work a little too quickly for my liking. For one thing, the simplicity of my life, my very solitude, was destroyed when I found myself in the position of responsibility which I had been hoping to avoid. Two of James's ex-wives turned up at the funeral in widow's weeds; neither of them shed a tear, nor did they attend the wake afterwards, but they seemed very friendly towards each other for two women who had been vying for extra money for several years and whose alimony payments had just come to an abrupt end. Some of his children were there, although the ones from whom he was estranged were notable by their absence. I spoke an oration in the church, citing his professionalism and excellence at his job as reasons why our business would suffer without him, and our own personal friendship as a reason why I would. It was brief, to the point, and I hated delivering it, knowing only too well the manner in which my former managing director had met his death and feeling like a hypocrite as I pretended otherwise. Alan put in an appearance, looking extremely agitated, but P.W. had already disappeared off to his home in the south of France, leaving his daughter Caroline with his power of attorney.

At the wake, I ended up in conversation with Lee, James's son and, within a few minutes, I wished that I could feign illness and return home immediately. He was a tall, gangly lad of about twenty-two, and I had been watching him for some time, as he appeared to be working the room quite professionally, with a few words or a joke for everyone. He did not appear to be behaving like a son in mourning. He was full of jokes and cheer and was refilling everyone's glasses as he moved around.

'It's Mr Zéla, isn't it?' he asked me when it came to my turn for an interview. 'Thank you for coming. You said some very nice things in the church.'

'I could hardly have stayed away,' I said quietly, looking at his straggly blond hair with distaste and wondering why he could not have shaved for this day or at least got a haircut. 'I had a lot of respect for your father, you know. He was a very talented man.'

'Was he?' asked Lee, as if the very idea was news to him. 'That's good to know. I didn't really know him very well, to be honest. We weren't close. He was always too caught up with work to be interested in any of us, which is why there are only two of us here.' He spoke as if this was the most natural conversation in the world, as if this type of scenario, this very setting, was one in which he took part on a regular basis. 'Can I get you another drink at all?'

'No, I'm fine,' I said as he refilled my wine glass anyway. 'It's a pity that you didn't know him better,' I added. 'It's always sad when people die and we haven't told them how we really feel towards them.'

He shrugged. 'I suppose so,' he said, the epitome of filial love. 'Can't say I'm too bothered to be honest. Got to be stoical about these things. It was you who found him, wasn't it?' I nodded. 'Tell me about it,' he said after a long pause when there appeared to be a battle of wills taking place between us to see who would give in first. Eventually I shrugged and looked over his shoulder slightly as I spoke.

'I came into work,' I began, 'around seven, I suppose. I went to—'

'You start work at seven?' he asked in surprise and I hesitated before saying anything.

'A lot of people do, you know,' I told him cautiously, a friend to the working classes, and he just shrugged his shoulders and smiled slightly. 'I came in around seven and went to my office to go through my tray. After a few minutes, I went down to James's – to your father's – office and found him there.'

'Why did you do that?'

'Why did I do what?'

'Go down to my father's office. Did you want to speak to him?'

My eyes narrowed. 'I can't remember, to be honest with you,' I said. 'Your father always showed up early in the mornings – I knew that he'd be there. I think I just grew weary of all those letters that were sitting on my desk in need of reply, and felt like a cup of coffee to ease me into the day. Thought your father might have some. He usually kept a pot bubbling on his sideboard, you see, throughout the day.'

'So you *can* remember after all,' said Lee. 'Would you like something to eat, Mr Zéla? Are you hungry at all?'

'Matthieu, please. And I'm fine, thank you. So what do you do anyway, Lee? I'm sure James told me at some point but there are so many of you that it seems hard to keep track.'

'I'm a writer,' he said quickly. 'And there's only five

of us actually, which probably isn't as many mouths to feed as my father pretended. He seemed to be under the delusion that he was responsible for the feeding of the five thousand. There's three different mothers though. I'm Sara's. The only child as it were. And the youngest.'

'Right,' I said, nodding. 'Do the other four gang up on you then?'

'They could try,' he said doubtfully. There was a silence for a few minutes and I looked around nervously, desperate to get away from him but wondering about the etiquette of deserting one of the chief mourners during his moment in the spotlight. He was staring at me and smiling lightly and I wondered what it was that he found so amusing. I desperately wanted to think of something to say to him.

'So what do you write?' I asked. 'Is it journalism like your father?'

'No, no,' he said quickly. 'God, no. There's no money in that. No, I write scripts.'

'Film scripts?'

'Some day maybe. Right now, it's for television. I'm trying to break in.'

'And are you working on something now?'

'I'm not *employed* on anything, if that's what you mean. But I am working on something, yes. A television drama. A one-off, one-hour black comedy. It involves a crime. I'm just in the middle of it right now but I think I'm on to something good with it.'

'Sounds interesting,' I muttered, a standard response. I am more than used to having writers approach me at parties, offering to tell me their plots and treatments, expecting me suddenly to write them out a cheque there and then for their works of genius. I half expected Lee to pull his manuscript out of his pocket and try to pitch it to me but he made no moves to continue talking about it specifically.

'It must be great to be actually working in television all the time,' he said, 'to know you're getting a steady paycheque from it, I mean. To be able to think up ideas and see them realized. That's what I'd love to be doing.'

'I'm just an investor really,' I said. 'Your father was the man who knew about the industry. I just put up some of the money and don't have to work very hard. It's a fine life.'

'Really?' he asked, stepping a little closer to me now. 'So why were you in your office at seven a.m. then? Should you not have been at home in bed, or off checking your investments somewhere?'

We stared at each other and I wondered why he was continuing with this line of questioning, behaving like some dogged detective off an American crime show. For a brief moment I felt as if he knew there was more to his father's demise than met the eye, but of course that was impossible as the police had gone through the place thoroughly and found no cause for suspicious comment. 'I *was* checking my investment,' I said. 'I have a lot of money invested in that station. I come in once a week and spend the whole day in there.'

'The whole day? Jesus. That must be rough.'

'Usually I ate lunch with your father on that day. I shall miss that.' He ignored the platitude as I had ignored his sarcasm and so I continued. 'I'm afraid when it comes to the actual day to day operations of running a television station, I'm not the man to talk to. My nephew, maybe, but not me.' I bit my lip the moment those words were out of my mouth but there was no pulling them back in.

'Your nephew?' asked Lee. 'Why, does he work at the station too?'

'He's an actor,' I admitted. 'He's been in television for quite some time. He knows the business quite well, I imagine. Or so he's always telling me anyway.'

Lee's eyebrows shot up and he inched a little closer to me still, the way people generally do when they know they're talking to someone who has some connection with celebrity. 'He was an actor?' he asked, curiously employing the past tense. 'I mean he *is* an actor? Who is he? Would I know him? I can't think of any Zélas in television.'

'He's not a Zéla,' I said quickly. 'He's a DuMarqué. Tommy DuMarqué. He's in some—'

'*Tommy DuMarqué?*' he shouted and a few people turned around to look at him in surprise. I swallowed and wished I was elsewhere. 'Tommy DuMarqué from—' He mentioned the name of Tommy's soap opera – sorry, recurring drama – and I shrugged and admitted that was the one. 'No fucking way!' he roared now and I couldn't help but laugh. He was his father's son all right.

'Afraid so,' I said.

'Jesus, that's unbelievable. You're his uncle. That was . . .' He trailed off as he thought about it.

'So to speak.'

'That's mad!' he said, running his hand through his hair, incredibly energized by the news, his eyes practically popping out of their sockets in his excitement. 'Everyone knows him. He's like one of the most famous—'

'Actually, I'm sorry but I have to use the bathroom,' I said suddenly, seeing an escape route. 'You don't mind if I leave you for a moment, do you?'

197

'OK,' he said, deflated now as his speech proclaiming my nephew's level of fame was prematurely ended. 'But don't leave without saying goodbye, all right? I still want to hear about how you found my father. You haven't told me that bit yet.'

I frowned and disappeared upstairs to throw some water on my face, knowing full well that my next move would be to take my coat and hat from the hall stand and disappear through the front door without having to see him again.

May and June turned out to be stressful months. With the death of James, there was a vacancy for the position of managing director at our station and, since P.W. had all but vanished from our lives, we were suddenly left in a state of some disorder. Alan came in and out to meet with me, usually unable to offer anything constructive by way of advice, constantly repeating the fact that he had most of his money invested in the station until it became something of a mantra for him, much as P.W. had been inclined to do before his disappearance. I returned to work on a daily basis, each day growing longer and longer until I began to think that, if I wasn't careful, it would start to age me. I couldn't remember working quite so hard since just after the Boer War, when I had a brief involvement with a hospital for soldiers who had returned from the front unable to cope with civilian life again. As I owned the place and was chiefly responsible for the employment of doctors who could help these boys, I became almost ill with worry myself and came close to ending up as a patient there before I hired the right person to lessen my workload and gradually wean me away from the quotidian business. That was what I had in mind as I was thinking about

James's replacement: someone who could do the job, lessen the workload and turn up before I went quite mad.

In the second week of May, I received a phone call from Caroline Davison, P.W.'s daughter, who arranged an appointment to meet with me. I suggested dinner in my club but she declined, preferring to meet in my office during the daytime. It wasn't a social visit, she said, but a professional one and her crisp, imperturbable tone on the phone intrigued me. I didn't think too much about it, however, and only remembered that she was actually coming in a few hours before she arrived when I noticed her name written in my desk diary.

She arrived at precisely 2 p.m., a well-dressed young woman sporting a simple black bob, a few strands of which fell down gently over her forehead. She had a very pretty face, with pale brown eyes and a small nose, her cheekbones emerging delicately through a thin layer of make-up. I guessed she was in her late twenties – although if anyone should know that you can't judge someone's age by their appearance then it should be me. For all I knew, she could have been 550; she could have narrowly missed out on being the seventh wife to Henry VIII.

'So,' I said as we sat opposite each other, drinking tea and sizing each other up through polite conversation, 'have you heard from your father lately?'

'Apparently he's somewhere in the Caribbean,' she told me. 'I got a phone call from him last week and he was doing some serious island hopping.'

'Lucky him.'

'I know. I haven't had a holiday in two years. I wish *I* could go to the Caribbean. It seems that he's met a woman there too, although from the sound of her she's more of a girl than a woman. Some nineteen-year-old bimbo with a lau, probably.'

'That's Hawaii,' I said.

'Pardon?'

'Hawaii. It's Hawaii where you get laus. The garlands you hang around your neck. It's not the Caribbean. I'm not sure what traditions they have there.'

She stared at me for a moment. 'Well, whatever,' she said eventually. 'He's obviously having some sort of mid-life crisis, which is extremely predictable. Did you ever have one of those?'

I laughed. 'Yes, but it was years ago,' I said. 'I can hardly remember it. And to call it "mid-life" would be stretching a point.'

'Anyway, I doubt if we're going to be seeing him returning to this miserable city any time soon. Who needs tubes and smog and millions of people and Richard fucking Branson mugging away on the telly every night when you can have tropical beaches, sunshine and cocktails all day and all of the night? Lucky for him that he can afford it. I can't on my money.'

She was being remarkably forthright but settled back in her chair after this mild outburst. I stroked my chin as I attempted to size her up. 'What *do* you do?' I asked her, wondering why P.W. had never spoken to me before about this self-assured daughter of his. She was the kind of girl whom most fathers would be proud to call their own.

'Music stores,' she told me. 'I'm an area manager with a retail chain. London and the south-east. That's forty-two shops in all.'

'Really,' I said, impressed by such responsibility. 'That must be—'

'I've been there since I left school, to be honest

200

with you,' she continued. 'Skipped all that university palaver. Been working my way up the ladder ever since. Salesgirl, assistant manager, branch manager. I got the area manager's job because everyone else who went for it was either incompetent or lazy. Now I'm their boss,' she added.

I smiled. 'And how do you treat them?' I asked her.

'With amazing fairness, all things considered,' she said, 'although I'd give my left nut to see about half a dozen of them leave or lose their footing as they stroll around the top of a very, very tall building. I'm trying to guide them towards alternative careers but they seem settled for life there. I, on the other hand, feel like a change. Ambition is all I really have. It's what I have instead of a life.'

'And is that enough for you?'

'That and ability. I'm looking for alternative employment, you see, Mr Zéla. I feel I've gone about as far in *retail* as I'm ever going to go.' Her face took on a slightly sour expression as she employed the dreaded R-word.

'Matthieu, please,' I said, predictably.

'So this has come as a godsend to me, you see.'

I nodded and finished my tea, wondering how much longer we would have to chat politely before we could say goodbye when that last sentence finally sank in. 'What has?' I asked her, looking up. 'What has come as a godsend?'

'This,' she said, smiling. 'This opportunity.'

Another pause. 'Sorry, I'm not with you.'

'This television station,' she said, leaning forward and looking at me as if I was an idiot. 'It's the right opportunity at just the right time for me. I've been in the same job for eleven years now. It's time I got out.

201

Got involved in something different. It excites me. I feel challenged by it.'

'You want to work *here*?' I asked, surprised by the idea, wondering what exactly I could offer her but sure already that she was the kind of woman that it would be good to have on board. 'But what exactly do you want to do?'

'Look, Mr Zéla,' she said, putting her cup down on my desk and her cards on the table as she crossed her legs in a quick movement. 'My father has given me his power of attorney and wants me to represent him in this business. Basically, his shares are now being operated by me. I *already* work here, you might say. So I will of course want to be kept up to speed with all the company's plans and transactions while at the same time learn very quickly about the history and needs of this place. You can see that, I'm sure. I'll need to look at budgets, projections, productivity, ratings, market share, that type of thing.'

'Right,' I said, very slowly and very suspiciously, as I tried to look quickly into the future and into what all of this might mean. I probably should have expected it but had never considered someone else stepping into P.W.'s shoes until now. I had always assumed that he would remain a sleeping partner, doing no work and drawing on his profits every quarter. He had barely been more than that before all of this business began anyway. 'Well, I suppose that can be arranged,' I said. 'You have all the necessary documentation, I presume.'

'Oh, yes,' she replied confidently. 'There're no problems there. I'll bike them across to you later this afternoon for your legal department to read through. No, the important thing is that I want to actually work

202

here. Not just be employed here, not just be paid from here, but to *work* here.'

'On air, you mean?' For a moment I could almost see it. She was the right age, she was attractive, intelligent. A possible replacement for Tara, I thought. Weather? News? Documentaries?

'No, not on air,' she replied with a laugh, knocking that idea on the head immediately. 'Behind the scenes obviously. I want James Hocknell's job.'

I blinked. Although I admired her forthrightness, I was amazed by her arrogance. 'You have to be kidding me,' I said.

'Not at all. I'm perfectly serious.'

'But you have no experience.'

'No experience?' She looked at me in amazement. 'I've worked in a management role in a high profile organization for over nine years. I deal with an annual turnover of sixteen million pounds. I have authority over a staff of almost six hundred people. I administer—'

'You have no experience in the media world, Caroline,' I said. 'You've never worked for a newspaper, a television station, a film company, a PR agency – nothing. You said yourself you've been in retail since you left school. Well? Am I right?'

'You're right, but—'

'Let me ask you this,' I said, raising a hand to silence her for a moment and she sat back with a slightly sulky expression, folding her arms like a child who hasn't been given what she wanted. 'In your business, if someone came to you from another company, a company where they may well have done very well for themselves but in a completely different industry all the same, and asked to be employed at the very highest level, would you consider it for more than a moment?'

203

'If they seemed like they could do the job, yes. I'd ask them to put together a—'

'Caroline, hold on. Answer me this question as if you were in the very position you aspire to.' I leaned forward and joined my hands together as I looked her directly in the eyes. 'If you were me, would *you* hire you?'

There was a long silence as she thought about it and realized that the best answer to that question was not to answer it at all. 'I'm an intelligent woman, Matthieu,' she said. 'I'm good at what I do. And I can learn quickly. And at the end of the day, I *am* a major shareholder,' she added, a hint of a threat in her voice, as if this was going to swing the vote in her favour.

'And I'm an even more major one,' I replied without hesitation. 'And with Alan on my side, as I assure you he will be, I am the *majority* shareholder. No, I'm sorry. It's out of the question. James Hocknell may have been many things and he may have come to an unpleasant end, but the man was a professional and absolutely brilliant at his job. He's helped advance this company and bring it to the point where it is today. I can't afford to see all that work go to waste. I can't take the risk. I'm sorry.'

She sighed and sat back in her chair. 'Tell me this, Matthieu,' she said, 'do you want to go on working here?'

'Oh, God no,' I said honestly. 'I want things to go back to the way they were. I want to be able to come in once a week, sure that I've left someone in charge who can handle any situation that presents itself. I want a little peace and quiet. I'm an old man, you know.'

She laughed. 'You are not,' she said. 'Don't be ridiculous.'

'Trust me. I don't look my age.'

'All I want is a chance, that's all I ask. You can always fire me. You can put it in my contract that I can be fired at any time for any reason and I can't sue you. What do you say? I can't say fairer than that.'

I pushed my chair back a little and looked out of the window. On the pavement below I could see a small child waiting with his mother for the traffic to stop so that they might cross the road. They weren't holding hands and I watched as he suddenly made a break for it, only to be whisked back by his mother before he was run over, whereupon she gave him a sharp slap on the back of his legs. Then he burst out crying although I couldn't hear him from this distance. I could just see his little eyes scrunched up tightly and his mouth twisted into some sort of wide open contortion. Hideously ugly. I looked away. 'I tell you what,' I said, turning back to her, and thinking, 'What the hell?'. 'It really looks like *I'm* going to be doing James's job for the foreseeable future. So how about you come to work here as my assistant. I'll teach you what I know about the place, for what it's worth, and after a few months we can re-evaluate the situation. See whether it's the kind of thing you really want to do or not. Maybe you'll prove me wrong. Maybe you'll be excellent at it. Or maybe your father will come home and we'll all be right back where we started.'

'I think that's unlikely somehow,' she said. 'But that sounds fair enough, I suppose. At least I'm willing to accept that arrangement for now. One last question.'

'Yes?'

'When do I start?'

It was splashed across the front pages of all the tabloids, and even hit a broadsheet or two. A colour photograph, slightly off-kilter, of Tommy and Barbra clinched in a passionate embrace, eyes closed, lips locked together, blissfully unaware of the paparazzo snapping away in the distance. The location was a dark corner of a famous people's nightclub; Tommy looked rather smart in his now apparently trademark black shirt and jacket, while Barbra was definitely not looking her age in a simple white blouse and culottes. He had one hand in her shoulder-length blonde hair as they kissed; their bodies could hardly have been closer together without risk of consummation and the whole picture represented the word 'lust'. The papers could hardly contain their excitement.

'I don't know how it happened exactly,' Tommy explained to me as we sat drinking cappuccinos in a top-floor café off Kensington High Street, hidden slightly behind a fern in order to escape from prying eyes. 'It was just one of those things. We met, we got talking, one thing led to another, we kissed. I know it seems odd but it felt perfectly natural at the time.'

'Honestly,' I said, amused by the boyish look of smug self-satisfaction he was giving me, 'she's old enough to be your mother.'

'Maybe, but surely the most important thing is that she's not.'

I laughed. 'Do famous people only make love to other famous people?' I asked him, intrigued now by the world which he inhabited. 'Explain it to me. Is that why famous people want to be famous?'

'Not always,' he said, shaking his head. 'Look at Andrea. She's not famous.'

'She's not famous *yet*, Tommy. Give her a couple of months and come back to me on it.' Andrea was Tommy's current girlfriend, who had already announced that she was two months pregnant with his child. They had met at a television awards ceremony, where Andrea was working as a junior sound recordist with the television station responsible for its broadcasting. According to him – well, according to her originally – she didn't know who he was when they met, never having seen an episode of his television show. Apparently, she doesn't even own a TV, which I find unusual for someone who actually works in the medium.

'It's true,' Tommy told me. 'There isn't a single TV in her apartment. It's wall to wall books, that's all. She's not like those other girls. She's not interested in who I am.'

I wasn't convinced. Even if she really didn't have a TV, it was impossible to conceive of an existence in this country over the last few years where, somehow or other, the name of Tommy DuMarqué did not creep into your consciousness. His many ventures into different areas of the entertainment world – television, music, theatre, *Hello!* magazine – have made him such a ubiquitous presence in the cultural mêlée that it seemed ridiculous that a normal person with eyes and ears could travel from day to day without having made his acquaintance, metaphorically speaking, at some point or another. And yet this girl, this Andrea, this now pregnant twenty-four-year-old sound recordist, was claiming that very thing.

'She's all right really,' said Tommy, defending her to me with his usual lack of superlatives. 'She's a nice girl. I trust her.'

'Do you love her?'

'Christ, no.'

'But you're still together?'

'Of course we are. We're having a baby, remember?'

'I remember.' What he didn't realize was that, to me, hearing of his impregnating someone was like watching someone sign his own death warrant. I picked up the newspaper again and waved it at him. 'So what about this then?' I asked. 'How do you explain this? To *Andrea*, if to no one else.'

'I don't *have* to explain it to her,' he said with a shrug, twirling his cappuccino around inside his cup carelessly. 'We're not married, you know. Things happen. We're young. What are you gonna do?'

'I'm not going to do anything, Tommy. I just want to try to understand why you're allowing yourself to get more and more deeply involved with some girl who you don't really care about, while you go around smooching with ageing movie stars whenever you get a chance. It seems to me that, if this Andrea really cared about you, she'd take exception to your behaviour.'

'Stop calling her "this Andrea". It's just Andrea.'

'Who has become pregnant with your baby. A rich and famous television personality. I wonder what particular qualities she first saw in you,' I added sarcastically.

Tommy looked irritated and paused before answering, in a slightly higher tone of voice. 'Who are you calling rich anyway?' he asked me. 'I haven't got two fucking pennies to rub together, surely you know that better than anyone. She's not after me for my money, you know.'

'Tommy, you're in a unique position. You may not currently be wealthy but you have the ability to make as much money as you want whenever you want. You are one of the elite. You are a star. People who never have and never will meet you look up to you, dream about you, have sexual fantasies in which you are involved. People will pay to see you. You belong to the extraordinary

208

social group of the professional celebrity. Can't you see that? You could make £100,000 tomorrow simply by allowing someone to take photographs of your gracious drawing room.'

'I don't have a gracious drawing room.'

'Well, then, go out and get one, for heaven's sake. Look one up in the Argos catalogue. Have one delivered and invite a photographer over to take a few shots of it. But if you want to make some money, then take advantage of your celebrity while it still exists.' I felt as if I had got off the point rather, as I had started with the photograph, moved on to Andrea, and was now giving out free financial advice. I relaxed in my chair and looked around. The place was mostly empty for it was the middle of the afternoon, too late for lunch, too early for dinner. Of those people who were present, I could make out a junior minister talking animatedly with his mistress at one table – the last time I had seen him was in a privately circulated photograph where he was playing the back end of a pantomime horse. Unfortunately the front end had forgotten to wear any clothes; there was talk of a scandal but no one was yet willing to publish. At another table there was a middle-aged couple eating cream cakes and drinking tea, looking right past each other in silence, as if they had already said every single thing that they had to say to each other in this lifetime and it was just a question of muddling through from now on. At another there was a teenage boy with his spotty girlfriend, both of whom were being loud. The boy's T-shirt said, 'My name's Warren Rimbleton and I won eight million quid on the lottery in March. And you didn't!' He was so covered in awful gold jewellery that I suspected this statement was one of fact. I looked away quickly as their lips met and they began to kiss in a rather strange, inexperienced manner, chewing on each others' mouths like toffee. As I glanced back at my nephew, he was scratching his arm and his shirt was lifted slightly above his wrist. The marks caught my eye and I looked at him quickly.

'What are those?' I asked him.

'What?' he replied, immediately rebuttoning his shirt.

'Those marks,' I said. 'Those marks on your arm. What are they?'

He shrugged and went slightly red, cringing on his seat. 'They're . . . they're nothing. I'm sorting it out, all right?' he added, apropos of nothing.

I shook my head in amazement. 'You were there, remember?' I said to him, leaning forward to whisper. 'You saw what happened to James Hocknell, right? You saw how he just suddenly—'

'He was some old fart shooting up to impress a teenage hooker who he picked up off the street. He didn't have a fucking clue what he was doing.'

'Yes, and he died because of it.'

'I'm not going to die, Uncle Matt.'

'I bet he thought the same thing.'

'Look, I don't do it that often anyway. I'm in a pressurized business. I need to blow off steam sometimes, that's all. I'm twenty-two years old and I know exactly how much of this stuff I can do without risking it all, OK? Trust me.'

I shook my head. 'I'm just worried about you, Tommy,' I said, a rare moment of conciliation between us. 'I don't want to see anything bad happen to you, that's all. Can you understand that?'

'Yeah, I can. And I appreciate it.'

'This baby . . . it means the worst.'

'It's just a baby, Uncle—'

'I've seen it all before. Too many times. Stop taking drugs, please. Can you do that? Don't live up to your ancestry. Pull yourself together, boy!'

Tommy stood up and threw some money on the table unnecessarily, as if to prove a point. 'This is on me,' he said. 'But I've got to go. I have to be back on set in about twenty minutes. Don't worry about me. I'll be fine.'

'I wish I could believe that,' I said, watching the heads turn as he walked out, the sudden moments of recognition, the way they looked back at him when he was already gone, their lives a little brighter for having seen him, ready to tell their friends of the encounter later in the evening. And he was oblivious to how important he was to complete strangers, let alone to me.

Chapter 13

Working with Dominique

I often tried to discover the derivation of the town name Cageley, but without much success. It remains, however, one of the most appropriately named places that I have ever come across, for I have rarely seen any town or city in 256 years which seemed so caged in, so soul-entrapping, as this small place was. Driving into Cageley, the first thing one saw was the set of large iron gates which had been constructed at its boundary, and through which all traffic passed. It was an unusual and strangely redundant sight, for both gates were simply placed solidly into the ground on either side of the road, and even if they were closed – which they never were – one could simply walk around them in order to gain access to what lay beyond.

It was primarily a self-sufficient town, with no more than five or six hundred inhabitants, each of whom appeared to contribute something to the common good. There were several all-purpose stores, a blacksmith, and a market in the centre of the town where the farmers' young children would generally position themselves from one end of the day to the next, selling their produce to each other's families. There was also a church, a schoolroom and a town hall, which saw annual productions from the local amateur dramatic group as well as the odd concert or solo performance.

Mr and Mrs Amberton brought us to their home on our first night in Cageley and we were all so tired that we went immediately to bed. They owned a relatively large house for two people living on their own and, to my disappointment, there was room enough for Tomas and I to share one room, and for Dominique to take the other. The next day, Mrs Amberton offered to show us around the town to help us make up our minds whether we wanted to stay there for the time being or continue on to London. As soon as I started walking around and seeing what I took to be an idyllic home setting before me, filled with families and relative prosperity and general satisfaction, I was keen to stay put and I could tell from Dominique's face that she was also being won over by the prospect of a stability that neither of us had ever known before.

'What do you think?' I asked her as we walked side by side along the street, Mrs Amberton moving a little ahead of us with my younger brother. 'It seems so different to Dover.'

'It does,' she agreed. 'There'd be no chance you could continue your previous life here. Everyone appears to know everyone else and we'd be strung up if you stole from them.'

'There are other ways to make a living. There have to be jobs here, don't you think?'

She didn't answer, but I could tell that she liked what she saw. Eventually we agreed that we would stay on for the time being, dependent on our abilities to find jobs, and that we would begin our search for those immediately. Both Mr and Mrs Amberton were delighted – I felt a little like some *naïf* being recruited into a cult – and said that we could stay with them for now and pay them a portion of our wages once we were secure. Although I found them both a little repugnant in their behaviour and manners – for even then I was beginning to believe that there was going to be more to my life than I was currently experiencing – we had no choice but to agree. Their offer was, after all, extremely generous and there was no telling when we would begin to achieve an income of our own. On those first couple of evenings, the five of us would sit around the Ambertons' fireplace, Tomas snoozing, Dominique brooding, I listening, Mrs Amberton talking and Mr Amberton alternating between coughing and spitting in the fire and taking long, noisy swallows of whiskey, while our hosts told us more about themselves and how they had become husband and wife in the first place. I began to feel that the three of us were becoming their surrogate children – I could see from the way they looked at us, particularly at Tomas, how fond they were growing of each of us – and found to my astonishment that I enjoyed that feeling. I had never known a sturdy, happy family unit before and that all too brief time that we spent in Cageley probably represents the closest I have ever come to knowing one in all my extended life.

'Mrs Amberton's father didn't want me to marry her,' Mr Amberton told us one evening. 'He had ideas, you see, about himself that weren't always fulfilled.'

'He were a good man, though, my father,' interjected his wife.

'He may have been a good man, my dear, but he had very high opinions for a man who spent the majority of his life milking cows and was only fortunate to come into a little money when he reached his middle age, on account of a legacy that an old aunt from Cornwall left to him, you see.'

'My great-aunt Mildred,' said Mrs Amberton. 'She lived alone all her life and never changed her clothes. She wore a black dress with bright red shoes and always wore gloves when she had company. They say she was a little disturbed in the head, something to do with an early grief, but I always thought she just enjoyed being the centre of attention, for what it's worth.'

'How and ever, she left her money to Mrs's father,' he continued. 'And from then on you would have sworn he were one of the landed gentry. "How exactly," he asked me the night that I came to ask him for Mrs Amberton's hand, "how exactly do you intend to keep my daughter in the style to which she has become accustomed, and you just starting out in life?" Well, of course I told him my plans and that I were going into the construction business in London – lot of money to be made in that back then, you know – and he just sort of sniffed the air as if I'd just let off a nasty smell, which I hadn't, and said that he didn't think it were a suitable match and maybe I should either look elsewhere or reapply when my prospects were a little higher.'

'As if I was some sort of job that he was interviewing for!' cried Mrs Amberton, looking angry at what was probably an age-old grievance.

'Well, in the end we just upped and went. Got ourselves married and went down to London and for a while her father wouldn't speak to either of us but then he just seemed to forget all about it and when we would come to visit he acted as if he couldn't remember there ever being a disagreement between us in the first place and even mentioned on one occasion the ham that he had eaten at our wedding dinner. Said it gave him stomach ache.'

'He went a little . . . at the end,' said Mrs Amberton in a whisper, making circular motions with her finger around her head as she left out the crucial word. 'Believed himself to be everything from George II to Michelangelo. I always worry the same thing will happen to me one of these fine days.'

'Don't even joke about it, my dear,' said Mr Amberton. 'That's a terrible thought, it really is. I'd be obliged to leave you if that's what happened.'

'So after he went,' continued his wife, 'we came into a little money and moved here, to Cageley, where Mr Amberton started his school. My sister lives in the next town, you see, with her husband, and I liked the idea of being nearer to them. And Mr Amberton is very popular with the children too, aren't you, Mr Amberton?'

'I like to think I am, yes,' he said with an air of self-satisfaction.

'Right now he's got forty young 'uns in his school-room and they're getting the best education they could possibly get with Mr Amberton as their master. What lives they'll get to lead, eh?'

And so they continued for our first evenings, filling us in on their history as if this would enable us to melt into their newly designed family life more easily. And as exhausting as their constant talking, coughing, fart-ing and spitting became, I found myself becoming more and more comforted by them and would have gladly stayed in front of their fire night after night had not the inevitable finally happened. At the age of eighteen, I was suddenly thrust into the unwelcome world of legal employment when I finally got a job.

Just outside the main town boundary in Cageley stood a large house wherein lived Sir Alfred Pepys and his wife, Lady Margaret. They were the local aristocracy, celebrities of a kind, and their family had lived there for more than 300 years. Their wealth was inherited but their business was banking and it generated enough money for them to run their 300-acre estate in Cageley as well as a townhouse in London and a holiday home in the Scottish Highlands not to mention who knew what other holdings around the country. A few years before we arrived there, Sir Alfred and his wife had retired to the ancestral home and left their business interests in London in the hands of their three sons, who visited them occasionally. The parents led a quiet life, with shooting and hunting their only real activities of any great extravagance, and neither lorded it over the locals nor encouraged any closer ties with them.

It was Mr Amberton who secured jobs for both Dominique and me on the estate, I as a stable boy and my so-called sister as a kitchen hand. He told us of our salaries, which were low but none the less the first we had ever received, and we were thrilled to be starting respectable working lives at last. The only disappointment to me was that Dominique's position required her to board in a small room in the servants' quarters of the house, while I had to continue living with the Ambertons. This devastated me almost as much as it thrilled her, who was suddenly achieving a level of independence to which she had been aspiring for some time. Tomas, on the other hand, began to attend Mr Amberton's school and showed a flair for reading and drama, which was of some consolation to me. His nightly accounts of what had taken place during the day, as well as his perfect mimicry of not only his schoolfriends but also his teacher and landlord, were always entertaining and perfectly drawn; he showed a gift for the dramatic which his father had sadly lacked.

My day began at 5 a.m. when I would rise and walk the twenty minute journey from the Ambertons' home to the stables at the back of Cageley House. Along with another stable boy of around my own age, Jack Holby, we would prepare a breakfast for the eight horses under our care before we had even eaten our own and, after they finished it, we would spend several hours cleaning and brushing the horses down until their coats shone as if they had just been polished. Sir Alfred liked to ride in the mornings and always demanded that his horses look immaculate. We never knew which particular steed he might choose, nor whether he would have guests with him that morning, so each one of them had to look their best at all times. While Jack and I worked there, they must have been the best cared for horses in England. By around eleven, we would be set free for an hour to eat something in the kitchens and we would follow this by sitting outside in the sun and smoking our pipes for twenty minutes, a new affectation that Jack had introduced me to.

'One of these days,' Jack said, sitting with his back against a bale of hay as he drew on his pipe and drank intermittently from a cup of steaming hot tea, 'I'm going to take a hold of one of them horses and I'm going to climb on its back and ride it all the way out of this place. And that's the last any of them will ever see of Jack Holby.' He was aged about nineteen and had bright blond hair which hung down over his face, forcing him to keep sweeping it away from his eyes in what became almost an instinctive gesture, a twitch of self-grooming. I wondered why he didn't just cut his fringe instead.

'I like it here,' I confessed. 'I've never been anywhere quite like it. I've never had to actually work before and it's a good sensation.' I was telling the truth; the constancy of each day, the knowledge that I had certain tasks to do and for which I would get paid, pleased me enormously, as did the envelope of money I received from the coffers every Friday afternoon.

'That's because it's a novelty to you,' he said. 'I've been doing this since I was twelve and I've got almost enough money saved up to get me away from here once and for all. My twentieth birthday, Mattie, that's when I'll be off.'

Jack Holby's parents both worked in Cageley House, his father as an under-butler, his mother as a cook. They were pleasant enough people but I did not see them often. Jack, on the other hand, fascinated me. Although he was only about a year or eighteen months older than I was, and although he had in fact led a much more sheltered existence than my own, he seemed a lot more mature and far more aware of where he saw his life going than I was. The difference between us, I think, was that Jack had ambitions while I had none, ambitions which his unchanging existence throughout his youth had forced him to create. He had spent enough years at Cageley House to know that he did not want to be a stable boy for ever; I had spent enough time travelling around to appreciate a little stability for once. Our differences helped us to become friends quickly and I looked up to him with something approaching hero worship for he was the first male peer I had known whose life did not revolve around stealing from other people's pockets. Where we had greed and idleness, he had dreams.

'The thing about this place,' Jack told me, 'is that there's about thirty different people all working their arses off to make sure that the house and the estate stay in proper order. And right now there's only two people who actually live there, Sir Alfred and his wife. Thirty people for two! I ask you! And every so often one of them swanky sons comes down here on a visit and they treat us all like horseshit and I won't have that.'

'I haven't met any of them yet,' I confessed.

'You don't want to, believe me. The oldest one, David, he's a beanpole who walks round here with his head in the clouds all day long, never so much as deigning to speak to anyone who works for a living. The next one down, Alfred Junior, is twice as bad only he's got religion which makes him even worse 'cos I've never known anyone with the power to speak down to you as them who thinks they've got God's ear on their side. And the youngest one, Nat, well he's the pick of the litter. He's got a nasty side to him has Nat. I've seen it on more than one occasion. Tried it on with my Elsie once and wouldn't let it go till she caved in. Then he just threw her away and doesn't even speak to her any more. She hates him but what can she do? She can't quit because she has nowhere to go. I've come close a few times to wanting to kill him myself but I'm not sacrificing my life for his, no sir. I like her, but not that much. One of these days though – he'll get his.'

Elsie was Jack's sometime girlfriend and she worked as a cleaning maid in the house. The story, as far as Jack told it, was that Nat Pepys had made advances towards her on one of his visits to Cageley and had reappeared every weekend from then on with gifts for her until she let him have his way with her. It had killed Jack at the time, he said, to see what was going on; not because he was in love with Elsie – he wasn't – but because he hated to see the way that wealth could get Nat anything he wanted while he, Jack, was stuck shovelling horseshit from barn to bin. For all his hatred of his employer's son, what really galled him was the fact that Nat Pepys didn't even know that he existed. For this, Jack was eaten up with bitterness and it was a strong factor influencing why he wanted to get away from Cageley and start his life afresh.

'And then,' he said, 'no one will ever order me around again.'

For my part, I didn't want him to go as our friendship began to be of great importance to me. In the meantime, I simply got on with my work and continued to put a little money aside each week so that if the day ever came when I wanted to leave as much as Jack did, I might have some chance of being able to do so without having to begin again from scratch.

I missed having Dominique in the house with me; it was the first time since we had met on the boat to Dover that we had been separated. Every Sunday evening she would come to dinner at the Ambertons' and every week, I sensed a little more distance growing between us and I didn't know how to fill that gap. True, it was a rare day that we did not see each other at all, for Jack and I would get our own meals from the kitchen and often she would be the one who would have prepared them for us as part of her work She always made sure to be generous with our portions and became friendly with Jack as well, although I think he found her beauty

221

intimidating and the fact that we were 'related' somewhat surprising.

'She's some looker, your sister,' he confided in me one
day, 'although I must admit she's a little on the skinny
side for my tastes. You don't look much like each other,
though, do you?'

'Not much,' I said, not really wishing to discuss it.

The Ambertons, on the other hand, were fascinated
by the lives that we led out at the house, so enthralled
were they by the very existence of the aristocracy
in their neighbourhood. It was a curious thing to
Dominique and me that a whole village could be in such
bewildering awe of one man and his wife. The whole
thing seemed ridiculous to us but every Sunday both
Mr and Mrs Amberton would quiz us for information
about our employers, as if by sucking details from
us they were bringing themselves one step closer to
heaven.

'I hear she has a carpet in her bedroom that's three
inches thick and lined with fur,' said Mrs Amberton of
Lady Margaret.

'I've never been in her bedroom,' confessed
Dominique, 'but I know she favours floorboards.'

'I hear he has a collection of guns which rival that
of the British Army, let alone a London museum, and
he employs a man to spend all his time cleaning and
polishing them,' said Mr Amberton.

'If he has, I've never met him,' I said.

'I hear that when their sons come to visit they serve
a small suckled pig to each one of them and they only
drink wine which is more than a century old.'

'David and Alfred Junior hardly eat anything at all,'
muttered Dominique. 'And they both claim that alcohol
is the devil's work. I haven't met the youngest one yet.'

After these meals, I would always walk Dominique back to the house and it was about the only time in the week when we got to spend any time together alone. We walked slowly, sometimes resting for a while by the lake if it was a warm evening. It was the time of the week that I most enjoyed for we were able to catch up with each other's lives without having to worry about anyone listening in or having to keep one eye on the clock at all times.

'I can't remember being so happy as I am right now,' she told me one evening as we walked along the road, the Ambertons' dog Brutus scampering along beside us as noisily as his owners. 'It's so peaceful here. There's no troubles. Everything seems so nice. I could stay here for ever.'

'Eventually things will change,' I said. 'We can't stay here for ever as much as we may want to. After all,' I told her, adopting some of Jack's independent beliefs, 'we don't want to see ourselves as being someone else's lackeys for the rest of our lives. We could make our own fortunes.'

She sighed and said nothing. I found that I was often forced to continue with the idea of an 'us' between Dominique, Tomas and me. Our one-time solid family unit had come slightly apart with the new arrangements in Cageley. I was sure that there were new aspects to Dominique's life of which I knew nothing. She spoke of friends she had made within the house and the village and of time they spent together from which I as a mere stable boy was naturally excluded. I would tell her about Jack and try to interest her in the idea of her and I and Jack and Elsie taking a picnic together somewhere, but she always agreed without appearing to care less. We were growing apart and it worried me for I did not want to arrive at Cageley House one morning only to find that she had left it for ever the night before.

On a bright summer afternoon, Mr Davies, who was the stable manager in charge of Jack and me, came to see us as we were cleaning out the stables. A dreary, middle-aged man, he spent most of his time – it seemed to me – ordering supplies and sitting in the kitchen, rarely bothering to speak to either of us. He had basically allowed Jack to take charge over the way in which the stables were run and, although he kept nominal control, all questions or queries came through Jack. His disdain for all the house employees was obvious, even though he was no more than a hired hand himself. He avoided speaking to us most of the time and when he did it was usually simply to point out our flaws. On one occasion, when there was a fire in the kitchen which ruined a day's cooking, he made a point of hovering around us until he eventually muttered the phrase 'at least the fire wasn't my fault', as if either Jack or I cared even a jot. For a man who was so keen to be seen as our superior, he was very concerned that we should see him as a competent manager, a phrase which could rarely have been applied to him. It came as a surprise therefore to see him approach us that afternoon and tell us to put away our pitchforks for a moment as he had something important to tell us.

'Next week,' he began, 'Sir Alfred's son is coming down here for a few days with some friends of his. They're going to be organizing a hunt and we'll have several more horses for you to take care of during their stay. He's made it clear that he wants them to look their very best each morning so you'll have to work extra hard.'

'We can't make them look any better than they already do,' said Jack, matter-of-factly. 'So don't ask for more because that's as good as it gets. You don't like what we do, you can give it a go yourself.'

'Well, you'll need to stay on longer then to make sure that these other horses get the same wonderful treatment then, won't you, Jack?' said Mr Davies sarcastically, grinning through his broken teeth at Jack. 'Because you know what he's like when he gives his orders, especially when he has his friends down with him. And he's the master after all. Pays your wages.'

And yours, I thought. Jack grunted and shook his head as if the very word 'master' offended him. 'Which one is it anyway?' he asked. 'David or Alfred?'

'Neither one,' said Mr Davies. 'It's the young one, Nat. Apparently it's his twenty-first birthday or some such thing and that's what the hunt is organized for.'

Jack cursed under his breath and kicked the ground in frustration. 'I know what I'd like to give him for his birthday,' he muttered, but Mr Davies ignored him.

'Later on, I'll give you your hours for next week,' he said. 'And don't worry, you'll be getting paid a little extra for them at the end of it. So no late nights, all right, because we'll need you here on your toes.'

I shrugged when he left. It seemed all right to me. I enjoyed my work and the way that the physical exercise was improving my body. My arms and chest had swelled a little and Mr and Mrs Amberton remarked upon what a handsome young man I was turning into. No longer the boy who had arrived there a few months earlier, I had already noticed that I was attracting a few flirtatious looks from the village girls. And a few more pounds for my savings couldn't hurt.

It was the first time I began to feel like an adult and it was a sensation I enjoyed. It was also fortunate that I felt that way, for no childish behaviour could have allowed me to survive my first encounter with Nat Pepys.

Chapter 14

The Terror

The year 1793 was a turning point in my life for it is about the year at which I believe I stopped the physical act of ageing. I cannot pin it down to a particular date or an event – I cannot even be sure that 1793 was the exact year – I just believe that it was around this time that my body's natural inclination to decline became dormant. It was also during 1793 that I had one of my least pleasant personal experiences, an event of such distasteful memory to me that I feel a strange misery for the human condition descend upon my mind even as I recall the manner in which that year turned out. But, unpalatable as it was, it remains one of the most memorable times of my life.

In 1793, I turned fifty years old and, with the exception of a few distressing fashion trends of the time such as the tendency to wear a small ponytail at the back of one's hair and to dress in a ridiculously effete manner, there is no great difference between the man I was then and the man I am today, 206 years later. My height of six feet and one half inch had not begun to shake off an inch or two as I wizened down to the shrunken frame of an older man as it might with another; my standard body weight of between 190 and 220 pounds was fixed at a pleasing 205 and my skin resisted the temptation to sag or grow wrinkly as with so many of my contemporaries; my hair had thinned slightly and turned a shade of grey which lent a distinguished air to my comportment and this was a condition which pleased me. All in all, I settled into an attractive middle age from which I have yet to be released. In 1793, when the French Revolution was at its height, I began the process which was to make me a thief of time.

I had been back in England for about twenty years. My third decade had been spent in Europe, where I began to work in banking and had some good fortune along the way. At the age of thirty, I returned to London and, after my initial success in business, I invested wisely and befriended credible people in the banking world there who assisted me with my initiatives. In time, I owned a house and had a decent capital from which to earn my income. I worked hard and spent wisely. Those years were passed with a clear intention on my part to make my life comfortable and I rarely gave much thought to either my personal or spiritual happiness. All I did was work and earn money, and eventually I felt that I wanted more from life.

It had never been my intention to stay in London for ever and as I turned fifty I began to regret the fact that I had not travelled very widely during those years. Of course, at that stage I believed that my life was cruising slowly towards its close as it was not particularly common for a man to live past a half century in those days; at times I felt that I had missed my chance to know more of the world. I grew a little disconsolate, examining my life and seeing money where a happy family life might have been. Little did I know how many wives were to come, how much travelling, how many years would remain for me. I began to feel that I had wasted my life.

I was living in a fine house in London which was far too large for my needs and I had recently agreed to allow my nephew Tom to stay with me. Tom was my first true nephew, the son of the half-brother I had brought to England with me in 1760, and like so many of his descendants he was a difficult lad who showed no great interest in creating a life for himself and instead drifted from job to job until time caught up with him. I believe he was waiting for me to die so that his inheritance might finally come through. Little did he know that this was not something that he should have been relying upon. I was sitting at home one evening with Tom, who was aged around twenty at the time, and feeling considerably depressed with the turn my life had taken when we decided on a whim to take a trip.

'We could go to Ireland,' suggested Tom. 'It's not too far and it might be a pleasant place to live for a while. I've always fancied a country existence.'

I shook my head. 'I don't think so,' I said. 'It's poor and miserable and it rains all the time. No use for the constitution. It would depress me even more than I already am.'

'Perhaps Australia?'

'I think not.'

'Africa then. There's a whole continent there waiting to be explored.'

'Too hot. And too underdeveloped. You know me, Tom, I like my home comforts. No, at heart I am a European. That's where I feel at my happiest. On the continent. Although I haven't seen much of it, I grant you.'

'Well, I've never even been outside of England.'

'You're young, I'm old. You have plenty of time ahead of you.'

Tom thought about it and said nothing for a while. Wherever we went, it would be on my money so he perhaps felt a twinge of conscience about proposing a trip. Or perhaps not.

'We could try Europe,' he said in a quiet voice after a while. 'There's got to be a lot to see there. We could try Scandinavia. I've always liked the sound of it.'

We discussed it further for some time until it was agreed. We would spend six months travelling around Europe, visiting some of the sites of great architecture which existed there – also the art galleries and museums, since I have always had an artistic bent. Tom would be my companion and secretary, for there would still be many business affairs which I would have to deal with while I was away. Letters to be written, telegrams to be sent, moneys to be wired. He was quite efficient, for one of the Thomases, and I felt that I could trust him entirely with this task.

One evening some months later, while relaxing outside our hotel in Locarno, Switzerland, after a long day climbing around the mountains with some ladies, each of whom showed more energy and commitment to the task than either of us did, Tom expressed a desire to see France. I shuddered slightly as it was the last place in the world I had intended visiting owing to the less than pleasant memories that I had of the place, but he was adamant.

'I am partly French, after all,' he told me. 'I'd like to see where my father grew up.'

'Your father grew up in Dover and then a small village called Cageley,' I told him irritably. 'We could have stayed in England if you wanted to see where

230

your father grew up, Tom. He left Paris when he was an infant, remember.'

'Nevertheless, it's where he was born and where his earliest experiences were. And my grandparents, they were both French, were they not?'

'Yes,' I said, grudgingly, 'I suppose so.'

'And you're French through and through. You haven't been back there since you left as a boy. Surely you want to see it again. See how it's changed.'

'I never cared for it much in the first place, Tom,' I told him. 'I don't see why I'd want to go back and feign a little romantic nostalgia.' I shrugged the idea off and wondered how I could dissuade him, so sure was I that I did not want to return to that country. The urge to learn more about one's heritage, however, is a powerful one and he claimed it was cruel of me to prevent him from seeing the streets where we had grown up, the city where my parents had lived and died, the place that we had left in order to begin our new lives.

'What if I just told you about them?' I asked. 'There are plenty of tales I could tell you about our early days in Paris and what went on there, if that's what you want to hear. I could tell you how your grandfather met my mother, if that would interest you. It happened one afternoon when she was leaving the theatre and a boy—'

'I know this story, Uncle Matthieu,' he said, interrupting me with a look of frustration upon his face. 'You've told me all those stories already. Many times.'

'Not all of them surely.'

'Well, a lot of them anyway. I don't need to hear them again. I want to see Paris. Is it too much to ask? Isn't there any part of you that wonders how the place has changed in thirty years? You ran away from it once with nothing, don't you want to go back now that you have made a success out of your life and see what it has become without you?'

I nodded. He was right, of course. Despite myself, my mind had often turned to France in the intervening years. Although I had no great patriotic feelings towards the country, I was none the less a Frenchman; although I had nothing but bad memories of Paris, it remained the city of my birth. And while I had occasionally had nightmares about our lives there, about the day my father died, the afternoon my mother was murdered, and the morning my stepfather was executed, it carried a strange and wholly understandable fascination for me. Tom was right; I did want to see Paris again. And so an arrangement was made to visit the city and late in 1792 we began to move slowly across Europe, stopping at places of interest for a few weeks at a time, and by the spring of the following year we had arrived at our destination, the city of my birth.

Tom was a bloodthirsty lad and it was a flaw that would eventually prove to be his undoing. Although not personally sadistic – he was never brave enough to be the person actually inflicting pain on others – he enjoyed watching others suffer, playing the role of voyeur in another person's misery. In London, I knew that he attended the cockfights and would return home after them with a slightly crazed expression in his eyes. He enjoyed boxing bouts and competitions where men would end up bloodied and beaten. And so, in order to satisfy this perversion, Paris in 1793 was not a wholly unpleasant place for him to be.

The Bastille, that massive, stinking, infected

prison where the aristos had been placed by the new Republicans, had fallen in 1789 and from then on there was a near endless series of demonstrations in the capital which forced the king, Louis XVI, to quit Paris with his family later that year. Over the course of the early 1790s, as the National Assembly strove harder and harder to force the king to accept their constitution and push through greater reforms that would sting his absolutism, it became clear that the atmosphere of the Terror was about to begin. In 1792, a year before we arrived in the city, Dr Joseph-Ignace Guillotin convinced the National Assembly to introduce the device – created not by him but by his colleague Antoine Louis – to deal with offenders and shortly after that the great killing machine was set up in the Place de la Concorde where she held sway over her citizens for the following few years.

It was into this atmosphere of distrust, betrayal and abject fear that Tom and I arrived in the spring of 1793. The king had already been beheaded and, as we drove into Paris, I felt a strange lack of feeling for the place which betrayed my anticipation of returning to my native city. I had expected to be moved by my return, particularly by the manner in which I was coming back after my long exile; no longer a poor orphan who saw pickpocketing as the only way to make a life for himself, but a successful businessman who had risen above the station of his birth to become a wealthy man. I thought of my parents and to a lesser extent of Tomas, but hardly gave Dominique a thought, as our relationship had been one solely based in England and, although we shared a birthplace, we never met in France at all and had rarely spoken of it.

We immediately settled into a boarding house as far

to the outskirts of the city as possible and it was my intention to stay there for about a week before moving south to explore a portion of the country with which I was unfamiliar.

'You can feel it, can't you?' asked Tom, coming into my room on that first day, his thick, dark hair practically bouncing away from his skull in his excitement. 'The atmosphere in the city. There's a real stink of blood in the air.'

'Charming,' I muttered. 'It's always one of the more pleasant aspects to a modern city. It's just the phrase they should use in the guidebooks. Really makes the holiday memorable.'

'Oh, come on Uncle Matthieu,' he said, bounding around the room enthusiastically like a little puppy dog who has just been unleashed from a tiny garden into a large open park. 'You should be thrilled to be here and at such an important time too. Don't you have any feelings for Paris? Remember the way you were brought up here.'

'We were poor, certainly, but—'

'You were poor because no one was interested in feeding you. Everything went to the rich.'

'The rich simply *had* everything in the first place. It was the way of the world.'

He shrugged, disappointed by my refusal to be drawn into the debate. 'Same difference,' he said. 'The aristos taking everything, leaving everyone else with nothing. It's not fair.'

I raised an eyebrow. I had never seen Tom as the revolutionary sort before. Indeed, it was my belief that given the chance he would much prefer to live his life as a wealthy, idle, drunken aristocrat than a poor, stinking, sober peasant, even if his ideals may have tended more towards the latter. Still, I suppose in retrospect that his basic belief – why should they have when we have not – was true enough in theory, even if it did not exactly apply to him, who was living off my money quite comfortably and without complaint.

It was shortly after we arrived that we first met Thérèse Nantes, whose parents owned the boarding house where we were staying. She was a dark haired girl of around eighteen and, to her obvious irritation, an only child, a position which required her to take an added weight of responsibility in her parents' business. I suspected that in healthier times the Nantes family had employed a small coterie of maids and cooks, for at peak capacity the boarding house could have held up to thirty guests. Now, however, with visitors to the city at an obvious decline, there was only an old French couple who had lived there for years and a couple of passing tradesmen in residence along with Tom and me. Thérèse wandered around her home with a permanent scowl on her face and responded to her parents with little more than monosyllabic grunts. When serving food, one learned not to ask for anything which was not already on the plate lest the dinner itself should drop mysteriously into one's lap.

Her mood improved immeasurably, however, as her friendship with my nephew developed. At first it was difficult to notice any signs of her thaw, but gradually, as the weeks passed, she would greet us for our evening meal with a look that bore a suspicious resemblance to a half-smile. The morning my breakfast was served to me with the phrase 'enjoy your meal' was a revelation and, when she offered to top up our wine glasses one night as we sat in the parlour, it felt like nothing short of a breakthrough. I took this as an encouragement towards conversation.

'And where are Monsieur Lafayette and his wife tonight?' I asked, referring to the elderly couple who shared the boarding house with us. 'They've surely not deserted their usual seats for the evening air.'

'Oh, didn't you know?' asked Thérèse, putting her wine bottle down on the sideboard and fingering it for dust. 'They've left us. Gone to the country, I believe.'

'The country?' I asked, surprised, for we had struck up an awkward friendship, the four of us, and I was taken aback that they would leave without saying goodbye. 'Well, how long are they going for? I thought they would be here 'til they were in their shrouds.'

'They're gone for good, Monsieur Zéla,' she replied.

'Matthieu, please.'

'They packed their bags early this morning and took a coach towards the south. I'm surprised you didn't hear them. Madame made a fuss about who should be carrying her bags. I told her there are certain things I'm paid for and certain things I'm not but she—'

'I never heard a thing,' I said, cutting her off before she could continue with her grievance and my abruptness merited a look of anger from the girl. Tom coughed in order to break the moment and turned around in his chair to look at her.

'At least you should have some more time to yourself with two less mouths to feed,' he said and she continued to stare at me for a moment before averting her gaze to my nephew and smiling at him.

'It's no trouble,' she said, as if he had suggested that it was. 'I enjoy it here.' My burst of laughter, quickly muffled, earned another look from Thérèse, whose eyes

236

narrowed into thin slits as she considered a response. I decided to forge a reconciliation.

'Why don't you sit down?' I said, standing up and pulling out the spare armchair that formed a triangle between my nephew's seat and my own. 'Enjoy a glass of wine. Your day's work must be over by now.'

Thérèse looked at me in surprise before turning to Tom, who nodded his approval and encouraged her to join us. She shrugged and with great dignity walked to the armchair and sat. Tom reached for another glass and poured her a healthy measure which she accepted with a smile. The gesture made, I wondered where our conversation could go from here and sat back, racking my brain for suitable topics. Fortunately the silence lasted only a moment as the wine immediately loosened Thérèse's lips.

'I never liked Madame anyway,' she began, referring to our recently departed housemate. 'She had some ways of which I could never approve. Sometimes her room in the mornings . . .' She shook her head as if she didn't want to cause us any horror by informing us of the devastation the Lafayette family could inflict upon their small room.

'She was always quite polite to me,' I muttered.

'She invited me into her room once,' said Tom suddenly, his voice overly loud as if we were in danger of not hearing him. 'She said that she was having some difficulty with her curtain rail. When I stretched to replace one of the hooks, she took a step towards me and . . .' He suddenly blushed a crimson red and I guessed that he had not thought this story out in advance. 'She behaved inappropriately,' he muttered, his voice low now. 'I . . . I'm . . .' He looked around at us in confusion and, for the first time ever, I heard Thérèse laugh.

'She thought you a handsome young man,' she replied, and I thought I saw her give my nephew a wink. 'I could tell from the way she would look in your direction when you entered a room.' Tom frowned, as if he regretted the turn this conversation had taken.

'My God,' he said, clearly appalled. 'She must be forty if she's a day.'

'A veritable Methuselah,' I muttered, but neither of my companions acknowledged the comment.

'She treated me with contempt,' said Thérèse, 'because she was jealous of my youth, no doubt. And my beauty. She has several entries in my occurrences book.'

'Your what?' I asked, unsure whether I had heard her correctly. 'What is an occurrences book?'

Now it was Thérèse's turn to look a little unsettled, having perhaps said more than she intended. 'It's a silly thing,' she said apologetically, refusing to look me in the eye. 'A thing I keep for my own amusement. Like a diary.'

'But a diary of what?' asked Tom, like me intrigued by the phrase.

'Of people who offend me,' she said with a slight laugh, but I could tell that she took it very seriously indeed. 'I keep a log of anyone who treats me badly or offends me in any way. I have done so for years.'

I stared at her. I could think of only one question. 'Why?' I asked.

'So that I don't forget,' she replied with perfect equanimity. 'What goes around comes around, Monsieur Zéla. Matthieu,' she added before I could protest. 'It may sound ridiculous to you, but to me—'

'It's not ridiculous,' I said quickly. 'It's just . . . unusual, that's all. I suppose it's one way to remember

. . .' I couldn't see where my thoughts were headed and brushed them off quickly with the phrase '. . . things that have happened.'

'I hope I don't feature too heavily in your occurrences book, Thérèse,' said Tom, his face breaking into a broad smile, and she shook her head, smiling back at him as if the very idea was impossible.

'Of course you don't,' she said, reaching out and touching his hand for a moment, stressing the word 'you' to deliberately exclude me. She shot me a reproachful glance to reinforce her point and I shifted uncomfortably, wondering what I could possibly have done to offend the girl. I stayed silent for a time, refilling the three wine glasses, as the two young people flirted with each other, both ignoring me completely, and I was about to make my excuses and leave when something that Thérèse had said came to my mind and I wanted to ask her about it.

'What goes around comes around,' I said loudly, in order to interrupt the pair, and they looked at me, perhaps surprised that I was still there. 'Do you believe that, Thérèse?'

She blinked and considered the question for only a moment. 'Why, certainly I do,' she said. 'Don't you?' I shrugged my shoulders, unsure whether I did or not, and she took advantage of the moment to explain herself further. 'Here, in this city,' she said, pausing dramatically between each clause, 'at this time, how could I not?'

'Meaning . . . ?' I asked.

'Well, look around you, Matthieu. Look at the streets today. Look at Paris. Don't you think that those things which have gone around are, in a manner of speaking, coming around again?' Again, my silence betrayed my confusion and she sat forward, turning away from Tom and looking me directly in the eyes. 'The deaths,' she explained. 'The guillotine. The aristocrats. My God, the head of the king himself has fallen into the basket. There is some justice beginning in France, Matthieu. You cannot be oblivious to it.'

'We haven't yet seen any beheadings,' said Tom. 'My uncle feels it is barbaric and won't allow us to go.'

'Do you feel that, Monsieur Zéla?' she asked, looking at me in surprise and reverting to my formal name as if to dissociate herself from me. 'Do you feel it is barbaric?'

'The method itself is quick and clean,' I said. 'But do you really need the method in the first place? Do these people need to die?'

'Of course they do,' said Tom, picking up on Thérèse's attitudes and pandering to them. 'Filthy aristos.' I shot him a withering glance and Thérèse had the manners to ignore him and continued to look at me.

'They have led bountiful lives,' she explained. 'And they have exploited us. All of us. You are a Frenchman, are you not? You must see what their behaviour has been responsible for.' I nodded. 'Their time has come,' she said simply.

'Have you seen the guillotine in action yourself?' asked Tom, his bloodlust returning now as she talked of death. I could feel the growing tension between the pair as she spoke and knew that if they were not a couple already it would not be long before they were.

'I have seen many,' she said with pride. 'I saw the king himself die and he was a coward at the end of course. As are they all.' Tom raised his eyebrows as his tongue licked quickly across his lips and he encouraged her to tell us of that day.

'He was found guilty of treason by the National Committee,' began Thérèse, as if to justify what was to follow. 'It seemed like half the city wanted to be at the Place de la Concorde for the fateful moment. I arrived early, of course, but stood near the sides. I wanted to see him die, Monsieur Zéla, but I do not like the baying of the crowds. But there were thousands there and it was difficult to get a good view. Eventually, the tumbrel entered the square.'

Tom raised an eyebrow and looked at her, unfamiliar with the word.

'The wooden cart,' she explained. 'It is the feeling of the citizens that the simplicity of the cart makes it clear that the traitors are to die like citizens of France, and not in the manner of rich layabouts. I remember them distinctly: a young woman, with long, dirty hair. She didn't know what was happening and didn't seem to care; perhaps she was already dead inside. Behind her, a teenage boy who was crying in convulsions, afraid to look up to see the instrument of his demise even as the middle aged man behind him screamed and screamed and screamed in fear, pointing towards the guillotine with the most abject horror as his jailers held him tightly to prevent him from jumping out into the crowd and making his escape, although he probably would have been torn limb from limb if we had thought we were going to lose the biggest traitor of them all. That's when I saw him, dressed in dark trousers and a white shirt open at the neck. The king of France, the convicted traitor, Louis XVI.'

I looked at Tom, who had eyes only for Thérèse, and the look on his face, the absolute thrill he was getting from her storytelling, the almost erotic excitement he was feeling, bothered me. And yet I must admit that it was difficult not to want her to continue, for there was a certain addictiveness to the drama of death which held us both. We weren't to be disappointed as she continued.

'My eyes were focused upon his face, watching for any reaction that might come from him. He was pale, whiter than the shirt that he wore, and he looked exhausted, as if he had spent his entire life battling to prevent this moment from taking place and now that it was upon him he simply had no more energy left to fight it. As the tumbrel stopped before the steps, the six covered men who guarded the great machine stepped forward and took the young woman roughly by the shoulders, pulling her dress sharply so that it ripped at the top, exposing a pale, full breast to the crowd, who screamed in delight at her nakedness. These men . . . they are great exhibitionists, performers of a kind. The largest of them nestled his head into the breast for a few moments before turning back to face us with a grin. For her part, she barely moved as she was led to the scaffold, her hair shorn quickly and her head placed within. The wooden semi-circle which held her in place was dropped and at that moment she suddenly came to life, her hands reaching to the sides to try to lift herself up, not realizing that she was already caged in. Within a moment it was over, the blade whistling downwards and slicing her head off in a perfect motion but her body gave a quick spastic movement before collapsing backwards on to the platform, where it was quickly taken away.'

'Thérèse!' gasped Tom, and there seemed to be no sentence to follow it; he merely wanted to cry out her name, as if engaged within a moment of passion.

'One of the jailers reached forward then and showed

the head to the crowd. We screamed, of course. The *tricoteuses* at the front kept knitting away contentedly. We were waiting for the main attraction,' she said with a smile. 'Before that, however, the teenage boy was carried to his death. Before being placed with his head on the block, he stood weakly before the crowd, looking out at us, appealing for help, his tear-stained face unable to cry any more. I could tell that, unlike his predecessor, he knew exactly what was going on and it terrified him. He couldn't have been aged more than about fifteen and I realized that his thin trousers were growing more and more stained as he pissed on himself one last time, the thin material sticking to his leg with a coward's indignity. He struggled as he was placed inside the guillotine but he was too weak for these men and, within a minute, his life had ended too.'

'And what was he guilty of?' I asked in disgust. 'This boy. Who had he betrayed?'

Thérèse stared at me and her lips formed a thin smile. She ignored the question. The climax was approaching. Despite myself, I wanted her to continue. 'For once,' she said, 'the crowd went quiet as the king marched up the steps. He looked out, his face a mixture of stoicism and abject fear. He opened his mouth to speak but no words came and so he was led quickly and nervously to the guillotine. I admit that the atmosphere was that of horror, as if no one was exactly sure what might happen the moment his head was severed, whether the very world itself might come to an end. There seemed to be some confusion on the scaffold as none of the men wanted to be the one who actually put the king's head on the block but eventually one of them stepped forward and the wood was again lowered for the third time. Struggling to look at us, I watched as his head lifted slightly and his eyes caught the sunlight. Then he spoke for the last time.

'"I die innocent, and I forgive my enemies," he shouted, no doubt hoping these platitudes could grant him an escape. "I wish that my blood—"'

'The blade fell, the head fell into the basket, the body squirmed, the crowd bayed, the screaming was all around me. He was dead.'

A silence fell among us. I could see Tom's face in the firelight glowing with perspiration and even Thérèse shook slightly as she sat back in her chair and took a drink from her glass. I looked from one to the other, wondering whether there was any suitable response to this story. I could find only one thing to say.

'And you, Thérèse,' I asked. 'How did that make you feel? Seeing those people die. An innocent woman, a young boy, a king. How did you feel at that moment?'

The wine glass balanced against her lips and its reflected rouge seemed appropriate to the conversation. In a quiet, deep voice she looked away and answered me with a single word.

'Avenged.'

We stayed in Paris longer than I had anticipated. Thérèse's influence on Tom had become so strong that her own revolutionary ideals were almost eclipsed by the sudden ardour of his own. Although I appreciated the fact that he was not quite the wastrel he had been some months earlier, I was nervous about the direction in which his passions were being focused. I travelled back and forth from the country, preparing to sever ties with my nephew if necessary and return home but finding myself unable to do so when he relied upon my charity so much. I spent a little time in the south of the country – where the atmosphere was almost as highly charged as it was in the capital – before travelling to the Alps for a few weeks, where peace reigned and the sea of white snow provided a welcome relief from the familiar red, white and blue of the city. By the time I returned to Paris in late 1793, Tom was a fully signed up revolutionary.

In a short period of time, he had managed to infiltrate the ranks of the Jacobin powers and was working as a secretary with Robespierre, the chief antagonist of the Terror. His relationship with Thérèse had blossomed and they had left the boarding house together. Now they shared an apartment near the rue de Rivoli and it was there that I met them on a dark Friday night shortly before Christmas.

Physically, he had changed somewhat since I had last seen him. In six months, it seemed as if he had aged six years; he had cut his hair short, which accentuated the line of his cheekbones and made his face appear more masculine and serious. His body had grown strong and muscular through the physical workouts he put himself through on a daily basis. What in the past had been the traditionally almost feminine beauty of his line had been sculpted into a figure of true revolutionary power and one would not have wanted to cross him easily. Thérèse had changed too. Having converted her lover to her beliefs, she seemed content to turn away from them a little and allow him to take control of their destinies. She was extremely tactile with him, taking every opportunity to stroke his cheek or rub his leg, her busy hands going almost unnoticed by him, it seemed, as he talked to me.

'What amazes me,' I told him, relaxing after dinner by the fireplace, 'is how you had never even been to France this time last year, and now you fight continuously for its survival. This new-found passion for an unknown country. Strikes me as a little odd.'

'It must have always been in my blood,' he told me with a smile – more talk of that word. 'I am partly French after all. Maybe it was just waiting to get out, citizen.'

'It's possible, I suppose,' I acknowledged. 'You are half French and half English, as you say. A troublesome combination. You'll find you're always at war with yourself. Your artistic and mundane sides will tear you in two perhaps.'

'I have only one passion now,' he said, ignoring my statement, which I meant only in jest. 'And that is to see the French Republic grow stronger and stronger until it is among the most powerful in the world.'

'And the Terror achieves that?' I asked. 'Growth through fear?'

'Tom believes in the cause, citizen,' said Thérèse quickly, her pronunciation of her lover's name throaty and warm, 'like we all do. Those who have died have contributed just as much as those who live on. It is part of nature's cycle. An entirely natural process.'

Nonsense, I thought. Absolute nonsense.

'Let me tell you a story,' said Tom, settling back in his chair as Thérèse nestled herself in on his knee, one hand slung carelessly about his groin. 'A few weeks ago if you had come here and asked me who my best friend in the world was, the man I respected the most, I would have told you it was a fellow named Pierre Houblin, who worked with me until recently in the National Assembly. He'd been there longer than I and was of course in a far more senior position. But Pierre was a young man, about my own age, maybe a little older, and somehow we became friends and he took me under his wing, introduced me to some people who could help my advancement. He was one of those who had been pushing for reforms from right back at the time when Louis XVI was still alive and in power. Pierre had worked closely with both Robespierre and Danton and had taken many chances to ensure that the full power of the Revolution would be realized. I looked up to him with the greatest of respect. He was like a brother to me. A wise, older counsel. We would sit for hours on end, the two of us, in the very chairs that we are sitting in now and talk about everything that interested us. About life and love and politics and history and what we were doing in Paris, for Paris, where the future would take us. No greater man, I thought, existed in France, for he opened up my mind to so many possibilities that I cannot even begin to explain them to you.'

I nodded, unconvinced. Sudden crushes, whatever form they may take, are almost always transitory. Their victims inevitably return to their senses and wonder what they were thinking of in the first place. 'So?' I asked him. 'And where is he now then, this Monsieur Houblin? Why are you telling me this? Citizen,' I added sarcastically.

'I'm telling you this,' he answered with some irritation, 'to highlight to you my commitment to this cause. A few weeks ago, Pierre and I were sitting here in this apartment – Thérèse, you were here too, weren't you?' She nodded but said nothing. 'And we were talking about the Revolution as ever. Always, always the Revolution. It obsesses us. And Pierre pointed out that over the course of the past month, over four hundred people had been guillotined in the city. I was a little surprised by the number, of course, but acknowledged it as being about correct, and then we sat in silence for a few more minutes. I could tell that Pierre was growing agitated and I asked him whether everything was all right, whether I had said something to upset him. Suddenly, he stood up and started pacing around the room in frustration.

'"Don't you sometimes think", he asked me, "that things are beginning to grow out of control? That too many people are dying? Too many peasants and not enough aristos for one thing?"

'I was shocked of course that he could feel this way when surely everyone knows that the way to achieve our final goals is to get rid of so many traitors that there will be only true Frenchmen left, equal and free. I protested for some time with Pierre that he was wrong and eventually he let the matter rest, but it concerned me for I worried that he might no longer have the stomach to take part in history in the way that he once had.'

'Perhaps he was simply growing a conscience,' I suggested, and Tom shook his head.

'That's not it!' he shouted. 'This has nothing to do with conscience! When one is fighting for change, to alter an unfair system that has existed for centuries, one must do everything in one's power to make sure that right wins through. There is no place within this struggle for half-heartedness.' He sounded as if he was making a political speech and even Thérèse had stood up now to allow his gesticulations to gain better freedom.

'But a balance in the Assembly might turn out to be a good thing,' I said slowly, afraid that he would suddenly leap off his seat and throttle me if I were to disagree with him. 'To hear both sides of this concept. You might find that Monsieur Houblin has more to contribute now than ever before.'

Tom laughed bitterly. 'Hardly,' he said. 'A few days later I sent word to Robespierre and told him of our conversation. I said that I believed Pierre was becoming too much of a moderate to be entrusted with any portion of state secrets or important documentation. I simply reported our conversation word for word and allowed Monsieur Robespierre to act as he saw fit.'

I stared at him and blinked quickly, sure that I knew where this was leading but afraid to see it actually reach there. 'And he was . . . dismissed from his post?' I asked hopefully.

'He was arrested that afternoon, tried for treason the next day, found guilty by a court of law – a court of law, Uncle Matthieu! And then he was guillotined the following morning. There's no place for half-hearts, you see, in a Revolution. It's all, the full mind, the entire heart' – he paused for dramatic effect before continuing, slicing his hand through the air quickly, like the very blade itself – 'or nothing!'

I sighed and felt myself grow a little ill. I looked towards Thérèse who was smiling slightly, watching for my own reaction. Her tongue extended slightly and moved around the edges of her lips and I looked back at my nephew and shook my head sadly. I thought they seemed a perfect match.

'You informed on him,' I said quietly. 'That is what you're telling me. You informed on your best friend, the man you claim to have respected the most in the entire world.'

'I committed an act of extreme patriotism,' he replied. 'I suffered the death of my best friend, my virtual brother, to help the Republic. What more can I do than that? You should be proud of me, Uncle Matthieu. Proud.'

As I left the apartment that evening, sure that the time was right for me to leave my nephew, Paris, France, Europe entirely, I turned to Tom and asked him one final question. 'This friend of yours,' I said, 'this Pierre. He had a good position within the Assembly, am I right?'

He shrugged. 'But of course,' he said. 'He was a man of some importance.'

'And when he . . . died. After he was guillotined. Who replaced him?'

There was silence for a moment as Tom stopped smiling and stared through me with something approaching hatred. For a moment I wondered whether my own life might not be in danger, before thinking, no, I am his uncle, he could never betray me, before once again changing my mind and thinking, fool! Of course he could. Thérèse looked shocked by my question, as she already knew the answer and just wanted to see whether Tom would tell the truth or not.

'Well,' he said, after what seemed like an eternity, 'someone has to do the essential jobs of the Republic. Someone whose loyalty is beyond reproach.'

I nodded slowly and went back out on to the street, wrapping my scarf around my neck tightly as I went, the better to keep my head attached to my body.

Seven months later, in July 1794, I received a most unexpected letter. I had returned to London and was following the Revolution only through the newspapers which spoke of Paris as the very blood-filled vein of Europe, leaking and haemorrhaging across its own society. I shuddered when I thought what life must be like there and worried for Tom, even though I had left Paris with no more illusions about his character. I had decided that it would be best for me to stay out of the city entirely; for one thing, I didn't trust my nephew not to take it into his head one day to denounce me for a traitor, at which point I could be destined for a wholly undeserved appointment with the guillotine, and for another, I simply did not want to have any part of such great bloodshed. However, my plans were suddenly altered when I received the following missive:

Paris, 6 July 1794

Dear Monsieur Zéla,

I write to you with some regret, Monsieur. Things have gone in an unhappy direction here and it is important that you come to see me – I fear for three lives right now and cannot persuade Tom to see what is going on – he is mad, Monsieur, on his power – there is trouble to come – he speaks of you often and would like to see you – please come if you can.

Yours,

Thérèse Nantes

Naturally, I was surprised, for I did not expect to hear from my nephew again, let alone the woman with whom he lived. I spent a day or two mulling over the contents of her letter, my mind swaying between a desire to stay as far away from Paris as possible and my inability to refuse her request, which she had made sound so urgent. A few days later, I arrived at her door.

'All has changed and Tom is too closely aligned to Robespierre now,' she told me, settling into her chair breathlessly, her features more bloated than I remembered them, owing no doubt to her pregnancy.

251

'He has become the most loyal general the man has, but the tide is turning against them. I have tried to convince Tom to leave Paris but he refuses.'

'But how can that be?' I asked. 'Surely he holds so much power here still? The newspapers say that—'

'There is too much going on,' she said, glancing towards the window nervously, as if at any moment a counter-Revolutionary might spring through the glass and slit her neck from ear to ear. 'Everyone in control – Saint-Just, Carnot, Collot d'Herboid, Robespierre himself – they are at each other's throats. Their alliance is falling apart around our ears and they will not all survive it, I promise you that. Now Robespierre is not even attending the meetings of the Committee of Public Safety after yet another argument and they are sure to try to arrest him because of it. It is inevitable. And if he falls, we all do.'

'It's nothing like inevitable, citizen,' said Tom, suddenly appearing in the doorway and surprising us both. 'Hello, Matthieu,' he said coldly, dropping the 'Uncle' now. 'What brings you back to Paris? I thought we disgusted you over here.'

I looked at Thérèse in surprise before staring back at him. 'You didn't know I was coming?' I asked. 'I assumed that—'

'He came because he was worried about you,' said Thérèse. 'Even in England they can tell what is going on here right now. They are not so far away as you think.'

'What's going on,' he said angrily, 'is that we are go-ing to win through. Robespierre is inspirational at the moment. He is going around forming alliances with even those who once opposed him. He will lead alone, just mark my words.'

'In this atmosphere?' she screamed. 'You are fooling

yourself! The very nature of life here now is to distrust anyone with power. He will end up with his head on the scaffold the moment he achieves anything. That will be his reward. And yours too if you are not careful!'

'Don't be ridiculous,' he said. 'He is too strong for that. He has the army after all.'

'The army don't care any more,' she cried, collapsing in pain as she held on to her stomach. 'We have to leave Paris. We have to get out now, all of us. Matthieu can take us with him, can't you? You can take us back to London. You can see the condition I am in,' she added, referring to her swelling stomach. 'I want to leave before the baby is born,' she said firmly.

I shrugged. 'I suppose so,' I said, fully aware that it was not as simple as her just saying it. Tom would have to be persuaded.

'I'm not going anywhere,' he said. 'Not a chance.' The argument continued for some time, back and forth between two stubborn people. Eventually I left, saying that I would return over the next few days to see how she was but I could stay no longer than that. I assured Thérèse that she was welcome to join me on my trip back to England if she wanted to but she claimed that, no matter what happened, she could not leave Tom. It seemed that, in the face of love, all her revolutionary principles of a year earlier had become unimportant.

A few days later, Robespierre, with Tom by his side, launched a bitter attack on his former friends and colleagues, those who were still in a position of authority in Paris. He claimed that they were trying to undo the work of the Republic and demanded that both the Committee for Public Safety and the Committee for General Security, both of which he had been a member of himself, be destroyed and new committees set up to organize the political process. There was little response from the members at the time, so amazed were they by his arrogance and fearlessness, his stupidity, but I myself was present the following evening at the Jacobin club when he repeated his charges and demands.

'You're a fool,' I hissed at Tom, grabbing him by the arm as he passed me by on the way out. 'This man is signing his own death warrant. Can you not see that?'

'Let me go,' he said, pulling away from me, 'unless you want me to have you arrested on the spot. Do you want that, Matthieu? Because I could see you executed tomorrow morning if I wanted to.'

I stood back and shook my head, horrified by the look of insane power in the eyes of my nephew, this mere foot soldier. And although it hurt me, I was less than surprised when, within twenty-four hours, the arrests were made. Several of the other leaders attempted to kill themselves before the guillotine could take them, only one, Lebas, having the ability to do it right. Robespierre's brother Augustin jumped from a top storey window but succeeded only in breaking his thigh, the incompetent fool. The paralysed revolutionary Couthon threw himself down a stone stairway and was stuck there, unable to escape, his wheelchair mocking him from the top stair, until the soldiers came to arrest him. And Tom's hero, Robespierre himself, put a gun to his head and succeeded merely in shooting off the lower part of his jaw, thus ensuring that his last twenty-four hours on earth were filled with pain. Beneath his eyes he saw a constant run of blood similar to the one he had himself helped to create.

Thérèse insisted on going to the Place de la Concorde on the morning of the executions. I racked my brain to think of some way to save my nephew but knew that it was impossible; he was already doomed. As the tumbrel arrived in the square, I was reminded of the days when we had first come to the city, he almost as innocent then as his unborn child was now, and remembered those people we had ourselves seen beheaded, including the man whose actions had begun all this in the first place, Louis XVI.

As the cart made its way through the crowd, the people went crazy, baying for the blood of their one-time hero, who sat at the front of the tumbrel screaming back at them in his madness, his face half collapsed from the bullet he had sent through his jaw the previous day. He grasped the sides of the cart and jumped from side to side like a wild animal, screeching at the crowds until his eyes were almost falling from his head. All around him, the seeds he had sown. In the air, the bloodlust he had created for France. Behind him, sitting stoically, looking more disgusted with the people on whose part he had become a revolutionary, sat my nephew Tom. Thérèse was in tears, and I feared that she would give birth there and then. I tried to convince her to leave but she refused. Something made her want to stay until the end, to see this through to its natural conclusion, and nothing I could have said would have made her change her mind.

Robespierre was first for the blade and, when he reached the platform, the makeshift tourniquet holding his face together was pulled away and he had to be held into the scaffold by force, this sometime orator's screams and shrieks becoming more and more incoherent until they were finally silenced by the guillotine. Tom, on the other hand, shrugged off his captors and placed his own head on the block, not even so much as glancing upwards before it landed in the basket on top of Robespierre's.

Such a great cheer accompanied the former's execution that hardly anyone noticed Tom's similar fate, except of course for Thérèse and me, whose hearts sank as he lost his head. Paris stank of blood. I imagined the very Seine becoming red with the innards of the city's so-called citizens. Before my nephew's body had even turned cold, Thérèse and I were sailing back to England, away from the Revolution, away from that city of death, and leaving our fallen, bloodthirsty boy behind us.

Chapter 15

July 1999

It was my first visit to the set where Tommy's soap opera was filmed and the security precautions that I found in place as I attempted to gain entry struck me as preposterous. Arriving on foot at the studio, I was first name-checked on a security guard's clearance list. He looked me up and down with something approaching outright contempt before acknowledging with a snort that I was in fact expected. When I made it through to the reception area I was pushed through a metal detector to make sure that I was not carrying any recording or photographic equipment or, possibly, sub-machine guns. I then had to sign a declaration regarding the same thing and promise that any scene or action that I saw take place on set would not be revealed or spoken about outside of there. I was not allowed to profit financially from any aspect of television business which I might become privy to upon access, nor was I ever to speak of these things to anyone. I began to wonder why we did not have similar security restrictions at our own television station, before realizing that the reason was because they were ridiculous, and in place purely to massage the egos of the actors beyond.

'For heaven's sake,' I told the young bored-looking

guard who talked me through all the above rules in advance. 'Do I really look like I'm going to be selling your ridiculous secrets to the tabloids? Do I look like that sort of person? I mean, I barely know the name of the show.'

'I don't know what that sort of person looks like, to tell you the truth,' he responded gruffly, scarcely looking at me as he made some notes on his clipboard. 'All I know is that I have a job to do and I do it. What's your business here anyway? You auditioning?'

'*No*,' I said, offended by the very suggestion.

'It's just that I heard they're looking for a new love interest for Maggie.'

'Well, it's not me.'

'I thought about going up for it myself, but my agent said I'd be cutting off younger roles that might come along if I became well known playing a middle-aged man.'

'Right,' I said. Even the security guards there had agents. 'Well, I am not auditioning, thank you very much. And I am *not* middle-aged. I was invited here by my nephew to see the filming in progress. He thinks it will broaden my experiences, which I doubt. They're not exactly narrow as it stands.'

'Who's your nephew?' he asked me, handing me back my watch and keys, which had set off the alarm system on the metal detector a few moments earlier.

'One of the actors,' I said quickly. 'Tommy DuMarqué. Thank you.' I put my watch back on my wrist.

'You're Tommy's uncle?' asked the security guard, a broad smile crossing his face now as he stepped back to look me up and down, searching for a family resemblance no doubt. There was hardly any point in him doing that; any similarities between myself and any of the Thomases were watered out many generations ago. Each successive one is far more handsome than I could ever dream of being, although my physical solidity is a condition which none of their number has ever succeeded in achieving. 'That's a surprise, Mr . . .' – he looked down at his clipboard – 'Zelly.'

'It's Zéla.'

'I didn't think he had any family at all, to tell you the truth. Just girls. Lots of girls, the lucky son of a—'

'Well, he has me,' I said quickly, looking around to see where I should go from there, whether a strip or cavity search was going to be the next indignity. 'But I'm it. There's just the two of us left.'

'You want to go down that corridor there and you'll come into another reception room at the end,' he said, anticipating my next question now that the formalities of who I actually was were out of the way. 'There's a girl at the desk there and you can just ask her to page Tommy for you from there. He knows you're coming, yeah?'

I nodded and thanked him and walked down the corridor he had indicated. On either side of me there were large, framed photographs of who I assumed to be the actors and actresses in the show, past and present. Each of them had two names printed under their frames, their real name and their character's name, as well as the years of their appearances in the show. I barely recognized any of them, except for one or two I had seen before in sitcoms of twenty years ago or in the tabloids of today. Towards the end of the corridor there was a dark, moody shot of my nephew with the words 'Tommy DuMarqué – Sam Cutler – 1991 – date' inscribed underneath it. I looked at it for a moment and couldn't help but feel a surge of pride, not to mention a slight smile cross my face, at my nephew's success. The photo was stylized and professionally shot – no one, not even my nephew, could look that good – but it was nice to see none the less. I pushed the door open and introduced myself to the girl at the desk, who made a quick phone call before pointing me in the direction of the armchairs where I sat for a few moments waiting for him to appear. I noticed that in all the time that I sat there, she rarely took her eyes off me but continued masticating on her chewing gum noisily, a habit that never fails to disgust me.

Another door swung open and I did a double take as my nephew came through it, looking in my direction sheepishly, his eyes barely raised off the ground. The receptionist sat up straight as he entered the room and stuck her gum behind her ear before beginning to tap away at her word processor fervently, watching the star out of the corner of her eye all the time.

'Tommy,' I said as he approached me, wondering what fresh horrors were about to appear now. 'Good Lord! What on earth happened to you?' He was wearing faded blue jeans and a small black T-shirt which accentuated the toning of his chest as well as the definition of the trapezoid muscles around the neck. His forearms were strong and tanned and I wondered how someone in such good condition could get himself into such scrapes, for his left eye bore the signs of an all too recent beating – it was half closed in upon itself and there were ugly purple stains swelling above it like a small hill of unattractive colour. His cheek was inflamed, and the corner of his upper lip was split in two, a dried line of blood sticking to his chin in a most ill-favoured fashion. I shook my head in dismay. 'How did this . . . ?'

'It's all right, Uncle Matthieu,' he said, leading me back through the door from which he had appeared a moment before. 'I'm all right. It happened this morning. Carl found out about what was going on between Tina and me and he was waiting for me when I came home and beat the crap out of me. So relax, I'll survive.'

'Carl . . .' I said, wondering whether this was an acquaintance of his whom I may have met at some point and forgotten, for he said the name in the most nonchalant manner. 'Carl did this to you?'

'Tina's pregnant, you see,' he continued, as if it was the most natural thing in the world. 'Of course we don't know whether Carl or me or this new barman in the pub is the father and we can't do a test 'cos Tina's got some weird genetic condition that means it might cause the baby some trauma or something if we try to find out. So we have to wait until it's born. Bit of a cliff-hanger, I suppose.'

I stared at him, unsure what on earth he was talking about, before the penny dropped. 'Carl,' I said, relieved, laughing now. 'He's some relation of yours, isn't he?'

'Sort of. He's my mother's ex-husband's adopted son by his second wife. We're not really related but we share the same surname. Sam Cutler, Carl Cutler. People think we're closer than we actually are. We've never really got on. He resents me for—'

'I *have* to start watching your show,' I said again, for the hundredth time, interrupting his character history. 'I can never remember who any of these people are.'

'Well, that's why you're here today,' he said and we were now on a familiar set, one I had seen before on a few occasions, the living room of the Cutlers' small terraced house in the East End of London.

'Two minutes, Tommy,' said a small, bearded man

with an earpiece as he passed us by, patting my nephew on the bicep with some familiarity.

'OK, you go sit over there,' said my nephew, indicating a chair in the corner. 'And stay very quiet. I've just got to wrap this scene up and then I'm all yours.'

I nodded and went in the direction he had indicated. There were four cameras at various points around the set and about fifteen technicians. Seated at the table in the living room, having her make-up touched up by what looked like a twelve-year-old girl, was a familiar figure, Tommy's screen mother, a woman who had made something of a name for herself in the 1960s as a comic film star. Her career had gone downhill in the seventies and mid-eighties but she had returned to prominence from the first day of the show's transmission and was now cordially referred to as a national treasure. Minnie was her character's name, and Moanin' Minnie her affectionate nickname in the tabloids. Also seated at the table was a young lad of about fifteen whom I had never seen before and who I suspected was the new teen idol who had been drafted in to help boost ratings with a certain quarter of the audience. While she shrugged her shoulders quickly to assume the body of her character, he sat hunched up over a magazine, chewing his nails, his right hand stuck halfway down the throat it seemed to me.

The director called for quiet on the set, the boy's magazine was whipped away to his protests, the technicians all stepped out of the shot and the playback began. Minnie and the boy sat up straight and chatted briefly while we all waited for the director to cry 'Action!' When he did, the scene burst into life.

'I don't care,' said Minnie, lighting a cigarette. 'You can say what you like about that Carla Jenson. She's a bad lot and I don't want you 'angin' aroun' with 'er, do you 'ear me?' Her accent was very East End, very Cockney, while I knew that in real life she spoke like a blue-blooded aristocrat. Nobody probably had the first clue as to what her real voice actually sounded like.

'Oh, Aun'ie Minnie!' cried the boy in despair, as if the entire adult world was ganging up against him and conspiring to keep him in short trousers and lollipops for ever. 'We weren't doin' anyfink wrong. We were just playing my new Nintendo game, thass all.'

'Yes, well,' said Auntie Minnie. 'That's as may be. But if that's the case I don't see why she 'ad to 'ave her blouse unbuttoned down to her navel, do you, showin' off her belongin's as if they were there for all the world to see.'

'That's the way girls wear 'em now, inni'?' he replied in disgust at her traditionalism. 'Don't you know any-fink?'

'I don't *need* to know anyfink, Davy Cutler, 'cept that you ain't to see that tar' no more! Do you 'ear me?'

'She ain't no tar', Aun'ie Minnie. I wish she were!'

Throughout their dialogue, two of the cameras rotated slightly on their dollies while the other two shot both characters from over each other's shoulder. As they got to the end of that part of the scene, one of the cameras spun around in preparation for the next shot and aimed towards the door. From behind me – as opposed to behind them where he was about to appear from – the sound of a door slamming was heard, and then my nephew appeared in the living room, slumping down on the ground before them, groaning loudly.

'Flamin' 'eck!' shouted Minnie, jumping up and go-ing over to where her 'son' lay, even more blood having been applied in the minute or two since I had left him. 'What the 'ell's after appenin' to you then, our Sam?'

'That'll be that Carl,' said Davy, looking remarkably pleased now that the heat was off him and his tar' for a few moments. 'He'll have found out about our Sam doin' his missus.'

'You keep that out,' shouted Minnie, pointing towards the boy's nose. 'That's not it, is it son?' she asked quietly, her face slowly moving from disbelief to disappointment in three well-trained movements.

'You shut it,' groaned Tommy to Davy, who was possibly a younger brother or a cousin or a foster child or just some stray who'd walked in off the streets and moved in with them.

'It's the troof,' said Davy defensively.

'I said . . .' long pause from Tommy. 'Shut it.' Another pause. 'You 'eard.'

Minnie looked from one boy to the other as she cradled Tommy's head in her hands and then, mysteriously, looked out towards me – or what I can only assume to be 'the distance' – and her face contorted into a sudden release of misery. The tears came, she dropped Tommy's head on the floor where we could all hear it bang suddenly and then she ran through the living room door crying and, a moment later, the sound-effects man behind me slammed another one once again.

'And cut!' cried the director. 'Lovely, people. Absolutely lovely.'

I was pleased by Tommy's invitation to spend an afternoon with him on the set of his soap as I desperately needed a break from my own affairs. Caroline and I were developing a somewhat tempestuous relationship and I was beginning to regret her presence. I couldn't fault her for her work ethic; she arrived before I did in the mornings and was always still there when I went home

– although it was perfectly possible that she was simply waiting for me to leave before calling it a day herself. She buried herself in short reports on the relatively brief history of our station and long ones on the condition of the broadcasting world in Britain today. When she spoke to me, she used terms such as 'market share', 'demographics' and 'core audience' as if they would be new to me, slowing down and speaking up when she used them in case I wasn't keeping up with her, when in fact I had been thinking in such terms – if not actually using those very words – two hundred years before. She kept three small pocket-sized televisions on her desk, with their volumes turned down, one tuned in to our own station, the other two tuned in to the BBC and another rival. Every so often she would glance up, look from one to the other and decide which programme would be more appealing to her if she was simply sitting at home, her feet up on the settee, settling down for an afternoon's viewing. She made a note of how many times our programmes won out and presented her results to me at the end of each week.

'Look,' she said, 'only twelve per cent of the time is there something on here that I actually want to watch. The other two stations pull in an eighty-eight per cent share between them.'

'Well, twelve per cent is a lot more than our current market share, Caroline, so I find that terribly encouraging.'

She frowned and stared at me, unsure if she was wrong to condemn our programming after that response and retired to her desk to do some further analysis. I found that I enjoyed winding her up, to use the current parlance, and that her extreme enthusiasm made her an easy target for jokes. She appeared to be devoting every moment of her day to her work which, in general, is no bad thing in a senior employee, but then I have never been the kind of man who has seen constant and unrelenting work as the ultimate test of a person's character. Caroline was attempting to convince me that she was the right woman for James's job, when all she was really doing was proving how far from that position she currently was.

In the meantime, I continued to slave away for six, sometimes seven, days a week. I grew tired of working, and the fact that I was less than interested in the mundane, day to day aspects of our business did not help matters any. I continued to hold weekly meetings with Alan, which Caroline also attended in her capacity as P.W.'s representative, but I broadened them now and sought opinions from our various department heads as well. Caroline always sat on my right hand at these meetings and tended to want to direct the manner in which the conversation went. I gave her a fairly free rein most of the time because her opinions, while not always correct, were generally interesting and everyone agreed that she was bringing a fresh point of view to the station.

'Of course,' she pointed out at one of our regular meetings, when we were discussing a 5 per cent drop off in market share between 6 and 7 p.m., 'the big mistake you made around here was getting rid of Tara Morrison. She was perfect for pulling in the tits 'n' ass crowd.'

'We didn't get rid of her,' I snapped back, noticing how she liked to impress the male dominated room by acting like one of the boys. 'She left of her own volition.'

'Tara Morrison was one of this station's few true stars,' she said.

'There's Billy Boy Davis,' said Alan predictably. 'The Kid.'

'Oh, please,' she said. 'I've got grandparents who are younger than him. Sure he's a *name* and he's got something of a *history* but that doesn't cut it any more. We need new, fresh talent. *Raw* talent. Now if we could just lure Tara back . . .' she said quietly, and I shook my head.

'I don't think so,' I said. 'She seems quite happy at the Beeb. Roger?' I looked towards Roger Tabori, the head of our news department, who looked like a member of Michael Corleone's family with his swarthy Italian looks and slicked-back hair.

'I've heard some things,' he said, shrugging lightly. 'She's not ecstatic about what's going on there but she's under contract so . . .'

'She was under contract here,' said Caroline.

'No,' I said forcibly, irritated now by the manner in which she was speaking of something that she didn't fully understand. 'Her contract came to an end. She chose not to renew it. She got a better offer.'

'Then you should have offered her more money, shouldn't you?' she asked sweetly. I stared at her, blinking a little, and my smile faded.

'Apparently she wanted six o'clock,' continued Roger, defusing the situation slightly. 'But they wouldn't give it to her because Meg would have walked if they had. So she asked for one o'clock and they said no. Not sure why 'cos she could have worked there. They wanted her for Breakfast TV and she balked at that of course. They've lined up a few documentary things, some "Celebrity Ready, Steady, Cook", a few segments like that. Nothing solid as yet.'

'She should have sorted these things out before she

left us then, shouldn't she?' I muttered, smiling at Caroline now. 'Who knows, maybe she'll walk out on them and come running back here with her tail between her legs.'

'I doubt it,' said Caroline and, in truth, so did I, although I found that I did miss her a little for, if nothing else, she was always good company. As James had been. But he was dead and she was working for the competition. 'But, anyway, there is one other issue we should discuss. We have to get rid of Martin Ryce-Stanford. And quickly.'

There was an audible intake of breath around the room when she said this and I leaned back and tapped the edge of the desk quietly with my pencil. Martin Ryce-Stanford was the man who lived in the upper three storeys of the house in which my own basement apartment was located. He had been a senior minister during the middle period of Mrs Thatcher's reign of terror and had lost his job when he got on the wrong end of his boss during a debate about the future of the coalmines. Martin thought they should close them all down and hang the consequences. Mrs T. felt the same way but knew that it would be too dangerous a thing to do; better to announce the closure of many, then give in slightly after the inevitable outrage and allow some to remain open while succeeding in closing the ones that she wanted to get rid of in the first place. Curiously, considering his own position, Martin thought this was the ultimate act of political cynicism and gave a scathing account of Mrs Thatcher's plans on *Newsnight* one evening. By midnight she had phoned him, fired him and threatened to have him castrated, after which he became something of a *bête noire* for her during her remaining years in power. He was one of those characters who helped John Major to power in 1990, despite the fact that the pair could not tolerate each other, and he had hoped that this unexpected assistance would secure him a place in the Lords. Unfortunately for him, favours do not always get repaid and so he was reduced to writing scathing articles about the leadership in whatever newspaper would have him. He developed a previously untapped skill at political cartooning and began to illustrate his articles with line drawings of ministers as different types of hybrids, their bodies the bodies of appropriate animals, their faces their own. Thus, John Major himself waddled around with the gait of a small duck, Michael Portillo stretched out his arms to reveal the plumage of the peacock, and Gillian Shepard scampered around the page with the body of a small Rottweiler. Eventually, it became clear that Martin's writing was a little too one-sided – he criticized absolutely *everything*, no matter whether it was a good idea or not. He was the ultimate no-man. He was considered politically unsound, incredibly biased and ridiculously prejudiced against anyone still in any position of power. There were those who believed he was mentally unstable. Naturally, the time had come for his promotion to television.

I got to know Martin quite well after I moved into the apartment in Piccadilly. He invited me to dine with him from time to time, along with his young, shrewish wife Polly and whichever partner I could muster up for the evening, and our evenings were always absurdly hilarious. His right-wing beliefs were so far gone that they could only have been an affectation. He appeared to take a delight in outraging people with the things that he said; Polly barely listened to him. I believed I had the mark of him and wouldn't fall for his games, but whatever lady I brought with me to the table inevitably found herself growing more and more outraged as the night wore on, to the point where she would either stand up and leave or attack him in return, a terrible social *faux pas*, the very kind of extreme reaction into which he enjoyed goading his guests in the first place.

It occurred to me shortly after the launch of the station how entertaining it would be to translate the madness and provocation of those dinner-time conversations to the television and I invited Martin to host his own thrice-weekly political chat show. The format was simple: a thirty-minute show, twenty-four not including commercial breaks and titles, with two guests each episode. Usually a political figure and an Outraged Liberal. The political figure would say all the right things for the sake of their own career. The Outraged Liberal – usually an actor, singer, writer or some such thing – would run the politically correct line. And Martin would throw in nuggets of bad taste just to rile them both. As the show progressed it became clear that the politician was doing all he or she could to embrace the party line while never going so far as actually to *condemn* Martin's obviously ridiculous points of view. And at the same time, the Outraged Liberal would grow more and more furious, using phrases such as 'this whole thing disgusts me' or 'my God, man, how can you continue to think like that?' and there was always a chance that the O.L. would throw their glass of diet-still-water-no-ice-no-lemon over the monstrous figure sitting before them. All in all, it was great fun and one of my better ideas.

Eventually, however, the fun simply wore off. Martin Ryce-Stanford began to appear not so much provocative as just plain stupid. Quality news shows caught up with him and his brand of personal right-wing bias took on the appearance of a man who was simply out of time. It became more and more difficult to find credible guests for his show; its nadir coming when the political figure was the wife of a political secretary to a newly elected health spokesman from the Liberal Democrat party, and the Outraged Liberal was a young man who had enjoyed a number three pop record six years earlier and hadn't been heard from since, but who was suddenly relaunching his career as an author of children's books featuring a hobgoblin with a variety of magic powers. Market share didn't just decline so much as evaporate. The show was a dud and we all knew it. But, still, Martin was my friend and I for one still enjoyed his company and didn't relish the idea of giving him the boot.

'We have to get rid of Martin Ryce-Stanford, Matthieu,' repeated Caroline. 'The show's a joke.'

'Agreed,' said Roger Tabori, nodding his head wisely.

'I didn't even know we still ran that show,' said Alan, looking surprised by the revelation.

'We need change,' said Marcia Goodwill, head of light entertainment, tapping a pen on her blotter.

'Something to bring the young people in,' said Cliff Macklin, director of imported programming, joining in the Greek chorus.

'You need to fire him. And soon,' said Caroline.

I shrugged. She was right, I knew she was right, but still . . . 'Isn't there any way that we could just change the format of the show?' I asked. 'Bring it a little more up to date?'

'Yes,' said Caroline. 'We could get rid of the host.'

'But isn't there anything else we could do? Other than firing him, I mean?'

Caroline thought about it. 'Well, I suppose we could

271

have him shot. That might bring back the viewers. Create a bit of publicity. Bring in a new host then. Someone with a little sex appeal.' I stared at her in surprise, unsure whether she was being serious or not. '*Kidding*,' she said eventually, seeing my expression. 'Honestly, it's like you're auditioning to be the Outraged Liberal yourself.'

'It seems to me,' said Roger Tabori, 'that the problem isn't so much with the format of the show as with the host. I think the political chat show still has some life left in it. We just need to find a new front for it. Someone with a little more . . . I don't know . . . appeal to the public. Someone with balls, frankly.'

'And tits,' said Caroline. 'If we can get someone with balls and tits, we'll have a winner on our hands.'

I laughed. 'Right,' I said. 'Balls and tits. What exact corner of Amsterdam do we travel to in order to find someone who fills that description?'

'Oh, I don't think we need go as far as Amsterdam, Matthieu,' said Cliff Macklin.

'Not when we know someone who can bring back the viewers in their droves,' said Marcia Goodwill, warming to the attack. I began to feel like I was being ambushed, as if this entire conversation had been rehearsed in advance, only with my part being spoken by an actor.

'Who exactly are you thinking of?' I asked with a sigh, looking directly at Caroline, their ringleader, who I began to think might have rather more going for her than I had realized before.

'Well, it's pretty bloody obvious, isn't it?' she said. 'We have to win her back. No matter what the cost, we have to win her back. Pay her whatever she wants, make whatever deal she asks for, make the station revolve around her if we have to. But win her back, that's what we've got to do. Tara says: it's time to come home.'

I shook my head and sighed, closing my eyes and blocking them all out for a few moments. I never wished that James was still alive more than at that exact moment.

'It's very impressive,' I told Tommy as we sat in his dressing room after the close-ups and point-of-view shots were finished. 'I never realized it took so many people to make a show like that. It was a lot simpler in the old days.' I had never told my nephew about my NBC days, for obvious reasons, but the differences between the two could not have been more pronounced.

'Don't you ever leave your office and see what's going on at your own station?' he asked me with a smile.

'Most of our stuff is imported,' I said honestly. 'Dramas, comedies and so on. All the home-grown product is news programming and current affairs stuff. It's just a couple of people sitting around desks talking. We don't need an awful lot for that.'

I watched as Tommy took off his make-up, seated in front of a Broadway-style mirror, a row of lightbulbs presented in an archway around the star's face. He saw me watching him in the mirror and smiled, not turning around as he spoke but speaking directly to my reflection instead. 'Last year, Madonna used this dressing room before appearing on the National Lottery,' he said with a grin. 'She sang "Frozen" and left behind a demo of her new album. I sent it on and never got so much as a thank you in return.'

'Really,' I said in a dry voice. 'How very impressive.'

'I had to clear the whole place out in advance for her but she left a whole pile of her shit behind afterwards for me to clean up. I held on to some of it, of course, but don't tell anyone.'

273

I shrugged and looked around me. There was a lot of television paraphernalia to be seen there. Pictures, posters, tapes and reels. There were so many scripts littered around the floor, each printed in a different colour to signify updates and revisions, that the place resembled a Montessori school. I wondered whether there was a little man sitting somewhere in the building, surrounded by a rainbow of paper, deciding which day would be signified by which colour and filling them all in on an enormous chart in order to justify his existence. I flicked around in them for a moment, pulling a few out to glance at their content but found the dialogue so risible that I was forced to toss them aside again.

'Do you like working here, Tommy?' I asked him after a while.

'Like it? How do you mean?'

I laughed. 'How do you think I mean it? Do you enjoy it? Do you enjoy your job? Do you like coming in here every day?'

He thought about it for a moment and shrugged. 'I *think* so,' he said. 'Turn around if you don't want to see this, by the way.' He was blading what I took to be a small amount of cocaine on a jagged mirror and his concentration on refining it was immense.

'Really, Tommy,' I said. 'How many times do I—'

'*Don't* start,' he said quickly. 'I've cut down, I promise you. Just don't go on about it, all right? I've spent the morning having the crap beaten out of me by an irate stepbrother who thinks I've got his wife up the spout. I need a little relaxant.' I sighed and said nothing more as he leaned down, snorted the entire amount into his nose through a thin cylinder of paper he kept in a drawer in his dressing table and, after a moment's hesitation, shook his whole body as if he was having a fit, his arms outstretched, fists clenched, eyes shut tight. 'Goddamit,' he said eventually, tugging at his nose violently and opening and closing his eyes many times. 'What a fucking day.' He started to put all his paraphernalia away and I turned away from him, not wishing to see any more. I wondered what would be the result if someone just happened to walk in while he was doing that, whether he would even care.

'By the way,' he said, his face free of its make-up now, his Sam Cutler clothes changed into his regulation Tommy DuMarqué ones, 'I've a bone to pick with you.' I looked across at him in surprise. What? I wondered. Had another one of my cheques not lodged into his account in time to pay off his debts? 'I got a script sent to me this week. Recommended by you, apparently.'

I stood back in surprise. 'What?' I asked, not having the first clue what he was talking about. 'What sort of a script?'

He shrugged and started rooting around his mess, looking for something. 'I don't know,' he said. 'I didn't *read* it of course. It's more than my career's worth. We have a hard and fast policy here. If anyone sends us a script, we have to return it to them the same day with a standard BBC statement maintaining that neither I, nor my agent, nor anyone appointed by my agent, nor any agent appointed by me, nor any representative of the BBC or *its* agents, has even opened it past the first page. Otherwise there's all sorts of legal difficulties involved with unsolicited manuscripts.'

'But what's that got to do with me?' I asked, confused by what he was saying.

'Well *I* don't know,' he said again, finding his keys now in the rubble and reaching for his coat. 'I mean I read the letter that went with it before sending back the script and it was from some guy who said that he met you at a party, talked to you about the thing, and you'd recommended that he send it on to me. That I might be able to do something with it somehow.'

I shook my head. 'That's ridiculous,' I said. 'I haven't met any such person. What was his name?'

He thought about it. 'Can't remember. He just said you'd talked recently at a party and you'd liked what he'd—'

'Dear God,' I said, a penny dropping in my mind which I was sure could not be the right one. 'It wasn't Lee Hocknell, was it?'

Tommy clicked his fingers and pointed them at me. 'Yeah, that was him,' he said. 'Name stuck in my head because it was the same as that guy who we sorted out a couple of months ago. Guy who OD'd and you got dragged into it.'

'That was his *father*,' I said, astonished. 'And we didn't meet at a party, we met at his father's *funeral*! Jesus!'

'Well, that's what he said.'

'And I *never* told him to send you anything. That's bizarre. I remember him saying that he was writing some crime story or something. Some drama for TV. Somehow your name came up but I never dreamed that he'd actually send it to you.'

Tommy shrugged and switched off his lights as we went through the doors to go to lunch. 'No harm done,' he said nonchalantly. 'Like I said, I returned it to him anyway.'

'Still, it's strange that he should send it,' I said. 'And a little rude. I promise you I never told him that he should.'

He laughed. 'It doesn't matter, honestly,' he said.

'Forget about it. So tell me,' he continued, changing the subject. 'What's new with you?'

Now it was my turn to laugh. 'Well,' I said. 'You're never going to believe who I'm supposed to go out and charm the pants off next week.'

Chapter 16

Missing Dominique

Nat Pepys was not a handsome man but from the way he carried himself it was easy to see that he had the self-confidence of a man completely at ease with both his appearance and his status in the world. He strode around the grounds like a peacock, his legs stretching further ahead of his body than seemed entirely natural; his neck bobbing back and forth like a consumptive turkey. He arrived at Cageley House alone one Tuesday afternoon, riding his horse so hard down the driveway that when he pulled up in front of us at the stables, the poor creature had to call on all its reserves to stop itself from falling over. The damn fool might have been thrown head forwards where he would have undoubtedly broken his neck and I could see the horse's face break into an expression of surprise and pain and I felt sorry for her; although I had never met Nat before, Jack had already filled my head with his contempt for the man and I was quick to resent his behaviour.

It was a drizzly afternoon and, as he jumped off his horse, he looked up towards the heavens as if one cold stare at the skies above would piece the clouds back together above his head. I watched as he strolled towards us without a care in the world, sniffing the air as if he owned it and was pleased to come back to Cageley to claim it as his own. He was not as tall as either Jack or I – standing in his riding boots he commanded no more than five foot seven or eight – and although it was only his twenty-first birthday upon him, his long brown hair was falling out to reveal great clumps of empty scalp beneath. His face bore the scars of an adolescent acne, although his eyes were of a deep blue colour and were the first thing one noticed about him; perhaps his only attractive characteristic. Above his lip was a pencil thin moustache which he pressed flat every so often, as if he suspected it might have fallen off during the ride.

'Hello, Colby,' he said, ignoring me completely as he strode towards Jack, who stopped shovelling out the stables for a moment and leaned on his pitchfork instead, squinting at Nat with barely concealed distaste. 'Doing all right, are you?'

'It's Holby, Mr Pepys,' said Jack in a cold tone. 'Jack Holby. Remember?'

Nat shrugged and smiled up at him in a condescending manner. The differences between them were obvious; Jack was tall, strong and handsome, his fair hair glistened in the sun, his whole body testified to the fact that he spent most of his time outdoors; Nat was none of these things. His complexion was sallow, his build slight. It would have been clear to anyone which of these two boys, not far separated in age, had worked throughout his youth and which had not. Knowing Jack's dislike of him, I wondered why Nat was acting in so cocksure a fashion; any fight between them could have had only one outcome. But then I remembered Jack's ambition; he wanted to make something of his life and, if kowtowing to a creep like Nat Pepys for a few years was what it took to see those dreams fulfilled, then he had the strength of character to do that very thing.

'Now I can't be expected to remember the names of every man, woman and child in my employ, can I, Holby?' he asked cheerfully. 'Man in my position in life,' he added as an afterthought.

'Don't matter much considering I'm not in your employ, am I?' asked Jack, keeping his tone polite even as his words grew more insolent. 'It's your father who pays my wages; always has been. Same as he pays yours, I expect.'

'Yes and who do you think makes sure there's still money in the coffers for him to use every month?' asked Nat with a wide grin, spinning around to look at me now, probably not wanting to get into a war of words with an underling only seconds after his arrival. I didn't know for sure what conversations had passed between these two in the past, but I knew one thing that this fellow also knew – that Jack was not one for standing on ceremony where Nat Pepys was concerned. 'So,' he asked, looking me up and down carefully, his mouth twisting a little as he decided whether or not he liked the look of me, 'who the devil are you then?' His tone wasn't as aggressive as the words sounded but for some reason I wasn't quite sure what was the right way to address him. I'd never had any dealings with his father or mother and he was the closest thing to an employer who had spoken to me since my arrival at Cageley. I looked over his shoulder at Jack for some reassurance.

'That's Matthieu Zéla,' said Jack after a moment, coming to my rescue. 'Stable lad now.'

'Matthieu what?' asked Nat, looking back at Jack in surprise. 'What did you say his name was?'

'Zéla.'

'Zéla? Good God, man, what kind of name is that? Where are you from, boy, with a name like that?'

'I'm from Paris, sir,' I said quietly, my face growing hot with anxiety as I explained. 'I'm French.'

'I know where Paris is, thank you very much,' he said irritably. 'Believe it or not, I do have a little schooling in the basics of world geography. What brings you from Paris to here then, might I ask?'

I shrugged. It was a long story after all. 'I just seem to have ended up here,' I began. 'I left—' He turned away from me as I spoke, uninterested, and began to talk to Jack, removing his leather riding gloves and putting them in his pocket as he did so. I had yet to learn the meaning of the word rhetorical.

'I'm sure Davies has told you I've got some friends coming down for the weekend,' he said quickly and Jack nodded. 'Bit of a birthday bash and the city's not the place for it. Now there's seven of them in all and they won't be here until tomorrow so that gives you a little time to be ready for them. Clean the place up a bit, will you?' he added, looking around the ground with disdain even though it was about as clean and well kept as any stable ground should be. 'Make it look a bit respectable. You, boy,' he said, turning back to me, 'give my horse a wash and then stable her, will you?' I nodded and reached over to take the reins when she reared up at me in panic. 'Oh, for God's sake,' said Nat, coming over and grabbing the horse fiercely. It was clear that she was terrified of him. '*That's* how you take hold of a horse,' he said. 'You have to show her who's the master. Same as with anyone.' He smiled at me and I could feel his eyes looking me up and down again as if I was some peasant off the side of the road and it made me uncomfortable. I stared down at the ground and took the reins off him. 'You'll have room for seven extra horses, I presume?' he asked Jack, stepping away from me now.

'I dare say,' said Jack with a shrug. 'Plenty of room in number three and we'll fit another one or two in here easy enough.'

'Well . . .' said Nat, thinking about it for a while. 'As long as they have room to breathe, that's all. We'll be hunting so I need them in good condition. Take some of pater's horses out for the time being if necessary. They live far too well as it is. Eat better than some of the villagers, I dare say.' Jack didn't reply and I could tell there was no way on this earth he was going to sacrifice one of his beloved horses' comfort for the horses of any of Nat Pepys's friends. 'All right then,' said Nat eventually with a quick nod, taking his small carpet bag off his horse's back. 'Better go inside and pay the respects to the old ones. I'll see you both later, I expect.' He turned around and gave me a quizzical look once again, shaking his head as he muttered 'Paris' in disdain before walking away. I stepped closer to Jack and we watched as he headed out of sight and towards the old house. I noticed that Jack's jaw was set in grim resolution and as Nat left his eyes followed him with something close to pure hatred.

Nat's seven friends arrived the following afternoon and Jack and I were there to meet them when they came charging up the driveway with just as much speed and just as little concern for their steeds as Nat had had twenty-four hours earlier. They practically fell off their horses to greet their friend, who was standing no more than a few feet behind the two of us, going towards him with complete confidence that someone – namely Jack or I – would attend to their horses and prevent them from simply turning on their heels and galloping away to freedom. We brought them all into the stables and spent the rest of the evening washing and brushing them down, which was a long and tiring business. They had all travelled down from London in good time, so the horses were sweating and hungry. As I finished arranging the hay around each one, Jack made a large trough of hot oats for them, more than we had ever been obliged to make for the horses before. By the time we were ready to go home for the evening, we were both exhausted.

'How about we go into the kitchens and see if we can't help ourselves to a drink after all that hard work,' suggested Jack as we locked the stable doors and pulled on them quickly to double check. The last thing we could afford was a break-out in the night.

'I don't know . . .' I said apprehensively. 'What if—'

'Oh, come on, Mattie, don't be such a coward. Take a look; lights are off.' I looked in the direction of the kitchens and, sure enough, it was dark in there and there wasn't a soul to be seen. It wasn't against the rules for us to help ourselves to a bite to eat at the end of the day either so, without too much more encouragement, I agreed to join him.

'The doors are open,' said Jack with a smile as we stepped inside. 'Doesn't that sister of yours know she's supposed to lock them up before she goes off to 'er bed?' I shrugged and sat down as he went into the pantry, returning with two bottles of ale which he presented to me delightedly. 'There you go, Mattie,' he said, placing them down firmly on the table in front of me with a smile. 'What do you make of these then?' I picked one up gratefully and took a long drink from the bottle. I wasn't accustomed to beer and the bitter taste of it made me gag at first. I coughed a little, some of the drink dribbled down my chin and Jack laughed. 'Well, don't waste it, for God's sake,' he said, grinning. 'We're not supposed to be drinking this anyway. Last thing we need is for you to pour it all down your jersey instead of your throat.'

'Sorry Jack,' I said. 'It's just that I've never drunk this before.' We lit our pipes and settled back in our chairs, the picture of relaxation. It dawned on me how wonderful it must be to be a man of leisure, relaxing like this whenever you felt like it, eating, drinking and smoking your pipe in peace. Even the working man was able to sit back at the end of the day and enjoy the fruits of his labour. All my money went into my savings, for the day that Dominique and I might leave Cageley and start our lives together somewhere else.

'I'll need a lot of this over the next few days,' said Jack thoughtfully. 'What with that bunch of wastrels floating around, shouting at us wherever they go. I swear to you, I've half a mind to . . .' He drifted off, not finishing his sentence but biting on his lip in suppressed anger.

'What exactly happened between Nat and your Elsie?' I asked him, using the word 'your' only because he had referred to her as 'his' on every single occasion that he had mentioned her name during my time at Cageley House and not because I myself had ever noticed any particular relationship existing between the two. He shrugged and looked as if he wasn't sure whether he wanted to discuss it or not.

'Thing is,' he said, 'I've tried to put that whole business behind me now. I suppose it's going back a bit anyway. Two years it must be since it all took place.' I looked at him and raised an eyebrow, urging him to go on and eventually he did. 'You see, I've been at Cageley House since I was about five years old,' he told me. 'On account of my olds working for Sir Alfred. I were brought up here and ol' Nat there, we used to play together a bit as kids. All that stuff he does now, calling me 'Colby' instead of using my real name. He's only known me most of his life. He only does it to annoy me.'

'But why?' I asked. 'If you were friends once?'

He shook his head. 'We were never really friends,' he said. 'We just happened to be both here at the same time with not that much difference in our ages. Sir Alfred spent most of his time in London back then; they only came to Cageley at weekends and they didn't even come then half the time. We were more like caretakers here than anything else. The real work began when Sir Alfred retired. So I only saw Nat from time to time. And he tended to stay in the house while I was always out-side. No, the real trouble started when my Elsie came here.'

'She wasn't here from childhood too then?'

'Oh no,' said Jack, shaking his head. 'She's only been here a few years. Maybe three years. Well, me and Elsie, we became friends right from the start and we started going for walks and things together, you know the lark. Pretty soon we were more than friends but it weren't more than a casual thing. We could take or leave each other most of the time, I think. You know how it is.' I nodded; I did, after all, know a little of how it was. For although the only true romantic relationship I had known had been far from casual, all my other sexual exploits had been either paid for or with the street girls in Dover. 'Anyway,' he continued, 'then Nat comes down here one weekend, takes one look at my Elsie and thinks he could do worse than have a go at her. So he starts coming on strong to her and I told you already what happened next.'

'He got her,' I said simply.

'Oh, he got her all right,' said Jack, 'and then he barely spoke to her again. Near broke her heart. She thought she was about to become the lady of the manor, the stupid tart, what was she doing falling for a short-arse dog like him?'

At those words the door to the kitchen opened and the short-arse dog himself stepped inside, bearing a tall candle. I jumped, wondering whether he'd been outside all that time, listening to us. 'Hello, boys,' he said, stepping towards the pantry and barely looking at us as he walked by. I guessed he hadn't or he just didn't care about our opinion of him. 'What are you two doing in here so late? Finished your work, have you?'

I waited for Jack to speak, him having the authority in the case as it were, but an embarrassing amount of time passed by without him saying a word. I stared across at him, urging him to answer, but he simply took a long swig from his bottle and smiled at me.

'All finished, sir,' I said eventually. 'The horses are ready for tomorrow.'

Nat stepped out of the pantry, peering at the labels on the two bottles of wine he had taken before looking with just as much discernment down at me. He waited a while before speaking, as if he was trying to figure out exactly why he was holding a conversation with someone as far down the food chain as myself, before stepping closer towards us both. I could smell the smoke and alcohol on him already and wondered what condition he would be in in the morning by the time the hunt began.

'We'll be riding out at eleven tomorrow, boys,' he said. 'I don't know what instructions Davies has given you but that's when the hunt starts so we'll need the horses ready in plenty of time prior to that.'

'We're here from seven, sir,' I said.

'Well, I suppose that will be time enough.' He glanced at his watch. 'Hadn't you ought to be getting off to bed then if you have to be up that early? I don't want you late.' He smiled down at us and I smiled back in order to make myself agreeable but Jack barely moved. I noticed that Nat kept looking across at him a little apprehensively, as if he was worried that he might suddenly overturn the table and throttle him. The atmosphere of sheer distaste was palpable in the room. 'I'll be off then,' he said eventually. 'Until tomorrow.'

He closed the door quietly behind him and I breathed a sigh of relief. I was sure that he was going to make some mention of the fact that we were both drinking his father's beer when he knew just as well as we did that it was off limits to us, but he had either not cared or not noticed.

'You're not scared of him, are you, Mattie?' asked Jack after a moment, eyeing me suspiciously. I laughed.

'Scared of him?' I said. 'You've got to be kidding me.'

'He's just a man, after all,' he replied. 'Hardly even that.'

I sat back in the chair and thought about it. I *wasn't* scared of him, Jack was wrong about that. I'd come across a lot more threatening individuals than Nat Pepys in my time and managed to see most of them off. But I was intimidated. I wasn't much used to authority and I certainly wasn't used to it when it was only a year or two older than I was myself. I couldn't quite put my finger on it, but there was definitely something about

Nat Pepys that made me nervous. I looked up at the clock on the kitchen wall as it struck midnight.

'I'd better be off,' I said, draining my bottle and putting it in my pocket as I stood up in order to discard it in a ditch on the way home to the Ambertons'. 'I'll see you tomorrow.'

Jack raised his own bottle to me in salute but said nothing as I opened the door, letting in a sudden brace of moonlight, and stepped back out into the cold. As I turned the corner to go down the driveway I could see the window reflecting the entertainment that Nat was putting on for his friends; it was noisy and boisterous and I could hear a man's voice shouting about something and then silence as a young girl began to sing. In the half-light, I looked around me at this vast house in which I worked and wondered whether I would ever be able to live like that myself. How are some people born into lives like this? I wondered. And what does one have to do to attain such wealth?

But I was wrong if I thought it could never be my turn.

Dominique and one of the more presentable kitchen maids had been hand-picked by Nat to stand near the stables with trays of port on the morning of the hunt. They were dressed in the smartest outfits which could be provided for them and it was clear that the attention of most of the males in the party was directed towards my 'sister'. She was aware of it, I think, but barely looked at any of them as she moved from person to person, offering drinks, smiling politely, enjoying the attention. I had grinned when I saw her emerge from the kitchen, in the way that one often smiles to see a friend dressed to the nines, but she practically ignored

288

me, obviously perceiving some sort of professional superiority to me.

Jack and I led the horses out and tied them at various stages around the yard. As Nat and his friends wandered around, helping themselves to drinks from Dominique's tray, they also ignored both of us, complimenting the horses on their fine appearance, as if they had had anything to do with it. Jack didn't care – he barely noticed, I think – but it bothered me a little, for I had worked hard and felt as if some recognition of that fact was in order. I was young.

Eventually the hunt began and the troop of dogs and horses disappeared through the gates of Cageley House and into the vast countryside that lay beyond with no small amount of commotion. For minutes afterwards I could hear the incessant yapping of the dogs as they chased out over the hills, and the hollow notes played by the horns which followed them. As Dominique and her friend Mary-Ann began their work in the kitchen, preparing the food for later and clearing away the glasses which had already been used, Jack and I stepped inside for our morning break. The two girls were giggling about something as we entered but stopped suddenly as they saw us, throwing knowing glances towards each other which, by their very nature, excluded Jack and me. As usual, he headed straight for the pantry to help himself to whatever was on offer while I took my seat at the table, hoping for some friendly words from Dominique, something that would prove to me that she still cared.

'I'd like to go on one of them hunts myself,' said Mary-Ann, pulling a huge sack of potatoes in from the pantry and collapsing in a kitchen chair with a large pot of water by her feet as she started to peel them. 'The way they all get to dress up like that and ride around the countryside. Beats sitting here peelin' spuds, that's for sure.'

'You'd fall off your horse if you tried it,' said Jack quickly. 'You'd break your bloody neck. When was the last time you sat on the back of a horse?'

'I could *learn*, couldn't I? It can't be that difficult if the likes of Nat Pepys can manage it.'

'He's probably been doing it all his life,' I said, standing up for Jack's position, and Dominique shot me a look of disgust. 'But you could probably manage it anyway,' I muttered then in order to appease her.

'You heard about his engagement, of course,' said Mary-Ann after a few moments, her face contorting into a mask of I-know-something-you-don't-know. We all looked at her in surprise.

'Nat's getting married?' asked Jack; it was clearly news to him.

'Not any more he ain't,' said Mary-Ann. 'It was said that he was about to become engaged to some tart in London. The daughter of one of his father's friends, I heard. But they say she found out that he'd gone and got himself drunk and gone off to one of them houses where no gentleman should be seen going and she broke it off with him because of it.'

Jack snorted a laugh. 'Lucky her,' he said. 'I mean, after all, who in their right mind would want to marry that ugly—'

'Oh, I don't know,' she replied. 'He ain't so bad. Plus he's got a third share of this place coming to him one day and that can't be bad. Money has a wonderful way of distracting you from a man's face, you know.'

'That's what you like about him then, is it, Mary-Ann?' asked Jack, shaking his head contemptuously.

'There's a lot more to a man than the things he owns, you know.'

'Funny that,' she replied, sniffing slightly as she concentrated on her potatoes. 'Usually it's only them that has things that comes out with lines like that. Not those who haven't got two pennies to rub together.'

I looked around at my surroundings and thought how wonderful it would be to be simply born into money, to inherit it without having to do a single thing along the way. 'A man like him could never make a woman happy,' I said then, anxious to please Jack, who barely acknowledged what I was saying anyway. Mary-Ann let out a loud laugh.

'And what would the likes of you know about pleasing a woman?' she screamed, the tears rolling down her cheek. 'You've probably never so much as held a girl's hand. You're just a baby still.' I said nothing, just looked down at the table, blushing furiously, aware that Dominique had turned around to the sink and was standing with her back to us all. 'What about it, girl?' asked Mary-Ann, looking at her. 'Has this brother of yours ever known a woman, do you think?'

'I don't know,' she replied gruffly. 'And it's not something I want to think about, thank you very much. Some of us have work to do even if others haven't.' I noticed that she was adopting some of the speech patterns of the area and wondered whether I was as well. Mary-Ann simply laughed some more and, when I did look up again, I could see Jack staring at Dominique's red face and back at me with an expression which mingled surprise and amusement. I stood up quickly and went back out to the stables.

When Nat and his friends arrived back at Cageley House later on that evening, they brought with them news of a casualty. I heard them coming from some distance and stood at the top of the driveway, watching as the dogs stormed towards me in a pack, followed by the exhausted horses and their riders. Nat had a passenger on his horse, a young lady whose face was quite pale, except for her eyes which betrayed the fact that she had been crying. The riders all descended and one of the taller young men, not Nat himself, helped her down and carried her into the house. I watched in surprise, wondering what had taken place, as Nat came towards me, his face contorted in worry.

'Bit of an accident,' he said, not actually bothering to look at me but watching as his friends all went inside, where they were immediately met by the butler. 'Janet, Miss Logan that is, took a bit of a leap from her horse when it refused at a fence. Sprained her ankle, I think. Poor thing never shut up squealing about it for half an hour.'

I nodded and looked around me, counting the horses. Eight had gone out but only seven had returned. 'So where's her horse?' I asked quietly.

'Ah,' said Nat, pressing his lips together briefly before scratching his head and giving an innocent shrug. 'Horse is in a bit of bother actually. It took a bit of a tumble when Janet flew over the top. It fell and gave itself quite a nasty knock. It's in a bad way.'

My heart sank inside. Although these were not the horses that I had been attending to over the previous few months, my connection with those belonging to Sir Alfred had instilled in me a love of the creatures which had never existed before. There was a raw strength to them which I admired, a power which we had harnessed and which had become ours to command. I loved the smell of the horses, the feel of them, the way their enormous, wet eyes could stare at you with complete trust. My favourite task at Cageley House was brushing down the horses, pressing the brushes hard into their skins until they whinnied in ecstasy and returned a walnut shine from their shanks which gave credit to our commitment and their beauty. To hear now of an injured horse, any injured horse, upset me. 'You had to kill it?' I asked expectantly, and Nat gave an uncaring shrug.

'Didn't have a gun with me, Zulu,' he said, mis-pronouncing my name somewhat. 'Had to leave the poor creature where she was, collapsed on the ground.'

'You *left* her there?' I asked, amazed.

'Well, she couldn't get up. I think her leg was broken. And, as none of us had a gun and we weren't about to bash its brains in with a rock, there was nothing we could do. Thought I'd come back here and fetch one of you boys. Where's Holby anyway?'

I looked around and could see Jack talking to Dominique through the kitchen window. He took a glance at us and came out slowly, heading towards the seven horses with the intention of beginning our work on them. I went over and explained to him what had happened and he looked at Nat, shaking his head in fury.

'You just *left* her there?' he asked, almost echoing my own words. 'What were you thinking of, Nat? You should carry a gun when you go on a hunt like that in case of emergencies. *Any* emergencies.'

'It's *Mr* Pepys to you, Holby,' said Nat, his face flush-ing with anger at the insolence. 'And I never carry handguns if I can avoid it. For God's sake,' he added quickly, 'all we have to do is go back and kill the creature. It won't take long.'

293

Jack and I stared at him, our bodies erect as his slumped slightly in humiliation. For the first time it became clear to me how much more of a man I was – or Jack for that matter – than this fool. Any deference which existed in me out of a sense of respect for his position left me in that moment and it was all that I could do to keep control of my temper.

'I'll go,' said Jack eventually, heading towards the house for a gun. 'Where did you leave her anyway?'

'No,' snapped Nat, finding his strength again and refusing to allow himself to be pushed around by two inferiors, 'Zulu can go. And I'll go with him to show him where she is. You stay here and tend to these horses. I want them watered, fed and cleaned, all right? And make it sharpish.'

Jack's mouth opened as if to protest but Nat was already going towards the house himself by now and all I could do was stand there and shrug at him. I went to the stable and took out two of Sir Alfred's horses, as I didn't want to exhaust the hunters any more, and led them out just as Nat emerged with a pistol, whose chamber he checked before mounting the horse. He didn't so much as look at Jack as he rode away and I followed quickly, a far less experienced rider than he, not entirely sure that I could keep pace with him.

It was a good twenty minutes before Nat found the spot where the horse had fallen. We pulled up at some distance and walked carefully towards her. I was afraid what condition she might be in, whether she might have already died, and hoped inside that she would not in fact even be there; perhaps the injury was not so serious as Nat had thought and she had managed to stand up again and was wandering around lost. But I was not so lucky. The mare, a hazel-hued three-year-old with a large white circle around one of her eyes, lay shaking on a mat of leaves and branches, her head bobbing around spastically, her eyes staring out blindly towards the distance, her mouth foaming slightly in her pain. I recognized the horse from that morning – the white patch gave her away – and she was a beauty, strong and muscular with taut legs in which the muscles and tendons could be identified as she walked. Nat and I stared at the poor creature for a few moments before looking at each other and I thought I could see an iota of regret in his eyes. Once again, I wanted to say, 'I can't believe you just left her here', but realized that the moment for insolence had passed and that I could instead receive a beating from his whip if I wasn't careful.

'Well?' I said eventually, nodding at him and looking towards the pistol which stood out in his jacket pocket. 'Aren't you going to do it?'

He took out the gun and his face grew a little pale. He stared at the butt and licked his dry lips before looking at me. 'Ever done this, have you? Ever had to kill a horse?' I shook my head and swallowed hard.

'No,' I said. 'And I don't want to now, if it's all the same to you.'

He snorted and stared at the gun again for a moment, and the horse, before thrusting it at me. 'Don't be such a bloody coward,' he said quickly. 'And do as you're told. Do . . . what has to be done.' I took the gun and knew immediately that he had never done this himself either, 'Just aim it directly at the beast's brains and pull the trigger,' he announced and I could feel the anger swelling within me. 'Try and get a clean shot though, Zulu, for Christ's sake,' he continued. 'We don't want to create too much of a mess.'

He turned around, lifting his boot and wiping at the toe of it with great concentration, waiting for me to take the fatal shot. I looked at the horse, whose movements were as shaky as ever and I knew that for her sake there was no more time to waste. I reached out my hand and settled it around the unfamiliar pistol – a shape I had never had to make before – and covered it with my left hand in order to stop it from shaking. Stepping closer to her head, I looked away and the second I could feel the gorge rise within me, I pulled the trigger and was immediately thrown back with the unfamiliar recoil. Neither of us said anything for a moment – I was stunned and the ringing in my ears took away all memory of the incident for a few seconds. I looked at my work and was pleased to see that the horse had stopped shaking. Through great fortune, I had achieved a clean shot and, with the exception of a smoking circle of red, whose colour leaked down into the horse's white-patched eye, there did not seem to be any great difference between the scene of a few moments earlier and the one that presented itself now.

'Is it done?' asked Nat, who had not turned around. I looked at his back and said nothing for a moment. I could see his whole body shaking and, without knowing why exactly, my hand lifted again and I aimed the pistol at the back of his head. 'Is it done, Zulu?' he asked.

'It's Zéla,' I said, my voice calm and steady now. 'My name is Matthieu Zéla. And yes, it's done.'

He turned around then but avoided looking at the body. 'Well,' he said eventually as we went towards our own horses. 'I suppose that's what you get for not doing what you're told.' I looked at him quizzically and he smiled. 'Well, she wanted the horse to jump the fence,' he explained. 'Miss Logan, that is. She wanted her to jump and she reared on her. And now look at her. That's what she gets. When we get back, you'd better tell Holby to organize someone to clear her off to the knacker's yard, yes?'

He didn't look at me or speak to me again as he mounted his horse and rode back in the direction of Cageley House. Suddenly I was forced to steady myself against a tree, where I felt my knees give way beneath me and my stomach turn over until its contents were on the ground at my feet. When I stood up again, my forehead was perspiring and the taste in my mouth was hideous. And, without quite knowing why, I started to cry. Small sobs at first, then great, dry heaving sounds, empty of noise for moments at a time, then filled with misery. I rolled myself up in a ball on the ground and lay there for what seemed like an eternity. My life, I thought. My only life.

It was dark when I returned home to the Ambertons' that night, and I went there only after Jack and I had disposed of the mare's body ourselves.

297

Chapter 17

With the Bulls and the Bears of 'The Great Society'

After the death of my eighth wife Constance in Hollywood in 1921, I decided to move as far away from California as possible, while yet remaining in the United States. Constance's death had left me depressed – she had died in a senseless car crash immediately following our wedding, an accident which had also seen off my nephew Tom, a teenage starlet and her own sister Amelia – and at the age of 178, I was left floundering, wondering where my life could possibly go from there. For the first, and perhaps only, time in my 256 years, I questioned my body's ability to continue its rigorous insistence upon being locked into a middle-aged appearance and vigour. I felt like giving up, removing myself from the tiresome existence which I seemed destined to be stuck within for ever, and it took a certain strength of will to prevent myself from going to the nearest doctor's office, explaining my situation, and seeing whether he could help me to age, or simply to end it all there and then.

However, this depression, such as it was, eventually passed. As I have said, I do not in general feel that my condition is a negative one; without it I would most

298

likely have been dead by the beginning of the 1800s and never had as many experiences as I have been blessed with. Age can be a cruel thing but, as long as you still have your looks and a little financial security, there's always an awful lot to do.

I stayed in California until the end of the year as there seemed no point beginning a fresh life so close to the holiday season, but then moved to Washington DC in 1922 where I bought a small house in Georgetown and invested in a chain of restaurants. Their owner, Mitch Lendl, was a Czech immigrant who had come to America in the 1870s and, in traditional style, made his fortune and bastardized his first name, from Miklôs to the more American moniker. He was looking to expand his chain around the capital but could not afford to do so. His credit rating with the banks was good but he didn't trust them not to recall any loan that they might give him and lay claim to his empire so he decided to look for an investor instead. I got to know him quite well from the simple fact that I enjoyed dining in his establishments and we hit it off; eventually I agreed to go in on the venture myself and it became profitable. Lendl's restaurants began to pop up around the state and through Miklôs's knowledge of good chefs – I always called him Miklôs, never Mitch – we established a fine reputation and a successful business.

Food has never been an abiding interest of mine; I like to dine well but then that is not a trait that singles me out from the masses. However, during this era, my one foray into the restaurant trade, I learned a little about food, particularly about the importing of fine delicacies and speciality foods from other countries, which was something in which we at Lendl's specialized. I became concerned about what we were actually serving in our restaurants and soon we made it a policy that nothing unhealthy would ever be served from our premises; indeed, it became something of a catchphrase for us. Through Miklôs's talent and skills, we served the most tender vegetables, the choicest cuts of meat and the most delicious cakes known to man. Our tables were full every night.

In 1926 I was invited to join an executive committee of the Food Administration and it was while I was a member of that panel, analysing the dietary habits of Washingtonians and putting together a common policy which could help improve them, that I met Herb Hoover, who had been a member of the same committee some years earlier under President Wilson. Although now serving as Secretary of Commerce, Herb had maintained an interest in our work, as it had been one of his abiding passions throughout his career. We became friends and would dine together frequently, a difficult business when everyone in the restaurant wanted to speak to him on some personal matter every time they passed by.

'They all think that I can help them out in some way,' he told me one evening as we sat at a secluded table in Lendl's, nursing our brandies after a large meal prepared to the very highest standards by Miklôs himself. 'They think that because I'm Secretary of Commerce I can give them some sort of tax break or something if they become my friends.'

Some chance. Herb was well known to be one of the straightest and most incorruptible men in the cabinet. How he had even ended up in such an important financial job was beyond me, considering his history of humanitarianism and, some might say, charity. When the Germans had overrun the Low Countries after the outbreak of the First World War, Herb had been in London and had been entrusted by the Allies with the task of getting food through to the Belgians, something he did with great success; the country might have starved without him. He had taken a great personal gamble a few years after that when, in 1921, he had seen to it that aid had been extended to Soviet Russia at the very height of their famine. When criticized for thus lending a helping hand to Bolshevism, he had roared back from the floor of the House, 'Twenty million people are starving. Whatever their politics, they shall be fed!'

'I don't know how I got it myself,' he acknowledged, referring to his current position. 'But I seem to be doing it all right!' he added with a wide grin, his jowly, cheerful features extending across his face and crinkling his eyes at the corner. And he was right; the country was prosperous and his tenure in the cabinet seemed secure.

I enjoyed his company enormously, I must admit, and was excited when he was elected president in late 1928 for it had been some time since I had a close connection with someone in a position of power, and there had never been anyone quite like Herbert Hoover in the White House. I attended his inauguration in March 1929, the day before I was due to leave for New York, and listened as he praised the country for rebuilding itself after the Great War and admitted pride in his fellow citizens as they faced the peacetime years ahead. His speech, although a little long and heavy on the kind of detail that the American people did not necessarily need to hear, was optimistic and cheerful and boded well for the four years to come. I had very little time to speak to him afterwards, of course, but wished him well, believing that the respect which the American people held for him, his own humanitarian nature, and the peaceful, economically prosperous country that he was inheriting bode about as well for him as for any of his predecessors. I little thought that, by the end of the year, the country would be entering into a great depression and that his presidency would be destroyed before it had even got off the ground.

I expected even less the personal price that those close to me would pay because of it.

Denton Irving loved to take risks. His father, Magnus Irving, had been the head of a large New York investment firm, CartellCo., which he in turn had inherited from his late father-in-law, Joseph Cartell. At the age of sixty-one, Magnus suffered a stroke which incapacitated him and Denton, who had spent the best part of his thirty-six years on the planet working as an investment specialist and vice-president with the firm, took over. Herb, then President Hoover, had brought us together a couple of years earlier in Washington and we had become friends; I looked him up immediately after I descended upon New York, told him of my plans for the future and sought his advice.

Miklôs and I had received a generous offer from a consortium of investors for our restaurant chain and we had decided to accept it, a decision which precipitated my departure from the capital. The offer was over and above what we could have ever expected to receive from a single buyer and far surpassed the kind of money that we could make together in a (regular) lifetime. Also, Miklôs was not getting any younger and did not have any children who possessed quite as much instinct for the catering industry as he did and so it seemed like the right time to sell up. However, it meant that, in addition to my regular shares and accounts, I now had a large stockpile of money which I needed to invest. When the time came, Denton seemed to be the right man to talk to.

This was in March 1929 and within a week he had put together a reasonably solid investment portfolio for me, dividing my money between perennial bloomers such as US Steel and General Motors, fresh growers such as Eastman Kodak and a few new and innovative companies as well, which we believed could take off and turn a profit for a man willing to take a chance or two. Denton was an intelligent man but I found that he had no patience and, on that point, we were quite different from each other. From the moment he knew that I wanted to invest a substantial amount of money, he was calling all his contacts, trying to find the best options for me, the wisest ventures, as if he himself was going to be the beneficiary of whatever profits I eventually made. His enthusiasm entertained me, and gave me great confidence in his abilities, and I found that I enjoyed his company enormously.

At the same time, a young woman whom I had never met before entered my life. Her name was Annette Weathers and she was a thirty-three-year-old post office clerk from Milwaukee. She arrived at my apartment near Central Park on a wet April evening with two bags and an eight-year-old boy by her side. I opened my door to find her standing there, a soaking rag who was doing all she could to keep herself from crying as she held the hand of her small son tightly. I looked at her in surprise, wondering who on earth she could possibly be and what she wanted from me, but I only had to take one look at the boy to figure it out.

'Mr Zéla,' she said, putting a bag down and extending

303

me her hand. 'I'm sorry to bother you but I wrote to you in California and I never heard back from you.'

'I haven't lived there in some years,' I explained, still standing in the doorway. 'I moved to—'

'Washington, I know,' she replied firmly. 'I'm sorry to come all this way but I didn't know what else to do. It's just that we're . . . we're . . .' She never made it to the end of her sentence as her battle to keep control of her tears was lost and she collapsed in a heap at my feet. The boy stared at me suspiciously as if I had been the one who had caused his mother to cry and I wasn't quite sure what to do. My last experience with a child his age had been about a century and a half before, when my own brother Tomas was a lad; in general I had steered clear of children ever since. I opened the door and ushered them inside, leading her towards a bathroom where she might regain her composure with a little dignity and seated the boy in a large armchair where he continued to stare at me with a mixture of awe and disgust.

An hour or so later, relaxing in front of the fire, freshly washed and wearing a thick, woollen dressing gown, Annette explained both her visit and her existence in the most apologetic of terms, even though I already knew exactly who she was.

'You contacted me after your wedding, you remember,' she began, 'when your poor wife died.'

'I remember,' I said, a vision of Constance rearing up in my head; it occurred to me suddenly how long it had been since I had spared her a thought and I despised myself for it.

'My poor Tom died that day too. It's not been easy without him, you know.'

'No, I can imagine. I'm sorry I haven't been of more help.' Annette was Tom's widow; I had hardly known

304

the boy but he had attended my marriage to Constance and lost his life because of it. I remembered him well from the day itself; even now I can see him working the room, introducing himself to Charlie and Doug and Mary, people he had seen on the big screen and in the newspapers and movie magazines. He had attempted to ingratiate himself with some teenage girl who had appeared in a few Sennett shorts and had been unfortunate enough to be standing in the spot where Constance and Amelia's car had landed after their accident. It was his own name that had appeared in the papers the following day. Annette had not been present; she had been pregnant at the time and hadn't wanted to travel from Milwaukee to California, although I suspected from what Tom had said that he had refused her permission to accompany him. From his behaviour on that one single day, I suspected that their marriage was not a strong one.

She was a fresh looking girl, with short, frizzy blonde hair and pale cheeks, the kind of girl who usually got tied to the train tracks by evil old men in the movies. Her eyes were wide with small pupils and her features were gentle and unaccentuated, with the most unblemished skin I had seen in a century. I felt instantly protective of her, not just for her son's or her husband's sake, but for her own. She had struggled for eight years without coming to me, even though she knew that I had money, and I guessed that for her to arrive now was not an act of greed on her part, but a simple act of necessity or desperation.

'I feel terrible,' I admitted, raising my palms in the air in a desperate gesture. 'I should have got in touch with you myself, if for no other reason than that this boy here is my nephew. How are you, Thomas, anyway?'

305

'We call him Tommy. But how did you know his name?' she asked me, no doubt running through our conversation in her mind to recall whether she had mentioned it. I shrugged and smiled at her.

'Lucky guess,' I said. The boy said nothing. 'Doesn't say much, does he?' I asked.

'He's just tired,' she replied. 'Perhaps he could take a rest for a while. If there was a spare bed at all?'

I jumped up immediately. 'Of course he can,' I said. 'And there is. Just follow me.' He leaned over towards his mother in fright and I looked at her, unsure what to do for the best.

'I'll take him in if that's all right,' she said, standing up and lifting the child from the floor with an easy movement, even though he was an average sized eight-year-old and didn't need picking up or carrying around by anyone. 'He gets nervous around strangers.' I didn't mind, and showed her the room and she stayed with him for fifteen minutes or so until he fell asleep. When she reappeared I gave her a brandy and told her that they must stay the night.

'I don't want to bother you,' she said and I could see her eyes fill with tears again. 'But I would appreciate it. I have to be honest with you, Mr Zéla—'

'Matthieu, please.'

She smiled. 'I have to be honest with you, *Matthieu*, the reason I've come here is because you are my last resort. I don't have a job any more, I haven't had one in a while. Some of the clerks were laid off about a year ago and I've been struggling through on my savings ever since. Then I missed a payment on our small home and we had nowhere to go. My mother died last year and I had hoped that we might inherit something then but her house was mortgaged to the bank and there

306

was nothing left after they were paid off. And I have no other family, you see. I wouldn't have come, but Tommy . . .' She drifted off and put a hand to her mouth as she sniffled slightly.

'The boy needs a home, of course,' I said. 'Listen to me, Annette. You mustn't worry. You should have come to me earlier. Or I should have come to you. One or the other. But either way, he is my nephew and you're my niece of a sort, and I'm happy to help you. Thrilled to help you.' I paused. 'What I mean is,' I added, as if further clarification was needed, 'I'm *going* to help you.'

She stared at me as if I was more than she could have ever hoped for, then put her glass down and came over to give me a hug. 'Thank you . . .' she began before giving up the fight completely and letting the tears come. And, when they came, it was like a downpour.

Fate has a way of bringing the most unexpected people together. I made an appointment with Denton to discuss a few questions I had regarding some investments and he had to cancel our meeting to attend a funeral.

'It's my secretary,' he explained over the phone. 'She's gone and got herself *murdered*, would you believe?'

'Murdered?' I asked in surprise. 'My God. How did that happen?' I remembered the woman from my meetings with Denton in the past; a plain sort with a constant odour of cold cream about her.

'Well, we're not quite sure yet. Seems she got herself involved with some man who moved in with her, some actor type I'm told, and they were talking about getting married. Then he came home one night after having missed out on an audition for some Broadway part and hit her one too many times. Poor thing didn't stand a chance.'

I shivered. 'That's terrible,' I said quietly.

'Sure is.'

'Has he been caught?'

'Oh, he's locked up in a city cell even as we speak. But I gotta go, all right? Her funeral's in about an hour and I'm dog late as it is.'

I'm not a man who likes to take advantage of another's misfortune but it occurred to me shortly afterwards how suitable Annette would be for the vacant position. She had several years' experience working as a postal clerk, which I assumed brought her into contact with a lot of office administration, and over and above that she was an intelligent girl, friendly and helpful, who I believed could be an asset to his firm. By then, she had been staying with me for a few weeks but had managed to land herself a job as a waitress while Tommy was at school. It didn't pay much and she insisted on giving me a portion of her earnings for her keep, even though I tried to decline, for the pittance she earned could hardly have been divided down any further.

'But I don't *need* it, Annette. I should be supplementing you.'

'You are, by allowing us to live here rent free. Please, just take it. It would make me feel better.'

Although it bothered me, I could see how important it was for her to feel that she was contributing to the household in some way. She had spent all of her son's life being self-sufficient, being solely responsible for his upkeep, and she had succeeded brilliantly. Although he was a very quiet child, he was intelligent and likeable; once we got to know each other a little better he became relaxed around me, as I did around him, and I found that I enjoyed returning to my apartment in the evening after wherever my day had taken me and discovering the two of them there, Annette preparing a little dinner for us all, Tommy sitting quietly with a book. Our domestic life quickly settled into an easy, unpressurized routine, and I felt as if they had been there for ever. As for our own relationship, although Annette was an extremely attractive girl, I immediately saw her as how I had described her on our first night – a niece – and our relationship was clear and relaxed.

Denton agreed to meet with Annette about the job, and she was more than keen to meet with him, having discovered that the joys of waitressing are not enormous, and the interview must have gone well for he offered her the position immediately and she was overjoyed. She thanked me profusely for my help and bought me a new pipe with her first week's salary.

'I wanted to buy you something that you'd appreciate,' she said. 'And I saw your collection of pipes over there. And, although you really should quit for health reasons, I got you one anyway. How long have you been smoking, might I ask?'

'Too long,' I said, recalling the first time Jack Holby had introduced me to the joys of the pipe. 'Many, many years now. But look at me: I'm still here.'

I kept a close eye on the economy. Investments were taking up most of my business life then and I read the newspapers and listened to the analysts carefully. I had a lot of money invested in various enterprises and, while Denton was a great adviser to me, I made sure to keep track of where everything was going myself. I attended a public meeting given by the National

309

Association of Credit Men at a hall in TriBeCa where they warned about the state of the public finances, claiming that the level of investment credit in the country was at its highest in history. Their advice to both businessmen like myself and the banks' lending institutions was to exercise caution as any credit pinch could, they claimed, have the most devastating consequences.

'Don't worry about it,' Denton told me. 'They're right in what they say – the level of credit *is* far too high – but it's not exactly going to bankrupt the country. Look at Herb, for Chrissakes. He's got his hand shoved so far up the ass of the Federal Reserve that it would take about ten tonnes of dynamite to shift it.'

'I think I want to liquidize a little,' I said, charmed as ever by his turn of phrase. 'Just a few things here and there. Nothing too substantial. I've been hearing stories and I don't much like what I hear. This Florida business for one . . .'

Denton laughed and slammed his hand down so hard on his desk that not only did I jump in surprise, but Annette ran in from the outer office to see what had happened. 'It's all right, honey,' said Denton quickly, smiling across at her warmly. 'I'm just making my point in my usual boorish manner.'

She laughed and pointed her pencil at him before leaving the room. 'You'll give yourself a heart attack if you're not careful,' she said flirtatiously, turning on her heels and closing the door behind her. I turned around – even though she was clearly no longer there – surprised by the intimacy of their brief remarks and, when I turned back, Denton was staring at the closed door with puppy dog eyes.

'Denton,' I said cautiously, trying to redirect his attention. 'Denton, we were talking about Florida.'

He looked at me as if he wasn't sure either who I was or what I was doing there before shaking his head, as a wet dog might do to dislodge the rain, and returning to the conversation. 'Florida, Florida, Florida,' he said, lost in a daydream as he tried to recall what the word meant, and then: *'Florida!'* he roared for no apparent reason. 'I told you, don't worry about Florida. You know, what's happened down there is about the biggest financial bust in the history of the so-called sunshine state and up here in New York City, where the real money is, you know who gives a damn?'

'Who?' I asked, although I knew what he was going to say even before he said it.

'Jack F. Squat,' he said. 'That's who. No one at all. Not a soul.'

I frowned. 'I don't know,' I said. 'I still hear talk about the same thing happening here.' I wasn't prepared just to let the matter drop when my entire future financial stability could be at stake.

'Look, Matthieu,' he said slowly, rubbing his eyes as if he was dealing with a child. One of the things I liked about Denton was his absolute belief in himself and the completely arrogant manner with which he dismissed anyone who questioned him. 'You wanna know what went on down there in Florida? I'll tell you what went on. 'Cos I don't know what your sources are or where you're getting your information from but I do know that they're probably all screwed up. Down there in Florida the last few years have been like a re-enactment of the Oklahoma land rush. Anyone with ten cents down there has been buying up land like it's been going out of style. You want to know something, and this is top secret 'cos I got this from a guy I know in Washington and I think we both know who I mean so there's no

311

going outside of this room and talking about it, but the fact is that over the last few years investors have staked out more house lots in Florida than there are families in the entire *U*-nited States of America. What do you think of that?'

I laughed. 'You're kidding me,' I said. Even I hadn't heard that fact, and wasn't entirely convinced of its veracity.

'It's the case, my friend,' he said. 'Florida is one of the most underdeveloped states in the union and people have been just cottoning on to that fact over the last ten years or so. But they've sold and sold and sold and sold until there wasn't anything left to sell. So then you know what they did? They sold it all over again. Millions upon millions of house sites sold that there isn't even the room for, but worse, not even the people in the whole Goddam country to fill, even if you could get everybody to relocate to Florida which' – here he snorted and bounced back in his chair – 'is even less likely. Do you know that if every man, woman and child in America was to suddenly descend on Florida the earth would be thrown off balance and we'd all go floating off into outer space?'

I hesitated and my eyes flickered from side to side nervously. 'No, Denton,' I said. 'No, I was not aware of that.'

'And! And!' he shouted, hitting the desk again in excitement. 'I'll tell you something else too. If everyone in China jumped up at the same moment, the same thing would happen. The whole axis or whatever it is would just break down, gravity would stop, we'd all go flying off to Mars. So, if you ask me, China could be the most powerful country in the world if only they'd think about it. They could hold the entire planet to ransom, just by threatening to jump up a few centimetres. Think about that!'

I thought about it and hoped that he was finished. 'That's all very interesting, Denton,' I said, stating his name with some firmness to make it clear that we were finished discussing China's global strategies for world domination. 'But I think we're getting off the subject somewhat. I just think it's important to do a little liquidizing and I'm sorry, but that's how I feel.'

'Hey, it's your money,' said Denton, leaning back with a smile. 'I'm just here to serve you,' he added graciously.

'Well,' I said, unable to prevent a laugh from escaping my mouth. 'Let's get on to it then. A little here and a little there, that's all. Let's not go crazy. Just come up with some ideas and let me know.'

'Will do,' he said. I stood up to leave, shook his hand and made for the door. 'One last thing, Matthieu,' he said suddenly before I could open it. 'And then I'll let you go.' I smiled and raised an eyebrow as if to say yes? 'That Florida thing. You know it wasn't the overspeculation that blew them out, don't you?'

'It wasn't?' I asked, surprised because that was what I had assumed had caused their troubles. 'What did then?'

'The hurricane,' he said. 'It's that simple. One son-of-a-bitch hurricane came flying through Florida late last year and caused millions of dollars' worth of damage. When it was all counted the truth about the overspeculating came out. Wasn't for that they'd still be doing it today. It was all the hurricane's fault. And I can't see any hurricanes coming down Fifth Avenue, can you?' I shrugged, unsure. 'And you know what the

313

moral of the story is, don't you?' he asked as I opened the door and prepared to leave.

'Go on,' I said, glad that I had paid for an hour's entertainment if nothing else. 'Tell me. What's the moral of the story?'

'The moral of the story,' he repeated, leaning forward and placing his hands flat on the desk in front of him, 'is that every so often a natural disaster comes along, an act of God, and it blows all the dust away and when it does people can see that whatever's left underneath ain't so pretty. You get it?'

Denton Irving was Old Money. Although his own father had inherited the firm from his father-in-law, the money on that side went back generations, almost to Pilgrim days. And despite the fact that his father's stroke meant that he could no longer compete in the day to day world of the firm, he pulled a lot of strings from the sidelines, watching most of his son's moves carefully and commenting on them in about the most ungracious manner possible.

I knew that Denton lived both in awe and in terror of his father. A giant of a man who had worked out in his private gym every day of his life – and this was long before such things were fashionable – I knew that he had been a strict father by the way Denton sat up straight in his chair or got a look of tension across his face whenever he phoned.

As 1929 went on, I continued to liquidize a lot of my portfolio, just as Denton himself buried his firm deeper and deeper into options which he claimed could never go wrong for him – solid firms like Union Pacific or Goodrich. As summer approached, the economy slipped as industrial production and prices began to fall. President Hoover forced the Federal Reserve to raise its discount rates in order to discourage speculation in the stock market, but nothing that he did seemed to work. The amount of money being poured into the stock market simply rose and rose until it was near to reaching saturation point. To calm nerves, both Hoover and the New York governor, Franklin Delano Roosevelt, declared their optimism in the Stock Exchange, Hoover himself referring to 'The Great Society' which could never be overcome; whether he was referring to the country or Wall Street I wasn't so sure.

At the same time, I became aware of a romance which had developed between Denton and Annette. She would often return home late from work in a flurry of excitement after he had taken her out to dinner or dancing. She seemed happy and excited by this new relationship and I encouraged it, for I was fond of Denton and he could certainly afford to give her and her son a happy lifestyle if things developed that far.

'I little expected to be playing matchmaker,' I told her one evening as we sat in my home, a rare evening when Denton was not with us. I was reading the new Hemingway novel, *A Farewell To Arms*, which had just been published, while she sat sewing new buttons on to some of Tommy's shirts. 'I thought I was just setting you up with a job, not a husband.'

She laughed. 'I don't know how far it will go,' she admitted, 'although I am very fond of him. I know he blusters around a lot and tries to make everyone think that he's so in control, but inside he's a lot quieter.'

'Really,' I said, finding it hard to imagine.

'It's true. That father of his . . .' She shook her head and looked back down at her work. 'I really shouldn't speak of this,' she said quietly.

'Whatever you prefer,' I said, 'but remember you're not involved with his father, just himself.'

'He interferes, you see,' she continued, clearly wanting to talk about it anyway. 'He breathes down poor Denton's neck every minute of the day. You'd think he was still running the place.'

'He has a lot of money tied up there,' I said, playing devil's advocate. 'And a lifetime of work too. It's only natural that he would—'

'Yes, but he asked Denton to take over the firm. When he had his stroke. And it's not as if he doesn't know what he's doing. My God, he's worked in the firm since he was seventeen.'

I nodded. She was probably right; I barely knew Magnus Irving at all, having only met him once or twice and even then he was only a shadow of the man that I knew he must have once been. But shortly afterwards, on Saturday 5 October, a great party was held at the Irving estate and when all the guests were assembled – everyone who was anyone in the New York financial world as well as a great many friends and relations – the engagement between my friend and my niece was announced. I was delighted for them both, for they looked deliriously happy, and congratulated them warmly.

'Good job my last secretary was murdered, eh?' he said to me, his face falling the moment he uttered the words. 'My God,' he said, shaking his head. 'That came out completely wrong. I meant that if it hadn't been for—'

'It's all right, Denton,' I said suspiciously. 'I know what you meant. Fate. Chance. All those sorts of things, I expect.'

'Exactly.' He looked across at Annette who was

holding court on the dance floor with a succession of bankers. 'Just look at her, eh?' he said, shaking his head in disbelief at his own good fortune. 'I can't believe she said yes. I can't believe my own luck.'

I noticed Magnus Irving dressed in a regulation tuxedo, sitting in his wheelchair at one of the tables, and nodded towards him. 'Your father,' I said, 'what does he make of the match? Does he approve?'

Denton bit his lip and looked momentarily angry, but composed himself quickly, not wishing to let anything spoil his evening. 'He's a bit concerned about the boy,' he said eventually.

'Tommy?' I said in surprise. 'Why? What's wrong with him?'

'Nothing's wrong with him,' he replied quickly. 'We get along fine. I've been getting to know him quite well recently in point of fact. No, I think that my father feels that, what with Annette having been married before, and having a child – I mean I hope you don't mind me saying this, with you being family of hers and everything, but—'

'He thinks she's a gold-digger,' I said simply.

'Well, in a word. He's just concerned that—'

'Well, it's simply not the case,' I said, stopping him in his tracks, determined to stand up for my niece-in-law's honour. 'My God, when she first got here she wouldn't even let me—'

'Matthieu, Matthieu, relax,' said Denton, placing a hand on my shoulder. '*I* don't think that's the case for even a moment. I love her, you see. And she loves me. I know she does. Everything's fine.'

I nodded and did relax, for I could see by the smile on his face that he was telling the truth. I also knew from my conversations with Annette how strongly she felt towards him. 'Good,' I said eventually. 'That's all right then.'

'And what about you?' he asked me. 'When are we going to fix you up with some charming young thing, eh? You've never remarried, have you?' he asked, believing Constance to have been my first wife.

'Several times,' I said. 'Marriage and I don't seem to agree.'

'Well, plenty of time,' he laughed, with the self-congratulatory arrogance of one who has found the love of his life. 'You're a young man still.'

Now it was my turn to laugh.

By the middle of October, I had very few stock options left on the books of CartellCo., and my relationship with Denton had changed from being a business one to a purely friendly one. I still called on him for lunch, enjoying our debates about the economy, the stock market, politics; we began to criticize Herb for never contacting us any more, although I suppose he had a lot more important things on his mind than the injured feelings of a couple of old friends. I liked my association with this happy couple and Tommy, enjoying the idea of playing the benevolent uncle in their lives. On 23 October, however, things started to go awry.

Although the market had closed on the upside for the previous few days, there was a sudden spate of selling on the 23rd that appeared to come out of nowhere. By the following day, Black Thursday, prices had all crashed to their lowest levels and did not appear to show any sign of improving. I was in Wall Street, in the stock exchange itself that afternoon with Denton, and watched as the traders on the floor screamed at each other, trying to make sales, their very hysteria helping the market to fall lower and lower. Denton was beside himself with anguish, unsure of what he could do to help matters, when a most extraordinary incident occurred.

Below us there was a sea of red jackets and young and old men all holding their tickets in the air as they tried to offload anything they could; however, not a single share was being traded. And then from the left-hand side of the exchange a young man – he couldn't have been more than about twenty-five – walked into the centre of the floor and raised his hand aloft. Over the din, which somehow seemed to lessen as his self-assurance grabbed people, he shouted out that he wanted to buy 25,000 shares of US Steel for $205 each. I looked at the board quickly.

'What's he doing?' asked Denton, his hand clutching the rail in front of himself anxiously so that the knuckles became white with the pressure. 'US Steel is down to $193.'

I shook my head. I couldn't quite grasp it myself. 'I'm not sure . . .' I began as the young man shouted out his order again to one of the traders who immediately sold the shares to him greedily, with the look of a man who could not believe his luck.

'He's steadying the market,' I said then, shaking my head in disbelief. 'The most audacious . . .' I found that I couldn't complete my sentence, so impressed was I by the gesture which within minutes saw more tentative sales taking place on the floor and a slight rise in prices. Within about half an hour they had steadied completely and it appeared as if the panic was over.

'That was incredible,' said Denton afterwards. 'I thought we were finished there for a moment.'

I wasn't so sure. I couldn't quite see what was going to

happen next but it seemed obvious that the worst was far from over. Over the next few days, the state of the stock market was on the tip of everybody's tongue and Denton himself was under siege from his father with constant questions of what he was doing to help salvage the firm's fortunes. However, as the consequences of Black Thursday began to settle in investors' minds, most people attempted to recover their losses and the dramatic selling began again. On Tuesday 29 October, the day of the Wall Street Crash, more than 16 million shares were dumped in an afternoon of trading. On that one single day, as much money was lost on the New York stock exchange as had been spent in its entirety by the US government on fighting the First World War. It was a disaster.

Annette phoned me from CartellCo. to tell me that Denton was acting crazy. His father had been phoning all day but Denton had refused to take any of the calls, finally locking himself in his office. The firm was bust – I knew that much already. Everything he owned was gone, as was most of his investors' money. I was the fortunate man in a city of terrible tragedies that day. By the time I arrived at his offices and made my way to the top floor, where his own suite was located, Annette was in a terrible state; Denton wouldn't open the door but we could hear him inside, breaking things. I could hear the sound of lamps crashing to the floor as he paced around, the incessant ringing of the phones his accompaniment as he moved.

'That'll be Magnus,' said Annette, ripping the line from the wall and silencing it at last. 'He thinks the whole fucking thing is Denton's fault.' I stared at her in surprise, having never heard her utter such a profanity before, but sure that it was called for at this point. 'You have to break the door down, Matthieu,' she said and I nodded.

I stepped back and shoved against it but it was solid oak and by the time I felt I was starting to get anywhere I could feel the bruising coming out on my shoulder. Eventually, with one last push and a kick to the lock, it fell through and Annette and I ran inside, to find Denton standing by the open window, his face contorted with madness and disarray, his clothes torn, his eyes on fire.

'Denton,' screamed Annette, tears rolling down her face as she started to run towards him, but I prevented her by holding on to her arm for I could see him edge ever closer to the window as she approached him. 'We can fix this,' she said. 'You don't need to—'

'Stay away!' he roared, jumping up on the ledge now, and my heart skipped a beat because I knew from the look on his face that all was lost. He took a look outside, licked his lips and in a moment he was gone. Annette screamed and charged to the window, leaning out so far that I feared she might fall herself but we could only barely make out his broken body on the ground below.

In time, the unfortunate Annette recovered from this tragedy although Magnus Irving suffered another stroke when he heard about what had happened to his son and he died shortly afterwards himself. I was lucky still to have my fortune pretty much intact and when I left for Hawaii for a couple of decades that Christmas I settled a decent amount on Annette and Tommy, who declined to join me but instead returned to Milwaukee where they lived out their days.

Annette and I kept in touch but she never married

again and after her son's death in Pearl Harbor she moved in with her daughter-in-law and grandson, until they in turn moved back to England where that child also fathered a son, who was to become a well known television soap opera actor and singer. Eventually we lost touch but I received a letter from her neighbour after she died, telling me that it had been quite peaceful after a long illness. She forwarded on to me a letter of gratitude from Annette which she had left in her possession, thanking me for whatever I had done for her in New York in the twenties and also sent a photograph of the three of us, Denton, Annette and I, at the ball which announced their engagement a few months before the Crash. We all looked very happy in it, very optimistic about our futures.

Chapter 18

August-September 1999

London, 12 August 1999

Dear Mr Zéla,

I have meant to call you several times since my father's funeral to thank you for the heartfelt words you said in the church that day. I can tell you that it has been a great source of comfort to all of us to know that our father was so well respected and liked within the industry.

I very much enjoyed our chat after the funeral and was only sorry that you seemed to disappear before we could finish it. You may recall we were having a discussion about my work – my writing – and you seemed keen to hear more about it. You also mentioned your nephew Tommy who you said would probably know more about the workings of the television industry than you did.

Following your advice, I finished my script and sent it along to your nephew, care of the BBC, and I'm sorry to tell you that he returned it to me, unread, with a rather terse note attached. Perhaps you forgot to mention to him that the script was on the way?

I never got a chance to talk to him or you about it, so in the best tradition of the Hollywood money-makers, I thought I'd 'pitch' it to you in one quick paragraph! So here goes:

A couple of middle-aged friends are out drinking one night and on the way home they pick up some teenage tart to take back with them. When they get there they start dabbling around in drugs, which they're not used to, and one of them ends up dead. One of the friends goes to pieces, but the other one keeps his head and phones up a young guy who owes him a few favours and asks for help. Together, they take the body elsewhere and when the guy is discovered, everyone thinks it was an accident and he was the only one involved and so no one gets dragged into the scandal. What they don't know is that in the middle of the commotion that night, the dead man's son woke up – they didn't even know he was in the house – and hears their plans and sees what they do. He thinks about calling the police to report them all but decides against it in the end because he knows that these two guys can help him out. They see the sense in it and life goes on as normal for everyone involved. No one ever finds out a thing.

That's it, Mr Zéla! You like? Well, as you can see I've sent you a copy of the full script and I've sent it to your nephew again with a better note of explanation. I'm sure you'll be able to help in raising the finance to make it and I look forward to hearing from you at your earliest convenience.

With best wishes,
Lee Hocknell

I invited Martin downstairs to my apartment for a drink, feeling that the warm, familiar surroundings of my home would be a better place to break the bad news to him about the cancellation of his show than the relatively sterile atmosphere of the station's offices. I considered his situation and how he would take it; a late middle-aged man, used to the spotlight, accustomed to people hanging on his every word, however ridiculous those words might actually be, suddenly unemployed and left to his own devices. He'd go crazy. And it wasn't the money because we didn't pay him all *that* much and he was already quite comfortable. He'd made enough as a politician to keep him for the rest of his life; he owned his house and had filled it with good paintings and *objets d'art* which hadn't come cheap. He had the kind of lifestyle that he liked to ridicule in others but enjoy for himself. I hoped he'd take the news well but, somehow, I doubted it.

I hadn't counted on Polly, his wife, coming downstairs with him and it rather threw out my prepared speech. Polly is Martin's second wife and they've been married for seven years. Needless to say, she's quite a bit younger than him – he's aged sixty-one, she's only thirty-four. His first wife, Angela, whom I have never met, was with him through most of his parliamentary career but they broke up shortly after he became a private citizen again. Not needing to pursue the public necessity for a happy marriage, he divorced her and chased after the next generation, managing to find Polly without very much difficulty, for celebrity inspires attraction. I know little about her background except to note that she has a very good eye for art – she used to work in a gallery in Florence whose construction I helped to finance in the 1870s – and an ear for music in which ladies of her generation are often lacking. She married him for his money, of course, but he's gained something out of it too. He clearly enjoys being seen as the ageing squire of a young, beautiful woman and, assuming that she allows him anywhere near her, I dare say there's still a thing or two that she can teach him.

'Martin,' I said, opening the door cheerfully, and 'Polly,' I muttered then, my smile freezing slightly as I tried to weigh up how this might affect the meeting. 'I'm so glad you two could make it.'

'Delighted to,' he replied, stepping inside and shooting his head in every direction quickly in order to see whether there was anyone else present or anything new which he could examine. He has a habit of picking up my belongings and giving them the once over, and then informing me either how he has a better one himself or how he could have got me the same thing for only half the price. It's one of his less endearing traits.

I led them both to the living room and offered them drinks. Martin took a whisky as ever but Polly absurdly asked for a mint julep.

'A what?' I asked in surprise for I had never intended upon this becoming a cocktail party or a scene out of *The Great Gatsby*.

'A mint julep,' she repeated. 'It's bourbon, mint leaves, caster—'

'I know what's in it,' I replied quickly. 'I'm just surprised to hear you ask for one, that's all.' It occurred to me that I hadn't had a mint julep since the twenties. 'And I doubt if I have any mint, to be honest with you.'

'Have you got bourbon?'

'Of course.'

'I'll have a glass of that then. Straight.' From a cocktail to a straight shot; odd. I went into the kitchen and fixed

326

the drinks. When I returned, Martin was standing in the corner with a wrought iron candleholder in his hands; it was inverted and he was examining it carefully, holding the three candles in place carefully even as small shavings of hardened wax drizzled effortlessly on to the carpet. I put the tray down noisily, hoping he would replace it as well.

'Where did you get this then?' he asked me, returning it right side up but scratching at the iron to see whether anything would come off. 'I've got one just like it but the colour comes off when you scratch at it.'

'Then you shouldn't scratch at it,' I said with a slight smile, sitting down as Polly twisted around in her seat to observe her husband more closely. 'It's like the old story of the man who goes to the doctor and says it hurts when I do this with my arm.' I watched as he put it back on the side table and came over to join us, and remembered that the candleholder had been a wedding present from my sometime mother-in-law Margerita Fleming, whose psychotic daughter Evangeline I had been foolish enough to marry some time in the early nineteenth century. It was one of my few mementoes from that miserable Swiss marriage, which had ended with Evangeline throwing herself from the roof of the sanatorium to which she had been confined. I had placed her there myself, of course, after she had tried to kill me – foolish girl – believing me to be in league with Napoleon, of all people, with whom I never had any dealings whatsoever. After her death, I rid myself of most of our joint possessions, not wishing to remember that sour, psychotic dervish, but held on to the candlestick for it was a particularly fine piece and one which always brought comment from visitors.

'It was a wedding present,' I replied when he asked

me again where I had come across it, 'from my former mother-in-law, may she rest in peace.' They both nodded in sorrow, looking at the ground for a moment out of respect to both the dead parties, even though they'd been gone for almost two hundred years. They presumably thought that it was my most recent wife to whom I was referring. It was like a moment of silence in their joint memories and I made sure to interrupt it for they deserved no such marks of respect. 'It seems like ages since we've all got together,' I said cheerfully, recalling our many entertaining dinners upstairs. 'And who knows how long it's been since I've invited you down here.'

'Are you still seeing Tara Morrison?' asked Polly, leaning forward and something made me glance at her hands to see whether she was holding a dictaphone or not.

'Oh no,' I said, laughing. 'We haven't been together in quite some time now. I'm afraid that really wasn't destined to be.'

'What a shame,' she replied; I suspected that she was something of a fan of the 'Tara Says:' column. I imagined she followed Tara's rules for living with something close to an obsessive-compulsive disorder. She had barely been able to keep her eyes off the celebrity the last time we had dined with them and had cornered her afterwards, looking for marital advice from a woman who had never held down a steady relationship in her life. 'I thought you seemed like the perfect couple,' she added generously.

I shrugged. 'I don't know,' I said and it amazed me how my mind was suddenly drifting on to Tara now with an emotion akin to regret. It occurred to me how often I thought of her, how much she had both delighted and infuriated me in equal measures, and how pleased I was by the prospect of winning her back to our television station. I shivered quickly. 'We both lead very busy lives,' I said, 'especially Tara. She has so many commitments that it was difficult to find time together. And she spends so much of her time trying to think up her next opinion; it can't be easy for her. Also, there was the age difference.'

'Oh, nonsense,' said Polly furiously, and I quickly realized my *faux pas* as I looked at the mismatched couple before me. 'Age has nothing to do with it. And it's not like you were *that* much older than her. She has to be in her mid-thirties if she's a day. And I bet you weren't even around during the war.'

I opened my mouth and thought about it. 'I was born in 'forty-three,' I said honestly.

'Well, then. What's that after all? Fifty-six?'

'Fifty-six,' confirmed her husband, nodding his head like a human calculator.

'Well, then,' she repeated, unwilling to let this one pass without hammering her objections into the ground. 'You see? That's not so much of a difference.' I shrugged and decided to change the subject. I could see that Martin was feeling uncomfortable with it as it stood, age being a subject which has always bothered him. He confided in me once how from the age of about nineteen he had gone into a state of depression every time he saw another year pass him by. Birthdays destroy him; he looks back now, of course, from the age of sixty-one at occasions ten, twenty, thirty years before and realizes just how young he was then but it doesn't show him that it's all relative. He should imagine how it feels to be looking forward to entering a fourth century; then he really would feel old.

Perhaps one of the things which made the age question most difficult for Martin was the business of Polly's fidelity to him. Over a late night of drinks a few months earlier, he had mentioned to me that he thought Polly was having an affair with a runner from his own television show. The lad in question – and I sought him out a few days later – was no more than about nineteen years old, and he was tall and handsome, with an air of smug arrogance which apparently charmed those with whom he worked. Martin wanted me to fire Daniel, for that was his name, but I had refused and it had tested our friendship for a little while. I felt that I could not fire him if he was doing a good job, and from what I heard from his supervisor he was doing an excellent job, particularly when the allegations against him were completely without evidence or proof. I subsequently learned from a source at the station that Polly and Daniel, while not actually having an affair, had enjoyed an 'incident' but I never brought the subject up with Martin again, who seemed keen to pretend that it had never happened. Either way, I could tell that youth – Youth by its very nature – irritated the hell out of him.

'I wanted to talk about the show,' I began, after all this small talk had been got out of the way, 'where you see it developing. Where you see the format going from here.' I heard the words come out of my mouth and found them startling as I had prepared a perfectly adequate opener and instead said something which implied that I saw his programme as a going concern.

'About time too,' said Martin, always keen to discuss his career. 'I don't know about you, Matthieu, but I think we've done about all we can with the show the way it stands. I have to be perfectly honest with you on that.'

'You do?' I asked surprised.

'Absolutely I do,' he replied firmly. 'It's something I had intended talking to you about in fact. Polly and I have been discussing it for quite some time, if you want to know the truth, and we've come up with what I think is a pretty good idea. A real way forward. I hope it makes sense to you,' he added with the air of a man who was actually saying that he hoped I would *understand* how much sense it made.

He's going to retire, I thought joyfully. He's going to retire!

'We need to move into prime time,' he said eventually with a smile, holding his hands palm out and away from his face, as if he could suddenly see his name up in lights. 'We put the show into prime time and make it an hour long. A panel of guests every week. A studio audience.' He leaned forward as if he was about to put the cherry on top of the icing on the cake. 'I could roam around with a microphone!' he said joyfully. 'Think of it. It'll be huge.'

I nodded. 'Right,' I said. 'That's certainly one idea.'

'Matthieu,' said Polly in a soft voice and for some reason I could tell that if I agreed to this absurd idea, she would be putting herself forward for the position of producer. I can recognize a job pitch when I see one. 'The format we've been working with . . . it's had its day. Anyone can see that.'

'Oh, I agree,' I said. 'There's no question about that.'

'But we still have a lot to offer. We still have an audience out there. We just need to modernize it, that's all. The politicians are getting further and further away from anyone with any power, and the Outraged Liberal . . . well, I mean to say, did you see who we had on last week?' I shook my head; I never watched the

331

television if I could avoid it, least of all my own station. 'A children's TV presenter,' she said, shaking her head sorrowfully. 'Some kid of seventeen with curly blond hair and dimples. He looked like he was auditioning for the part of Oliver. We asked him his views on the Euro and all he suggested was that we adopt it but drop the queen's head in favour of Sporty Spice's.' (Again with the 'we'.) 'I mean honestly, Matthieu. Martin should not be interviewing people like this. It's beneath him.'

'It is. I know it is,' I said. I did agree with her too. In his heyday, Martin was excellent at his job. He gave great value entertainment with his insane points of view but he never shirked away from asking an appropriate question or looking to discover a hidden nugget of hypocrisy beneath a well-scripted, carefully prepared, Central Office-designed, Chief-Whipped-into-place answer. There was no question that what he was doing now was an insult to his past glories. But then he was getting older and he was not as sharp as he had once been; recently I had begun to wonder whether he actually believed the things he came out with, as opposed to saying them purely for shock value, and I suspected that he did. Age had embittered him. I discarded all my previous plans and decided to try a different, potentially more dangerous, tack.

'Don't you ever feel . . . old?' I asked quietly, sitting back in my chair and pouring a little water from a bottle into my glass. A drop bounced upwards to my cheek which I wiped away slowly to avoid catching their immediate expressions.

'Don't I ever *what*?' asked Martin in surprise. 'Don't I ever—'

'Sometimes,' I said, my voice rising above his as I looked off into the distance, 'I feel terribly old and I just want to give everything up and move to, I don't know, the South of France or somewhere. A beach. Monaco perhaps. I've never been to Monaco, you know,' I added pensively, wondering why I never had. Plenty of time, of course.

'Monaco,' said Polly, looking at me as if I had gone mad.

'Don't you ever want to just take it easy?' I asked then, locking my eyes on Martin's. 'Don't you ever get the urge to sleep in in the mornings? To do whatever you want with your day? Not to have to check the ratings all the time. To wear an open-collared shirt *all day long*.'

'No,' said Martin, uncertainty creeping into his voice now. 'Well, no, not really. I mean, I enjoy my . . . Why do you ask?'

'The show's not working, Martin,' I said clearly. 'And it's not the guests and it's not the time-slot and it's not the seventeen-year-olds with dimples and it's not the format and it's not even you. It's just had its day, that's all. Look at all the great TV shows over the past thirty years or so. *Dallas*, *Cheers*, *The Buddy Rickles Show*. Eventually the time came for all of them to end. It doesn't take away from how great they were or how much entertainment they provided. Sometimes you just have to know when it's over. When to say goodbye.'

There was silence for a moment as they both considered this. It was Polly who eventually spoke first.

'Are you saying you're *cancelling* the show?' she asked and I said nothing for a moment, just raised an eyebrow slightly.

'Well, now let's not go overboard,' said Martin, his face growing a little red, no doubt wishing he could go back about twenty minutes and prevent this conversation from ever having taken place at all. 'All I said was that we could jazz it up a little, that's all. I didn't mean for you to think that—'

'Martin,' I said, cutting him off, 'that's why I brought you here today, I'm afraid. Both of you,' I added generously, even though I had never intended being the person to speak to Polly on this matter. I'd figured he could do that himself. 'I'm sorry to say that the show is over. We're cancelling it. We've discussed it and we feel the time has come for a dignified exit.'

'And what will I do instead?' he asked, his whole body appearing to sink back into the chair, his shoulders sagging, his skin pale and blotchy, looking at me as if I was his father or his agent, someone responsible for his future celebrity in some way. 'You're not going to give me some bloody awful quiz show or something, are you? And I've no patience for documentaries. Anchorman, I suppose. I could do the news. Is that what you're thinking?' He was grasping at straws now and, for one horrible moment, I thought he was going to cry.

'Nothing,' said Polly, stating the obvious for me. 'You'll do nothing. You've just been fired. That's it, isn't it Matthieu?'

I breathed heavily through my nose and stared at the floor. I hated this kind of thing but I had done it before when it was necessary and, by God, I would do it again. 'Yes,' I said in a matter-of-fact voice. 'I'm afraid that's the long and the short of it, Martin. We're terminating your contract.'

Any self-respecting pig would refuse to live in my nephew Tommy's apartment.

A couple of years ago, when he was enjoying some hit records alongside his acting career, he had the good sense to invest in a little property and bought a two-bedroom penthouse overlooking the Thames. It's the only item of any value which he possesses and I find it extraordinary that in all this time he hasn't sold it in order to finance his chemical needs, instead of constantly borrowing from me and incurring my disapproval. I suspect the property gives Tommy what little stability he requires in his life.

His apartment has high ceilings and the most splendid windows which look out over the river. They take up almost an entire wall, from floor to ceiling, and like a child I stood back and leaned forward, my hands resting on the glass in front of me as I looked down, waiting for the exciting feeling of dizziness to overcome me. The living room in which I stood was badly named, for I couldn't help but wonder who or what species of amoeba could possibly live in it without feeling the need to shower every fifth minute. A decent couch was covered in newspapers and fashion magazines, the floor was strewn with bottles, overturned cans and glasses, the majority of which also contained the stubbed-out remains of cigarettes and/or joints. In the corner, behind a large overstuffed armchair, sitting on the ground for all to see, was a used condom and I stared at it in bewilderment, amazed by the filth which surrounded me. This, I thought in amazement, is a man's home.

I opened the window – it slid across leading to a thin, rail-floored balcony – and stepped outside. Below, a boat sailed down the Thames and couples and families walked by the river's edge. In the distance, I could see Tower Bridge and the Houses of Parliament, a sight which always impresses me.

'Uncle Matt.' I spun round and saw Tommy emerging from the bedroom now, pulling a – for once – white T-shirt over his head and down over his shorts. He had trapped his shoulder-length hair back into a ponytail but a few strands were escaping and circling his face, which was so pale as to be ghostly. His eyes were red-rimmed and dark underneath, but nothing like his nose which twitched nervously, inflamed from its recent misuse. I shook my head and felt sorry for him; every time I think that we may be growing closer and he may yet survive, something happens, something like this, and I know that it is absolutely futile. He looked – and I do not use the phrase casually – like Death.

'How can you . . . ?' I began, looking around at the Vietnam which surrounded me, but he cut me off quickly before I could berate him any further.

'Don't start, please,' he said irritably. 'I'm feeling fragile enough as it is. Had a bit of a party last night. Very late getting to bed.'

'Well, thank God it's not like this all the time,' I said. 'You'd catch the Black Death or something in here. And I've seen what that can do to people and it's not pretty.'

He cleared some spaces on the couch and armchair and I sat down nervously on the former as he took up the lotus position on the armchair, tugging his feet closely beneath himself for warmth. I considered offering to close the window but simply didn't want to – I appreciated the oxygen – and, as I looked at him, my attention was once again drawn to the prophylactic, which sat miserably shrivelled up not far from him. He followed my eyes with his own before picking up a newspaper and throwing it on top of it, hiding it from view with a thin smile. I wondered how long it would remain there, breeding with the newsprint, creating who knew what bacterial worlds on his carpet.

'We have a problem,' I told him and he yawned heavily.

'I know,' he said. 'I got a letter too.'

'From Hocknell?'

'The very same.'

'With the script?'

'He sent it, but I haven't had a chance to read it yet. Too busy getting ready for the party and everything *plus* I've had, like, eighteen-hour days at work all week. But I read the treatment. It's pretty clear what he's saying in it.'

'Well, I've read the script.'

'And?'

'Oh, it's absolute rubbish,' I said, laughing despite myself. 'I mean there's nothing to it at all. There's absolutely no way that we could ever think about producing it. I mean the *idea* is all right, I suppose, but the way he handles it . . .' I shook my head. 'Some of the dialogue . . .'

The door to one of the bedrooms opened and a figure emerged, a young woman clad in a pair of man's boxer shorts and a T-shirt. She didn't come out of Tommy's room and she was clearly not pregnant so I knew it couldn't be Andrea. She was familiar to me though; a singer or actress or some such person. I knew her from the tabloids or celebrity magazines, her natural home. She took one look at us, seated deeply in conference, slumped her shoulders in misery and returned to her room with a groan, closing the door firmly behind her. Tommy watched her disappear before reaching for a packet of cigarettes and lighting up. His eyelashes fluttered slightly as the first of the day's nicotine entered his lungs.

'That's Mercedes,' he said, nodding towards the closed door.

'Mercedes who?' I asked.

'Just Mercedes,' he replied with a shrug. 'She doesn't use a surname. Like Cher or Madonna. You must know her. She's had *only* the biggest selling dance record of the year. She's in there with Carl and Tina from my show. They all hooked up last night. Lucky bastard.'

I nodded. 'Right,' I said after a suitable pause, unwilling to involve myself in the sexual theatrics of the young. 'Getting back to Lee Hocknell then . . .'

'Fuck him,' said Tommy casually with a flick of his hand. 'Tell him his script is shit and there's not a chance in the world that either you or I are going to touch it, that's all. What's he going to do, go to the police?'

'Well, he might do,' I said.

'With what? He's got no proof of anything. Remember, *you* didn't kill his father. Neither did I. We just sorted a situation, that was all.'

'Illegally though,' I said. 'Look, Tommy. I'm not all that concerned about what he might or might not do. I've met much tougher cookies than him in my time, believe me, and I've been in far worse situations than this one too. I simply don't like being bribed, that's all, and I want to get rid of him out of my life. I don't like . . . complications. I'll sort this situation out myself, you needn't worry about that, but I just wanted to make sure that you were aware of what was going on.'

'All right, thanks,' he said and lapsed into silence for a moment. I stood up to leave.

'How's . . . Andrea?' I asked, realizing that I had never inquired after her health before.

'She's great,' he said, his eyes lighting up as he looked at me. 'She's almost six months now. Starting to show pretty well. She'll be up soon if you want to hang around and meet her.'

'No, no,' I said, making a move for the door, hoping to

part the red sea of rubbish that stood between me and it. 'That's all right. I'll have you both over for dinner or something soon.'

'That'd be good.'

'I'll be in touch,' I said, closing the door behind me and re-emerging into the relatively sterile atmosphere of the stairwell. I took a deep breath, banished Lee Hocknell from my mind for the rest of the afternoon, and jogged downstairs into the daylight and fresh air.

'So how was it? Did he go gracefully or put up a fight?'

I sighed and looked up from the notes that I was making for a later meeting. It occurred to me that, although I generally left my door open, Caroline was the only employee at the station who didn't even make the slightest illusion of a knock on it as she walked through. She simply pushed it out of her way, leaving manners and respect on the other side.

'Martin was a good friend of mine,' I said, reproaching her for her attitude and tripping over my tenses as I did so. '*Is* a good friend of mine. It's not a question of grace or fights. It's a man's job that has been taken away from him. Some day that might happen to you and you won't be so quick to crow about it.'

'Oh, please,' she said, collapsing in an armchair in front of me. 'He was a washed up old has-been and we're better off without him. Now we can get someone in with a little bit of talent instead. Put this place on the map. Now that kid, Denny Jones? The one who Martin interviewed last week on the show? With the dimples? He'd go down well with a young audience. We *have* to get him in here somehow.' She looked at me and must have caught the fury in my eyes, my desire to pick her up by the ears and simply throw her out the window, because she relented immediately. 'All right, all right, I'm *sorry*,' she said. 'I'm being inconsiderate. He's a friend of yours and you feel you owe him. Fine, whatever. How did he take it then, badly?'

'Well, he wasn't happy,' I said truthfully. 'But he didn't say very much to be honest. It was Polly, his wife, who put up the most protest. She seemed much more aggrieved than he was.'

After I had told Martin that his services were no longer required, Polly had indeed been the one to show the most anger. As her husband had slumped back in his chair, one hand resting over his brow as he contemplated his future – or lack thereof – she had gone on the attack, accusing me of disloyalty and downright stupidity. She said that we owed her husband for all his years of service, which was, I felt, overstating his case somewhat, and that we were fools if we couldn't see how much of an asset he was to the station. I could tell from her behaviour that what most concerned her was the idea of no further income from her husband and the prospect of his being excluded from showbusiness parties, functions and awards shows as his star grew ever dimmer until an introduction was always followed by the phrase 'Didn't you used to be . . . ?' She was a young woman and she was stuck with Martin now, day and night.

'Fuck her,' said Caroline. 'She's the least of our problems.'

'She had ambitions towards producing,' I pointed out, and she laughed out loud. 'Why is that so funny?' I asked her, baffled.

'Well, tell me this,' she replied. 'Does she work in television?'

'No.'

'Has she ever worked in television?'

'Not as far as I am aware.'

'Has she ever, in fact, worked at all?'

'Yes. She's worked in the art world. And she's always taken a great interest in Martin's show,' I said, wondering why I was explaining myself to Caroline.

'In his bank account, more like,' she said, shaking her head. 'In where he could take her. Producing!' she scoffed. 'The very idea's ridiculous.'

I stood up and came around to the front of my desk, sitting on its edge as I stared down at her angrily. 'Have you forgotten our first conversation?' I asked her. 'Have you forgotten how you tried to convince me to give you the top job in this organization even though you had absolutely no experience of it whatsoever?'

'I had years of management experience in—'

'Selling records, I know,' I shouted, losing my temper with her now, a rare thing. 'Well, this is a whole different world, baby. It may have escaped your attention as you sit out there tuning into television from around the world, but we don't sell records. Or books or clothes or stereo systems or posters of twelve-year-old pop stars with perfect skin. We are a television station. We produce televisual entertainment for the masses. And you knew nothing of that when I took you on, did you?'

'No, but I've—'

'No but nothing. You asked me to give you a chance and I gave you one. Nice to see you won't extend the same courtesy to someone else. Isn't there a parable about that somewhere in the Bible?'

She shook her head and I could see her tongue bulging in her cheek as she thought through what I had said.

'Hold on a minute,' she said eventually. 'What exactly are you saying here?' She looked at me in dismay. 'You didn't . . . you didn't actually . . . don't tell me you sacked him and hired her? Please, Matthieu, don't tell me you did that?' I smiled at her and raised an eyebrow slightly. I let her stew. 'Oh for God's sake,' she said. 'How on earth are we ever going to—'

'Of course I didn't hire her,' I said, cutting her off in mid-explosion, just before the stream of lava could escape her mouth and spill out all over me. 'Believe me, Caroline, I will *never* give someone a job for which they are completely inexperienced. An assistant's job, sure, but nothing more than that. To perform at this level, you'd have to know what you were doing.'

She curled her lip in distaste and I walked over to the window and stayed there, staring out at the street below until I heard her leave, her high heels clop-clop-clopping on the wooden floorboards beneath her.

Chapter 19

Fighting with Dominique

Jack and I divided the weekend work at Cageley House between us, with each of us working every second one. It meant a longer day, of course, because one would be obliged to do the work of two people, but it was worth it in order to have an alternating weekend of idle pleasure. It was on one such Saturday, while I was lazing around the Ambertons' house playing cards with my younger brother and generally feeling a boredom that almost sent me back to the stables, that Mrs Amberton prevailed upon me to join her for a shopping expedition in the village.

'I want to stock up the pantry,' she told me, bustling through the kitchen, arcing the juices from her chewing tobacco into the spittoon as she passed it. 'And I'll never be able to manage it on my own. Mr Amberton's down with one of his chests so you better come and help me.'

I nodded and finished the game before getting ready to join her. I didn't mind; the Ambertons rarely asked anything of me and had been very good to both Tomas and me during our stay there. They took a parental interest in my younger brother, whose schooling had come on remarkably well since he had actually started attending one, and they appeared to care for me as well for no other reason than the fact that they liked me. In the months since the hunting weekend and the death of the mare, little had changed in Cageley, except for the fact that Nat Pepys was spending more and more of his weekends at the house, to the point where it would have hardly been a Friday evening at all if we had not seen his short, stooped-over frame, charging up the driveway on horseback as dusk fell.

'He's up to something,' Jack confided in me. 'Like as not he thinks the old man's going to snuff it soon enough and he wants to make sure that he's in for a larger share of the pot come the day.'

I wasn't so sure; we hadn't had very many dealings since the incident with the horse – I think he realized that I had seen through his cowardice that afternoon and was unsure how to deal with a feeling of humiliation when it involved someone whom he perceived as a subordinate. In general, we ignored each other completely; I tended to his horses, he tended to his business, and in that manner we co-existed comfortably.

On this particular Saturday, a recent cold spell had finally lifted and the village was drowned in a warm golden light which seemed to bring all the residents out of their hiding places, blinking in the sunshine. They hovered around the few shops that existed in the village and chatted sociably. Mrs Amberton greeted all whom she passed and it occurred to me how these people, all of whom knew each other very well, never called each other by their Christian names, preferring to use the full 'Mr' or 'Mrs' appellation all the time. We stopped and chatted with some of our neighbours, making small talk about the weather or the condition of each other's clothing. I began to feel as if I was Mrs Amberton's son, pausing by her side whenever she wanted to speak to someone, standing silently beside her as I waited for their conversation to end. It made me uncomfortable after a time and I wished that she would simply hurry up and allow us to be on our way. I realized that stable village life was beginning to lose its appeal for me.

It was while we were standing at the corner of one street, talking to a Mrs Henchley who had recently lost her husband to pleurisy during the bad weather, that I saw something which made my stomach sick with anger. Mrs Amberton and Mrs Henchley were chatting twenty to the dozen, patting each other on the arm from time to time, reassuring each other of just how fond they had been of the late Mr Henchley, when I spotted Dominique standing outside the small teashop in the centre of the street, just under an outstretched shade, chatting with a young man who bore a cast upon his leg. She was wearing a smart Sunday outfit which I had never seen before and a bonnet, from the sides of which hung a few long curls which she had recently fashioned into her hair. They were chatting animatedly and, as they did, Dominique would laugh from time to time, always putting her hand to her mouth as she did so, in a ladylike affectation that she had no doubt picked up at Cageley House. I turned back to look at Mrs Amberton, who was oblivious to my presence by now as she and her friend picked over the corpse, like a pair of vultures looking for a little unspoilt meat, before walking towards Dominique slowly, squinting in the sunlight.

She looked in my direction several times, it seemed to me, before she even realized who I was, at which point she stopped laughing and physically pulled herself together, giving a small cough as she remarked on something to her companion before nodding in my direction. He turned to look at me also and I immediately met the eyes of Nat Pepys, who I had thought had other business this weekend when he had not shown up by the Friday evening.

'Hello, Dominique,' I said, bowing slightly before her in a cavalier manner. I was aware that my clothing was less than clean and that I hadn't washed in a couple of days, while these two were quite the young gentleman and lady in their Sunday best. My hair needed both cutting and washing and was curling around my collar limply. 'We missed you last night.' She regularly came to dinner with the Ambertons, Tomas and I at the weekend but had missed it the previous evening for no apparent reason.

'I'm sorry, Matthieu,' she replied cordially. 'I had other plans which I had forgotten about.' She nodded towards Nat after a moment. 'You know each other, don't you?'

'Of course,' said Nat, grinning broadly as if our previous experiences had been all but forgotten. 'How are you, Zulu?'

'It's Zéla,' I replied, gritting my teeth in irritation. 'Matthieu Zéla.'

'Of course, of course,' he said quickly, shaking his head as if he was trying to force himself to remember it, even though he probably knew my name only too well. 'It's that bloody French language. I can't keep it straight in my head. My brother David, now he's the man to talk to you. French, Italian, Latin, Greek. He knows 'em all.'

I nodded curtly and looked at his leg which was encased in white plaster; he was supporting himself with a fine mahogany walking stick. 'What happened to you?' I asked, resisting the urge to add the word 'Nat'

346

to the end of that phrase, not quite having the courage of Jack Holby, even if I did share his opinion of the stupidity of this cushioned fool. 'An accident, was it?'

He laughed. 'It's the damnedest thing, *Zéla*,' he said, emphasizing the name carefully. 'I was attempting to install some new light fittings in my home in London and fell off the ladder that I was standing on. Wasn't even up very high either but somehow I landed on my leg the wrong way and broke one of the bones in it. It's not too serious, I'm glad to report, but I have to keep it in plaster for a few weeks yet.'

'Right,' I said. 'There was someone else there to help you then?' He stared at me quizzically and cocked his head to the side. 'When you fell,' I continued after a moment, 'there was someone to fetch help? You weren't just left lying there?' A slight smile spread across his features and I could see his deep blue eyes grow a little colder as he attempted to figure out whether I was being offensive or merely making conversation.

'I had a few servants there,' he answered. 'But then,' – and here he enunciated each word carefully – 'I'd be lost without all of you to wait on me hand and foot, wouldn't I?' The words hung in the air between us. He had insulted me, and Dominique too, who stared at the ground in embarrassment, her face growing a little pink with discomfort as we waited for someone to break the silence.

'I wondered why I didn't see you arrive by horse yesterday evening,' I said, choosing my words carefully, wishing to allude to our last meeting without mentioning it outright.

'I took a carriage,' he said hesitantly. 'Quite late at night, as it happens.'

'It'll be some time then before you get on a horse again,

yes?' I said, nodding towards his leg. 'It's fortunate we don't equate the same attitudes towards injured humans as we do towards injured beasts, isn't it?'

There was a pause. 'Meaning?' he said eventually, his lips growing thinner as he began to draw them in contemptuously towards his teeth.

'Well,' I said, laughing quickly, 'if you were a horse and had injured yourself like that, we'd have to shoot you, wouldn't we? Or at least I would.'

Dominique stared at me and slowly shook her head. The expression on her face – which I had expected to be one of admiration for my ability to insult Nat, albeit in a slightly roundabout way – reflected irritation, as if she wanted no part of any childish games between the two of us. I swallowed and felt my face flush as I waited for one of them to say something. Eventually Nat broke the silence.

'Your brother's a smart young man, isn't he?' he said eventually, looking at her and she raised her head and smiled, looking at me as if she wanted to apologize for her part in any of this tension even as she refused to take my side within it. 'Never forgets a thing.' He gave a sharp intake of breath and rebalanced his body to take the weight off his leg. 'Sometimes it's best to forget though. Can you imagine how much we would have in our heads if we remembered every single thing that ever took place?'

A panting Mrs Amberton took this opportunity to reappear at my side, her tongue sticking out of the side of her mouth as she looked at Nat Pepys in awe; they had never met before but he was part of Cageley House, she knew that much, and she would have gladly dropped to her knees to shine his shoes had he so required it.

'Mrs Amberton, this is Nat Pepys,' I said after a moment, feeling that an introduction was called for. 'My employer's youngest son. This is Mrs Amberton, my landlady,' I added, looking at him.

'Charmed,' he said, shooting me a glance of distaste for that second last remark even as he began to hobble away. 'I'm afraid I must be on my way though. Dominique, I suppose I'll see you back at the house.' He uttered this last phrase in a quieter tone, directing it towards her but intending for me to hear it too. 'Zulu, Mrs Amberton,' he said, nodding in our direction as he walked away.

'What a pleasant young man,' said Mrs Amberton, watching him depart with great joy in her eyes. 'Wait until I tell Mr Amberton who I was talking to!' I simply looked at Dominique who stared back at me solidly without blinking, raising an eyebrow slightly as if to say 'Yes?'

Jack was sitting with his back to a tree with a heavy lump of wood on his lap, chipping away at it with great concentration with a knife. I came towards him slowly, curiously afraid of startling him, and watched as his eyes bore into his work, never looking aside for a moment as the blade took small nicks from it here and there, fashioning something which I could not as yet decipher. I waited until he stopped for a moment, holding the wood up to the light and blowing the chipped dust away, before coming closer, stepping heavily on the ground so that he might hear me without my having to say a word.

'Hello there,' he said, squinting at me in the sunlight as he looked in my direction. 'What are you up to then?' I pulled my arms out from behind my back to reveal a couple of flagons of beer which I clinked together in the air, mugging a drunken face as I grinned at him. He laughed and put his equipment down for a moment as he shook his head. 'Matthieu Zéla,' he said, biting his lip now, 'stealing from Sir Alfred's pantry. I've trained you well, grasshopper.' He took one of the bottles gratefully and with a quick, careless movement snapped the lid off it with the heel of one hand and the thumb of another.

'Nat's back, I see,' I said after a few moments, enjoying the sensation of the liquid whistling down my throat, chilling my insides as it passed through my body. 'Did you believe that story about the lights that he's telling?'

He shrugged. 'I was barely listening when he told me it if you want to know the truth. He seemed intent on telling me though and, since he's told you as well, I doubt it. Who knows what he really did.' He hissed and looked down at his hand; as he had been speaking he had put the bottle down by his side and started to carve away on the wood again, missing a beat while talking to me and nicking his finger. The blood appeared in a sudden spout at the tip but stopped as he pressed his thumb on top of it for a moment, waiting for the flow to clot. 'Have you ever seen the sea, Mattie?' he asked me and I laughed in surprise.

'The *sea*?'

'Yeah, sure, why not?' he asked, shrugging. 'Have you ever seen it?'

'Of course. We had to sail to get from France to England in the first place. I saw it then. And I spent a year in Dover, I told you.'

He sighed and nodded, remembering my stories about life in Paris and when I had first reached England. 'Of

350

course, of course,' he said. 'Well, I've never seen the sea. I've heard about it though. The sea, the beaches. I've never gone swimming, you know.' I shrugged. In truth I hadn't done much swimming myself. 'I'd like to do something like that.'

I took a long drink and looked out ahead of me. The grounds of Cageley House opened up before us, the green grass almost wet with the light which fell upon it as far as my eyes could see. In the distance I could hear the horses whinnying in their paddocks and the odd shout of laughter from back at the house where the servants were beating out the rugs in the summer air. I felt a rush of contentment and happiness devour me, filling my body with a warmth that made me feel almost like crying. I looked at my friend and he had his head pressed back against the bark of the tree, one hand pulling back his bright blond hair from his forehead and holding it in place, his eyes shut, his lips moving quietly as he sat there.

'A couple more months, Mattie,' he said after a moment and I jumped back out of my reverie. 'A couple more months and that's the last you'll see of me around here.'

I looked at him in surprise. 'How do you mean?' I asked and he sat up straight again, looking around to make sure that there was no one listening.

'Can you keep a secret?' he asked me and I nodded. 'Well,' he began, 'you know I've been saving up, don't you?'

'Sure,' I said. He had spoken of it often.

'Well, I've got quite a bit put aside now, you see. I've been saving since I was about fifteen if you want to know the truth. And a couple more months and I'll have all I need. I'm going to take it, go down to London

351

and set myself up for life. No more shovelling horseshit for Jack Holby.'

I felt sad and even as he spoke of leaving, although I felt such genuine contentment with Cageley, my mind bounced quickly to an idea of whether we could all leave together some day. 'What will you do?' I asked him.

'I can read and write,' he said. 'I got some schooling before coming to work here. I'm going to put myself out as a clerk. Find a good business that will take me in and let me do some study. Maybe the law or book-keeping, I don't mind. Something solid. Something regular. I've got enough now to buy my way into a firm and let them pay my way from there. Get some rooms somewhere. I'll be set for life.' His whole face positively beamed with excitement at this prospect.

'But won't you miss it here?' I asked him and he laughed out loud.

'You haven't been here that long, Mattie,' he explained. 'You still see it as a bit of stability, something you've never known before. I've been here all my life. I grew up here. And why should the likes of Nat Pepys get to live the high life and roll around in his money and boss other people around when I can't do the same? Difference between him and me is I'll have earned my way out. I'll have worked for it. And, one of these days, that bastard's going to be calling *me* "sir"'.

The antipathy between the two, an antipathy which it had to be said existed mainly on Jack's part, had never been as obvious to me as then. It wasn't just the manner in which Nat had mistreated his friend Elsie, nor was it the way he lorded it over us all the time. It went deeper than that. It went down to the fact that Jack couldn't stand the idea of someone feeling they had authority over him. He didn't believe in the very concept. He'd been in near servitude all his life and it disgusted him. He was the original revolutionary. Only he wasn't hot headed; he would never have just upped and left until he felt the time was right for him and he could make it on his own.

'You want to start thinking about it,' he said after a few moments. 'You can't stay here for ever, I mean. You're young, though, so you should start saving your—'

'Well, I've got Tomas to think about,' I interrupted. 'And Dominique. I can't just get on a horse and ride off to wherever I choose. I've got responsibilities.'

'But don't them Ambertons look after Tomas?'

'I wouldn't go without him,' I said firmly. 'He's my brother. We stick together. And Dominique.' He snorted a laugh and I spun around and stared at him. 'What?' I asked. 'What was that for?'

He shrugged and looked as if he didn't want to answer. 'It's just . . .' he began, hesitating and thinking about his words carefully. 'I don't think she necessarily needs you to look out for her, that's all. She looks like she's able to take care of herself if you ask me.'

'You don't know her,' I said.

'I know she's not your sister,' he said, his words coming out so clearly and unexpectedly that they didn't even register with me for a few moments. 'I know that much, Mattie.'

I stared at him and felt my face drain a little, unsure of what to say. 'How do you . . . ?' I began. 'How did you know that?'

'It's obvious from the way you look at her,' he said. 'I've seen it. And the way she looks at you sometimes. It's the look of two people who've been a little bit more than just brother and sister if you ask me. I may have

353

spent my whole life holed up in this cage but I do know a thing or two about that.'

I slumped back against the tree and wondered for a moment why I had never bothered to tell him before. Why we hadn't explained it to everyone. Perhaps it was because we had at first been so fearful of being separated that we had concocted the lie but, once we had settled in there so well, an opportunity had never arisen where we might clear up the deception.

'Does anyone else know?' I asked him and he shook his head.

'Not so far as I've heard. But the point is, whatever you feel for her, you can't let your whole life be run by it. Make your own life yourself.'

I nodded. 'We *will* leave some day,' I said. 'When we're ready.'

'Do you love her then?' he asked and, to my irritation, I blushed furiously. Although it had been the primary emotion in my mind for a couple of years now, the all-consuming desire which racked me from morning till night, whenever I saw her and whenever I didn't, I had never come out and just told someone about it and it seemed odd to be suddenly asked the question and find that I was stuck for words.

But: 'Yes,' I said eventually. 'I do. It's that simple.'

'And do you think she loves you?'

'Absolutely,' I said, this time without hesitation, although I was less convinced. 'What's not to love?' I added with a smile in order to lighten the moment.

'I don't know,' he said pensively and for a moment I wasn't sure whether he meant that he didn't know what was not to love or whether she loved me or not.

'The thing is,' I continued, oblivious to his doubts, wanting to reassure myself of her feelings now more

354

than anything else, 'the thing is she sees me as her . . .' I paused, trying to figure out exactly what she saw me as. 'As her . . . her . . .' And for the life of me I couldn't finish the sentence. Jack simply nodded and finished his drink before jumping up and stretching out his limbs.

'She believes it, you see,' he said. 'The lie. She's managed to convince herself that it's true.' I looked at him quizzically. 'That you're brother and sister,' he explained. 'She's come to feel that that's the natural relationship between the two of you.'

'She's just hiding her feelings,' I said. 'You don't know her like I do.'

He laughed. 'Not sure I want to, Mattie,' he said.

I jumped up and stared at him furiously. 'What's that supposed to mean?' I asked, my fists clenching automatically by my side even as I willed him to back down.

'I just mean that, whatever you feel for her, there's no guarantee that she feels the same way, that's all. Maybe she's playing on that fact. You're a safety net for her. She knows she can count on you without her having to give anything back.'

'But what could she give back?' I asked, infuriated, and he hesitated before answering.

'Well, when was the last time you spent a night in her room, Mattie?' The words were barely out of his mouth when I swung the first punch. He stepped back quickly and my arm flew past his face without connecting. Instead he grabbed me by the arm and gave a half-laugh. 'Take it easy,' he said, perhaps a little unnerved by my reaction.

'Take it back,' I shouted back, my face red, particularly since he had my right arm in a tight clench and

355

seemed unwilling to release it. 'You don't know her so take it back.'

He pushed me backwards and I tripped over a root of the tree, falling hard on the ground. I groaned as I felt a jabbing pain run through my back. Jack stared down at me and kicked a foot in the dirt angrily. 'Now look what you've done,' he said. 'I didn't mean any harm, Mattie. I was only saying, that was all. There's no need for any of this.'

'You take it back,' I repeated, probably in no position to issue orders to him but willing none the less to stand up and face off once again if necessary.

'Fine, fine, I take it back,' he said, sighing and shaking his head. 'But you think about what I said. It might stand to you at some point. Here,' he continued, throwing the piece of wood at me, and I looked at it now and held it up, realizing what it was for the first time. He had carefully scored out the insides of the wood, leaving a frame around emptiness and a solid cube cage in my hand. It was like a puzzle or game and I stared up at him feeling a mixture of anger at how he had talked about Dominique and frustration with an argument I had never expected. I wanted to continue our talk, to convince him how much she loved me, to make him say it, but he was already heading back towards the house and within a couple of minutes he had vanished over the hill, leaving me there alone, the wooden box in my hand.

'She *does* love me,' I muttered before getting up and dusting off the seat of my pants roughly.

The sand was golden brown beneath my toes and I buried my feet down into it as deeply as I could until it became too heavy for me to push any further. I lay back, my body creating an image of itself in the sand below, and allowed the sun to burn down on top of me. I had just emerged from the cold water and my skin was wet, droplets sitting casually about my chest and making my legs appear darker as the hairs stuck gently to the skin. I ran a hand down towards my centre, my fingers enjoying the feel of my warm skin, my eyes closed to block out the light as my body stretched within itself. I could lie there for ever, I thought. Then my hand came back up towards my head until it was contorted in upon itself, shaking my shoulder, dragging me back to consciousness.

'Matthieu,' said Mrs Amberton, her nightdressed form a ghoulish figure to awaken to. I licked my mouth, creating unpleasant sounds as it snapped open, and stared at her in confusion. Why was she there? I asked myself. I'd been having such a lovely dream. 'Matthieu,' she repeated, her voice louder now as her rough hands shook my bare shoulder beneath the sheet. 'You've got to get up. It's Tomas. He's not right.'

My eyes opened now and I sat up in the bed, shaking my head and combing my hair roughly away from my eyes with my fingers. 'What's wrong with him?' I asked. 'What's going on?'

'He's in the kitchen,' she said. 'Come on. Come and see him.'

She left me alone and I stumbled out of the bed, pulling on my trousers quickly before stepping inside. Tomas, just turned eight years old, was sitting in the rocking chair by the fire on Mr Amberton's knee, groaning dramatically.

'Tomas?' I asked, leaning over him and putting a hand to his forehead to check his temperature. 'What's wrong with you?'

'Don't,' he hissed, brushing my hand away. His eyes were closed and his mouth was wide open. The brief touch I had had of his forehead had been warm and I looked at Mrs Amberton in surprise.

'He's burning up,' I said. 'What is it, do you think?'

'Summer 'flu,' she said. 'I saw it coming. He just has to go through it, that's all. Only he don't seem to be 'appy about it right now, does he? Should be in bed but he won't go.'

'Tomas,' I said, shaking him now in the same way that she had awoken me, 'come on, you need to go to bed. You're not well.'

'I want Dominique,' he said suddenly. 'I want her to put me to bed.'

'She's not here, you know that,' I replied, surprised that he had asked for her.

'I *want* her,' he screamed, making us all jump back in fright. He was not a tempestuous child and it was rare that he behaved in this manner. 'I want *Dominique*,' he repeated.

'I think you'd better go get her,' said Mrs Amberton.

'At this time of night? It's nearly one o'clock in the morning.'

'Well, he's not going to get any sleep until she gets here,' she answered angrily. 'I've been trying to get him off for thirty minutes since but she's the only one he asks for. Just tell her it's an emergency. Look at him, Matthieu! He's got a fever. He has to get to bed.'

I sighed and nodded before returning to my room to finish dressing. The bed looked warm and inviting and I was sorry to have to leave it. I put on two shirts and a jumper to stave off the cold. As I stepped out into the night, wrapping one of Mr Amberton's scarves around my neck beneath my coat, I shivered and wondered how Dominique would react to this urgent summons.

Tomas could barely remember his mother. He had only been five when Philippe had killed her and, by the time he reached the age of reason, where he could remember the things that took place, we had already fallen in with Dominique. She had taken some charge of him then, halving my responsibilities towards him during those early days, and had been his sole daytime protector while we lived in Dover and I had earned the money for our dinners through my pickpocketing experiences. They were friends, they got on well, but it had never really occurred to me – or to Dominique, I expect – how much he saw her as a maternal figure, which in turn made me realize how much he must have seen me as his true father. And, since we had arrived in Cageley, that 'mother' had all but vanished out of his life. True, he saw her once a week at dinner and they would often run into each other in the village but by and large he did not have the same connections with her as he once had. I didn't think that he had ever even *been* to Cageley House, where both Dominique and I spent most of our time, and it occurred to me how little I knew about his own days and what he did to occupy them. Mr Amberton had accepted him into his schoolhouse and from all accounts he performed well there, but what of his friends? What of his interests, his pastimes? I knew nothing of these. I felt guilty about this as I walked down the driveway towards the rear of the house and regretted my neglect of my brother in recent times.

Dominique and Mary-Ann had a habit of leaving the side door to the kitchen unlocked at nights; if anyone should want to go out and return, it was far easier to go through this way than to have to unbolt the locks on the house's main door. There was little chance of burglary as Cageley was always a peaceful place and no one would have dared risk the dogs in the driveway had they not been as well acquainted with them as I already was.

As I turned past the stables towards the kitchen, I imagined Jack asleep in one of the upstairs rooms, dreaming of his escape from this place, and envied him his ambition. I was surprised to see a candle burning in the window of the kitchen and for a moment I thought I could see movement from within; my pace slowed down and quietened as I came closer. I hesitated outside and peered through, and I could see two figures at the table sitting close by each other and recognized them immediately as Dominique and Nat Pepys, whose head was bowed down as he held her hand. He was shaking visibly.

Shocked, I unlatched the door and stepped inside. There was a sudden rustle and they separated, Dominique standing up and smoothing down her simple dress as she looked at me, Nat barely acknowledging my presence.

'Matthieu,' she said in surprise. 'What on earth are you doing here?'

'It's Tomas,' I replied suspiciously, looking from one to the other. 'He's not well. He's asking for you.'

'Tomas?' she asked, her eyes widening and, despite everything else, it occurred to me how much she must have cared for the lad. 'Why? What's wrong with him? What's happened?'

'Nothing,' I said, shrugging my shoulders. 'He's just sick, that's all. Running a fever. Refuses to go to bed until you come to him. I'm sorry that it's late but . . .'

My voice trailed off. I was unsure what to say about the scene that I had witnessed, whether I had even actually seen what I thought I had seen. By now, Nat was over by the counter lighting a candle and looking at his watch.

'It's very late, Zéla,' he said irritably, getting my name right for once. 'It might have waited until the morning.'

'He's *sick*, Nat,' said Dominique quickly and I noticed he didn't flinch when she spoke to him in such a familiar fashion. 'And he's my *brother*.' She took her coat from behind the door and followed me outside. I walked a few steps ahead of her and said nothing. All the way back to the Ambertons' house, we barely spoke and I made no mention of what I had seen, so unsure was I by now that I had even seen anything. She got Tomas to sleep and left shortly afterwards and it was I who lay awake most of the night then, tossing and turning, wondering, thinking, considering.

I tried to return to my warm, peaceful beach but it was lost to me now.

It was the following afternoon before I could get Dominique on her own again to ask her about the events of the previous night. I was tired and irritable from my lack of sleep but furious with her at the same time, having convinced myself that there was something untoward going on between her and Nat Pepys.

'Oh, just stay out of it, Matthieu,' she told me, trying to get away from me, but I blocked her route back to the house. 'This doesn't concern you.'

'Of course it concerns me,' I shouted. 'I want to know what's going on between you two.'

'There's *nothing* going on between us,' she said. 'As if there would be! A man in his position would never get involved with someone like me!'

'That's hardly the—'

'We were just talking, that's all. There's more to him than you realize. You just see black and white, that's all. Whatever your friend Jack tells you, you believe.'

'Over Nat? Any day. Any day, Dominique,' I said firmly.

'Listen to me, Matthieu.' She leaned in close and I could see from the flaring in her eyes that she was growing more and more angry by the minute and I was wary of pushing this to so far a point that there was no room to come back. 'You and I . . . there is nothing there. Do you see that? I care for you, but—'

'It's this place,' I said, spinning around, not wanting to hear any of this. 'We've both become so involved in this bloody place that we've forgotten where it all started for us. Remember the boat from Calais, do you? Remember that year in Dover? We could go back there. We were happy there.'

'I'm *not* going back there,' she said firmly, a brittle laugh escaping her mouth. 'Not a chance.'

'And Tomas,' I said, 'we have a responsibility towards him.'

'I don't,' she said. 'I care for him, yes, but I am sorry. My responsibilities are only towards myself, no one else. And, if you don't stop this, you're going to push me away for ever, can't you see that, Matthieu?'

I had nothing else to say and she pushed past me. I felt sick inside; I hated her and loved her at the same time. Maybe Jack was right, I thought. It was time to get out of Cageley.

Chapter 20

The Fictionalist

I arrived in London in 1850 a wealthy man. Incredibly, the Roman authorities had eventually paid me most of what they owed me for my work on the unfinished opera house and I came back to England burning with ambition. My experiences in Rome had left me feeling ill at ease; Thomas's unnecessary murder at the hands of Lanzoni was causing me some sleepless nights and I was angered by the fact that the machinations of one woman – Sabella, my bigamist wife – had resulted in two deaths, that of her husband and my nephew. I placed a sum of money at the disposal of Marita, Thomas's fiancée, and quit Italy with great haste.

I began to feel depressed and unfulfilled by my experiences there. I had worked hard on the opera house and on my plans to give Rome a centre of culture and all my efforts had come to nothing. The internal strife of that country made it seem impossible that I could ever go back and complete the tasks which I had been employed to do. I wanted to undertake something which I could feel proud of; to create something which I could look back on in a hundred years' time and say *I did that*. I had money and I had ability and so determined to keep my eyes open for any opportunities which could test me.

In 1850, that which we subsequently came to know as the Industrial Revolution in England was in full swing. The population had risen dramatically since the end of the Napoleonic Wars thirty-six years earlier; newly created machinery meant better farming practices, which led to a better quality of food and improved standards of living. The average life expectancy then rose to forty years old, although I, of course, was heading towards my 109th birthday and proving an unexpected exception to that particular rule. There was a gradual shift in the populace from the country to the city, where more and more factories and industrial settings were emerging on an almost monthly basis. By the time I myself arrived in London, more people were living in urban dwellings than rural ones, for the first time in history. I arrived with the masses.

I took a set of rooms near the Law Courts and happened to be living above a family named Jennings, with whom I became quite familiar over the subsequent months. Richard Jennings was working as an assistant at that time to Joseph Paxton, the designer of the Crystal Palace, and his every working moment was devoted to the upcoming Great Exhibition of 1851. After some initial shyness on both our parts I became familiar with Richard and spent many happy evenings taking a glass of whisky with him at either his kitchen table or my own, listening to his tales of the exotic delights which were being brought to Hyde Park for what then sounded like the most ludicrous display of conspicuous consumption in the history of mankind.

'What exactly is the idea behind it?' I asked Richard on the first occasion that we spoke of the Exhibition, which was already the talk of the country despite the fact that it lay several months off in the future. Many people were mocking the building, the very structure, and questioning why so much taxpayers' money was being poured into something which was little more than a display of national achievement. Whether it would serve any earthly purpose after that was open to conjecture.

'It's to be a celebration of all that's good in the world,' he explained to me. 'A massive structure containing works of art, machinery, wildlife, everything that you can possibly think of; too big to see it all in one day. Something from every corner of the empire. It'll be the greatest living museum that the world has ever seen. A symbol of our unity and ability. Of what we are, in other words.'

The greatest living museum; I thought his home was already that. I had never seen a house so crammed with belongings before, nor known a man so keen on displaying his every possession. There were shelves running along every wall, each one holding books, ornaments, outlandish cups and teapots, every different type of collection known to man. One sudden gust of wind through the room could have caused chaos. Remarkably, there was not a speck of dust to be found and I came to realize that Betty Jennings, Richard's wife, spent her entire life cleaning it. Her very existence revolved around a feather duster and a sweeping brush, her *raison d'être* to keep the place spotless. Whenever I entered their home she would greet me in her familiar apron, wiping the perspiration from her brow as she rose from washing the kitchen floor or sweeping down the stairs. She was always friendly with me, but kept a polite distance as if whatever business her husband

and I had – more often than not the simple business of drinking and good conversation – was the business of men and she was better off left out of it. For my part, I would have enjoyed her company on some occasions as I suspected there was more going on behind that human cleaner than she was letting on.

Richard and Betty were the proud parents of what they called 'their two families'. A middle-aged couple, they had brought three children into the world by the time they were nineteen, a daughter and twin boys, and eleven years later had given birth to another set of twins, this time daughters. The difference in age between them gave the impression that the baby daughters were a second family and that the first three children were more in the role of aunt and uncles than older siblings.

Although I have never much concerned myself with children, I grew to know the eldest daughter, Alexandra, quite well during my time there. The Jenningses had high ambitions for their children and had named them accordingly; the twin boys were George and Alfred, the girls Victoria and Elizabeth. They were regal names but, like so many of the offspring of the European royal houses of the time, they were sickly children, those four, forever coughing or running temperatures or splitting their knees open simply by running down a road. I rarely called on the family without discovering that one of them had taken to their bed with some disease or ailment. Bandages and rubbing oil were familiar products on their sideboards. Theirs was a house of constant nursing.

Unlike her siblings, however, Alexandra never displayed a day's illness in all the time that I knew her. Not physical illness anyway. A headstrong girl of seventeen, she was taller than both her parents and slim, with the kind of body that turned heads in the street. Observed in the right light, her long dark hair became almost auburn and it appeared to me that she must brush it a thousand times every night in order to extract the perfect shine which glistened from its surface. Her face was pale, but not in a sickly sense, and she had the ability to control her blushes, waiting for an opportunity to impress and captivate with the charms that she had developed so naturally.

I became interested in Richard's work and he invited me to Hyde Park one day to view the Crystal Palace as the preparations continued for the May opening. It was agreed that I would walk the short distance to the park with Alexandra, who was also interested in viewing the structure. She had heard so much from her father about the delights which lay within that it surprised me that she had never asked to visit it before. I collected her from her home on a fine February morning, when the air was just a little frosty and the ground had only the slightest covering of smooth ice.

'They say it is so big that even the great oak trees in Hyde Park are contained within its surface,' said Alexandra as we walked along, our arms linked in a platonic, parental-style lock. 'They thought about cutting down any trees within the Crystal Palace but decided to just build the ceiling higher instead.'

The fact struck me as impressive. Some of those trees had stood rooted to the same spot for hundreds of years. Most of them were even older than I was; an impressive achievement. 'You've been reading up about it then,' I said, making casual conversation with the girl. 'Your father would be impressed.'

'He leaves plans around the house all the time,' she

announced haughtily. 'You know he's had several meetings with Prince Albert, don't you?'

'He did mention it, yes.'

'The Prince consults my father on almost everything to do with the Great Exhibition.' Richard had mentioned to me on several occasions that he had taken part in some meetings concerning the manner of the Exhibition, meetings which were generally jointly chaired by the Prince Consort and Joseph Paxton, the chief designer. Although he clearly enjoyed speaking of his contacts with royalty, he never overstated the connection, always insisting that his role in the business, while a senior and important one, was mainly supervisory of plans which Paxton had already put in place. There had been some disagreement over which side of the structure to place the British goods with relation to light, air and visibility. Albert had asked several people for their advice and eventually a section on the western half was chosen.

'You'll be his guest on the day it opens, of course,' I said, naturally ignorant of the chain of events which would follow over the coming months. 'It will be a proud day for him to have his family there at such an important occasion. I hope to attend myself.'

'Between you and I, Mr Zéla,' said Alexandra then, leaning in towards my shoulder in a conspiratorial fashion as we entered the great gates of Hyde Park, 'I'm not sure whether I will be in attendance or not. I'm engaged to be married, you see. To the Prince of Wales. And there's a good chance that we shall *elope* before the summer is over, for his mother would never agree to the match, you know.'

* * *

Two hundred and fifty-six years is a long time to be alive. With such a life-span, one gets to meet many different kinds of people. In my time, I have known honest men and crooks; I have met virtuous men who suffer moments of crippling madness which have led directly to their downfall, and mendacious rascals whose singular acts of generosity or integrity have cleared a path for their salvation; I have acquainted myself with murderers and hangmen, judges and criminals, workers and sloths; I have been brought into contact with men whose words have impressed me and stirred me into action, whose conviction in their own principles has ignited the spark in others to fight for change or the simple rights of man and I have listened as charlatans read from scripts, proclaiming great ambitions which they have failed to enact; I have known men to lie to their wives, women to cheat on their husbands, parents to curse their children, offspring to damn their ancestry; I have seen babies born and adults die; I have helped those who are in need and I have killed; I have known every type of man, woman and child, every facet of human nature which exists on the shores around me and I have observed them and listened to them and heard their words and seen their deeds and walked away from them with naught but my memories to translate them from my head to these pages. But Alexandra Jennings was a girl who barely fits into any of these descriptions for she was an original, a true singularity in my time, the kind of girl one meets only once in a lifetime, even if that lifetime happens to last for 256 years. For she was a fictionalist, in that every word, every single phrase that ever escaped her mouth, was based upon a fiction. Not a lie exactly, for Alexandra was not a deceitful girl or a dishonest one, she simply felt the need to create a life for herself which was absolutely at odds with the one which she was actually leading and a compulsion to present that life to others as the plain truth. And it is that fact alone which holds her memory – despite the brevity of our time together – alive in my mind even today, a century and a half later.

'I'm engaged to be married, you see. To the Prince of Wales.' These were the words that Alexandra had spoken. The year was 1851. Prince Albert, later crowned King Edward VII, was aged ten and in no condition to marry anyone, although an arrangement for the future had most likely been already made by his mother. (Ironically, he eventually married another Alexandra, the daughter of the King of Denmark.)

'I see,' I replied, more than a little surprised by this announcement. 'I was not aware that there was an understanding between the two of you. Perhaps I have not been paying as close attention to the Court Circular as I might.'

'Well, it is imperative that we keep it secret,' she said casually, tossing her hair a little as we walked through the park, able now to see the great glass and iron building which stood in the distance. 'His mother has a rotten temper, you know, and would be terribly angry if she found out. She's the Queen, you see.'

'Yes, I know,' I said slowly, looking at my companion suspiciously as I tried to ascertain whether she was completely convinced by what she was saying or whether this was some form of youthful entertainment with which I was not familiar. 'But there is something of an age difference between you, surely,' I added.

'Between the Queen and I?' she asked, frowning slightly. 'Yes, I expect there is, but—'

'No, between the prince and yourself,' I said irritably. 'Isn't he just a child? Nine or ten perhaps?'

'Oh yes,' she answered quickly. 'But he intends to grow much older. He's hoping to turn fifteen by the summer and perhaps make it into his twenties by Christmas. I, on the other hand, am only seventeen, and I must admit that I quite like the idea of an older man. Boys my own age are so stupid, don't you agree?'

'Well, I don't know very many,' I admitted. 'But I'll take your word on it.'

'If you like,' she added after a few moments' silence, and she spoke now with the tone of a person who is unsure whether this is a good idea or not but is going to say it anyway, 'if you like, we could invite you to the wedding. I'm afraid it won't be a grand, state affair – neither of us want that – just a simple ceremony, followed by a pleasant reception. Family and close friends only. But we would be delighted to have you there.'

I wondered where she had picked up her speech pattern, which mirrored that of society ladies almost perfectly. Her parents, while relatively well-off and suddenly mixing in elevated circles, came from simple London stock and their accents gave their ancestry away. They were regular folk who had enjoyed some luck, Mr Jennings's abilities and business sense giving them a fine home and a higher standard of living than many of their peers. Their daughter was obviously hoping to take it a step further.

'Of course, it means I'll be queen myself one day, which is tiresome,' she said eventually as we approached the dome. 'But when one is called to duty—'

'Alexandra! Matthieu!' The voice of her father reached the great doorways of the Crystal Palace a few moments before he did himself and he ushered us in excitedly. I

371

was delighted to see him at last, unsure how much more of his daughter's bizarre ramblings I could endure before either bursting out laughing or stepping cautiously away. 'I'm so glad you got here,' he said, opening his arms wide to signify the majesty of what we saw before us. 'So. What do you think?'

I had not known quite what to expect and this enormous structure with its walls of iron and glass was without a doubt one of the most impressive sights I had ever laid eyes upon. We were standing inside and there was still an incredible amount of work to be done, however, so what we saw resembled a building site more than the great universal museum which it was no doubt intended to be.

'It's hard to get a good idea at the moment,' said Richard, guiding us along one path, on which we were surrounded by enormous glass cabinets which were currently empty and at the time covered in enormous dustsheets. 'They're not staying there,' he said quickly, indicating the cases with a flick of his wrist. 'I think they're going to the India section for a display of their local pottery but I'd have to check the chart to be sure. Over here we're going to have an astronomy section. Ever since they discovered that new planet a few years ago, what do you call it . . . ?'

'Neptune,' I said.

'That's the one. Ever since they discovered that, there's been huge interest in that whole field. That's why that display's going there. When it eventually arrives, that is. There's still so much to be done,' he added, shaking his head in worry. 'And we've only got three months left.'

'I never expected it to be so big,' I said, catching sight in the distance of the very trees which Alexandra had mentioned on the way here, rooted in the ground and continuing to grow within the glasshouse effects of the palace. 'How many people will fit in here?'

'At a guess?' he said, shrugging his shoulders slightly. 'Perhaps thirty thousand. Which is only a fraction of the number who will want to attend.'

'Thirty thousand!' I repeated, stunned by the figure which, for the time, could have represented a large portion of any major city in England. 'That's incredible. And all these people . . .' I looked around at the tribe of workmen who were walking to and fro, carrying equipment and every type of wood, glass or iron known to man; the noise of their activities meant we were never speaking below a dull shout.

'There're a thousand people working here, aren't there, Daddy?' asked Alexandra, the future queen of England.

'Well, several hundred anyway,' he replied. 'I don't know the exact figure. I—' One of their number, a dark, swarthy man with a hunchback and a cloth cap, interrupted him, whispering something in his ear which was clearly bad news for he slapped his forehead dramatically and rolled his eyes with something close to music-hall theatrics. 'I have to go see about something,' he announced to us, cupping a hand to his mouth as he shouted. 'Take a further look around but be careful. I'll meet you back here in about thirty minutes. And, for heaven's sake, don't touch anything!'

An opening emerged in the protocol department and, although the salary was negligible, I accepted it, as I found the whole business of the Great Exhibition fascinating. There was to be a procession of foreign representatives brought before the Queen and the Prince Consort on the opening day and I had responsibility for making sure that all those who had been invited were in fact coming and would have a place to stay in London for the duration of their visit. This work brought me into some contact with Richard, for he was making sure that there was enough room between the various exhibits for the delegations to pass through.

I tried not to see too much of Alexandra during this period for, while I was baffled by her conversation on the day we had first visited the Crystal Palace, I was also less than happy about being a foil for her delusions. I wondered about her behaviour at home, whether she created as many fictions there about her life as she had with me that day, and resolved to ask her father about it. The thing which surprised me the most had not been *what* she had said, so much as her utter conviction in the things that she was saying, as if she truly believed them herself and was utterly serious when she implored me to keep her secrets for her.

'How is Alexandra these days?' I asked Richard one afternoon in as casual a manner as possible. 'I thought I would see more of her down here. She seemed so interested in your work.'

'Well, that's my daughter for you,' he replied, laughing. 'She takes a fancy to something one minute and it goes out of her mind the next. That's always been the case with her.'

'But what does she do with her days?' I asked. 'She's not still schooling, is she?'

'She's training to be a teacher,' he explained, poring over a detailed map of the ground floor of the Exhibition. 'She's under the tutelage of some of them who taught her in the first place. Why do you want to know?' he asked me suspiciously, looking at me as if I was considering making some illicit move on his daughter.

'No reason,' I replied. 'No reason at all. I just wondered why I hadn't seen her in so long.'

In fact, I did not have to wait very much longer, for there was a knock on my door late that night. I opened it, just a crack to see who was there for there were a great many robberies and murders taking place in London at the time and it was unwise to simply fling open one's doors to anyone. I saw her standing outside, looking around her nervously.

'Let me in, Mr Zéla, please,' she said in a nervous voice. 'I must speak with you.'

'Alexandra,' I said, opening the door as she rushed inside. 'What's wrong? You look quite—'

'Close the door, he's after me!' she shouted and I shut it quickly, looking at her in surprise. Her normally pale complexion had grown flushed and, as she sank down into an armchair, she put one hand to her throat as if to catch her breath. 'I'm sorry to come here,' she said, 'but I couldn't think of anywhere else to turn.' Considering her family lived only downstairs, I found this an odd statement, but let it pass, pouring her a glass of port to steady her nerves and seating myself at a safe distance opposite her.

'You'd better tell me what has happened,' I said and she nodded slowly, taking a careful sip from her glass and closing her eyes gently as it warmed her inside. Again, I could not help but notice how beautiful she was as she sat there, clothed in a simple blue dress with a pale grey shawl at her neck.

'It's Arthur,' she replied eventually. 'He has gone mad, I believe! He wants to kill me!'

'Arthur . . .' I said thoughtfully, running through the

members of her family in my mind, as if one of them might be the intended murderer. But the boys' names were George and Alfred, and her father's name was no more Arthur than my own. 'I'm sorry . . . who *is* Arthur?'

At this she burst into tears and buried her face in her hands until such time as I stood up and went to fetch her a handkerchief, which she accepted gratefully, blowing her nose loudly in it before wiping the tear stains from her cheeks. 'It's a terrible business,' she said then, helping herself to a little more port from the bottle. 'I'm afraid I have not any confidante in which to place my secrets.'

'Well, then, you must place them here,' I said hesitantly, 'unless you would prefer that I go downstairs for your mother, of course.'

'No, not her,' she said loudly, making me jump in my chair. 'She mustn't know any of this. She would throw me out of the house.'

Immediately, I suspected the worst. She had arranged another marriage, or worse, she had already undertaken one and was with child. Whatever it was, I wished that I had no involvement in the business. 'You must tell me how I can help you,' I said then, moved by her obvious unhappiness.

She nodded and took a deep breath before speaking. 'Arthur is in charge of the school where I am currently in training. Arthur Dimmesdale is his name.'

'Dimmesdale . . . Dimmesdale . . .' I said, sure that the name meant something to me, but not quite sure where to place it.

'We have been having an illicit romance,' she continued. 'At first it was innocent, it grew out of a mutual affection we had for each other. It was entirely

376

natural. We enjoyed each other's company, we would dine together sometimes, he took me on a picnic in the early months of our courtship.'

'The early months?' I said surprised. 'How long has this relationship existed then?'

'About six months,' she answered, a figure which pre-dated our own acquaintance and overlapped with her alleged affair with the Prince of Wales.

'And what about the young prince?' I asked her cautiously.

'What young prince?'

'Well,' I said, laughing slightly, unsure whether the conversation had ever really taken place, so absurd did it seem now, 'you mentioned that you had an under-standing with the Prince of Wales. That you were plan-ning on eloping together as his mother would never agree to the match.'

She stared at me incredulously, as if I was the worst kind of madman she had ever had the misfortune to meet, before bursting out laughing. 'The Prince of Wales?' she asked, between her convulsions. 'How could *I* be having a relationship with the Prince of Wales? Isn't he just a child?'

'Well, yes,' I admitted. 'I did say that originally my-self but you seemed convinced that—'

'You must be mixing me up with someone else, Mr Zéla,' she said.

'Matthieu, please.'

'You must have a veritable harem of young girls confiding their problems in you,' she added with a flirtatious smile. I sat back in my chair and knew not what to say to her. The conversation had taken place – I could remember it distinctly – and now here was another. It was now that her position as a fictionalist first became clear to me. 'Anyway,' she continued eventually, 'Arthur and I have become more than friends, I am ashamed to admit. He has . . .' – and here she paused for dramatic effect, her eyes darting from left to right as if she was already on the stage – 'he has *known* me, Mr Zéla.'

'Matthieu—'

'He has taken from me that which can never be restored. And I am damned to admit that I allowed it. For such was my own passion for him, you see. I am in love with him but now I fear that he does not love me.' I nodded and wondered whether I was expected to ask questions or not at this point. She was staring at me, wild-eyed, and it did appear to be my turn to speak so I asked her further about Arthur, whose name was swimming through my mind as I attempted to place it. 'He is in charge of our school,' she answered. 'And worse . . . he is a man of the cloth.'

'A priest?' I said, astonished and ready to laugh now as she took the deception further and further.

'A minister,' she replied. 'A Puritan minister at that. Ha!' she laughed, as if the very idea of Arthur's puritanism was no more than a joke to her. 'He has sought to deny our affair but the other teachers have gotten wind of it. There are moves to eject me from my position. The rest of the staff, they consider me a harlot, a woman of no shame and, because they fear divine retribution if they criticize Arthur, they have turned on me instead. They have demanded my dismissal and, if he does not agree to it, they intend to stand up in front of the whole school and denounce me for a wanton. When my parents hear of this, they will kill me. And as for Arthur . . . Why, his whole career could be at risk.'

Suddenly, like a lightning bolt, it hit me. I stood up,

ostensibly to get another bottle of port, for the one we had both been drinking from had been almost empty before and was drained now. Beneath my bookcases, which were on the far side of the room behind her, I took a bottle from the cabinet and reached up to take down the volume which I was sure lay behind this fiction. It was a new book, published only a year or so earlier, by the American writer Nathaniel Hawthorne, and had proved a popular success with readers. I skimmed through the pages, looking for the name, and I came across it quickly, on page thirty-five, the name whose scurrilous adventures had caused such a scandal in literary circles not twelve months earlier: '"Good Master Dimmesdale," said he, "the responsibility of this woman's soul lies greatly with you. It behoves you, therefore, to exhort her to repentance, and to confession, as a proof and consequence thereof."' Arthur Dimmesdale. Puritan minister and lover of Hester Prynne. I sighed and replaced the book on the shelf and the bottle in the cabinet; I suspected that Alexandra had no further need of alcohol.

'I saw him tonight,' she said as I returned to my seat, an elbow on the arm-rest, my cheek flattened to the heel of my hand. 'He was following me through the streets. He means to kill me, Mr Zéla. Matthieu, I mean. He means to cut my throat so that I might never be able to explain my side of this story to anyone.'

'Alexandra,' I said, 'are you sure that you are not just imagining things?'

She laughed. 'Well,' she replied, 'I realize that the streets are dark, but—'

'No, no,' I said, shaking my head. 'This whole relationship, I mean. Arthur Dimmesdale. His name is familiar to me, is it not?'

'You *know* him?' she asked, her eyes opening wide as she sat forward in her chair. 'He is a *friend* of yours?'

'I know *of* him,' I answered. 'I have read about him. Is he not a character in—'

'What was that?' she said quickly, a noise on the corridor outside alerting her attention, the simple creak of floorboards as a breeze passed through. 'He is here!' she declared. 'He has followed me! I must leave!' She jumped out of her seat and threw her coat on again before heading for the door. I followed, completely unsure of what I should do next.

'But where will you go?' I asked her and she touched my arm gently in thanks.

'Don't worry about me,' she said. 'I will go downstairs to my parents' home. With any luck they will not have heard of my behaviour yet. I'll sleep there tonight and make my plans in the morning. Thank you, Matthieu. You have been a great help.'

She kissed me on the cheek before disappearing through the door. Alexandra Jennings, self-styled bearer of a Scarlet Letter, sole inhabitant of a world which she created for herself on a daily basis.

May Day arrived and with it the opening day of the 'Great Exhibition of the Works of Industry of All Nations'. I was in the Crystal Palace from five in the morning, seeing to the final preparations, making sure that all those in the receiving line would be in their places in time for the opening ceremony. Although it was quite warm out, there was a slight drizzle in the air which I hoped would clear up by mid-morning, when most of the carriages would be en route. Over half a million people were expected to gather in Hyde Park that morning, awaiting the arrival of the foreign dignitaries along with the young Queen Victoria and her family. The building had been finally finished, with the very last touches added only hours earlier. As far as the eye could see were arranged the displays and exhibits, containing everything from chinaware to steam engines, hydraulic pumps to national costumes, butterflies to butter churns. The colours and ornaments stretched out in a rainbow of display beneath the glass surroundings and there was a constant sound of the intake of breath as the visitors passed through, amazed by the wondrous sights which greeted them at every juncture. The Queen herself arrived at lunchtime and formally declared the Exhibition open. The foreign delegates were presented to her before Sir Joseph Paxton himself gave her a tour of the British exhibits and she later wrote of the experience in her diaries with admiration for the craftsmanship that had gone into the preparations.

It was near midnight by the time I returned home to my rooms but I felt as if the time had passed by within about the space of an hour. I could hardly recall a day so filled with excitement and the luminescence of artistry as had been gathered before me then. The Exhibition was a success – eventually over six million people would pass through it – and all the hard work which had gone into it had paid off. Although I felt gratified by my work, I could see what a small hand I had actually played in the preparations and contented myself with the knowledge that I had managed to take even a tiny role in one of the great events of recent times.

I settled down with a book and a glass of wine; naturally I was exhausted but decided to wind down a little before going to bed. I was expected back at the Crystal Palace the following morning and so required sleep if I was to be of any use whatsoever. I thought I could hear a commotion coming from downstairs in the Jennings household but gave it barely a thought until footsteps came charging up in my direction and someone attempted to gain entry to my room, which I had locked after coming in.

I stepped quickly towards it and was about to shout out to ask who was on the other side when I heard the familiar voice of Richard, raised in anger for the first time, calling my name as he banged on the door with a clenched fist.

'Richard,' I said, opening it at once, fearing that he was being attacked on the other side and before I could say another word he pushed through, driving me against the far wall and holding me there with his hand pinning me by the throat. The room spun in my surprise and it was a few moments before I realized exactly what was taking place. I kicked out but, in his anger, his strength had increased and it took the sensible actions of his wife to pull him away from me. I collapsed on to the floor, coughing and spluttering, and holding my wounded throat with one hand.

'What in God's name—?' I began before he cut me off by kicking out at my prostrate form, cursing me for a dog and a traitor.

'Richard, get off him,' roared Betty, grabbing her husband with equal force and pushing him back until he landed on my sofa. I took advantage of this moment to struggle to my feet and prepare a defensive position for another attack.

'You'll pay for this, Zéla,' he roared and I looked from husband to wife in amazement, unsure what crime I could have possibly committed to receive such treatment from my sometime friend.

'I don't understand,' I said, looking to Betty for an explanation, expecting her to be slightly more open to reason than her husband. 'What's going on here? What am I supposed to have done?'

'She's just a *child*, Mr Zéla,' said Betty, bursting into tears, and I feared that she might attack me next. 'Couldn't you have left her alone? Just a *child*.'

'Who is just a child?' I asked, shaking my head, pleased to note that, although Richard had taken control of himself again and was looking furiously in my direction, he did not appear poised for another attack.

'You'll marry her,' he said to me before looking at his wife and speaking as if I was not in the room. 'Do you hear that, missus? He'll marry her. There's no other choice.'

'Marry *who*?' I begged, sure that I had caused no offence to anyone that could merit such a terrible punishment. 'Who on earth am I to marry?'

'It's Alexandra, of course,' said Betty, looking at me irritably as if to suggest that I should get past the denials and move straight on to the retribution. 'Who do you think we're talking about?'

'*Alexandra*?' I roared, finally unsurprised. 'Why on earth would I marry Alexandra?'

'Because you have tarnished her, you cur,' cried Richard. 'You stand there, look at the cut of him will ya, and deny it? Do you? Well?'

'I most certainly do,' I said firmly. 'I most *certainly* do. I haven't so much as touched your daughter.'

'The lying—' He sprang from his seat but this time I was ready for him and punched him in the nose as he leaped towards me. Although I had not intended on hitting him hard – merely hoping that the blow would

383

prevent him from attacking me again – I immediately heard the sickening crunch of a bone breaking and I gasped as he fell to the floor, blood pouring from the centre of his face as he cried out in pain.

'What have you done?' gasped Betty, rushing to her husband's side and screaming as she pulled his hands away to see the torrent of blood coming from his broken nose. 'Oh, call the police!' she cried out to no one in particular. 'The police, someone! Murder! Murder!'

By three o'clock the following morning the story was settled. Alexandra and I were both summoned to Richard Jennings's kitchen where we stood sullenly on opposite sides, staring each other down. I had explained privately to Betty Jennings the conversations I had already had with her daughter and she had shown little surprise by them. The doctor had treated her husband's nose and he sat there sulking, his face purple with bruising, his eyes baggy and bloodshot. 'Alexandra,' I said quietly, looking in her direction and pleading for honesty, 'you must tell them the truth. For both our sakes, please.'

'The truth is, he promised to marry me,' said Alexandra. 'He said that if I . . . if I let him have his way with me he'd take me away from here. Said he had all the money in the world.'

'A couple of months ago she was marrying the Prince of Wales!' I cried in annoyance. 'Then she was having relations with a character straight out of *The Scarlet Letter*! She's mad, Mrs Jennings, mad!'

'You promised!' roared Alexandra.

'I did no such thing!'

'You have to marry me now!'

'Child, shut up!' screamed Betty Jennings, most likely feeling that enough was enough. 'That's an end to it, both of you. Alexandra, I want the truth now and there's neither of us leaving this kitchen until I get it. Mr Zéla, you go on back up to your rooms and I'll be up to you presently.' I moved to protest but there was no arguing with her. '*Presently*, Mr Zéla!' I returned to my rooms.

I met Richard the following afternoon as I was supervising an area occupied by the Cornish Quilt-makers' Association. If anything, his face seemed even worse than it had the night before but he approached me sheepishly and immediately apologized for his behaviour.

'She's always been like that, you see,' he explained. 'I don't know why it is that I fall for it every time. But when a man thinks his daughter's been tampered with, well—'

'Really,' I said, 'there's no need to explain. But you realize that there is something wrong with the girl, don't you? She's told me some wonderful tales over these last few months. I believed some of them at first too. I promise you, she'll land herself in a heap of trouble one of these days if she's not very careful.'

'I know, I know,' he said, looking sad and dejected. 'But it's not as simple as all that. She's just blessed with an over-active imagination, that's all.'

'Please,' I replied, 'there's a difference between an imagination and a downright lie. Particularly when the person passing it off as the truth actually believes what they're saying.'

'Right enough,' he acknowledged.

'So what are you going to do about her?' I asked after an incredibly annoying period of silence had passed. 'You realize I'll have to move out because of this. She needs help, Richard. Medical help.'

'Well, sir,' said Richard, turning and taking my arm, pressing on the bone as if even now, despite his apology, it would have done him the world of good to knock me unconscious. 'If you ask me it's better to be the harmless child that tells the stories than the gullible fool who believes them.' I gasped in surprise. He was excusing her behaviour, was that it?

'Your daughter should be a novelist, sir,' I said angrily, pulling away from him. 'She could probably find a way to fashion a brand new story on every single page.'

He shrugged and said nothing as I walked away.

A few years later, while holidaying in Cornwall, I caught sight of Alexandra Jennings once again. It was in a newspaper report in *The Times*. The brief article, dated 30 April 1857, stated the following:

FAMILY DIES IN HOUSE FIRE

A London family were killed tragically when their house burned down during the night, Friday. Mr Richard and Mrs Betty Jennings, along with their four children, Alfred, George, Victoria and Elizabeth, all died after a burning coal caught with a rug, sending the entire house up in flames. The only survivor was another daughter, Alexandra, 23, who told our reporter that she had been away from the scene when the fire had taken place, staying with friends. 'I feel like the luckiest girl in the world,' she was reported to have said, 'although I have, of course, lost my entire family.'

Perhaps I was becoming an old cynic, but as I read it I found her alibi less than convincing. She had never been violent, in my experience, but I couldn't help but wonder what stories she had been spinning in the intervening time and what tales she would fashion from this disaster. I read a little further, but the article concerned itself with the events of the inquest, until the very last paragraph, which contained the following.

The former Miss Jennings, a widow herself and a teacher in a local school, has vowed to rebuild the house where she was born. 'It contains all my childhood memories,' she told us, 'not to mention the fact that it was where my late husband Matthieu and I were happy during our brief marriage.' Alexandra's husband died tragically six months after their marriage from tuberculosis. There was no issue.

She may have been a fictionalist – she may have been a downright liar – but she managed to do something that neither God nor man had been able to do for one hundred and fourteen years before that or one hundred and twelve years since: she killed me off.

Chapter 21

October 1999

On 12 October, at four o'clock in the morning, I took a taxi to the City Hospital where my nephew Tommy lay in a coma, following a drugs overdose. He had been brought in by an anonymous friend towards midnight the night before, and Andrea – Tommy's pregnant girlfriend – had been contacted an hour later by the hospital, following a phone call made to his apartment, the number of which was in his wallet. Shortly after that, she phoned me, waking me up with a sense of *déjà vu*, for it had been a similar late night phone call which had alerted me to James Hocknell's death a few months earlier.

I arrived, tired and bleary eyed, at the front reception desk, asked for directions to my nephew's room and was sent upstairs and towards intensive care, where I found him hooked up to a heart monitor with an intravenous tube inserted into a vein on his needle-marked arms. He looked perfectly peaceful, he even had a slight smile hovering about his lips, but I could see that his breathing was laboured and a little less than regular due to the uncertain movements of his chest. His heart rate and blood pressure were being constantly monitored and the sight of him lying there, a picture typically seen on a television medical show, was depressing but somehow inevitable.

While walking towards his room, I had noticed a small group of nurses hovering outside the window, staring in at him excitedly and I even heard one wonder how 'Tina' would take the news if he died. 'Perhaps she'd go straight back to Carl,' said another. 'Them two were made for each other.'

'He'd never forgive her. After what she did with his brother? Forget it,' said a third, but they all walked away when they saw me approach. I sighed. Such was the life my unfortunate nephew had set out for himself and such was the one he was damned to continue living.

A short history of the DuMarqués: they have been an unfortunate line. Every one of them has had their life cut short, either by their own stupidity or by the machinations of the times. My own brother Tomas had a son, Tom, who died in the French Revolution; his son Tommy was shot during a card game for stealing aces; his unlucky son Thomas died when a jealous husband tried to run me through with a sword in Rome and ran him through instead; his son Tom caught malaria in Thailand; his son Thom was killed in the Boer War; his son Tom was crushed by a speeding motor car in the Hollywood Hills'; his son Thomas died at the end of the Second World War; his son Tomas was killed in a gangland riot; his son Tommy is a soap opera actor, lying in a coma following a drugs overdose.

I stood by the window myself for some time and watched him. Although I had been warning Tommy for so long about the chances of his ending up in this very condition, it shocked me to see him finally laid so low. Gone was the handsome, self-assured, bright young man who was recognized wherever he went, the celebrity, the star, the fashion plate; replaced by a mere body in a bed, breathing with the help of a machine, unable to turn away now from the prying eyes. I should have done more, I thought. This time, I should have done more.

I met Andrea for the first time in the waiting room a few minutes later. She was sitting there alone, drinking a cup of hospital coffee, in the typically sterile atmosphere which hardly encourages relaxation. The stench of disinfectant surrounded us and there was only one window, which didn't open and was in need of cleaning. Although I had never met Tommy's girlfriend before, I guessed it was her by her obvious pregnancy and the fact that she was shaking and staring at the ground.

'Andrea?' I asked, leaning in towards her and touching her gently on the shoulder. 'Are you Andrea?'

'Yes . . .' she said, looking at me as if I might be a doctor come to bring her the bad news.

'I'm Matthieu Zéla,' I explained quickly. 'We spoke earlier on the phone.'

'Oh, yes,' she said, looking both relieved and disappointed at once. 'Of course. We meet at last,' she added with an attempt at a smile. 'Of all the places. Would you like some coffee? I could . . .'

Her voice trailed off as I shook my head and sat down opposite her. She was wearing clothes that looked like they had been lying beside her bed before she'd crawled out of it. Dirty jeans, a T-shirt, running shoes without socks. Her dark blonde hair was curly but needed a wash and as she wore no make-up, her face had a natural beauty which appealed. 'I don't know what happened to him,' she said, shaking her head miserably. 'I wasn't even with him when it happened. Some friend of his brought him here and then disappeared. One of those hangers-on that are always lurking, hanging out of his coat, getting into clubs for free, trying to get a part or pick up girls.' She paused and looked suitably angry. 'I *can't* believe he OD'd,' she said. 'He's always so careful. He's supposed to *know* what he's doing.'

'It's difficult to remain careful when you're high on drugs all the time,' I replied irritably. I find myself increasingly irritated by the young; the older I grow, the more distance that exists between myself and the current generation, the more maddening I find them. I had thought that the previous one – the generation born around the 1940s – was bad enough but everyone that I had ever encountered connected to my nephew, all of those born in the 1970s, seemed oblivious to the dangers the world presented them. It was as if they *all* believed they could live to be my age.

'It was never *all* the time,' she retorted, and I noticed that she was already using the past tense in reference to him. 'He liked a little something socially, that was all. No more than everyone else does.'

'*I* don't,' I said and I didn't have the first clue why I was behaving so puritanically; now I was irritating my-self as well.

'Well, then, you're a fucking saint, aren't you?' she shot back immediately. '*You're* not in an incredibly stressful job, working eighteen hour days, being stared at wherever you go and always having to put on this . . . this *display* for millions of people who don't even know you.'

'I realize that. I'm—'

'You don't know what it's—'

'Andrea, I realize that,' I repeated firmly, silencing her with my tone. 'I'm sorry. I know that my nephew leads a bizarre existence. I know it can't be easy for him. My God, I've heard him talk about it often enough. For now, though, I feel we should be thinking about his recovery and how we can prevent this from happening again, assuming he survives. Has a doctor spoken to you yet?'

She nodded. 'Just before you got here,' she said, quieter now. 'He said that the next twenty-four hours will be crucial, but I think they just train them to say that at medical school no matter what the situation is. It seems to me the next twenty-four hours are *always* crucial, whatever's going on. Either he'll wake up, in which case he'll be all right after a few days, or he could be brain damaged, or he'll stay like that. Lying there. In that bed. For God knows how long.' I nodded. In other words, the doctor had said nothing that a fool couldn't have diagnosed.

'You're shaking,' I said after a reasonable pause, leaning across to take her hand. 'And you're freezing cold. Shouldn't you get a jacket or something? The baby . . .' I muttered, not quite sure what I was trying to say but feeling that there was a good chance she shouldn't be sitting around catching pneumonia when she was six months pregnant.

'I'm all right,' she said, shaking her head. 'I just want him to wake up. I love him, Mr Zéla,' she offered, almost apologetically.

'Matthieu, please.'

'I love him and I need him. That's all there is to it.'

I stared at her and wondered. My problem with Andrea was this: firstly, I didn't know the girl so I didn't know what her qualities were, what her position at work was, who her family were, what kind of money she earned, where she lived in London and how many people she shared with. I didn't know the first thing about her so it was perfectly reasonable of me to be suspicious.

On the other hand, I could have misjudged her. She could love him. Simple as that. She could know the sickening, aching pain that goes with love. She could know how it feels to be aware of someone's presence in a building, even when you're not together; she could know how it feels to be hurt and damaged and crucified by someone and still be unable to shake them from your head, no matter how hard you try, no matter how many years you are apart; she could know that, even years later, all it would take would be one phone call and you would go to them, drop everything, desert everyone, put the world on hold. She could feel those things for Tommy and I could be denying her that right.

'The baby,' she said after a while. 'He has to live for the baby's sake. That's what will make him hold on, isn't it? Well? Isn't it?'

I shrugged. I doubted it. I know a little about the Thomases and their lack of resilience.

The lift opened on the ground floor of the hospital and I stepped outside, surprised by the number of people waiting near the main reception desk. I gave them a cursory glance – old men, sitting and rocking back and forth catatonically through some internal rhythm, young women in cheap clothes with greasy hair and tired faces yawning and drinking from murky plastic cups of tea, children buzzing around the floor noisily, alternating between tears and screams – and made for the doorway. They opened automatically as I approached them and the second I stepped outside I took a long, deep breath of fresh air and felt it recharge my body from within. The day was breaking, it was bright now but it would still be an hour or so before full service was restored, and the wind bit through me as I wrapped my coat closer around my body.

I was about to hail a taxi when, like a moment of revelation, I spun around and stared back at the hospital. I thought about it and shook my head – it couldn't be. After a moment, I walked back quickly through the doors and looked at the mass of seats once again, scanning the faces carefully this time, aiming directly for where I had seen him, but now he had been replaced by an old woman breathing from an inhaler. I looked around, my mouth open, and I had the sudden impression that I was in a film. The scene before me was opening up like a wide angle shot and I was carefully moving around the reception area before my eyes focused on the drinks machine where he stood, a finger hovering over the choices as he made his decision. I walked towards him, grabbed him by the collar and pulled him around. A fifty pence coin fell to the floor and he almost tripped over himself with surprise. I was right; I stared at him and shook my head.

'What the hell are you doing here?' I demanded. 'How the hell did you find out?'

The irony of watching a report of my nephew's overdose and currently comatose condition on my own broadcasting station's breakfast news show was not lost on me. I didn't sleep much when I got home; instead I collapsed into a comfortable armchair which could easily fit two average sized people and closed my eyes for a while, dozing fitfully before I realized that the night's sleep was lost to me. Afterwards, I took a long, hot shower, applying exotic shower gels with intriguing fragrances to my body and shampoos with heavy scents of coconut to my hair before emerging in a thick bathrobe a half hour later into the kitchen. It was refreshing and gave me a new energy for the day that I would have otherwise lacked. I prepared a light breakfast – a tall glass of cold orange juice, a toasted muffin with sliced kiwi – and ate it in front of the television as the coffee brewed.

A reporter named Roach Henderson was standing outside the hospital and he looked as if he would rather be almost anywhere else in the world than standing there in the freezing cold, worrying that his hairpiece might blow away in the middle of his broadcast. I knew Roach only slightly, his real name was Ernest but for some reason he had decided in his early twenties to call himself 'Roach'. I think he had been heavily influenced by the anchormen of the American news shows and believed that an exotic first name would lend him both credibility and a desk job in a warm studio. He had achieved neither in the twenty odd years since. It was interesting that he had chosen a bug's name for his own.

'Roach,' asked the *real* anchorman, Colin Molton, his brow furrowed in trademarked worry, a biro tapping against his lips as he himself stared at the television screen containing the reporter's image. 'What can you tell us of Tommy DuMarqué's condition? Roach,' he added once again to indicate that it was his turn to speak now.

'Well, as most of you know,' began Roach, ignoring the question and launching into his prepared speech anyway, 'Tommy DuMarqué is one of the nation's most *recognizable* actors.' Stress on the 'recognizable'. 'He began his career eight *years* ago, playing Sam Cutler on a leading soap opera—' Photographs and a brief scene from a few years ago were quickly played. 'Having also launched himself into the worlds of pop *music* as well as *modelling*, it's fair to say that Tommy DuMarqué's condition is one which will be monitored by the general public *as well* as entertainment insiders. Colin.' It was like saying 'over' at the end of every sentence on a walkie-talkie.

'So what *is* his condition then? Roach,' Colin repeated his question.

'Doctors say that he is *critical* but *stable*. We're still not quite sure what exactly *happened* to Tommy DuMarqué but reports are coming in to us that he collapsed at a fashionable night-club in London just after one o'clock this morning' – wrong, I thought – 'and was rushed here shortly after that. Although he was apparently *conscious* when he arrived here, he slipped into a coma soon afterwards and has remained in that condition since then. Colin.'

Colin looked incredibly upset now, as if this was his own son lying in the hospital. 'He's a young man, isn't he, Roach?'

'He's twenty-two, Colin.'

'And would you say that drugs played a part in these events? Roach.'

'Hard to say for definite right now, Colin, but it is well known that Tommy DuMarqué leads an *extravagant* lifestyle. He's photographed at clubs seven nights a week and I have heard reports that producers at the BBC wanted to put him through a rehabilitation course as his life was spinning out of control. He's been in trouble for continued lateness and also for an article written by a prominent *newspaper* columnist; he was widely believed to be the subject of a column detailing

396

his wild lifestyle and *sexual* habits. Colin.' I noticed that his head twitched with every stressed word.

'And I assume his family are gathered around his bedside this morning, Roach?'

'Unfortunately, both of Tommy DuMarqué's parents are dead but his girlfriend is here at the moment and I believe his uncle spent several hours in the hospital early this morning. No word yet on whether Sarah *Jensen*, who plays love interest and sister-in-law Tina Cutler on the show and whose television affair with DuMarqué has captivated millions over the last few months, has come to visit him but we'll let you know as soon as she gets here. Colin.'

Without so much as a goodbye, Colin's chair swivelled back round to face the camera and Roach's image vanished. Colin promised to keep us all in touch with the story throughout the day as it developed before his face changed entirely to tell us of a panda named Muffy which had just been born in London Zoo. I considered getting dressed and going out for the papers but I knew that Tommy's state would be front page stuff and couldn't be bothered. Instead I put on some music and closed my eyes, allowing my mind to drift away from these current problems, if only for a little while.

Lee Hocknell opened and closed his mouth like a fish as he stood before me, unsure what to say. His surprise at seeing me was typical of his stupidity for surely he would have known that I would arrive at the hospital as soon as I heard the news. I mean I might have had a lot of nephews in my time but Tommy was the only one of them who was still alive. Lee was dressed quite fashionably and I noticed that he had undergone a severe haircut since I had last seen him at his father's funeral. It was cut close to the scalp and stood out in tufted bunches, a definite improvement on the hippie look he had sported for the funeral.

'Mr Zéla,' he said when I let him go and stood staring at him furiously, 'I didn't see you—'

'What the *hell* are you doing here?' I repeated, edging closer towards him. 'How long have you been here? How did you find out about this?'

He stood back in surprise as if it should be obvious how he had found out about Tommy's overdose and in a moment, of course, it was. 'It was me who brought him in here,' he explained. 'We were at a club, you see, and he suddenly started to act weird. Collapsed on the floor. I thought he was dead. I called an ambulance and brought him here. He woke up on the way so then I thought he must be all right but now they say he's gone into a coma. Is that right?'

'Well, yes,' I said quietly, wondering why on earth Lee Hocknell had been in a club with my nephew in the first place. I looked around and saw a quiet corner of the reception area and led him firmly towards it, sitting him down beside me with as threatening an expression on my face as I could muster. 'Now,' I said, 'I want to know what you were doing with him in the first place. You don't know each other, do you?'

He looked at the ground and sighed. For a moment, he was like a little boy who had been caught doing something he shouldn't and was trying to think of how to lie his way out of it. When he looked back up at me, he was biting his lip and I could tell that he was nervous. Whatever they had been doing, it had clearly got out of hand.

'I phoned him, you see,' he explained, 'about the script. Somehow I thought I'd have a better chance with him than with you. I told the people at the studio my name and said that he'd take my call. And he did too.'

'Of course he did,' I said sternly. 'We both received your letters and the script.'

'Yeah,' he muttered in reply, unable to look me in the eye. 'Anyway, I spoke to Tommy on the phone and told him that I wanted to meet with him. He wasn't sure, suggested bringing you along, but I told him that I wasn't trying to bribe anyone or get them to do anything they didn't want to do. I just wanted to discuss it with him. Get some advice. It's like you said before, he knows a lot about the industry. I thought he could help me.' He sighed and paused before continuing, as if he genuinely wished that none of this had ever taken place. 'So he said OK, he agreed to meet with me and we got together for a drink last night. And it just escalated from that. We got on really well actually,' he added, his face lighting up, and I realized that his whole persona had changed overnight from that of blackmailer to that of star-struck groupie. 'We just had a really good laugh. We'd lots in common.'

'Really?' I asked in surprise. I couldn't imagine what.

'Oh, yeah. Well, like, we're the same age and everything. We're both, eh, artistic.' I raised an eyebrow but said nothing. 'We talked about my script of course.'

'And what did he say?'

'Tommy said it wasn't easy to get financing. Said he could put me in touch with some people though. He said it needed more work. That it would be a hard sell in its present condition.'

'He's not wrong there,' I said.

'He promised to help me,' he said quietly and, for a moment, I feared tears. He looked at me as if he was trying to convince me that my nephew, the celebrity, was his new best friend. From that position of glamour, I knew there was no such thing as a true friend. Spending time with someone famous is generally done for one reason and one reason only: because it's easier to get girls that way.

'Listen, Lee,' I said slowly, my head spinning with the possibilities that his character could take on now. What kind of person was he exactly? 'You were there that night, weren't you?'

'Where?'

'In the house. Your father's house. The night he died. You were there. That's what your script is all about, right?'

He nodded and blushed, which was bizarre. 'I was upstairs,' he said. 'I heard what happened. I know *you* didn't do it. But you should have called the police, that's all. You should have been honest about it. That story about him being at the office, well, it just wasn't true.'

'Just explain this to me,' I said, unwilling to be preached at by this boy, particularly when I knew that he was probably right. 'Are you actually expecting to blackmail Tommy and I with this information?' He didn't look at me, as if being actually faced with me, having to do this in person as opposed to through a letter, made the whole thing a lot harder. I suspected this was a good time to be having this conversation; when neither of us knew what was going to happen to Tommy and there was some possibility that Lee himself could be dragged into it.

'I just need a start,' he said, unwilling to commit himself to a yes or no answer on the blackmailing question. 'That's all I need. Just to get my career off the ground. I just thought one of you could help me. And, you know, I *may* have saved your nephew's life.'

'Or you may have killed him. Tell me. What exactly happened? How did he OD?'

Lee licked his lips and thought about it. 'We had a bit to drink,' he said. 'And it was strange for me, because everyone in the pub was looking at us all the time, because they recognized Tommy of course and, while it was incredibly strange to feel that, I started to imagine they were looking at me too.'

'Well, they probably were,' I admitted. 'People always look at the person with the celebrity. They want to know who that is too. They assume it must be Someone with a capital "s" or they wouldn't be together. And most of the time it is too.'

'Anyway, some people came over and asked for autographs. They looked at me and weren't sure whether they should ask me too. Some of them did and I signed. We pretended that I'd just joined the show. Tommy told them that in a month's time everyone would know who I was.'

'Oh, for God's sake.'

'It was just for fun, that's all. We didn't mean any harm. Eventually we decided to go on to a club and he asked me where I wanted to go. I named some place that I'd tried to get into a few times and always been refused and he just laughed and took me straight there in a cab. There must have been about a hundred people standing in a queue outside trying to get in but we went straight to the top and the bouncers just fawned all over him and let us right in without even having to pay. It was incredible! Every eye was on us. We got free drinks, a table. When we hit the dance floor, every woman in the place started coming on to us. It was amazing. The best night of my life.' He was staring at the floor as he spoke, and had taken on the look of a child in a toy store. Tommy had given him a glimpse of what it was like to be famous and he'd loved it. He was hooked now. We'd never get rid of him.

'So what happened next?' I asked. 'Where did the drugs come in?'

'Tommy hooked up with a guy he knew there and they disappeared off to the toilets for a while to shoot up. He came back and he was fine. We picked up a couple of women, had a lot more to drink and decided to all go back to my place for some more.'

'For God's sake,' I said. 'This is like a rerun of how your father died. Don't you kids learn *anything*?'

'I wasn't thinking about that,' he said, staring at me angrily. 'I was . . . All I wanted was . . .'

'You wanted to get laid,' I said. 'Thank you, but I figured that one out. With those girls, with Tommy, with whoever. You just—'

'Hey, hold on a second—'

'No, you hold on,' I said, grabbing his collar. 'You're an idiot, you know that? What drugs did you take?'

'I didn't take any!' he said. 'I swear it! It was just Tommy and this other guy. We'd only stepped outside the club and the air hit us and before I knew what was happening he was on the ground, rolling around. He didn't look too bad but then his eyes opened real wide and he wasn't moving and so we called an ambulance. That's it, that's the whole story. That's all that happened.'

'All right, all right,' I said. 'Fine.' Somehow, I felt sorry for him. All he wanted was to be somebody. He'd seen a chance for that and gone after it. He'd used some unfortunate tactics, granted, but rather than a vicious blackmailer, intent on squeezing us for everything he could gain, he appeared to me like a child, anxious for approval, looking for friends. I sat back and sighed. 'I'm going home,' I said eventually, handing him a small notebook and pen from the inside pocket of my coat. 'Write your number down in that,' I said. 'I'll be in touch with you. I'm making no promises though, all right? Tommy wasn't exaggerating. Your script needs a *lot* of work.'

He wrote his number down greedily and I felt like laughing at the absurdity of the situation. This boy, I thought, is only going to cause me trouble. He didn't seem to care about his father dying, he'd withheld the truth from the police, he'd tried to blackmail me and, the worst crime of all, he was a terrible writer. So why was I so sure that I was going to help him after all?

Chapter 22

Conspiring with Dominique

Months passed and I began to grow less weary of Nat Pepys, for his visits became more irregular with time and when he was present he did not seem as interested in Dominique as I had previously thought. I continued with my work but began to think more seriously about moving on; my two fears were first, how Tomas would take the news as he had settled into life there better than any of us, yet there was no way that I felt I could leave without him, and second, whether Dominique would come with me at all. She wasn't a child; unlike my brother she could make her own decisions.

It was summer now and a birthday party was taking place for Alfred junior, the religious second son of Sir Alfred Pepys. About fifty people had gathered for the festivities which were taking place outdoors. The morning dew left a shine on the grass which sparkled when the sun caught it. The flowerbeds were all in bloom and the estate looked as healthy and vital as it ever had.

Jack and I were tending to the carriages and horses which lined the driveway of Cageley House from the entrance right to the stables where we generally worked. We were carting bucketloads of water to the horses to prevent dehydration in the heat; in truth it was we who were feeling the effects of the heatwave as we went from one end of the estate to the other, carrying heavy buckets all the way. We were not allowed to take our shirts off when there was company present, so they were sticking to our backs through our perspiration. I began to lose track of my work, going to and fro without even realizing the time passing or the number of horses to whom we were attending. The day grew almost white with brightness before my eyes and I could see no one or hear nothing until eventually, as I filled yet another bucket from the tap beside the stables, I felt Jack's hand on my shoulder, shaking me lightly.

'Enough,' he said, collapsing on the grass beside me. 'We've done enough for now. They're all OK.'

'You think?' I asked, almost ready to cry with relief. 'We can take a break?'

He nodded. In the distance out towards the lawn, we could see some of the guests mingling, sipping glasses of ice cold lemonade. I heard footsteps behind me and grinned as I saw Dominique come towards us with a tray. 'You two ready for something to eat?' she asked, smiling at us, and I doubt if either of us had ever been happier to see a living soul. She had prepared some bread and meat for us and a tall pitcher of lemonade stood in the centre of the tray, with a couple of tankards of beer beside it. We ate and drank gratefully for a few minutes, saying nothing as our strength returned to us. I could feel the lemonade passing through my throat and into my body, its sweetness going some way to restoring my blood sugar levels, and I began to feel less shaky and, instead, tired.

'This is no way to live,' I said eventually, rubbing at the muscles in my arms, astonished by how much larger my forearms had grown in recent months. I was stronger than I had ever been but unlike Jack, whose body seemed naturally designed for strength and muscle, I was still sinewy, the brawn seeming almost too much for my still youthful frame. 'I need another job.'

'You and me both,' he said, although he was a little closer to it than I was. Jack had decided that he wouldn't stay at Cageley past the summer and privately he had told me that he was planning on handing in his notice the following week. He had enough money to make his way to London and to survive for several months if need be, although he was convinced that he would find work as a clerk relatively easily. I didn't doubt it. He had bought a brand new suit and when he dressed up in it late one night to show me, I was astonished by the transformation. The stable lad seemed more of a man than any of the Pepys boys, who had gained adulthood and respectability simply through age and money; he was tall and handsome and wore the suit with the air of a man who was born to wear one. As he was also intelligent and quick-witted, I could not envision a situation where he would not find employment within a matter of days.

'Don't you two have any work to be getting on with?' Nat Pepys appeared from behind us and we sat up, squinting in the sunlight, shielding our eyes with the backs of our hands.

'We're eating our lunch, Nat,' said Jack aggressively.

'Looks to me like you've already eaten it, Jack,' replied Nat quickly. 'And it's *Mr* Pepys to you.'

Jack snorted and lay back down; I wasn't sure what to do. Nat was afraid of Jack – that was easy to see – but it was unlikely that anything more than talk would ever happen. As if to reassert his authority, Nat poked the toe of his boot into my ribs, making me jump up angrily.

'Come on, Matthieu,' he said, using my given name for once. 'Get up and get this stuff cleared away.' He indicated the tray with the empty plates and tankards. 'It's a mess. You're like a couple of pigs, the pair of you.'

I wasn't sure what to do, but eventually I picked up the offending items and brought them towards the kitchen, depositing them abruptly in the sink, causing Dominique and Mary-Ann to jump in surprise.

'What's up with you?' asked Mary-Ann.

'Just wash 'em,' I said aggressively. 'It's your job, not mine.' With a loud curse, I marched out and walked back to Jack, who was reclining on his elbows now, watching as I came towards him, and Nat walked away. When I looked across again at the kitchen doorway, Dominique and Nat were close in conversation and she was laughing at something he was saying. I breathed heavily and felt my fists clench. A fly buzzed in my face and I lashed out at it, blinded momentarily by the sun as my head jerked upwards. When I saw again, I could see their heads bending closer together and Nat's hand moving towards the back of her dress, reaching lower and lower until she looked at him coyly and a horrible smile spread across his face. My whole body grew tense with the knowledge of what I was about to do next.

'Mattie, what's wrong?' Vaguely, I could sense Jack beside me, trying to grab my arm as I marched towards Nat and Dominique. 'Mattie, stop it, it's not worth it,' he continued, but I could barely see him, so intent was I on the object of my anger, which at that moment could have been either of them; it could have been the innocent Jack himself, so enraged was I within. I saw

Nat turn to look at me and a sudden recognition of trouble spread across his face. He could see that I had lost my reason and that position, employment, money or servitude would count for nothing now. He took a step backwards as I reached him, grabbing him by the lapels and pulling him around. He fell awkwardly on the ground and struggled to find his feet as I made beckoning motions towards him.

'Get up,' I said, my voice deep and emerging from a place within myself I barely knew existed. 'Get up, Nat.'

He rose and made to turn around but I took hold of him again, just as both Dominique and Jack took a hold of me. Without realizing it, they had grabbed me from both sides, lowering my defences, making me helpless as Nat found his footing, pulled one arm back and threw a punch at my face. It was not fierce or particularly strong, but it stunned me for a moment and I fell backwards, preparing to recover myself and lunge at him, to kill him if necessary. As I blinked back into the daylight, my right fist clenched and I walked towards him, pulling it back as Jack shouted at me to stop. He knew what the consequences would be for me if I knocked Nat Pepys unconscious and so, as Dominique ran between us, getting in my way for a moment, he did it himself. He found the same anger within his own body and, most likely unwilling to let a man like Nat Pepys destroy my life, he launched his own attack, felling him with a slap to his left cheek, a punch in the stomach and a final right hook to the face.

Nat collapsed, bloody and unconscious, to the ground and we all three stood over him, witnessing the effects of our actions with increasing horror. The whole episode had lasted no more than a minute.

Jack was gone before Nat even regained consciousness. He lay there on the ground before us, broken, his face covered in the blood that was gushing from both his nose and his mouth. Within a few minutes the guests from the party were coming in our direction. A lady screamed, another fainted. The men looked indignant. Eventually, a doctor came towards us and he bent over Nat in order to examine him.

'We have to get him into the house,' the doctor said, and some of the younger men lifted him and carried him indoors. Within a few minutes, only Dominique, Mary-Ann and I were left standing outside.

'Where's Jack gone?' I asked in a daze, incredulous at the chain of events which had brought us here. I looked around blankly for my friend.

'Took a horse and fled,' said Mary-Ann. 'Did you not see him?'

I shook my head. 'No,' I said eventually.

'Slipped away through the crowd a few minutes ago. No one noticed because everyone was looking at Nat lying there.'

I wondered whether Nat would be all right and pulled my hair away from my face in frustration; it was all my fault. I spun around and stared at Dominique angrily. 'What happened?' I shouted at her. 'What the hell happened here?'

'You're asking me?' she yelled back, her face pale now. 'You're the one who came charging towards us. You looked like you were going to kill him.'

'He was all over you,' I roared. 'I saw where his hands were going. You don't understand—'

'*I'm not yours to protect!*' she screamed, before turning on her heels and running back into the kitchen. I shook my head in frustration. Beneath my feet a pale puddle of water and blood had gathered.

By nightfall, the story was all around the village. Jack had attacked Nat Pepys, had broken his jaw and two of his ribs, knocked out most of his teeth, stolen a horse from his employer and disappeared. The local constabulary were already giving chase. I lay in my bed at the Ambertons', unable to sleep as I worried for my friend. All his plans, everything he had been intending to do over the next few months, all potentially vanished because of me. My jealousy. At least Nat hadn't died; that was something. All I could think of was how Jack had done it because it had to be done; he had acted so I wouldn't have to.

The next morning, I rose before five and went straight to Cageley House. I had no idea whether I still had a job or not – I suspected not. Yet, I wasn't so worried about the turn of events since I now knew that I did not intend to stay around much longer at Cageley anyway; my time there had run out. I wanted to see Dominique. I wanted her to tell me how she felt. I discovered her walking across the fields as the day broke, her face white and her eyes a heavy red. She had clearly not slept either.

'No sign of him yet,' I said, unsure whether I meant this as a question or a statement. She shook her head.

'He's long gone,' she replied. 'He'll be halfway to London by now. Jack's not stupid.'

'Isn't he?' I asked, and she stared at me.

'What's that supposed to mean?'

'He was leaving anyway,' I said. 'He'd saved up enough money. He'd bought a suit. He was planning on putting himself out as a clerk in London. He was giving in his notice next week.'

She sighed loudly and I thought she was going to cry.

'This is all my fault,' she said, her French accent slipping back into place as she began mentally to dissociate herself from Cageley. 'We should never have come here. We had plans. We should have seen them through.'

We. How long since I had heard her use that phrase? As much as I despised myself for it, I began to see a positive outcome to this: that things would go back the way they had been a couple of years before, back in Dover. We would leave together, live together, stay together, grow old together. I found myself pushing the thought of Jack to the back of my mind, like an inconvenience in my plans and, as much as I hated myself for it, I couldn't help it. I bit my lip in frustration.

'What is it?' she asked, stopping and taking my hand in hers. I felt tears welling behind my eyes and bit down harder.

'He's . . .' I began, rubbing the heel of my hand to my eye quickly to wipe them away. 'He's my friend,' I said simply, my voice catching slightly. 'Jack . . . he's . . . he's my friend. Look what he did for me. And look what I did to him. I'm . . . I've . . .' I collapsed in tears and fell to the ground, burying my head in my arms to prevent her from seeing me in this condition. The more I tried to stop, the stronger the convulsions grew until I was babbling a stream of nonsense and my mouth was contorted with misery.

'Matthieu, Matthieu,' she whispered, wrapping herself around me, holding me to her as I wept upon her shoulder. She shushed me and rocked me back and forth like a baby until eventually I could cry no more and pulled away from her, tugging my shirt from my trousers to dry my face with. 'It's not your fault,' she said but there was no conviction in her voice and I didn't even need to utter the words 'Of course it is'.

411

I had destroyed Jack, my true friend, and he had saved me. And all I could think about was getting us all away from there and leaving him behind.

'What kind of man am I?' I asked her, hesitantly.

We walked back towards the house slowly. We knew not what awaited us there. There was a good chance that Dominique's position would be safe for now but I feared what might happen when I arrived there. Sure enough, I saw Sir Alfred standing outside the front door with a constable. They stared at us as we came across the field, continuing to talk but not letting me out of their sight as I walked towards them. When we got to the point where we should turn off for both the stables and the kitchen, he shouted to me and I turned around; he beckoned me over. I sighed and looked at Dominique, taking both her hands in mine.

'If we can leave here without any trouble,' I said, 'will you come with me?'

She looked at me, exasperated, and threw her eyes to the sky. 'Where would we go?' she asked.

'London,' I said. 'Like we originally planned. You, me and Tomas. I have a little money saved. Do you?'

'Yes,' she answered. 'A little. Not much though.'

'We can make things right,' I said, unsure whether even I believed this. Sir Alfred called to me again and I turned to see him growing ever more agitated.

'I don't know . . .' she said, and again there was a shout. I released her and started to walk backwards towards Sir Alfred and the constable. 'I'll come here tonight,' I said. 'I'll speak to you then. I'll meet you after midnight, all right?'

She gave an almost imperceptible nod before turning and walking away, her head bowed in sorrow.

*   *   *

412

Sir Alfred Pepys was broadly built and overweight, his face an overripe pumpkin sitting atop a body of pure obesity. He found it increasingly difficult to walk owing to arthritis and we rarely saw him around the grounds of Cageley House as he generally preferred to sit indoors, reading his books, drinking his wine and eating his livestock.

'Come here, Matthieu,' he said to me when I was only a few steps away from him. He grabbed me roughly by the arm and pushed me towards the constable, who looked me up and down several times with distaste. 'Now, sir,' he continued, looking at the younger man, 'you'd better ask him your questions.'

'What's your name, lad?' asked the constable, a middle-aged man with a heavy red beard and remarkable orange eyebrows. He took a pencil and pad from his pocket and licked the tip carefully before writing down my answers.

'Matthieu Zéla,' I said, spelling the name out for him immediately afterwards. He looked at me as if I was something he had recently spat up. He asked me what my position was at Cageley House and I told him that I was a stable lad.

'So you work alongside this Jack Holby, do you?' he asked me and I nodded. 'What sort of lad do you take him for then?'

'The very best sort,' I said, standing erect before him, as if speaking Jack's name meant that I should offer some sign of respect. 'A good friend, a hard worker, a peaceful fellow. Ambitious too.'

'Peaceful, eh?' said Sir Alfred. 'He weren't so peaceful when he broke my son's jaw and ribs, were he?'

'That was provoked,' I said, and for a moment I thought he was going to swing for me himself before the constable intervened. He asked for my side of what had taken place the previous afternoon and naturally I lied, claiming that Nat had swung the first punch and that Jack had been merely defending himself. 'The fact that Nat wouldn't have a chance of taking Jack is his own fault,' I insisted. 'He should have thought of it before he started it.'

The constable nodded and I waited for Sir Alfred to tell me to get off his estate immediately and never show my face there again, but he didn't. Incredibly, he asked me whether I thought I could manage the horses on my own for the time being, even suggested that there'd be a little more money in it for me if I did, and I shrugged and said that it would be all right.

'I'll have to get someone else eventually of course,' said Sir Alfred, scratching his beard thoughtfully. 'To replace Holby, I mean. We won't see him back here again.' Although I already knew this, my heart sank a little at its confirmation. I decided to try to help Jack a little, even at this late stage.

'No,' I said. 'We'll probably never see him again. He's probably halfway to Scotland by now.'

'Scotland?' asked the constable, laughing. 'Why would he be in Scotland?'

'I don't know,' I shrugged. 'I just imagine he'll go as far away from here as possible. Start again. You'll never catch him, you know.' They looked at each other and smirked. 'What?' I asked. 'What is it?'

'Your friend Jack Holby is nowhere near Scotland,' said the constable, leaning towards me so that I could smell the foul stench of his breath. 'We captured him late last night. He's in a cell in the village awaiting trial for grievous bodily harm. He'll be spending the next few years of his life in prison, my friend.'

Dominique and I met as arranged late that night. 'Everyone's talking about Jack,' she told me. 'Sir Alfred says he's going to be spending at least five years in jail for what he did.'

'Five years?' I asked, appalled. 'You can't be serious.'

'They say it could be six months before Nat can speak again. And they'll have to wait until his jaw heals to start fitting him for false teeth. The doctors are afraid the lower half of his face will collapse in upon itself in the meantime.'

I felt a rush of sickness inside me. Even Nat Pepys hadn't deserved such a fate. It looked as if everyone had lost out – Jack had lost his liberty, Nat had lost his health, I had lost a friend. I was still blaming myself, and hated to think what Jack himself must think of me as he sat stewing in his prison cell.

'So have you thought about it?' I asked her eventually. 'About leaving?'

'Yes,' she said firmly. 'Yes, I'll leave with you. But we can't leave Jack like this, can we?'

'I'm working on it,' I said, shaking my head. 'I'll think of something.'

'What about Tomas?'

'What about him?'

'Well, is he coming with us too?'

I stared at her in surprise. 'Of course he is,' I said. 'You don't think I'd leave him here, do you?'

'Not by choice,' she replied. 'But have you spoken to him about it? Have you asked him what he wants to do?' I shook my head. 'Well, maybe you should,' she continued. 'He seems happy here. He's going to school. The Ambertons practically think of him as their own.

And, anyway, things will be difficult enough for us in London without having to worry about a—'

'I can't leave him here!' I said, amazed that she would even suggest it. 'He's my responsibility.'

'Yes,' she said doubtfully.

'I'm the only family he's got and he needs me. I can't just desert him.'

'Even if this is the best place for him? Think about it, Matthieu. Where are we going to go when we leave here?'

'London. All the way this time.'

'All right then. Well, London doesn't come cheap. We have a little money, sure. But how long will it last us? What if we don't find work? What if we end up in the same position we were back in Dover? Do you really want Tomas roaming the streets of London getting into who knows what kind of trouble?'

I thought about it. What she said made sense, I knew it did, but I wasn't comfortable with the idea. 'I don't know,' I said. 'I can't imagine not having him there. He's *always* been there. Like I said, I'm the only family he's got.'

'Don't you mean he's the only family *you've* got?' she asked quietly and I looked across at her in the dark. No, I thought. There's you too.

'I'll speak to him as soon as I can,' I said. 'We'll make our plans then. I've got something to do tomorrow though.' Dominique looked at me quizzically and I shrugged. 'I'm going to the jail to visit Jack,' I said. 'I'm going to work out a way to solve this problem or I won't leave. I can't be responsible for destroying the next five years of his life.'

She sighed and shook her head. 'Sometimes I wonder about you,' she said after a long silence. 'You can't see

416

that the answers to all our problems are staring you right in the face, can you?'

I shrugged. 'What?' I asked.

'All these things we're discussing. Getting out of Cageley. Getting to London. Starting afresh. You and I. *And* Tomas. The solution is there, only you don't want to open your eyes and see it.' I stared at her, waiting for this magical answer, unsure what she could mean, although somewhere at the back of my mind I suspected that I already did. '*Jack,*' she said eventually, a fingertip trailing down my skin from my throat to the point halfway down my chest where my shirt was buttoned. The touch of her hand upon my cool skin distracted me, and I glanced downwards, surprised by what she was doing, so long had it been since I had received any kind of human contact from anyone, let alone her. 'He was leaving, wasn't he?' she asked.

'Yes,' I said, the word catching in my throat. She leaned closer towards me and her whispered words filled my ear.

'And how was he going to survive up there, Matthieu?' I said nothing and eventually she removed her hand and took a step backwards. I stood quietly, rooted to the spot, unable to move a muscle until she was gone. As she disappeared back into the darkness of the night, her final words rang in my ears and I couldn't help but be seduced by them. 'Five years is a long time to be in jail,' she said.

Chapter 23

Off Pinks

My first foray into the world of television entertainment came not in the 1990s with the opening of our satellite broadcasting station, but in the late 1940s when I was living in Hollywood, not far from the house where I had first met Constance earlier in the century. I had moved to Hawaii after the stock market crash of 1929 and lived there quite comfortably until just after the war, when I grew weary of the life of a sloth and felt in need of a fresh challenge. To whit, I returned to California with my young wife Stina, whom I had met on the islands, and set up home in a pleasant, south-facing bungalow near the hills.

It wasn't just for my sake that I decided to leave Hawaii; Stina's three brothers had been killed in the closing months of the war and their loss had devastated her. We lived in the same village where they had grown up and she began to hallucinate, imagining them at every street corner or public bar, convinced that their ghosts had returned to say aloha. I consulted a doctor who suggested that a change of scenery might be appropriate, and I decided to take her to the very antithesis of the quiet, tranquil world which she had always known and introduce her to a town whose glamour and pretension were second to none.

We had met in 1940 at a public meeting to denounce F.D.R's apparent plans to bring the United States into the war. I was present as an interested observer; having been through several wars myself, not to mention having seen a couple of my nephews lose their lives in the fighting, I knew the devastation that they could inflict on people. At the time I was opposed to the United States becoming involved with what I perceived to be a little local difficulty on the European front; naturally, with the benefit of hindsight one can see that the only correct action was to take part, but my opinions at the time were echoed by the willowy girl on the platform who was speaking as I entered the hall. She appeared to me to be no more than fifteen years of age. Her skin was of a smooth caramelized brown and her long dark hair hung down thickly on either side of her head. My first thought was that she would be an extraordinarily beautiful woman if her looks did not change too much when the ravages of adolescence had their way. Then, of course, I wondered how a child could hold the audience in such thrall and I realized that I had underestimated her. In truth, she was almost twenty years old, a good deal younger than I – even if my age had mirrored my appearance – but I was mesmerized by her, despite my tendency to be attracted to ladies who have passed out of their immediate youth and into the flush of early middle age.

Stina was heartily opposed to everything to do with the war. She called Churchill a despot and Roosevelt an incompetent. She claimed that, even as she spoke, a war cabinet was being assembled in the White House to drag

419

the country into a needless struggle with a third-rate power – Germany – who were simply seeking retribution for the ills of the Versailles treaty twenty years before. She spoke passionately but her words focused more on her conviction to her anti-war principles than a clear understanding of why this particular war was in any way different from others. Still, she impressed me and I made sure to speak to her afterwards and congratulate her on the effectiveness of her public speaking.

'Your accent?' she asked me. 'I don't recognize it. Where are you from?'

'I was born in France,' I explained. 'But I've been travelling around most of my life. I dare say it has become a hotch-potch of dialects by now.'

'You consider yourself French though?'

I thought about it; it was not something I had ever really considered at all, as if after all these years my nationality had become incidental to the very fact of my existence. 'I expect so,' I said. 'I mean, I was born there and spent most of my childhood and youth there. But I've only been back a few times since.'

'You don't like France, then?' she asked, looking surprised. I have noticed throughout my life the romantic view that many people have of the French and their homeland; the decision to live away from it is one which confuses some. Usually those who have never actually lived there themselves.

'Let's just say that every time I go back there I seem to land myself in trouble,' I said, anxious to change the subject. 'And you? You have always lived in Hawaii?'

She nodded. 'Always,' she said. 'My parents are dead but my brothers and I . . . we cannot imagine leaving here. It is home.'

I sighed. 'I've never really found one of those,' I said. 'I'm not sure that I'd recognize one even if I did.'

'You're still young,' she said, laughing, which was an ironic statement on several levels. 'There's still time.'

Stina's brothers were gentlemen and, as I got to know her, I became fond of their company as well and spent many happy evenings in their home playing cards, listening to Macal, her eldest brother, play the guitar at which he was quite expert, or simply sitting on the porch drinking fruit juices or local wines into the night. Although they were initially put off by the age gap between us, or at least their perception of the age gap between us, we became friends quite quickly as they were intelligent young men and could see that I had no malicious intent or unpleasant designs upon their sister. On the contrary, our romance blossomed naturally and when we eventually decided to marry they were happy for us and fought for the privilege of giving her away.

Our wedding night was our first night together for Stina would never have consented to anything else, and out of respect for her and her brothers I never broached the question after the first refusal. We chose to honeymoon on the islands, for we were happy there, taking a kayak with us to tour the cluster of paradises which were scattered around the ocean. It was a glorious time, the closest thing I have ever known to an unspoilt Eden on this earth.

Then the war did come to America, and more particularly to Hawaii with the attack on Pearl Harbor and, despite the familial opposition to the war, each of Stina's three brothers registered themselves as privates within the United States Army. Stina was devastated, but more than that she was furious with them, believing that they were betraying every principle which they had ever held close. On the contrary, they explained individually, they still believed that the war was wrong and that Americans should not have to become involved, but since they *were* involved and since Japan had already struck inside their borders, and so close to their own home at that, the only right thing to do was to join the army. Oppose the principle, but answer the call to arms anyway. Nothing could make them change their minds; Stina begged me to make them stay but I barely tried, knowing that they were men of principle and that once they had made up their minds to do something – particularly something which caused them so much inner conflict – there would be no turning them around. And so they went, and so they were killed one by one before the war itself came to a close.

Stina did not lose her mind entirely. The hallucinations, while troubling and upsetting to her, were not symbols of a crumbling intellect or diseased brain. Rather, they were images of her grief and she knew that even as she saw them standing there before her, they were not real and were simply painful reminders of a happier time with which she had to find a way to come to terms. And so it was decided. We would take a break from Hawaii and settle in California, where I would return to work and she would maintain a house; there was some talk of children but this came to nothing; we would live the opposite life to the only one she had ever known and the one with which I had become happy over the previous twenty years, and we would see whether this did not return us to the previous state of happiness in which we had once revelled.

*   *   *

I had not lost the art of discovering the right circles within which to move and before long I became friends with Rusty Wilson, a vice-president at NBC. We met on the golf course and began to play regularly as we were neither one of us any better than the other and the outcome of our matches was always in question, right down to the eighteenth hole. I told him of my desire to find gainful employment once again and at first he was a little nervous about discussing the matter with me, no doubt concerned that I had only befriended him in order to find a job.

'The thing is, Rusty,' I explained, eager to disavow him of this notion, 'it's not that I need the money. In truth, I'm extremely wealthy and wouldn't have to work another day in my life if I chose not to. It's just that I'm *bored*, that's all. I need to be doing something. I've taken the last—' I was about to say 'twenty or thirty' but changed it necessarily – 'two or three years off and I'm itching to get involved again.'

'What experience do you have?' he asked, relieved now that I wasn't simply looking for a meal ticket. 'Have you worked in the entertainment industry before?'

'Oh, yes,' I replied, laughing. 'I've been in the arts, you might say, all my life. I've run various different projects, usually from an administrative viewpoint. Mostly in Europe though. In Rome I was entrusted with the building of an opera house to rival those in Vienna and Florence.'

'I hate opera,' said Rusty with disdain. 'Gimme a little Tommy Dorsey any day.'

'I worked on an exhibition in London which attracted six million visitors.'

'I hate London,' he said, spitting on the ground. 'It's cold and it's damp. What else?'

'The Olympic Games, the opening of several major museums, I had some involvement with the Met—'

'OK, OK,' he said, holding up a hand to get me to stop. 'I get the picture. You've been around. And now you want to try TV, is that it?'

'It's something I've never done before,' I explained. 'And I like to try different things. Look, I know what it is to have to put on entertainments of any sort and be constricted by budgets while doing so. I'm good at that sort of thing. And I learn quickly. I'm telling you, Rusty, you don't know *anyone* who has been in this industry as long as I have.'

It didn't take too much persuading; we enjoyed each other's company and fortunately he took my list of previous employments on word, not asking for references or phone numbers to contact those who had worked with me before. Just as well, as they were all dead and buried anyway. He brought me out to NBC and gave me a tour of the lot, and I was amazed by what I saw. There were several programmes in production while I was there and soundproof stage led into soundproof stage with audiences of every type gathered before them, watching the cue-card boy for directions on when they should laugh, clap or stamp their feet in appreciation. We saw the editing suites and I met a couple of directors who barely acknowledged me; they were mostly sweaty, balding middle-aged men with cigarettes sticking out of their mouths and horn-rimmed glasses above their noses. I noticed that the walls were filled mostly with pictures of movie stars – Joan Crawford, Jimmy Stewart, Ronald Colman – rather than their televisual equivalents, and inquired why that was.

'It feels more like Hollywood this way,' explained Rusty. 'Gives the actors something to dream about.

There's two types of TV star: those who are looking to break into movies, or those who can't get a job in movies any more. You're either on the way up or on the way down. It's not really a career for anyone.'

We ended our tour in his suite of offices, which were palatial in their design and overlooked the NBC lot where actors, technicians, secretaries and would-be stars were running around at a tremendous pace. We sat on a couple of heavily filled sofas around a glass-topped table by the fireplace, a good twenty feet away from his mahogany desk, and I could tell that he was enjoying displaying his wealth and position to me with such pride.

'Two days ago I was sitting right where I'm sitting now,' he told me. 'And you know who was sitting where you are, begging for a TV show of her own?'

I shook my head. 'Who?' I asked.

'Gladys George,' he said triumphantly.

'Who?' I asked again, for the name meant nothing to me.

'Gladys George!' he repeated. 'Gladys George!' he shouted now, as if this would lift the veil for me.

'I'm sorry, I don't know who she is,' I said. 'I've never—'

'Gladys George was a movie star a few years back,' he told me. 'She got nominated for the Academy Award in the mid-thirties for Valiant Is The Word For Carrie.'

Again, I shook my head. 'Sorry,' I explained. 'I haven't seen it. I don't get to the movies as much as I should.'

'The Three Stooges did a pastiche of it a couple of years later. You must have seen it. Violent Is The Word For Curly? Boy, was that a howl!'

I laughed gently. 'Oh, yes,' I said quietly, although it actually meant nothing to me whatsoever; still, I considered it was a bad idea to display such ignorance of the industry if I was looking for a position within it. 'That was a screamer. *Violent is the . . .* eh . . .'

'Gladys George was going to be a big star,' he continued, ignoring my attempts to recover the name of the movie. 'But she got on the wrong side of Louis B. Mayer. She went around telling everyone who would listen – and, believe me, that was *lots* – that he was having an affair with Luise Rainer behind her husband's back. Everyone knew that there was no love lost between Mayer and Clifford Odets – he'd called him a miserable commie a few years earlier – but there was no truth in the rumour. Gladys was just sore because Mayer kept giving all the best parts to Luise or Norma Shearer or Carole Lombard or some floozie he was screwing around with. Anyway, it all got back to Mayer who gave her no more work after that but he kept her on contract just to get his own back. She's only just got released from it but no other studio will touch her. That's when she came to me.'

'Right,' I said, trying my best to keep up with the train of events in all of that. It occurred to me how much I had to learn about Hollywood, how the town thrived on insider gossip such as the above and how it could make or break careers. 'So did you give her a job?'

'Jesus, no,' he said, shaking his head furiously. 'Are you kidding me? Girl like that means only one thing to a man like me. T. R. Ubble.'

I thought about it. 'Right,' I repeated, smiling now. His point, I supposed, was that people came to him looking for jobs all the time. That the seat where I was sitting had been used by a hundred people already that week and I was merely keeping it warm for its next occupant. All of this, the tour, the enormity of the soundstages, the regal nature of his offices, the name-dropping, the decision-making about who can or cannot work in Hollywood, it was all for my benefit. I stood up and reached across to shake his hand, assuming that what he was really saying was that it would take a lot more than a couple of games of golf to get a job in his studio. 'Thanks for the tour,' I said.

'What are you doing?' he asked, as I turned around to walk towards the door. 'Where do you think you're going? I haven't got to the good bit yet.'

'Look,' I said, not a man to be toyed with. 'If you don't have a position for me, that's fine. I simply wanted to—'

'Don't have a position for you? Matthieu, Matthieu!' he said, laughing and patting the seat opposite him once again. 'Sit down, my friend. I think I've found the very job for you. Assuming you are everything you claim to be. I'm going to give you a chance, Matthieu, and I don't expect to be let down.'

I smiled and went back to the couch where he filled me in on his idea.

The Buddy Rickles Show was big business. It was a prime-time, thirty-minute comedy on NBC every Thursday night at 8 p.m. Although it had been on the air for only just over one season, it was one of the most popular shows on television and, no matter what the other networks put up against it in the same time-slot, it won hands down.

It was a family comedy. Buddy Rickles himself, although now virtually forgotten by all but the most astute of entertainment historians, had been a bit-part actor from the mid-twenties to the mid-forties. He'd never headlined his own feature, but he'd played the best friend to James Cagney, Mickey Rooney and Henry Fonda and had once duelled on screen with Clark Gable for the hand of Olivia de Havilland (he lost). His work had dried up though and he had been offered this show by NBC and, not only had he accepted it, he had almost single-handedly turned it into a success.

It was a straightforward concept: Buddy Rickles (his character shared his own name, save for one small change – he was known as Buddy Riggles) was a regular family man living in suburban California. His wife Marjorie was a homemaker and they had three children, Elaine (seventeen) who was just getting interested in boys, much to Buddy's consternation, Timmy (fifteen) who was always trying to find ways to play truant, and Jack (eight) who mixed up the meanings of words in ever more hilarious ways. Each week, one of the children would get involved in something which could potentially lead them down the road of self-ruination, but Buddy and Marjorie would set them right, making them see the error of their ways just in time for supper. There was nothing particularly groundbreaking about it, but people enjoyed it, and that fact was mostly down to the writers.

The Buddy Rickles Show was written by Lee and Dorothy Jackson, a husband and wife team in their mid-forties who had been writing hit shows for the best part of a decade. They were popular and threw extravagant parties in their home to which everyone who was anyone tried to score an invitation. Dorothy was known for her sharp tongue and Lee was known for his drinking, but together they were considered to be one of the happiest couples in showbusiness.

'I'm looking for a new producer for *The Buddy Rickles Show*,' said Rusty to me that afternoon in his office.

'There's already two there but I need a third; they each have different responsibilities, and the last guy wasn't up to the job. What do you say?'

I exhaled loudly and thought about it. 'I have to be honest with you,' I said. 'I've never seen the show.'

'We've got all the reels here at the studio. We'll set you up for an afternoon and you can watch it from start to finish. What I need is someone to deal with the public image of the show. Someone who will handle all publicity and enquiries from the news organizations. Someone who will generate publicity for us so that the show grows even more successful. I'm going to launch a new show immediately after it in six months' time so I need it to still be on top of the ratings then. *The Buddy Rickles Show* has to be what people do on a Thursday night, you got it?'

'All right,' I said, warming to the idea. 'I can do that.'

'Yes, but can you start yesterday?'

It was a far more difficult job than I ever would have imagined. Although the show was already a success – the writing was witty and sharp, the acting was simple and appealed to the American public – there was never an attitude of complacency around the crew who produced the show. Rusty Wilson was a hands-on vice-president and he had regular meetings with the three producers of *The Buddy Rickles Show* to discuss our plans and vision for the future.

There was a mild flurry of trouble at the beginning of the third season, when ABC put a brand new quiz show up against us which offered regular folks the opportunity to win up to a million dollars over a period of time. However, it didn't catch on as the networks were deluged with quiz shows then and we regained supremacy of our time-slot.

Buddy Rickles himself was an odd fellow. Although immensely popular with the American public, he didn't like to do too much publicity and avoided both the talk-show circuit and anything but the most important of print interviews. When we did consent to these, he always spoke to me about them in advance and required me to sit in on them with him, which surprised me as he was a capable man and in no more need of help from me than I was in need of a life insurance policy.

'I don't want them knowing too much about my life,' he explained. 'A man's got a right to a private life, hasn't he?'

'Sure,' I said. 'But you know what these magazines are like. If you've got anything to hide then it won't be long before it all comes out.'

'That's why I like to keep my profile low. Just let people watch the show. If they like it, that's fine, that's all they need. They don't need to know much more about me than that, now, do they?'

I wasn't so sure but I couldn't see what he had to hide anyway. He was happily married to a thirty-five-year-old woman called Kate and they had two small children who were regular visitors to our set. As he had been in the business a long time there didn't seem to be anything about the last twenty years or so that wasn't in the public domain in one way or the other. I guessed he was just a private person and decided to allow him his privacy. And although the fanzines wanted more access to him, I limited it and simply granted them more interviews with the rest of the show's stars to compensate.

Stina's mood picked up after a few months of grieving

for her brothers. She began to grow more interested in my work and even attempted to watch the show on a number of occasions but she could never sit through the whole thing as she found the action beyond foolish. Television was not a popular medium on Hawaii and instead she began to grow more interested in local politics, much as she had been when we had first met at the anti-war meeting.

'I have a job,' she announced one evening over dinner and I put down my knife and fork in surprise. I didn't even know that she been looking for one.

'Really?' I asked. 'Doing what?'

She laughed. 'It's not much,' she said. 'Just as a secretary. At the *Los Angeles Times*. I was interviewed this morning and they offered me the job.'

'But that's wonderful,' I exclaimed, pleased that she was developing a new interest at last and leaving her mourning behind. 'When do you start?'

'Tomorrow. You don't mind?'

'Why should I mind? You could go places from there. You've always been interested in politics. You should train as a reporter. There have to be opportunities for young people in a place like that.'

She shrugged and let the idea pass although I suspected she had already considered this. Stina was not the kind of woman who was happy to settle for a desk job when she could be doing something active; her mind was alert and fertile and she would find a busy atmosphere such as the *Los Angeles Times* exciting.

'I know some people there,' I said, recalling a few entertainment reporters with whom I had regular dealings. 'I'm sure it's a good place to work. Perhaps I'll call them. Let them know who you are. Tell them to keep an eye out for you.'

'No, Matthieu,' she said, placing a hand above my own. 'Let me make my own way there. I'll be all right.'

'But they might be able to introduce you around,' I protested. 'You'll get to know people easier. Make some friends.'

'And then they will think because I am married to the producer of *The Buddy Rickles Show* that they will get easier access to it and to everything at the network. No, it's better if I just make my own way. For now, I am only a secretary anyway. We'll see what happens further down the line.'

We attended a party at the home of Lee and Dorothy Jackson, which was populated by many of the most important names in the television industry. Robert Keldorf was there with his new wife Bobbi – with an 'i', as she said every time you mentioned her name – and he made a great show of telling everyone how he had recently lured anchorman Damon Bradley away from the Eye to the Alphabet. Lorelei Andrews spent most of the party propping up the bar, a cigarette drooping limply out of her mouth, complaining to anyone who would listen about the way she was being treated by Rusty Wilson; needless to say I steered clear of that one.

Stina was looking devastating in a strapless pale blue creation modelled on a dress that Edith Head had designed for Anne Baxter for *All About Eve*. It was the first time she met many of the people with whom I worked on a day to day basis and she was excited by the glamour, her eyes opening wide whenever she saw a more devastating gown pass her by. Unfortunately, the people meant nothing to her; she so rarely watched television that I could have introduced her to Stan Perry himself and she would have smiled and asked him whether she could have another Manhattan.

'Matthieu,' said Dorothy, sweeping towards us from across the room, her arms outstretched to smother me with affection. 'How wonderful to see you. Still gorgeous, I note.' I laughed. Dorothy liked to play the part of the extravagant, asphyxiating those whom she liked with sparkling compliments while poisoning those whom she could not stand with her acid tongue. 'And you must be Stina,' she added playfully, sizing up my willowy wife carefully, taking in her gentle form, bronze skin and wide, hazelnut eyes. I held my breath, hoping that she would say something nice as I was very fond of Dorothy and didn't want a barb to come between us. 'You're wearing *quite* the most devastating gown in the room,' she said with a smile and I relaxed. 'Honestly, I feel like just walking around naked in order to recapture some of the attention which you have stolen away from me, you heartless tramp.'

Stina laughed, for Dorothy had uttered the phrase affectionately, rubbing her arm in a friendly manner as she spoke. Another habit of Dorothy's was her random decisions to take a *naïf* and forge that person in her own likeness. 'You mustn't mind me fawning all over your husband,' she exclaimed. 'But I'm the writer and without me he hasn't got a show.'

'Of course, Lee is the writer too,' I added, teasing her gently. 'And who among us can imagine *The Buddy Rickles Show* without Buddy Rickles himself, eh?'

'Come with me, Stina, if that is in fact your real name,' said Dorothy mischievously, winking at me as she took my wife's arm and led her away. 'I want to introduce you to a young man who I'm sure you'll fall hopelessly in love with. And just think of the alimony you'll be able to demand off this fellow when you finally cut him loose. Why, he must be getting ready to draw his pension any day now.'

If only she knew, I thought, but felt pleased that she was going to introduce Stina around as it would have been ridiculous for a husband to introduce his wife to everyone in the room. Better for the hostess to do it and make something of a show of it. Stina would enjoy it, people would get to meet her and Dorothy would feel that she was performing one of her official functions.

I made my way to the French windows and glanced outside, pleased to see Rusty and Buddy there – such American names, I thought – with an older couple, all of whom were engrossed in conversation. I decided to pester them and coughed slightly as I made my way through the doors. The lawn of the Jacksons' house stretched out magnificently before me and the thin spotlights on either side sent a shiver of brightness on to the central fountain that illuminated it and made it a thing of beauty. The sound of trickling water, always a favourite with me, seemed perfectly right in the cool night air and I was glad to see that, rather than giving me an irritated look for pressing my way into the conversation, Rusty looked pleased and beckoned me forward.

'Matthieu, there you are, good to see you,' he said, shaking my hand.

'Hello Rusty, Buddy,' I said, nodding across at him and waiting for the introductions to the other two people who stood by my side, twitching nervously.

'We were talking politics,' said Rusty. 'You're a man of politics, aren't you?'

'Oh, barely,' I said. 'I try not to keep up. I find that

whenever I involve myself in current affairs they drag me into their lair and make a prisoner of me.' There was a silence and I wondered whether I should leave the rhetoric to Dorothy. 'I keep myself to myself,' I added quietly.

'Well, we were just talking about McCarthy,' said Rusty, and I groaned.

'Do we have to?' I asked. 'We're not at work now.'

'We have to because it's important,' said Buddy firmly, which surprised me as I did not take him for a man with any political views whatsoever. Indeed, it would have surprised me if he could have named the occupant of the White House, let alone his state senators or congressmen. 'If someone doesn't act now, it's going to be too late.'

I shrugged and looked at the man and woman standing to my left and they both, as one, bowed courteously, as if they were Japanese, or I was a king. 'Julius Rosenberg,' he said, extending a hand towards me which I gripped tightly. 'My wife Ethel.' She reached forward and kissed my cheek, which was unexpected, but I liked her for it, particularly when she blushed slightly in its wake.

'Hello,' I said. 'Matthieu Zéla. I'm one of the producers on *The*—'

'We know who you are,' said Mr Rosenberg quietly, and he tapped his fingertips together quickly in a gesture which threw me off guard. I looked at Rusty, who immediately began talking again.

'Look,' he said, returning to his conversation, 'I guarantee you that McCarthy will have Acheson's head on a spike by Christmas. Metaphorically speaking, that is.' We all laughed; given the chance, we suspected that Senator Joseph McCarthy would have eliminated the metaphor. 'He needs support. Now, the question is, will Truman support him?'

'Truman can barely support his local football team,' muttered Buddy predictably, but I disagreed. I had never met President Truman and knew nothing of him save what I read in the newspapers and saw on the television but I took him for an honest man and one who would stand by his friends.

'Look at Alger Hiss,' said Mr Rosenberg after I had expressed this opinion. 'Did he support Alger Hiss?'

I shrugged. 'That's a very different case,' I said. 'It was up to Acheson to support Hiss, not Truman, and that's exactly what he did.'

'Which is why old Joe is getting ready to hang him out to dry,' said Mrs Rosenberg in a deep voice, much deeper than her husband's or any of ours for that matter. Indeed, the voice boomed out from so deep within her chest that I wondered whether she was indeed a woman at all. We all stopped talking and looked at her as she gave us her version of the Hiss case, a long and involved monologue which I suspected she had delivered on more than one occasion in the past.

Her version of the events ran something like this: Alger Hiss had worked in the state department and had been recently convicted of espionage in a disturbing display of what the country could do when it got its teeth into something it feared. There was a growing feeling in Washington – we heard of it all the time – that communists were lurking at the heart of every major business, corporation and government department in the land, including the entertainment industry – *especially* the entertainment industry – and Joe McCarthy was making it his personal campaign to expose them, or to tag innocents with the name of Red.

Ethel Rosenberg, while not an intimate of Hiss's, had known him well enough to know that his only crime was lying at his first trial, a perjury which led to his conviction at the second, and believed that McCarthy would destroy the country through his crusade. Of course, both she and her husband were prominent communists – they admitted as much to us that night – and I suspected that their fanatical hatred of the House Un-American Committee was in itself McCarthyism by a different name.

'It was that Californian congressman who did for Hiss,' said Mr Rosenberg. 'Everything would have been all right if it hadn't been for that slimy little toad.'

'Nixon,' said Rusty, spitting out the name of the then little-known representative.

'Now he's as tied up with McCarthy as anyone and they're out to get Acheson and the minute they do is the minute we all end up in jail.'

'What's Acheson got to do with it?' I asked innocently, proving that I really hadn't been paying attention to the times, for Dean Acheson was Truman's secretary of state. He had defended Hiss after his arrest, to his considerable political and indeed personal peril, stating to reporters that, whatever the outcome of the trial, he would not turn his back on him, adding that his own friendship was not easily given and even less easily withdrawn. Naturally, both Nixon and McCarthy had had a field day with that one.

'But I fail to understand why we need to involve ourselves in this,' I said naively. 'I'm sure the senator is a passing figure. He will have his day and, like any day, night will fall upon it.'

Buddy laughed and shook his head as if I was an idiot and my eyes narrowed as I looked at him, wondering what exactly I was missing here. Rusty took me by the arm and steered me back indoors to the party as the troika behind me melted back into one.

'Look, Matthieu,' he said, ushering me to a corner where he spoke in a controlled, quiet voice. 'There are those around you who are not communists but who will not stand by and let McCarthy do to their careers what he's done to others'. You've seen the blacklists, you've—'

'In the motion-picture industry, certainly,' I protested. 'But us?'

'It's coming,' he said, pointing a finger at me cautiously. 'Mark my words, Matthieu, it's coming. And, when it does, we'll all find out who our true friends are.' His words chilled me slightly as I felt that I was a mere observer in a greater drama which was unfolding before me – not an uncommon feeling for me – and I stood there, swallowing nervously, as he walked away.

'You know what Hugh Butler said about Acheson?' he asked me in parting, standing a few feet away from me now. I shook my head. 'After Acheson defended Hiss, he stood up in the senate and virtually exploded, shouting "Get out! Get out! You stand for everything that has been wrong in the United States for years!" That's what's spreading around here, Matthieu. Not a fear of communists or Reds or whatever you want to call them. Plain old rhetoric, that's what. You shout loud enough and forceful enough and sooner or later someone's gonna come and string you up.'

He winked at me, turned around and swept majestically into a waltz with Dorothy Jackson without so much as missing a beat. As I turned away I could see his head nuzzling in towards her ear as they danced, his lips whispering, her eyes paying attention to every word he said, analysing them and storing them away to consider later. A shiver ran though me and, for a moment, I recalled the Terror in Paris in 1793. This was how it had started.

Over the course of the next year or two things grew progressively worse. Many of the writers and actors who I knew to be at the very top of their profession were brought before the HUAC and challenged about their patriotism. Some denied everything and got away with it; some claimed innocence and were jailed anyway, some pre-empted their questioning by making a great show of their Americanism. I recall opening a newspaper one morning during the presidential election at the very start of the witch hunts to see a picture of Thomas Dewey denouncing communism from his latest platform, flanked on either side by Jeanette MacDonald, Gary Cooper and Ginger Rogers, who didn't allow the fact that she was from the same home town – Independence, Missouri – as Truman affect her rabidly republican, anti-communist viewpoint one iota.

Stina did quite well at the *Los Angeles Times* and became a reporter in due course, covering at first tame, local interest stories that the more experienced reporters didn't want to touch but in time her brief widened and she had the occasional stroke of good luck with regard to the stories she pulled down. She covered the three-month bus strike, focusing not on the politics of the drivers' complaints, but on those whose lives were affected by it and succeeded in writing some quite moving profiles. She even won a local news award for a series of articles on impoverished schooling conditions in central Los Angeles, and it was around that time that she became interested in television news. Although she had no luck at first, for she refused to work at NBC as she considered she was being offered the position not on her own merits but on mine, she eventually got a spot with a local channel.

The show had gone from strength to strength but eventually our audience plateaued out and we became as popular as we would ever be. Around this time, *The Buddy Rickles Show* was nominated for some Golden Globe awards and the whole team attended the dinner at the Beverly Wilshire Hotel, looking forward to some respite from the seemingly endless series of news stories and unsubstantiated rumours about what was taking place for our colleagues in Washington, the nation's capital and supposed seat of justice.

In the end, we didn't win any awards, despite our four nominations, and there was a sense of gloom at the table as there was a good chance that the current season would be our last and we would all be looking for work again before very long. Marlon Brando was sitting at the next table, toying with his award for *On The Waterfront*, and I could hear Jane Hoover trying to draw him on the current spate of inquisitions which were taking place but he wasn't going to bite; he was polite and gentle but had refused to discuss the HUAC since Elia Kazan's testimony earlier in the year. I had heard that he was in a state of bewilderment, unable to reconcile a natural loathing for the act with an honest adoration of his mentor, and pitied him for his predicament, for Jane was not a woman who was going to be put off easily. I slipped away to the bar where I found Rusty Wilson drowning his sorrows over his lost awards.

'This is the last time for us, Mattie,' said Rusty and I winced slightly; he had taken to calling me that in recent times, despite my best efforts to make him stop, and it brought back memories of a time long since past. 'We won't be here this time next year, you'll see.'

'Matthieu, Rusty. And don't be so pessimistic,' I muttered. 'You'll have a new show. An even bigger hit. You'll sweep the board.' Although I was saying this, I didn't really believe it. Rusty had introduced a number of new programmes to the schedule over the course of the last twelve months and all of them had failed; the smart money was on his being fired before the new season could begin.

'I think we both know that's not true,' he said bitterly, reading my mind perfectly. 'I'm finished around here.'

I sighed. I didn't feel like having this conversation go back and forth with his prophecies of doom countered by my optimistic sightings of the future. I ordered us both a drink and leaned back against the bar, survey-ing the hundreds of people mingling around the dance floor, a veritable Noah's Ark of celebrities, air-kissing each other and admiring dresses and jewellery. I was a long way from opera houses now.

'You heard Lee and Dorothy have been called,' he said eventually, and I spun around, slamming my drink on the counter in amazement.

'No,' I said, my eyes opening wide. At that time, one didn't need to expand on meaning any more than that; the simple phrase 'X has been called' said all that one needed to know about the state of one's future career prospects.

'Just today,' he said, downing his whisky in one shot and contorting his face in pain as he did so. 'They have to fly to Washington in two days' time to give testimony. So that's them out of the way. We may as well write the rest of the series ourselves.'

I considered this latest piece of news, which was about as devastating an event as I could recall. 'They never said anything,' I told him, straining my neck to try to see our two writers at their seats at the table. 'They never mentioned a word about this.'

'Didn't want to worry everyone, I suppose,' he said. 'Tonight of all nights.'

'Still . . . this is going to be very dangerous. I mean they're not going to give an inch, either of them.'

'You know Dorothy,' said Rusty with a shrug. 'They're going to try to tie them in to the Rosenbergs.'

I laughed. 'Well, that's just ridiculous,' I said. 'What connection could Lee and Dorothy possibly have to them?'

He looked at me now in surprise. 'You don't remember, do you?' he asked.

'Remember what?'

'The Rosenbergs. We all knew them. You met them yourself once.' I looked at him in surprise for it was only after he explained that I recalled the curious little man and woman at the Jacksons' party a couple of years earlier. Since then, however, they had become something of a *cause célèbre* and their case, although now over, still generated much discussion. They had been brought down after being linked to Klaus Fuchs, a physicist who was found to be passing American atomic secrets to the Soviets. It was claimed that the Rosenbergs were communist spies intent on destroying the US nuclear system while helping develop a more powerful one on the Soviet side. Although it had been a difficult case to prove, the courts, filled with an anti-Red terror, seemed unconcerned about the necessity for such a thing, and convicted them both for treason. Not long afterwards, they were executed as enemies of the state.'

I found it hard to believe that the apparently harmless couple whom I had met at that party had been the now infamous Julius and Ethel Rosenberg and was amazed it had never occurred to me before although, in fairness, I had barely exchanged ten words with either of them.

'So what's their connection to Dorothy and Lee?' I asked him and he looked around nervously, afraid that he might be overheard and dragged into the business himself.

'They were friends, good friends,' he said. 'The Jacksons aren't communists but they've dabbled in various political groups, certainly. But they're not Reds. Not at all. More like a couple of Off Pinks, to be honest. They like to dabble and find out about things but they're too fickle to ever fully involve themselves. They have a colourful past between them and, if Joe McCarthy brings all that up, that's the end of them. Not that it will be difficult for him to discover these things. He's got spies everywhere. You watch. It's only a matter of time before you and I get called.'

I considered it. I wondered whether my French citizenship would protect me from the inquiries of the HUAC. In truth, the so-called colourful past of the Jacksons was nothing compared to my own; although I have never been particularly political – for I have witnessed the eventual transience of all political movements – I could not honestly say that I had no contact with any form of different civic system as I had in my time been associated with them all. I was not afraid of what was to come, but it worried me that so many people could find their lives and their careers ended by the zealous mania of one opportunistic man.

'Are you going with them?' I asked Rusty. 'To Washington, I mean? For moral support?'

He snorted. 'Are you kidding? You don't think I've got enough problems here without being tagged as a Red as well?'

'But they're your friends,' I protested. 'Surely you'll take your chances in order to be able to show some sort of solidarity to the committee for your friends. You're in a position of responsibility. If you stand up and say that they're innocent, then—'

'Listen to me, Matthieu,' he said coldly, placing a hand on my arm as he dropped the diminutive this time. 'There isn't anything in this world which would make me get on a plane and fly to Washington right now. And there's absolutely nothing you can say here to make me change my mind so I wouldn't even waste my time trying.'

I nodded and felt saddened; if this was how he treated two friends whom he had known a lot longer than he had known me, I could tell that there was no chance of his ever showing any loyalty to me either. Our friendship ended at that moment and I turned away from him.

'Well, don't expect to see me around the lot over the next few days,' I said in parting. 'Because if you're not going to support them I certainly am.'

Dorothy and Lee were already testifying when I arrived in the House for the committee hearings. We had dined together the night before and tried to avoid discussing the upcoming grilling but it was difficult to keep away from the subject entirely. Nobody mentioned Rusty – I suspected that they had already had something of a run-in with him before leaving California for Washington – but his spirit hovered in the air like the ghost of trouble yet to come. Stina attempted to lighten the conversation with tales of hardship covering school prize-givings for her local television station but the mood was bleak among us and we drank heavily in an attempt to cover over the cracks in the conversation.

As a result I overslept the following morning – most unlike me – and didn't arrive in the committee room until after eleven o'clock, about an hour and a half after the proceedings had begun. Fortunately, my friends had not been called until a few minutes earlier so I hadn't missed much but nevertheless I cursed myself, for they had their backs to me at the front of the room and I wanted them to see that I was there and on their side.

'It's just a comedy show,' Lee was saying as I settled into my seat beside a large fat woman eating a bag of mints noisily. 'That's all it is. There's no subtext at all.'

'So what you're telling this committee is that you put no aspects of your own personality or beliefs into the characters of . . . *The Buddy Rickles Show.*' The man speaking was a thin, pale senator from Nebraska who had to consult a piece of paper to be sure that he was referring to the right show. About a dozen men sat in a line behind an enormous oak desk, with secretaries passing back and forth between them, placing notes or copies of relevant information before them. I saw Senator McCarthy sitting in the centre of his team, a fat, bulbous man, perspiring heavily under the lights and cameras which were directed towards him. He seemed hardly aware of either Dorothy or Lee and was engrossed in the day's edition of the *Washington Post*, shaking his head from time to time to signify his disagreement with what the paper said.

'Subconsciously perhaps,' said Lee carefully. 'I mean when you write anything you—'

'So you admit that you do infuse your own personal

beliefs into this television programme watched by millions around the country every week? You admit that?'

'Hardly beliefs,' countered Dorothy. 'We're talking about a TV show where the biggest dilemma faced by the characters is whether to upgrade the family motor car or use the money to hire a maid two mornings a week. It's just a TV comedy script, that's all. It's not exactly *The Communist Manifesto*.'

I winced when she said the words, and I dare say she did herself, for that was about the worst example she could have made to prove her point. The senator from Nebraska glared at her, wondering whether he should wait a few moments for her to try to pull back from that comment or whether this was a perfect opportunity to attack. In the end, he attacked.

'You've read *The Communist Manifesto* then, Mrs Jackson?' he asked, and there was a flurry of camera shots as she struggled for an answer.

'I've read the St James' Bible too,' she said carefully. 'And the constitution of the United States. Have you read that, sir?'

'I have,' he replied.

'I read many things,' she continued. 'I'm a writer. I love books.'

'But would you say you love *The Communist Manifesto* in particular?'

'Of course not, I just meant—'

'Mrs Jackson,' boomed Senator McCarthy suddenly and all eyes turned towards him. He was known for his incredible lack of patience with his witnesses and the televised proceedings were already beginning to damage what little credibility he had left by that stage. 'Please don't bother wasting the time of this committee

446

by giving us a needless trawl through your no doubt effusive bookshelves. Is it true that you socialized with Julius and Ethel Rosenberg, that you plotted with them ways to overthrow the legitimate government of these United States and that had it not been for a lack of evidence you and your husband may well have ended up in a similar unfortunate state as those two traitors?'

'Lack of evidence is hardly a cause for acquittal in these times, Senator,' said Dorothy sharply.

'Mrs Jackson!' he roared in response and even I jumped in my seat then. 'Did you socialize with Julius and Ethel Rosenberg? Were they present in your home on social occasions when you discussed ways that you could—'

'We didn't socialize,' she shouted over the din. 'They were there, perhaps, but we weren't close. I hardly knew them. Although having said that, there remains no firm evidence that—'

'Are you currently a member of the communist party?' he shot back, and this was usually the point where he would go in for the kill.

'No, I'm not,' she answered defiantly.

'Have you ever been a member of the communist party?' he asked in the same tone of voice and this time she could not help but hesitate.

'I was never a member,' she said carefully.

'But you admit to attending their meetings? Reading their literature? Disseminating their filthy ideas to corrupt the minds of America's young at a point in our—'

'That's not how it was,' she said, beginning to come apart now, for she had backed herself into a corner and everyone present knew it. She may well have never been a member of the party but she had of course learned about their organization and read about their ideals.

'You *were* a member of the communist party,' shouted Senator McCarthy as if she had just admitted it. He slammed his hand down on the desk and for the next few moments it was impossible to decipher all that was said between the two as they roared ever louder to get their points across.

'I have never said that I—'
'You were a cold-blooded—'
'And furthermore I question the—'
'You were in league with—'
'I don't believe I am under any—'
'You stand for everything that is—'

The meeting ended in chaos. Officers of the senate took the Jacksons from their seats and led them away from the committee room through a door at the back. The senator from Nebraska called the next witness and the stormy business of government continued.

Things moved quickly after that day. Lee and Dorothy were blacklisted and prevented from working in the entertainment industry. We brought in a couple of new writers but the show had run out of steam anyway, and once the investigation into Buddy Rickles himself began we had no choice but to close down production for good.

Within a few months, Lee and Dorothy were living apart. He began a romance with the daughter of a stationery tycoon and eventually spent the rest of his working life in that business, after his divorce and remarriage. Dorothy never really recovered from the witch-hunt years. She was so accustomed to being at the very centre of things, hosting parties and making sure that she said the cleverest things at them, that her exile from society hit hard. Stina and I saw a lot of her, of course, but we were the only ones. Everyone else who was still working in the industry had grown afraid of associating with those who had already been black-listed and those who had received the same treatment had mostly moved away from America, towards London or Europe, where they found a more moderate system of government in place.

By the time the blacklists were lifted, she was no longer the woman that she had once been and drifted into alcoholism; I lost track of her after I left America but always imagined her ending up in a nursing home somewhere, her face fully made-up, still drinking, still writing, still cursing McCarthy and Rusty Wilson, who was retired by NBC shortly after the end of *The Buddy Rickles Show* and given a comfortable golden handshake as he tottered off to old age and obscurity.

Stina and I stayed in California for some years, although I eventually got out of television production. We made our home there but travelled often and we remained happy until the beginning of the Vietnam War, when the memories of her dead brothers came back to haunt my wife and she became an ardent politicist once again. She travelled across the country campaigning against the war and was eventually killed in a riot at Berkeley, when she recklessly jumped out in front of an army vehicle in an attempt to halt it. Her death hurt me for we had enjoyed some happy times over twenty years or so and I packed up and left California once again with a heavy heart.

This time I decided to return to England and to a life of leisure. In the 1970s and 1980s I lived on the south coast, near Dover, and spent many happy days walking

449

the streets there, reliving my youth, recognizing hardly anything after a distance of two hundred-odd years. But it still felt strangely like home and those decades were rich with adventure and happiness and I was greatly amused to note the sudden rise to fame of my nephew Tommy towards the end of my time there. But eventually I knew that I had to leave for I grew restless, as is my habit every few decades, and returned to London in 1992, unsure of my plans for the future. I made the decision to rent a small basement flat in Piccadilly, for I did not want to be too heavily tied to the city should an opportunity arise elsewhere, and it was completely by chance that I found myself heading back towards the world of television with the creation of our satellite broadcasting station.

And that is where I have lived for these last seven years.

Chapter 24

Leaving Dominique

I waited until Tomas was out of the house, playing with friends, before speaking to Mr and Mrs Amberton. I hadn't been looking forward to this, and felt more than a little tense as I entered the room. We sat around their kitchen table, the three of us, their small wood-laden fire hissing and spitting with almost as much frequency as Mr Amberton himself, and I told them about what had taken place with Jack Holby. At first I was economical with the truth, not wishing to do anything which would cast the injured Nat Pepys in anything less than a despicable light; not wishing to say a word which would portray Jack in anything less than a heroic one. Mr Amberton said nothing, paying more attention to his whiskey than he did to me, while his wife drew in her breath in shock every so often, a hand rushing to her mouth as I reached the point in my story where blood was drawn, and by the end she was shaking her head in horror, as if we had assaulted God himself.

'What'll happen to him?' she asked. 'This is terrible. To inflict such an injury on Nat Pepys. Sir Alfred's son!' The fact that he was the son of a prominent man, as opposed to actually being a prominent man himself, was irrelevant to Mrs Amberton; the crime at hand was that someone from the lower orders had assaulted someone from the upper. 'I never trusted that Jack Holby anyway,' she added, sniffing loudly as she crossed her arms before her chest.

'It wasn't his fault,' I insisted, keeping my voice controlled but feeling concerned that I had not presented the case for the defence anything like as well as I should have. 'He was provoked, Mrs Amberton. Nat Pepys is a bully and a lech, that's all. He—'

'But I don't understand,' asked Mrs Amberton. 'Why would Jack be defending Dominique? Does he know her that well?'

'Well, we all work together,' I said doubtfully. 'But the thing was that he wasn't so much defending her as he was me.' She stared at me, baffled, and I was forced to explain. 'The truth is,' I said, feeling a little nervous inside as I prepared to tell two good people that I had been lying to them for a year, 'Dominique isn't actually my sister. In fact, we're not related at all.'

'There, I said so, didn't I?' said Mr Amberton triumphantly, slamming his hand down on the kitchen table with a grin as his wife shushed him and urged me to continue.

'We said that originally because we didn't think there was much chance of us finding work together if we said we were anything *but* brother and sister. Meeting you was pure chance and by then we had already developed the deceit. By the time it seemed needless, we had lied to everyone and we felt there was no point in changing our stories.'

'And Tomas?' asked Mrs Amberton, her voice controlled but an obvious anger bubbling up inside her. 'What about him? I suppose you'll tell me now that he was just some child you picked up off the streets somewhere in Paris. I mean you all have the same accent, so how are two poor fools like us to know the difference?' I could tell by the tone in which she spoke that she was hurt; it was one of injured pride.

'No,' I said, bowing my head in shame, unwilling to meet her eye. 'He really is my brother. Well, half-brother anyway. We have different fathers but the same mother.'

'Ha!' she snorted with distaste. 'And where is she then, might I ask, this mother of yours? Living in the village somewhere? Working at the house?' There were tears in her eyes, more for Tomas's sake, I suspected, than my own. It occurred to me how in all the time that we had been there we had told the Ambertons little about our past other than the barefaced lie that we were three siblings travelling together. In fairness to us, they had never asked for much more, accepting our fiction as worthy of their trust, and nothing had stepped in the way to dissuade them. But, finally, the truth had to be told. Staring into the fire, I told them of my early years in Paris; of my mother, Marie, and the senseless killing of my father, Jean; of the dramatist who had provided us with a little money to survive upon; of the child who stole my mother's bag one day as she left the theatre, resulting in a meeting with her second husband Philippe, Tomas's natural father; of his attempts at creativity, both on stage and off; finally I told them of the fatal afternoon when he had killed my mother and how I had run from the house to seek help. After telling of his execution and the subsequent meeting between Dominique Sauvet, Tomas and me on board the boat from Calais, I related how we had lived by our wits in Dover for a year before heading towards London, in order to seek our fortune. En route, we had

453

met them, the Ambertons, and they knew the rest. I neglected to tell them of the dreadful night on which we had encountered Furlong and left him to rot in a thicket as we made our getaway; it seemed senseless to add pointless trauma to the story. I told them all of that, and it took some time but they heard me out silently and maintained a respectful pause when I finally finished.

Eventually: 'Well, I still don't see why you had to lie to us,' said Mrs Amberton, maintaining her position as ranger of the moral high ground while allowing her tone to slip back from insulted outrage to disappointed understanding. 'But I suppose it's all come good in the end.'

'Good?' I said, staring at her in amazement. 'How has it come good? What *good*? Because of this, Jack Holby is left sitting in a prison cell, his entire future ruined. He had plans, Mrs Amberton. He was leaving Cageley.'

'He'll be going nowhere for a few years now,' said Mr Amberton, pulling a piece of gristle from between his two front teeth, the only teeth he possessed on the upper gum. 'He'll get five years for what he did to Nat Pepys. He won't have a job to come out to either when he gets released. He should count himself lucky that he didn't kill him or he'd be on the scaffold himself.'

'This is what I mean,' I said, incredibly frustrated by their lack of compassion for my friend, feeling as if I wanted to break up every item in the room to get them to understand how this made me feel. 'All these lies . . . if we hadn't lied, then none of this would have happened. Dominique and I could have sorted out our relationship and people would have known about it. Nat Pepys wouldn't have mattered. As it stands, Jack is only in jail because he didn't want to see *me* end up there. He's my *friend*!' I insisted, still shocked within myself at what he had sacrificed to preserve that friendship; in my two and a half centuries of life, I have never known a more selfless act. Although I never observed its like again, it made me value friendship. It made me believe that being true to one's friends and refusing to betray them was as important a trait as any other. The history that one can create with a friend, a lifetime of history and shared experience, is a wonderful thing and shabbily sacrificed. And yet a true friend is a rare thing; sometimes those whom we perceive as friends are simply people with whom we spend a lot of time.

'I thought there was something funny about you and Dominique,' said Mr Amberton eventually. 'I saw the way you looked at her. Didn't seem like the kind of looks you give your sister,' he muttered, but I hardly heard him for Mrs Amberton said something instead which made me sit up and open my eyes wide.

'Well, I never liked her anyway,' she said, catching my eye after a moment and seeing how shocked I looked. 'There's no point looking at me like that, Matthieu,' she continued. 'I speak as I find, I do. I always thought there was something a little shifty about the girl. Here we are, bring her here to this new life, put a roof over her brothers' heads – oh, I know you're not her brother but you know what I mean – and how does she repay us? Barely comes to visit us any more. Only speaks to me on the street out of politeness. I can see she's always itching to get away.'

'Mrs Amberton, please,' I protested.

'No, I'll have my say,' she said more loudly, drowning me out as she simultaneously raised a hand to silence me. 'If you ask me, she's sat around and let this whole thing develop around her. From what you tell me, she's been quite keen to encourage that Mr Pepys and his advances.'

'She has no interest in him whatso—'

'*He* might have no interest in *her*, certainly, for he'll be marrying into a better family than hers, but she's got ideas, oh yes. I can see them in her. Now she's got the whole village fighting over her—'

'It's hardly the whole village,' I said.

'And she's probably loving every moment of it. Nat Pepys is half crippled, Jack Holby's ruined and in jail and you . . . well, I don't even know what you're planning on doing.'

'Leaving,' I said quietly, allowing the word to settle in before continuing. 'I'm leaving is what I'm doing. I'm getting out of here and going on to London *as originally intended*.' She snorted and looked away, as if I was an idiot. 'And Dominique's coming too,' I added.

'You'll be lucky,' she said and I grew furious and determined to hurt her, this harmless, generous woman who had shown nothing but charity to me. I threw one final line at her to cause her pain as she was causing me pain by her attitude towards Dominique.

'And I'm taking Tomas too,' I said.

They both looked up, astonished. Mrs Amberton's hand went quickly to her throat as she gasped and her husband looked at her with concern in his eyes.

'You can't,' she said.

'I have to.'

'*Why* do you have to?'

'Because he's my *brother*!' I roared. 'Why do you think? You think I'm just going to desert Tomas? I would *never* do that!'

Suddenly, she was crying, her words becoming engorged by the choking in her voice. 'But he's just a child,' she protested. 'He needs his schooling, his friends. He's doing so well now. You can't take him away from us.' I shrugged and grew hard-hearted; those days were terrible. 'Please, Matthieu,' she begged, reaching across and taking my hand in her tough, gnarly claw. 'Please don't do this. You and Dominique go to London if you must, set up house, become rich and famous and send for him then. But let him stay here in the meantime.'

I looked at her and sighed. 'I can't do that,' I said eventually. 'I'm sorry but I won't leave him behind.'

'Then stay!' she cried. 'Stay at Cageley House, both of you. You both have good jobs. You're earning—'

'After what I've done to Jack?' I cried. 'I just can't, I'm sorry. Both of you, I'm truly sorry. I'm grateful to you both for all you have done for us, but I've made my decision. And Dominique has agreed. We're leaving for London, the three of us. And we will be a family again. I'm . . . I'm grateful to you both, naturally, but sometimes . . .' I couldn't think of the end of the sentence; I couldn't muster up a *sometimes*. Silence descended upon us and after a few minutes of unbearable tension I got up to leave. I went to my room for my coat, as I had somewhere else to go now, and as I left their house I could hear crying coming from the kitchen and for the life of me I couldn't make out whether it was hers or his.

The jail was no more than a small, purpose-built structure just outside the main village of Cageley. I approached it nervously, having never been there before, and felt somehow afraid that I myself would be dragged inside and locked up for my part in these troubles. Outside the main door, a group of children were playing, throwing a ball to each other and running away whenever one of their number was hit; when the ball came too close to the jail there was a noticeable concern among them regarding who should reclaim it. I kicked it back to them myself as I walked up the steps towards the entrance and they scattered, afraid now that I was actually going to open the door.

I had never been inside a prison before. When my stepfather Philippe was arrested in Paris, I had remained in our house with Tomas, waiting until the next day for an officer to return to speak to me regarding his trial which was set for more than a couple of weeks away. At the time I had considered going to visit him in jail, not to offer any comfort or support, but rather to fulfil some strange need that one last time I had to see the man who had killed my mother. Despite the fact that we had been living in the same house for some years and knew each other well, I felt as if I had never really known him at all. I thought that by looking at him in his prison cell, particularly after he had been found guilty and was sentenced to death, I would gain some insight into who that man really was; I believed I would see something evil in him which I had never seen before. However, in the end I didn't go, instead joining the throng on the day of his execution.

The jail was built in the shape of a 'T'. Along the main corridor as you walked in there was a desk, behind which the constable sat when he was present. At the end it branched off on either side into two prison cells which faced each other. As I stood at the door I couldn't see either cell, just the long corridor, and the turning to left and right. I presented myself to the constable who looked up at me in surprise.

'What are you doing here?' he asked me. 'Come to

join your friend, have you?' He was a tall, thin man with a shock of dark hair and a scar running along his jaw, which for some reason I suspected he was extremely proud of.

'Come to speak to him,' I countered, wanting to behave in a more aggressive fashion than was my normal manner but aware that I had a task to fulfil there and it wasn't worth jeopardizing that just to prove that I wasn't afraid of him. 'If that's all right,' I added deferentially.

He tapped his pencil on the desk rhythmically, leaning back on his chair until I was afraid he might topple over but he had the movement down to a fine art from years of trying. 'You can see him,' he grunted. 'But not for long. About fifteen minutes, all right?' I nodded and looked towards the end of the corridor, unsure which way to go but before I could even make a step in that direction he was in front of me, holding me by the arm roughly, his thick, dirty fingers pressing into the bone of my arm. 'Not so fast,' he said. 'Have to make sure you're not carrying anything, don't I?'

I looked at him in surprise. I was wearing trousers, boots and a loose-fitting shirt. There was hardly anywhere for me to be concealing a file or a gun. 'Do I *look* like I'm carrying anything?' I asked, biting my tongue to prevent myself from saying more.

'Have to be careful in this job,' he said, pushing me up against the wall and kicking my legs apart with the toe of his boot. I gripped the wall and tried not to kick backwards, as a horse might do under pressure, as his hands roamed around my body, checking for hidden equipment.

'Happy?' I asked sarcastically, and he shrugged and nodded in the direction of the cells. My opinion meant nothing to him.

'Down the end. Turn left,' he said. 'He's in there.'

I walked down the corridor and breathed in before making that final step which would lead me into sight of the two cells. For some reason I looked to my right first in order to see who was the occupant of that cell. It was empty and this pleased me. I turned around with a smile, but it fell as I saw Jack sitting silently on the floor of the facing cell.

It contained nothing more than a small bed and a hole in the corner of the room which served as a toilet. Jack was sitting on the floor, his back to the bed, staring at the wall. His blond hair hung limply around his face, a dirty brown now. He wore nothing on his feet and I could see that his shirt had been ripped slightly at the shoulder, revealing a purple bruise beneath. As he turned to look at me I could see that he was pale and his eyes were red-rimmed from lack of sleep. I swallowed nervously and moved towards the bars.

'Jack,' I said, shaking my head in dismay. 'How are you?'

He shrugged but seemed pleased to see me. 'I'm in trouble, Mattie,' he replied, dragging himself up now to sit on the bed. 'I've messed up.'

'Oh, God,' I said, unable to control my emotions as I saw my friend in such a state of disrepair. 'This is my fault,' I added.

'It's not,' he said quickly, looking irritated now as if the last thing he needed was for me to start feeling sorry for myself. 'It's no one's fault but my own. I should have just pulled you away, not laid into Nat myself. How is he anyway? Did I kill him? They won't tell me anything here.'

'Unfortunately, no,' I answered. 'You broke his jaw

460

and a couple of his ribs. He doesn't look too good to be honest.'

'He never did anyway,' Jack said with a shrug. 'And you? What's happening with you?'

'I haven't been fired yet if that's what you mean. I thought I would be but no one's said anything to me there yet.'

He looked surprised but said nothing for a moment. 'They still need someone to look after the horses, I suppose,' he said eventually. 'They'll keep you on for as long as it takes them to find someone to replace you. And me too. We're both finished there.'

I nodded and stared at the floor. I wasn't sure whether I should apologize to him or not, whether he even wanted to hear anything like that. I decided against it and told him instead of my conversation with the Ambertons, of how they had said they had never liked Dominique in the first place and how annoyed that had made me.

'I'm not surprised,' he said, looking away from me. 'She treats you like shit. And you're the only one who can't see it.'

I stared at him, my eyes opening wide. 'What?' I asked.

'It doesn't matter. I don't want to talk about her right now.' I opened my mouth to speak again but he silenced me by raising his hand. 'Mattie, I *don't* want to talk about her, do you hear me? I've got more pressing problems right now than your love life. Like the fact that I'm about three days away from ruining the next few years of my life. I need you to do something for me, Mattie. I need a favour.' I nodded and looked around me conspiratorially, although from where I sat there was nothing on either side of me but a wall. I pressed

461

closer towards the bars as he began to whisper. 'I have a plan,' he said, a sparkle coming into his eyes now as he smiled at me.

'Go on,' I said.

'Can I trust you?' he asked me after a pause, his eyes looking right through me.

'Of course,' I answered quickly. 'You know you—'

'I hope so,' he said, cutting me off, 'because you're the only one that I can *afford* to trust right now so I have to hope I'm doing the right thing. That constable out there,' he said, nodding in the general direction of the corridor, 'Musgrave. He's no friend of mine. We've had some run-ins in the past and he'd like nothing more than to see me swinging from the end of a rope.'

'Well, *that*'s not going to happen,' I said. 'You'll only end up doing time for—'

'I know, I know,' he said irritably. 'What I'm saying is that he won't help me, that's all. But the other constable, Benson. You know him?' I nodded. I knew him by sight. He was a younger man and popular with the villagers. His mother owned a local inn and his father's funeral earlier in the year had attracted the entire population of Cageley, even Sir Alfred himself. 'He's got a far smaller social conscience than Musgrave,' he said. 'And he's sick of living off his mother. He's open to persuasion.'

I shook my head and checked once again that no one could hear us as I looked at my friend, somewhat confused. 'You want me to persuade him to let you go?' I asked doubtfully.

'Listen, Mattie. I told you I was leaving Cageley, right?'

'Right.'

'And that I've saved up enough money over the years to get out?'

462

'Yes.'

'Well, I've got over three hundred pounds stored away now.'

'*Three hundred pounds?*' I said in amazement, for the figure was enormous to me. I could barely imagine such a sum and knew that he must have had great plans for his future to wait until he had that much saved up before making his escape.

'I told you; I've been putting it aside since I was about twelve. There's not much to spend it on here, you know. My aim was three hundred and then I was going to leave. I hit the amount last week. That's when I told you that I was going to hand in my notice. I need you to get it for me.'

My heart sank. I could feel a growing tension inside me and became afraid of what he was going to ask me to do. More than that, I remembered Dominique's phrase of the night before – 'Five years is a long time to be away' – and worried for my own integrity. 'Yes,' I said slowly.

'I know for a fact that Benson would let me out of here for a portion of that money.'

'He wouldn't,' I said, confident of *his* honesty, if not my own.

'He would,' said Jack clearly. 'I've spoken to him about it already. For forty pounds he'll let me out. He's always left alone here overnight, that's his regular shift, so you can be sure that he will be the only one we have to deal with. We just have to make it look like a break-out, that's all. That's where you come in.'

I hated the conflicting feelings that were running through my mind. I wanted to help Jack – I truly did – but I also wished that I'd never come here in the first place. I was about to bury myself in deeper and

463

deeper when I could have fled hours before. I thought about it, considered my options, and nodded to him. It could do no harm to hear him out. 'Go on,' I said.

'You get the money, you bring it here at night, we give some to him, he lets me out, then we have to knock him unconscious so that it looks as if you came in and attacked him and set me free.'

'He'll let you do that?' I asked, surprised.

'He'll let *you* do it,' he replied. 'Forty pounds is a lot of money.'

'All right,' I said, willing to go along with the story if not necessarily execute the plan. Friendship was one thing, but being implicated in the crime and potentially separated from Dominique and Tomas was another. 'Where do I find the money then?'

He paused now, realizing that this was the moment of truth between us. Everything he had been working for all his life, every penny that he had put aside after shovelling shit or rubbing down the horses since he was twelve years old, he was about to place in my hands. He would give me the information and trust me with it. He had no choice; it was either that or he would lose it all anyway.

'It's on the roof,' he said eventually, sighing as he said it, the final release of his security.

'The *roof*?' I asked. 'At Cageley House, you mean?'

He nodded. 'You've been up there, right?' he asked.

'A couple of times,' I said. In the east wing, where the servants' rooms were located, I knew that there was a corridor which led to a window from which one could gain access to the roof of the house. Just before the ascent to the slate and the chimneys, there was a flat portion where, in the summer, I had often seen Mary-

Ann or Dominique or Jack himself lying, relaxing in the shade.

'When you step out there,' said Jack, 'you turn right and you'll see a covering that leads to a drain. Open it up, reach below and there's a jewellery box in there. That's where I keep it. No one knows it's there, Mattie. It's my hiding place. It's safe there. I've never felt that I could trust anyone in that house. Except you now. That's all. And you can't tell anyone, you hear me?'

'All right,' I said, closing my eyes and nodding slowly. 'All right. I hear you.'

'I can trust you, Mattie, can't I?'

'Yes.'

'Because this is everything I have. Tell me I can trust you.' His hand darted out between the bars and he caught hold of my wrist tightly. *Tell me,'* he hissed, his eyes narrowing into slits with the frustration of being locked up.

'You can trust me, Jack,' I said. 'I promise. I'll get you out of here.'

To betray a friend. To accept that you can't save someone and so to decide to save yourself instead, that is the dilemma with which I was faced. Nat Pepys was sitting outside the front door of the house with a parasol over his head to prevent the sun from burning him. He watched me as I walked towards the stables, his head rotating slightly through design or pain as I made my way past him. I stopped and walked over towards this man who had caused so much trouble. His mouth was wired up and his face was multi-coloured; he looked truly dreadful. I knew that most of his injuries were simply surface bruising which would heal but nevertheless he wasn't a pretty sight.

'How are you?' I asked, before realizing that he couldn't answer me anyway. He grunted slightly and his head jerked in spasm which I took to be my cue to vanish. I shrugged – I was past caring about the likes of him – and went on my way, listening to the sounds of his increasingly loud grunts as I went. I wasn't sure if he was trying to call me back again or whether he was simply shouting abuse at me.

Dominique sat outside the kitchen, shelling peas. She glanced in my direction as she heard my footsteps approaching her but she didn't acknowledge me. I sat on the ground beside her and played with the pebbles, wondering which one of us would speak first and whether we were both thinking the same thing.

'So?' she asked eventually. 'Did you see him?'

'Yes.'

'And?'

'And what?' I asked, looking up at her irritably. Her hair was tied back behind her and she wore a low-cut dress which accentuated the pale smoothness of her neck. I sighed, exasperated with myself, and threw the pebbles away.

'And what did you discuss?' she asked patiently.

'Well, he's very worried,' I admitted. 'Needless to say. It's a terrible place. And he knows that he's thrown it all away. He's devastated.'

'Of course he is, but what else did you discuss?'

I hesitated and felt her hand on the back of my neck, squeezing tightly to massage away the knots of tension which were even then building up; it felt good. 'He has more than three hundred pounds,' I said.

'*Three hundred pounds?*' she cried in astonishment, echoing my reaction of a couple of hours earlier. 'Are you serious?'

466

'I'm serious.'

'That's a lot of money. Just think what he could have done with that. He could have put this entire place behind him. He could have disappeared completely. Found a new life. Anyone could. Money breeds money.' I looked at her and wondered whether she was using 'he' for 'we'. Neither of us had actually said it yet but I knew what we were both thinking. Finally, she cracked. 'It's of no use to him, Matthieu,' she said in a stern voice and I jumped up and began pacing the yard in front of her.

'So what do you suggest?' I asked her, raising my voice in anger. 'You think we should just take the money and run? Leave him to rot in his jail cell, is that it?'

'There's nothing you can do to help him,' she cried. 'He's made his own bed. And for God's sake, keep your voice down. The last thing we need is for someone to come out here right now.'

I was furious; I hated being in this position. 'But what if I could help him?' I asked her, my voice low now but filled with self-loathing; I didn't want to have to make this decision myself. 'What if I could use that money to get him out of there? What then? It is his, after all. He worked for it, not me, not you. Even if he stayed in jail for the next few years, it would still be there waiting for him when he came out. He'd have a chance to rebuild his life.'

She put down her bowl of peas and stood up. Coming towards me she took my face in her hands and looked deep into my eyes. 'Listen to me, Matthieu,' she said, her voice able to maintain the steady equilibrium that my own could not. 'You are not a child any more. You can make your own choices. But think of this: we have an opportunity here. You, me, Tomas. We have the chance we have always needed. We can do this. Jack is

467

not your friend. You think he is, but he's not. You owe him nothing.'

I laughed. 'That's not true,' I said. 'He *is* my friend. Look at what he did for me. He put himself in jail to prevent me from going there. He wouldn't have done that to Nat if he didn't care about me.'

'You think he was defending *your* honour?' she asked me, her hands on her hips. Her mouth opened and shut a few times as she wondered whether or not to continue with this. 'You think it was *your* honour, you fool? It was *mine*. It was *my* honour he was defending. Open your eyes, Matthieu.'

I took a step back in surprise. I didn't understand what she meant. 'Your honour?' I asked quietly, my brow furrowing as I tried to make sense of it. 'I don't . . .' Then it came to me and I looked at her in shock. 'What are you saying?' I asked her hesitantly. She said nothing for a time, simply looked down a little in shame and raised an eyebrow.

'Nothing ever happened, of course,' she said. 'I wouldn't let it. You know I love you, Matthieu.'

My head spun with the possibilities and I thought about simply jumping on a horse and riding away, leaving them all, Jack, Dominique, the money, far behind me. 'You're lying,' I said eventually, my voice cutting through the tension.

'Whatever you want to believe is fine,' she said casually. 'The fact remains that Jack Holby is no more your friend than he is mine. And he has something that we can have. We can take it and we can leave. It's up to you. Where is it, anyway?'

I shook my head, dazed. 'No,' I said. 'No, I want you to tell me what you mean by that. Why would he be defending your honour?'

She sighed and looked around, drying her hands in the apron she wore. 'It was nothing,' she said. 'You don't have to get angry about it.'

'Just tell me!' I shouted.

'It's just that sometimes, when you would go home in the evenings, we would end up talking. We both live here after all. We see more of each other than you see of either of us.'

'Tell me what happened,' I insisted.

'He liked me,' she said simply. 'He knew you weren't my brother, he could tell that, he said as much to me himself and he asked me what had taken place between us. Whether we were lovers.' My heart skipped a beat at the word and I stared at her, waiting for her to continue. 'I told him we weren't,' she said. 'There was nothing to be gained from it and it was not his business anyway. I said you had feelings towards me but, for me, this farce of being brother and sister was closer to the truth.'

I swallowed hard and felt tears well behind my eyes; I was afraid to ask whether she thought that was actually the case or whether she had simply said it for Jack's benefit. And somewhere deep inside, the childish, immature side of me wanted her to acknowledge the fact that we were lovers. For her to deny it to Jack wounded me and I knew not why.

'So what did he do?' I asked.

'He tried to kiss me,' she said. 'But I told him no. It was too complicated. Besides, he's just a boy.'

I laughed, irritated by her arrogance. Jack was older than I was – and older than Dominique as well – and for her to dismiss him in such a way maddened me. My mind was spinning with possibilities. Was she telling the truth about Jack or lying? And what of Nat? He was older than us, and uglier, but richer. Far richer. I shook my head to expel all such thoughts for now and looked at her in bitterness.

'I won't tell you where the money is,' I said. 'But we will take it. We'll take it tonight.'

She smiled. 'It's for the best, Matthieu,' she said quietly.

'Just . . . shut up, Dominique,' I said aggressively, my eyes closed as I battled between untrusting love and greed. 'I'll come here tonight. Around midnight. We'll take the money then and we'll leave then, all right?'

'And Tomas?'

'After we take it, we'll stop off for him. I'll speak to him this afternoon.' I turned on my heel and prepared to walk away and she shouted something after me that I didn't hear. I didn't know what to believe. No – that's not true. I did know. I knew she was lying. I knew by the way she had said it, when she had said it, that she was lying. Nothing untoward could ever have happened between them; Jack, for one, would never have allowed it. He was too good a friend for that. He would never have betrayed me. There was not a single doubt in my mind that she was lying and yet I chose to believe her anyway, because by doing so I could justify my actions.

If I pretended to believe that Jack Holby had betrayed me, then I could betray him too. With a new resolve, I walked home quickly, determined now. I would take the money and run.

Tomas was insistent; he didn't want me to leave Cageley. More importantly, he didn't want to have to leave either.

'But think of the new life we'll lead in London,' I explained, doing my best to sound excited about it. 'Remember we planned to go there in the first place.'

470

'I remember *you* planning on going there,' he said. 'I don't remember being consulted on it. You and Dominique were the ones who wanted to go there, not me. I'm happy where I am.'

He sulked, considering tears, and I groaned in frustration. I had never counted on him finding a home here and it surprised me. For although I too had been reasonably happy in Cageley, it had never meant so much to me that I could not imagine leaving it some day. And I envied him for finding that which had proved so elusive to me all my life: a home.

'Mrs Amberton . . .' I said, appealing to her for some help but she turned away from me with tears in her eyes.

'No point looking to me,' she said. 'You know what I think on the matter.'

'We can't be separated,' I said firmly, trying to take hold of my brother's hand but he pulled away from me. 'We're a family, Tomas.'

'*We're* a family too,' cried Mrs Amberton. 'And didn't we take you in, both of you, when you didn't have a place to go? You were grateful enough to have us then.'

'We've been through this,' I said, exhausted by the amount of work which was going into making these simple plans. I was growing annoyed by her unwillingness to help me persuade Tomas to change his mind too; it never occurred to me that she loved the boy. 'I've made my decision.'

'When would we be leaving?' asked Tomas, not caving in even slightly but anxious to know the timetable of these upcoming plans.

I shrugged. 'A couple of days,' I said. 'Maybe sooner.'

His eyes opened wide and he looked at Mr and Mrs Amberton in horror, his lower lip trembling slightly as he tried not to cry. I could see that he wanted to say something, to protest at my decision, but he was at a loss for words.

'It'll be fine,' I said. 'Trust me.'

'It *won't* be fine,' he said, giving up now and letting the tears flow. 'I don't want to go!'

I stood up furiously and looked around the room. Mr Amberton was sitting by the fire, for once in his life ignoring his whiskey bottle which sat on the mantelpiece, while his wife and my brother hugged each other for support. It made me feel as if I was the cruellest man in the world when all I was trying to do was to keep my family together. It was too much.

'Well, I'm sorry about it,' I said angrily, leaving the room. 'But that's my decision and that's what we're doing. You're coming whether you like it or not.'

There was a full moon but thin, wispy clouds were drifting across it and I stood in the woods, surrounded by trees, the smell of the bark surrounding me as I shivered slightly from nervousness. It was after midnight and Dominique had already emerged from the house; she was standing in our usual spot near the stables but I wanted to watch her for a few moments before making my appearance. It had been one of the longest days of my life and here I was, needlessly dragging it into the next as I prepared to rob the friend who had sacrificed so much for me. I stared at my sometime lover, wondering how our lives would develop in London once we were wealthy, and despite the amount of time I had spent looking forward to such a day, I could not see it now. I was blinded by the money. Three hundred pounds. Enough to set us up comfortably, but a high price to pay for the loss of one's honour.

'There you are,' she said, smiling in relief as she saw me emerge from my hiding place and come walking towards her. 'I was beginning to think you weren't coming.'

'You knew I would,' I said irritably. She reached across and rubbed my arm quickly.

'You're cold,' she said. 'It'll be all right. I've left my things over there.' She nodded towards the wall where one small case stood propped up against it. 'I didn't bring much,' she added. 'We can get new things once we get to London.'

'I'll go up and get the money,' I muttered, not feeling much like small talk, particularly when it involved the spending of our ill-gotten gains. I began to walk towards the entrance but she came after me quickly.

'I'll come with you.'

'There's no point,' I said. 'I can get it myself.'

'I *want* to,' she replied, her voice filled with a false gaiety, as if this was some sort of great adventure we were on. 'I'll keep a watch out for you.'

I paused and stared at her. The moonlight made her skin appear a bluish-white and she held my gaze steadily. 'Keep a watch out for me or on me?' I asked her. 'What do you think I'm going to do? Run away with it myself?'

'Of course not,' she said, shaking her head. There was a long pause as she pursed her lips, trying to decipher my mood. 'I'll come with you,' she repeated firmly, tugging at my shirt and this time I merely shrugged and continued to walk. Near the door I stopped, holding on to the series of spiked railings which cordoned off the basement washing room from my ground level and looked upwards towards the roof. It didn't look so very high up from where I was standing but I knew from experience that the view was a lot more troublesome from the top. It was easily thirty feet in the air and yet from this place I felt I could scale the wall easily, like an eighteenth-century Romeo.

'Come on,' I said, opening the door and stepping through into the darkness. Inside, the kitchen was black and I made my way to the stairway which led to the servants' quarters. With Dominique trailing me by a few feet I began to ascend them quietly and reached behind me to take her hand. At the next level up, a candle was burning on the windowsill and I stopped for a moment, considering whether I should take it with me, but decided against it. It threw a narrow corridor of light upwards and I could make out the steps without much difficulty. Unfortunately, Dominique stumbled and had I not been holding her hand she would have fallen and made some noise.

'Sorry,' she said, biting her lip, and I stared at her. My stomach was churning with fear, not so much for any apparent danger, for in truth there was little, but for what I was about to do, and for what? For her? For us?

'Be careful,' I muttered, continuing to climb. 'Go quietly.' At the next level, I could see the doors which led to several rooms, one of which I knew to be Mary-Ann's, one of which I knew to be Dominique's. At the turn of the spiral, six steps up, was a door standing slightly ajar and I hesitated, looking back as if to acknowledge a respectful moment. It was the door to Jack's room and something made me press against it lightly, causing it to open wider with the slightest groan which sounded to me as if it was echoing all across England. I drew in my breath, hesitating as I was sure that an alarm was about to be sounded, and as I stood there I glanced inside. A narrow bed, a wardrobe with one door hanging loose

474

from a lower hinge. A rug on the floor, threadbare. A fireplace still filled with cinders. A shelf filled with books. A waterbowl; a jug. I had seen it before of course but it struck me as ghostly now, knowing where its occupant currently resided and where he was likely to remain. We continued upwards.

A long corridor ended with a window, which in turn led out to the roof. I opened the window gently and stepped outside into the cold night air, reaching back to help Dominique step through as well. Her skirt was long and became briefly tangled on a splinter of wood extending from the lower frame but after tearing it loose we were out. We were standing on a flat platform, perhaps fifteen feet by ten, and to the right of us the slate roof extended upwards. I walked over to the edge and leaned slightly forward, looking down at the spiked railings below where I had been standing a few minutes earlier. I was transfixed by the height and felt my sense of balance begin to slip away from me as Dominique grabbed my arm and pulled me back towards her fiercely. We fell, pressed against the wall, our lips separated by no more than a hand, but she pushed me away, looking at me for all the world as if I was mad.

'What are you doing?' she asked angrily. 'Do you want to fall off? You'd kill yourself if you fell from this height.'

'I wasn't going to fall,' I protested. 'I was just looking.'

'Well, don't look. Let's just find this money and get out of here.'

I nodded and looked about me. Jack had said that there was a covering which led to a drain and that was where he stored his wealth. I was still slightly disorientated but saw the drain running along the roof and followed it with my eyes until I spotted the square black panel at the side.

'There,' I said, pointing at it. 'That's it.' I went over and knelt down beside it, attempting to prise it open, but the small circle from which one could access what lay beneath was too small for my fingers.

'Here. Use this,' said Dominique, handing me a hooked pin from her hair, which fell about her shoulders now. I stared at her for a moment before returning to the task at hand and lifted the cover effortlessly. Reaching in, I pulled out the box which lay below and we sat against the wall, staring at it in delight. That was the moment when I knew that I could take the money. I hadn't seen it yet, I hadn't been able to count it, I just knew that whatever lay inside that box I could take. I could steal it all.

'Open it,' said Dominique, her voice low and concentrated, and I did as she requested. It was a normal cigar box which he must have bought in the town or, more likely, stolen from a guestroom when he first began his savings. I opened it and we were greeted with a roll of banknotes and some coin. The musty smell of money filled my senses immediately and I laughed, amazed to see so much cash suddenly before me. I pulled out the enormous notes, which were held together by a clip, and marvelled at their size and thick texture. I had rarely held a note myself; my own small savings consisted of a bag of coins which had given me just as much enjoyment as I counted them in my room back at the Ambertons'. Flicking through this hoard, I could tell that there was just as much as Jack had said, potentially more.

'Look at it,' I said in awe. 'It's amazing.'

'It's our future,' she replied, standing up and this time

476

helping me to my feet. I put the notes back inside the box and closed it as I stood up, fastening the clip lest some God-delivered breeze whisked it from my hands and across the treetops of Cageley, scattering its contents down upon the houses below. I was ready now to go through the window and get out of Cageley for ever, already seeing the good life as it stood like a mirage before me, complete with its fine clothes and food, a decent home, a job, more money. And love. Above all, love.

We turned towards the window and I could not help but look back over my shoulder once. There are moments in life, simple still-framed scenes, that one can recall and, for me, this was one of them. Even after two hundred and fifty-six years on this earth, whenever I think of my youth, my childhood, the picture of my teenage self stopping before the window on the roof of Cageley House, and throwing one last look over my shoulder before I left, springs into my consciousness and my heart sinks with the conviction of my actions and the desolation which they caused me for so many years. For it was at that moment, between two blinks of my eyes, that I saw them across the courtyard down below: the stables. They were not directly in the path of the moonlight but I could make them out with no difficulty. I knew them so well by then, every inch of their flooring, every piece of wood in their walls, every horse contained within. I could hear them when I listened closely, one or two of the mares making whinnying sounds in their sleep. I saw the outside wall and the corner by the water pump where Jack and I always sat to drink a bottle of beer at the end of the day, the spot where the sun shone down best. I remembered the feeling of near hysterical delight it gave me to collapse there after nine or ten hours of work, knowing that the evening stretched before me like a long, lazy picture of possibility. I recalled how we would often sit there for hours, just talking, despite the fact that we had spent the entire day wishing we were elsewhere. I remembered jokes and laughter and insults and friendly mockery. And I knew that if I lived to be a hundred years old, I couldn't live with what I was about to do.

There was nowhere else for us to go and no one else to talk to. We were friends. I closed my eyes and thought of it. I did not know what it is to be hurt by those I thought to be my friends although I have felt it often enough since, and there I was, getting ready to do that very thing. All that money. He had worked for it. He had suffered, taken abuse, shovelled shit, brushed down horses ten thousand times; he had *worked* for it. And I was there to rob him. It was impossible.

'I'm sorry,' I said, looking at Dominique and shaking my head sadly, 'I can't do it.'

She cocked her head to one side. 'Can't do what?' she asked.

'This,' I replied. 'This thing that we're doing. This *stealing*. I can't do it. I just can't.'

'Matthieu,' she said in a calm voice, coming towards me slowly, speaking to me now as if I was a naughty child who had to be talked out of doing something dangerous. 'You're just nervous, that's all. So am I. We need that money. If we're going to—'

'No, *Jack* needs the money,' I said. 'It's his money. He needs it. I can get him out of jail with it. He could disappear off to—'

'And what about us?' she cried and I could see her eyes flickering towards the box, causing me to

478

strengthen my grip on it. 'What about our plans?'

'Don't you see? We can do them anyway. All we have to do is get back on the road, get—'

'Listen to me, Matthieu,' she said firmly and I took a step backwards for fear that she would make a grab for me. 'I'm not getting back on any road, you understand me? I'm taking this money and—'

'No,' I shouted. 'You're not. We're not. I'm taking it to Jack. I can get him out with it!'

She sighed and put a hand to her forehead for a moment before closing her eyes as she slipped away into concentrated thought. I swallowed nervously and my eyes flickered from side to side. It was her move. I waited for her to say something. When she took her hand away, rather than the look of fury which I had anticipated, she was smiling. Her lips flickered slightly and she came closer towards me, never once taking her eyes off my face.

'Matthieu,' she repeated in a quiet voice, 'you have to look at what's best for us. For you and me. For us to be together.' I cocked my head slightly to the left, trying to decipher what she meant. Her face came closer to mine and her eyes closed as our lips met gently, her tongue pressing softly against my closed lips which parted a little on instinct. I felt her hand against my back, a finger trailing down until she brought her hand around my waist, her palm massaging me lightly where she knew me to be at my most vulnerable. A sigh caught in my throat and my body shivered in anticipation as I prepared to put my hand behind her head, to kiss her deeper and stronger, but before I could her mouth slipped away from mine and she continued to kiss me at my neck. 'We can do this,' she whispered. 'We can be together.'

479

I struggled. I wanted her. And then I said no.

'We have to save Jack,' I whispered, and she pulled away from me furiously, her lips crooked with madness, her eyes filled with rage. I looked away for a moment, unwilling to see her greed personified before me. I gripped the cigar box full of money and I knew that we were both concentrating on it now.

And she pounced.

And – a reflex action – I jumped out of the way.

And then she was no longer there.

I blinked and shook my head in surprise. I had grown accustomed to the dark and I knew that she was gone but I stood there nervously for a moment, still clutching the box for all I was worth, unsure what to do now for the best. Slowly my stomach churned and after a few minutes my knees buckled; I fell and vomited on the roof. When there was nothing left to escape my system, my head slowly turned to view the results of my actions, and I could see her there, Dominique, thirty feet below, impaled upon a spike, dangling like a rag doll in the calm, cold night.

Before heading towards the jail house, I took Dominique down from where her body lay and placed her gently on the ground. Her eyes were open and a thin trickle of blood hung from the side of her mouth to her chin. I wiped it away and smoothed down her hair. I didn't cry, curiously, I felt very little at that moment other than a desire to get away. The self-recriminations and insomniac nights of reliving that scene over and over would come later – I have had two and a half centuries to recall it since then – for now, I was in shock and determined to get away from that house as quickly as possible.

I brought her into the kitchen, however, and from there back up the stairs to her own bedroom, which was musty and damp. I opened a window as I lay her on the bed and when I stepped away, my shirt was stained with slashes of red and my hands were wet and bloody. I jumped in fright, more afraid of the presence of her blood than I was of the dead body, and I felt strangely oblivious to her now, as if the corpse before me was not Dominique at all, merely a representation of her, a false image, and her true personality was deep within me and far from dead.

On this occasion, I did not look back as I left the room. I stopped by Jack's bedroom and took off my bloodstained shirt, putting on one of his instead. Outside I washed my hands under the pump and watched as the redness poured into the drain, her last essence slipping away from me effortlessly. I went to the stables then and untied two horses, the two fastest and strongest steeds in Sir Alfred's possession, and led them quietly to the end of the driveway, where I mounted one and held the reins of the other as we headed towards the outskirts of the village where the jail stood. I tied them up outside and drifted inside as if I was in a dream. A guard – a different one from the one I had seen earlier – was asleep at his desk but he jumped when I coughed and gripped the desk before him nervously.

'What do you want?' he asked, before his eyes lit on the cigar box in my hands. Jack had obviously filled him in on the plans earlier for he looked pleased to see it and glanced around the empty room nervously. 'You his friend?' he asked, nodding in the direction of the cell.

'Yes,' I said. 'Can I see him?'

He shrugged so I walked to the end of the corridor

481

and around the corner, where Jack was pacing in his cell. He grinned when he saw me but his smile quickly froze as he saw the expression on my face. 'Jesus,' he said. 'What happened to you? You look like you've seen a ghost.' He paused. 'That's my shirt, isn't it?'

I held up the cigar box so that he could see it, ignoring his question completely. 'Here it is,' I said. 'I got it.'

The guard appeared at my shoulder and Jack looked at him. 'So?' he said. 'Do we have a deal then?'

'Aye, forty pounds and I'll let you go,' he replied, rooting through his keys for the right one. 'That Nat Pepys deserves a good kicking anyway, if you ask me,' he muttered, justifying his actions to two people who had done worse. When he was released, Jack handed over the money and the guard steeled himself for the blow which would knock him out. 'Just try and do it quickly,' he said, turning back towards his desk and Jack, at that moment, lifted a chair and brought it crashing down about the back of his head. He fell to the floor, knocked out, and although the injury was less severe than the one I had seen tonight – the guard would, after all, live – I felt sick again and thought I might faint.

'Come on,' said Jack, leading me outside and looking around to make sure that no one was coming. 'You brought the horses?'

'Yes,' I said, pointing in their direction but not moving.

'What's the matter?' he asked me, confused by my attitude. I paused, unsure whether I should tell him or not.

'Will you tell me something?' I asked him. 'The truth now, whatever it is.' He looked at me blankly and opened his mouth to inquire further but changed his mind and simply nodded. 'You and Dominique,' I said. 'Did anything ever happen between you?'

This time there was a long hesitation. 'What did she tell you?' he asked eventually and I interrupted loudly.

'Just tell me!' I yelled. 'Did anything ever happen between you? Did you . . . make advances towards her?'

'Me?' he asked laughing. 'No,' he said, shaking his head firmly. 'No, I didn't. And if she told you I did, she's a liar.'

'She did tell me that,' I replied.

'It was the other way around,' he said. 'She came to my room one night. She made the advances, as you put it, towards me. I swear to you.'

I felt a stab of pain through my heart and nodded. 'But you did nothing,' I said quietly.

'Of course not.'

'For me? Because of our friendship?'

He exhaled loudly. 'Maybe a little because of that,' he said. 'But to be honest with you, Mattie, I never really liked her. I didn't like how she treated you. I told you that. She was a bad lot.'

I shrugged. 'I loved her though,' I said. 'Funny, isn't it?'

He frowned now and looked upwards. It was starting to get brighter and it was past time that we should be on our way. 'Where is she anyway?' he asked and I hesitated, unsure whether I should tell him the truth, whether I dared explain what had happened that night.

'She's not coming,' I said. 'She's staying here.'

He nodded slowly, somewhat surprised, but thought better of pursuing the topic. 'And Tomas?' he asked. I said nothing. There was a long silence. 'All right,' he said, mounting one of the horses. 'Let's go then.'

I put my foot in the stirrup of the second horse, jumped on her back and followed Jack Holby as he led the way out of town. I didn't look back once and, although I would like to describe the journey which brought us back to the south coast and on board a boat destined for Europe and our freedom, I cannot recall a single moment of it. My childhood had ended. And although I had many years of life yet to live – more than I could have ever possibly imagined – I became an adult the moment my horse set foot outside the gates which, a year before, had first brought me into Cageley.

And for the first time in my life, I felt completely alone.

Chapter 25

November–December 1999

It was Tara who suggested meeting in the same Italian restaurant in Soho where we had discussed her job prospects and the possibility of her leaving the station earlier in the year. I wasn't sure how I felt about this meeting and was slightly nervous as I sat waiting for her to arrive. We hadn't seen each other in over six months and I had rarely watched her on television in that time either.

Yet when I had phoned Tara, after much pushing from Caroline and her fellow conspirators at the station, she had quickly agreed to meet me. We chatted for about ten minutes before arranging a time and place to meet.

When she arrived, she took me quite by surprise. The last time I had seen her, she had been the very picture of the modern career woman. She had worn a designer suit – nothing off the rack for Tara (or 'Tart' as James had called her) – and her blonde bob had sat perfectly about her head as if her stylist had been sitting outside the restaurant, ready to give her one final touch-up before she made her appearance on the catwalk. But now, six months down the line, I barely recognized her. The suit had given way to an expensive pair of white jeans and a simple blouse, open at the neck. She had allowed her hair to grow a little and it hung above the neck, in a simple arrangement, brunette now with some gentle blonde highlights. She carried a Filofax, which was *de rigueur* I expected, and her face bore little sign of make-up. She looked fantastic; she looked her age.

'Tara,' I said, my breath quite taken away by the new grown-up look. 'I'd hardly have recognized you. You look fantastic.'

She paused and stared at me in surprise for a moment before breaking into a wide smile. 'Thank you,' she said, laughing now and, I thought, blushing slightly. 'That's nice of you to say. You don't look so bad yourself for a middle-aged man.'

I laughed – how many middle-aged five-hundred-year-olds did she know? – and shook my head to stop myself from looking at her. After the formalities were over and we had ordered a relatively light lunch, we sat back in our seats and an uncertain silence descended over us. Of course it was I who had invited Tara to lunch, and as such it was I who was expected to initiate the conversation.

'So how's life at the Beeb? Much better than with us, I expect.'

She shrugged. 'It's fine,' she said without much enthusiasm. 'It's different to how I expected it would be.'

'How so?'

'Well, they throw a lot of money at you but don't seem that keen on you doing any work half the time. It seems a strange way to go about doing business.'

'It's called keeping control of all the talent,' I explained. 'They're willing to pay an awful lot of people to be under contract to them, not so much to actually work for them, but to prevent them from working for someone else. It's an old practice. I've seen it done before.'

'Don't get me wrong,' she said quickly, eager not to appear unhappy with her new arrangement. 'I've a lot on. I have to go to Rio de Janeiro in a few weeks for a holiday show. I'm on *Question Time* later this week. And Gary Lineker and I are going to be redesigning each other's living rooms for an interior design special next month. We've only got two days to do it in so that should be . . .' She struggled to find an appropriate word, couldn't and so gave up. I looked down at the food which had just arrived and began to eat, not wishing to look at her in case her face bore an expression of utter misery.

'Well, it's good that it's going so well and you're keeping busy,' I said eventually. 'Although we miss you, of course.'

'Sure you do,' she replied. 'You couldn't get rid of me fast enough.'

'Now that's not true,' I protested. 'There was an awful lot going on at the time and it seemed to me that if you were getting a decent offer from the BBC then it was in your best interest to take them up on it. I was only thinking of your future.'

Tara laughed. She didn't believe that any more than I did. 'Oh, well,' she said. 'It hardly matters now, to be honest with you. I think I was a bit of a bitch about the whole thing anyway. There was more to getting out of the station than just job offers, as I'm sure you realize.'

I looked at her in surprise, but she was looking over my shoulder towards another table where a celebrity couple had just arrived. She nodded an acknowledgement towards them before returning to her pizza. 'Oh, how's Tommy?' she asked after a moment, looking across at me as if she had meant to ask this question immediately after she had arrived.

'Not so good,' I said.

'I was so sorry to read about what happened.'

'It was on the cards,' I told her. 'He was heading for it for a long time. History isn't on his side.'

'But he's out of the coma anyway?'

I nodded. 'Oh, yes. He's back home as well, which is a good thing. But he's very down. And there's no word as yet as to whether he's still going to have a job when he does get fully better again.'

'That's a tough break. I know his producer though, and she's a total bitch. Real moral high ground hypocrite. She doesn't mind showing every type of human behaviour or perversion on her TV show but, if a single person behaves like a human being in real life, she thinks it's the end of the world. Total nightmare of a woman. Not that I'm one to talk.'

'Oh, come on,' I said, smiling at her, uncertain whether she was looking for sympathy or simply playing me off against my better nature. 'You're not so bad,' I added mischievously.

'I was once,' she said. 'I was just like her.' She paused and bit her lip briefly, contemplating whether she had the courage to go through with a planned speech. Eventually, stuttering slightly, she continued. 'Look, Matthieu. There's something I need to tell you. It's something I've been meaning to call you about for quite a while now but every time I try to I can't quite work up the courage. Since you called me and since we're here, I expect I should eat humble pie and just get on with it.'

I looked at her and put my fork down. 'Go on,' I said.

'It's about what happened,' she explained. 'Between us, I mean. When I . . . became interested in your nephew.'

'That's a long time ago, Tara,' I said irritably, not wishing to drag the whole business up again.

'I know it is, I know it is,' she replied. 'But I have to get this off my chest anyway.' She took a deep breath and stared me straight in the eye. 'I'm sorry,' she said. 'I'm sorry for what I did. I was wrong. I was unfair to you and I was unfair to Tommy. I don't know what I could have been thinking of – I acted like a schoolgirl with a crush – but it's like you say, it *was* a long time ago now and I . . . I think I've changed anyway. So I just wanted to apologize, that's all. Your friendship always meant a lot to me and I've missed it. I behaved badly and I'm sorry about it. You were the first person—'

I reached across and placed a hand on top of hers. 'Tara, it's all right,' I said. 'It's all in the past. We're none of us perfect. You have no idea the mistakes that I've made in relationships over the years.'

She smiled and I started to laugh and shake my head. It surprised me just how much I appreciated hearing her say these things. We started to eat again and a pleasant feeling of happiness descended on the table. We were friends again and that was a good thing. More importantly, she seemed different from the Tara that I had fallen out of love with and closer to the Tara that I had fallen *in* love with in the first place.

'Give him my best anyway,' she said after a moment before trying to catch the words back. 'Unless you think that's the wrong thing to do. Maybe you shouldn't say anything about me. He's probably not my number one fan. Not after . . . Well, I didn't exactly help matters, now did I?' The 'Tara Says:' column that had caused him a certain amount of trouble at the time hadn't come up in the conversation. I changed the subject.

'Forget about it,' I said. 'Anyway. I didn't bring you here to talk about Tommy or any of that old business. This is actually supposed to be a business meeting, you know.'

'Really?' she said, although I didn't believe for a moment that she had seen it as anything but. 'All right then. How are things in my old haunt?'

'Busy,' I said. 'Extremely busy.'

'Did you get someone to replace James?' she asked and I shook my head.

'No. I've been doing the job ever since he died. And P.W. disappeared off to the Caribbean or some place and delivered his dervish of a daughter to me instead to take care of his shares and she's about the worst thing that's ever happened to me, which is really saying something.'

'How come?' asked Tara, and I found that I didn't mind discussing these things with her. Six months, even twelve months, before I would have been worried that anything I said would either be in a newspaper column or all around the office by dinner time but now, even though we had only been together for about half an hour, I trusted her again. I felt that I could get these problems off my chest and reveal how they made me feel. And I recognized that I didn't have anybody in my life that I could do that with. I told her about Caroline and how she was gradually trying to involve herself deeper and deeper in the business, even though I didn't believe she was particularly good at her job, and how she was still bucking for James Hocknell's old job.

'Well, she's not going to get it, is she?' asked Tara,

washing down the last of her meal with a long drink from her mineral water. I shook my head.

'Oh, no,' I said. 'But then neither am I. I've spent about six months doing it now and I've had enough. I need a break. I'm not a young man.'

'You want to return to your idle man of leisure days,' she said with a smile and I nodded quickly.

'I *do*,' I said, unashamed to admit it. 'I really *do*. I mean I want to maintain my involvement but not at this level. Not where I'm responsible for everything that goes on. I want the old days back.'

'Who doesn't?' she said quietly, and I stored that phrase away as I suspected it was a hint on her part as much as anything. 'So what are you going to do then?' she asked. 'Recruit from another station? I suppose I could give you the names of a few people who—'

'No, no,' I said. 'That's all right. I have a vague idea in my mind of what I might do but I have no idea whether it makes any sense or not. I have to think it through. Anyway, tell me about you. Honestly now. Are you happy with your job?'

'About as happy as you are with yours,' she said honestly. She sighed. 'I'm not exactly *stretched*, Matthieu. I'm bored with the shows I'm doing and the rest of the time it's all research and administrative things, which I have about as much interest in as you do. I want to be back in front of the camera. I want to present a solid news show, that's all I want to do. I want to put one together, design a fresh format, put together a professional team and work to make it successful. A good news show. That's all I want.'

I nodded and looked down at the table. I felt my whole body skipping with delight; this had gone so much better than I could ever have anticipated. 'Tara,'

491

I said, 'I think it's time we both put our cards on the table, don't you?'

I waited until Tommy had settled in at home again before calling over to visit him. Andrea opened the door and looked relieved to see me, even though we had hardly hit it off on our one previous meeting in the hospital. She was heavily pregnant by now and her cheeks looked a little puffy, but she seemed in good health, if a little tired.

'How's the patient?' I asked, stepping into the hallway and taking off my coat. 'I thought I'd give him a couple of days before visiting him.'

'I wish I could,' she said, leading the way through to the living room where Tommy was staring at the television. 'But now that you're here it gives me a chance to go out for a while. I'll see you later, Tommy, all right?' Her manner was rude and irritable, as if she had had just about enough of baby-sitting my nephew.

He grunted and she disappeared out of the room, leaving the two of us alone. He was lying down on the couch in front of the television wearing a T-shirt, a pair of sweat pants and thick, woollen socks. His hair was unwashed and looked a little greasy; his face was still pale and he barely glanced in my direction, turning the volume on the television up instead. Children's programming. Cartoons.

'You know how you can always tell a cartoon person from a real one?' he asked me from his prostrate position.

'Go on,' I said. 'How?'

'Their fingers,' he said quietly. 'Cartoon people always have four fingers. That's how you can tell. Why do you suppose that is?'

492

I thought about it. 'Well, yes,' I said. 'That and the fact that the cartoon people are generally *animated*. What's up with you, Tommy? Sit up and act like a grown-up, will you? I'm going to make some coffee. Do you want one?'

'Tea,' he muttered. I forgot; despite Tommy's addiction to various narcotic or addictive substances, the one drug to which he seemed indifferent was caffeine.

After bringing the drinks in, I walked across the living room and switched the television set off.

'Hey,' complained Tommy. 'I was watching that.'

'And now you're not,' I said, reaching across and putting the mug of tea in front of him. He frowned and covered his eyes with his hands as he lay there, waiting for me to say something. I sighed. 'So,' I said eventually, 'how are you? Feeling any better?'

'Oh, yeah,' he said sarcastically. 'I feel like a million dollars. Let me see, I overdosed, I nearly died, I'm on all these weird medications to wean me off drugs that make my stomach sick all the time and give me near constant diarrhoea, I've got no money, my girlfriend's about to leave me and I'm going to be a father in about a month's time. Oh, and I've been fired from my job. With all these things going for me, how could I feel anything less than deliriously happy? But you're a peach to ask.'

'You've been fired?' I asked in surprise. 'When did this happen?'

'Yesterday,' he replied quietly, slightly ashamed I thought. 'Stephanie phoned to see how I was, or so she said at the start anyway, and then she said that she thought I should take a break from the show for a while. Said that my extra-curricular activities, as she put it, reflected badly on them and they couldn't afford to have me there any more. So, like, thanks for nine

493

years' worth of your life but *sayonara* baby.' He ticked off his hand against his forehead, like a military salute.

I shook my head. I wasn't surprised but it annoyed me that they couldn't wait until a more appropriate moment to tell him this. After all, he would be on sick leave for the next month or so anyway, during which time he would *hopefully* be getting his life back in order. There was no need for such immediacy.

'I'm sorry,' I said. 'I'm sorry that's happened but—'

'But you knew it would,' he interrupted. 'Yeah, you don't have to tell me you told me so. You've been saying it for years.'

'That wasn't what I was going to say,' I said. 'I was going to say that maybe the time has come when you *should* leave the show. I mean you've been in it since you were, what, twelve?'

'Fourteen.'

'You don't want to spend the rest of your life playing one character, do you?'

'It's a job, Uncle Matt,' he said, sitting up now and staring across at me with a look of enormous self-pity on his face. 'The fact that I've been in it so long is what's going to hurt me. You think that any casting director from any TV show or movie is going to look at me and see Tommy DuMarqué? They don't! They see Sam Cutler. Stupid Sam. A heart-of-gold boy with about two brain cells to rub together. I'm typecast now. I mean whatever happened to Mike Lincoln, eh? Or Cathy Eliot? Or Pete Martin Sinclair? Where do you see any of them now?'

'Who?' I asked, not initially seeing his point, only grasping it a moment too late.

'Exactly!' he roared. 'They were just as big as I was once. And where are they now? Nothings! No ones!

494

Probably working in a restaurant somewhere, asking whether you want fries with that, sir. That's my future. No one will employ me in TV. I'm unemployable!' He bowed his head in his hands and for a moment I was afraid that he was crying, but he wasn't. He just wanted darkness. He wanted to see nothing or no one. He wanted to remove himself from the lot. 'I wish I'd died,' he said simply when he came back up for air. 'I wish that OD had killed me.'

'Now that's enough,' I said furiously, coming over and sitting beside him on the couch. I took his face in my hands but his eyes looked away; he looked so tired, so utterly exhausted by life, that my heart went out to him. And in his face now, this dying boy's face, I saw the faces of his ancestors, each of them in turn dead or on their way to dying by his age. Defeated, depressed, Tommy was ready to join their number. 'You're not going to die,' I said firmly.

'What have I got left?' he asked.

'A baby, for one,' I said and he shrugged. 'Tell me this,' I added after a moment. 'You've told me over and over again how much you hate the attention of being famous, how much you wouldn't miss it. You've said that you can't stand people looking at you all the time—'

'Well, not *all* the time,' he muttered, a gentle spark of humour still present in his misery.

'How much would you really miss it?' I asked him. 'How important is fame to you? Tell me, Tommy. How important is fame? How much does it mean? How much does it matter having dozens of celebrity friends hovering around you all the time?'

He focused for a moment and thought about it, as if he realized that his response could be important here. 'Not much,' he said, and it was almost like a revelation to himself. 'I've been famous. I *am* famous. It doesn't mean that much. I just want to be successful. I don't want to be a loser all my life. I've got . . . I don't know . . . *ambition*. I need to feel that I've succeeded in life. That I'm *somebody*. I can't remain static. I have to . . . *achieve!*' he roared. 'My life has to end up having some meaning.'

'All right,' I shouted triumphantly. 'Now do you mean that? Do you really mean that? You're looking for success?'

'Yes.'

'Good. Then this, all of this, means nothing. Forget about the show. There's so much more that you can do now. Look at you, you're in your early twenties, for Christ's sake. You've got your whole life ahead of you. You've achieved so much in the last decade, ten times more than most people your age have. Just imagine what you can do in the future! You pull yourself together or you're going to die. You're going to end up killing yourself just like you almost did.'

'Big fucking deal,' he said, sinking again.

'All right Tommy,' I said quietly. 'I want you to sit up and listen to me. I'm going to tell you about your family. Your father, and his, and his. Something I've never done before, believe me. I'm going to show you where they went wrong and, by God, if you can't change your life because of it then there's no point in either of us continuing on here. There're nine generations of DuMarqués whose destiny you know nothing about but who you're following into the grave so predictably. It ends now, Tommy. It ends here and now. Today.'

He stared at me as if I was mad. 'What are you talking about?' he asked.

'I'm talking about history,' I said.

496

'History.'

'Yes! I'm talking about you repeating the same old pattern of all your ancestors because you're too stupid to open your eyes and allow yourself to live! Every one of you didn't give a damn about life and so sacrificed it. I've been given all your years. And I've had enough, all right?' I was shouting and saying things I hadn't imagined I would before.

'What are you talking about?' he asked. 'How can you tell me any of that? I mean I know you must have known my father and, I guess, his, but how could you—'

'Tommy, just sit back and stay quiet and let me speak. Don't say anything until I finish, can you do that for me?'

He shrugged. 'OK,' he said in a defeated tone, leaning forward and picking up his cup of tea.

'All right then,' I said, moving back to the armchair and taking a deep breath. I would save Tommy's life, I decided. I *demanded* of myself that I save him. 'All right,' I repeated, taking a deep breath and gearing myself up to begin my story. 'Here's the thing, Tommy,' I began. 'This is the story. So just listen to it. There's one thing about me that you don't realize and it's probably not going to be easy to grasp but I'm going to try anyway. And it's this.

'I don't die. I just get older and older and older.'

Over the next few days I was surprised by the public reaction to Tommy's dismissal. Although the initial response to his overdose had been one of tabloid horror at the excesses of a spoilt youth who had thrown away so much – a predictable and entirely hypocritical reaction on their part, considering that they were the very ones to build him up in the first place – public

497

opinion slowly began to alter that viewpoint into one of sympathy and understanding.

The fact was that Tommy DuMarqué had become part of the nation's life over the previous nine years. They had watched him grow up from a violent, tortured adolescent, to a responsible, albeit sexually promiscuous, man – or rather they had watched Sam Cutler grow up, but the two names were interchangeable to most, as were their lives. They had followed his adventures in the newspapers, bought his records, pinned his posters to their bedroom walls, bought the celebrity magazines where they invented a house for him to pretend was his own. They had bought a magazine one week because the cover showed Sam Cutler and Tina embracing; they had bought it the following week because it showed Tommy DuMarqué and his latest girlfriend. The lines between the two were thin; the distinctions blurred. They had bought into this life, whoever's it was, Tommy's or Sam's, and they weren't going to give it up without a fight.

News stations began to carry reports on the number of letters which the producers were receiving, condemning them for cutting him loose at a time when he most needed help. Having nurtured him for so long and made him a star, these letters pointed out, it was despicable that they should fire him for embracing the very lifestyle which their programming demanded of him.

An appeal was made through one newspaper that all of those who were opposed to Tommy DuMarqué's dismissal should tune off from the Tuesday evening episode of his television show, and indeed the viewing figures on that night sank from their regular position of around fifteen million, to only eight. I had no idea what was going on at the show's production meetings, but I suspected it wasn't pretty.

I phoned Tommy to see whether he was encouraged by the news, but he wasn't at home. 'He had to go to a ground floor flat and out the side window,' explained Andrea. 'We've got what looks like half the world's media camped outside here. They're all waiting for some response from him.'

'Tell him not to make any,' I told her firmly. 'The last thing he needs right now is to get into a war of words with his producers. Tell him to stay quiet on the matter. If he really wants back in, that's his best shot.'

'Don't worry, that's what he's doing.'

'And how is he anyway?'

'He's not too bad actually,' she said optimistically. 'Much better than last week. He's gone back to the hospital for a check-up. Says he's going to join a group for reformed drug users, so that can't be bad.'

'Really?' I said, delighted to hear it. 'Well, that's good news.'

'*If* he actually sees it through. You know what he's like.' She paused. 'Do you think he's going to get his job back?'

I hesitated before answering. 'I don't know,' I said. 'I wouldn't hold out much hope. The public are fickle. This is big news right now but it won't be in a couple of weeks' time. All they've got to do is invent some enormous storyline to get everyone hooked again. Why, is he holding out for a phone call from them?'

'I think he's thinking about it, I'm not sure. He hasn't said much. He's been in a funny mood, to tell you the truth, ever since the other day, the day you were here. His whole attitude has changed since then.'

'Really,' I said, aware that she was in fact asking a

question but unwilling to supply her with an answer. Tommy's reaction to what I had told him had been one of disbelief at first, naturally enough. He was the first person I had ever told about my life and he had laughed, thinking that I was playing some joke on him.

We talked back and forth for hours and I told him many stories of his own forefathers as well as tales of incidents in which I myself had been involved. I told him of my youth and of an early, doomed love affair which had ended in tragedy. I even acknowledged how it is possible to fall in love with someone who is undeserving of that affection. I told him everything. I spoke of the eighteenth century, the nineteenth and the twentieth. The settings shifted from England to Europe to America and back again. I told him of people he had heard of from history and those whose names had vanished after their deaths, only to live on in the memories of their counterparts, who in turn had died, leaving only one, leaving only me, the eldest of them all.

In the end, while still not fully convinced, I left him in a state of bewilderment. 'Uncle Matt,' he asked as I made my way through the door. 'All of these people, my father, my grandfather, my great-grandfather and so on. Is it supposed to be some sort of metaphor for me? Are you making this stuff up to make a point?'

I laughed. 'No,' I said simply. 'Not at all. These things happened. They took place, that's all I'm saying. Make of them what you will. And now it's your turn, that's all. I'm telling you this and I promise you I never told any of your ancestors. Maybe I should have. Maybe the knowledge could have saved them. But, either way, you know now. What you do with the information is your own business. Just one thing, that's all—'

'Yes?'

'You keep it between you and I. The last thing I want is your level of fame.'

He laughed. 'You and me both,' he said.

'He's probably still feeling the effects of the last few weeks,' I told Andrea. 'Give him time. He'll come round. How are you feeling anyway? You can't have that long left.'

'A couple of weeks,' she said heartily. 'I just hope he or she isn't born on Christmas Day, that's all. Before or after, I don't mind. But not Christmas Day.'

'As long as he's healthy,' I said, as people do.

'Or she.'

'Right,' I said, as if there was any chance of that happening.

Caroline was becoming the bane of my life. Although she worked hard, she was too eager to please. She had an opinion on everything and in spite of being new to the industry, she didn't mind sharing every single one of them at the board meetings. Sometimes there was a naive charm to what she said – to be fair, she had an ability to cut through industry jargon and tended to take me to task for the wide chasm between what the public wanted to see and my perception of what they should actually be watching (which was nothing) – but more often than not her lack of experience shone through and she succeeded only in infuriating those colleagues who saw her as arrogant and incompetent. I had made a mistake in hiring her in the first place, at least at such a high level in the station, but in fairness I had been left with little alternative at the time. After all, she controlled her father's shares and P.W. remained an important member of the board as well as one of the owners of the station. Whether I liked it or not, she was there to stay. Unless I could persuade her father to return, of course, although that still wouldn't necessarily see her off.

I was working late on some scheduling problems and thought I was alone in the building when she came into my office, standing at the door and staring at me with a curious smirk on her face.

'Caroline,' I said, surprised and not entirely thrilled to see her there. 'What are you still doing here? I thought everybody had gone home.'

'What have I got to go home to?' she asked quietly, a smile flickering around her lips. I thought about it. I didn't know. We had never shared any personal information with each other.

'Matthieu,' she said then, biting her lip and disappearing back outside. 'Can you just stay here for a moment? There's something I want to get.'

I put down my pen and rubbed my eyes. I was tired and not in the mood for games or even for business discussions. Whatever she wanted, I hoped she would get off her chest as quickly as possible. I considered packing up my papers and taking them home with me instead but I have a golden rule that I work in the office and I live at home and even the possibility of a long conversation with Caroline was not enough to force me to change that.

She reappeared with a bottle of champagne and two glasses and kicked the door shut behind her with her heel. 'What's this for?' I asked in surprise, for it was the last thing I had been expecting.

'You mean you don't know?' she said, smiling at me as she laid them down on the desk before me.

'Are we celebrating something?'

'It's our anniversary, Matthieu. Don't tell me you've forgotten.' I thought about it. I was certainly no spring chicken but my memory was fine and I knew that while I had married a few duds in my day she had not been one of them. I shook my head and smiled awkwardly.

'I'm sorry . . .' I said. 'But . . .'

'It was five months ago today that we first met,' she explained. 'The day you talked me into coming to work here, remember?'

'And that qualifies as an anniversary?' I asked.

'Oh, come on,' she said, opening the bottle and pouring two glasses. 'We don't need an excuse to have a drink together, now, do we? We're friends.'

'Indeed,' I said hesitantly, accepting the glass and clinking it against hers. 'Well, here's to another five wonderful months,' I said dryly.

'And longer,' she said, slapping my arm. 'I see a big future for us here, Matthieu. You and I. I have so many plans for this place, you know. There's so much I can do here. I'm an extraordinary woman, you know. If you took the time to get to know me better, you'd realize that.'

I nodded slowly. Now I got the idea. Strange how after 256 years it still takes me a few moments to realize when someone is flirting with me. In this case it was probably because I suspected a subtext. Caroline was not the kind of woman who gave anything away without wanting something back in return.

'Look, Caroline,' I began, but she cut me off.

'Did you speak to Tara Morrison?' she asked and I nodded.

'Yes, yes. We had lunch a few days ago.'

'And did you offer her the job?'

'As directed.'

Her eyes opened wide. 'So?' she demanded. 'What did she say?'

'She said she'd think about it. She wasn't going to give me an answer on the spot, now, was she? But I think it's safe to suppose that we probably have her. She's changed, I think. She's still ambitious but in a different way. A better way.'

'We're all ambitious, Matthieu.'

'Yes, but she wants . . . what is it . . . ?' I tried to think of what it was about Tara that had most impressed me upon our meeting; what it was that made her different from the Tara I used to know. 'She wants to feel proud of what she's doing, you know? She wants to be . . .' I laughed. 'Well, she wants to be really good at it. I think she wants to achieve a little self-respect. Do something she can feel proud of.'

'Good,' said Caroline. 'I'll start working on some ideas for her.'

'Don't,' I replied firmly. 'I'll look after Tara. We're still in the delicate stages of negotiation. Don't jeopardize that, you don't even know her.'

'I just think if I put some programme ideas together for her—'

'Listen to me, Caroline,' I said firmly. 'I want you to stay out of this one. Just leave it to me and all will be well. Tara could eat you up and spit you out and you have to know how to handle her.' She sat back in her chair, looking a little miffed. I knew that she wouldn't interfere.

'I'm sorry,' she said eventually. 'I wouldn't do anything you didn't want me to do, of course.' I shrugged. 'It's just that I want to be proud of my work too. And I want you to be proud of me.' I glanced down at my desk and within a moment I felt her palm stroking across my cheek. 'I don't think we're as close as we could be, Matthieu.'

I pushed the chair back a little and held up both hands in protest. 'I'm sorry, Caroline,' I said. 'I really don't think that this would be a good—'

'I don't think you realize just how fond I am of you, Matthieu,' she continued, getting up and coming over to me now, her seductive manner forced and imitated from TV. 'I've always been attracted to older men.'

'Not this old, you haven't,' I said. 'Believe me. Now really, I—'

'Just try it,' she whispered, leaning forward to kiss me. I dodged out of her way.

'Sorry,' I said, touching her arm lightly. 'Really, I am.'

She brushed herself down and composed herself. 'Fine,' she said. 'I'm fine. I'm going now.' And with that she stormed towards the door, turning back for one final shot. 'Just remember I'm still a major shareholder here, Matthieu, and if I want to involve myself in things, then that's exactly what I'll do.'

I sighed and turned back to my work.

A few days later, the phone rang. It was Tara, eager and willing to take up my offer of employment. 'And the Beeb?' I asked her. 'They're willing to let you go?'

'Not quite,' she said. 'My agent's had some discussions with them. Lack of commitment on their part to my career and so on. He threatened to sue them and after some negotiation I'm basically out of a job right now.'

'Well, let's end that situation right here and now,' I said, delighted. 'I really am pleased that you'll be coming back to us.' I hesitated for a moment before adding, 'I've missed you.'

Now it was her turn to hold back. 'I've missed you too,' she said eventually. 'I've missed our friendship. Not to mention our arguments.'

'Well, things will be different this time. The station's going to be different. You can have a certain autonomy over what you're doing. I trust you.'

'The only thing I'm worried about,' she said, a certain tension creeping into her voice now, 'is exactly who's going to be leading the station.'

'Well, I am for the time being,' I said.

'You said you wanted to leave.'

'The day to day operations, certainly. I need another James Hocknell to run the place but I'll still be a share-holder and board member.'

'Right,' said Tara. 'But when do you think that will be? Have you started looking?'

'No,' I admitted. 'But like I said before, I have an idea what I'm going to do. I just haven't found the right opportunity yet to make the offer. Plus I have to be sure that I'm doing the right thing. Leave it with me. Whatever I do, I'll do it soon.'

'I should tell you,' she said, 'I spoke to Alan and P.W.'

'You did?' I was surprised. Even I hadn't spoken to Alan in a while and I hadn't heard from P.W. since he left the country. 'Where did you track P.W. down?' I asked.

'I have my sources,' she laughed. 'He's getting married in Bermuda, did you know that?'

'Good God, no. I bet she's some seventeen-year-old belly dancer, am I right?'

'Well, she's sixteen, but the age restrictions are a lot less severe there.'

Now it was my turn to laugh. 'I wonder what she sees in millionaire P.W.,' I said sarcastically.

'I wonder indeed. But, anyway, I felt I should speak to both him and Alan before coming back on board and it was all right except for something that P.W. said.'

'Oh, yes.'

'It turns out he wants to sell his shares altogether. Did you know that?'

This took me by surprise. It was the first I'd heard of it. 'No, I didn't,' I said. 'When did this happen?'

'Well, according to him, he's only recently made the decision but he hasn't done anything about it yet. Wants to wait until he gets this whole new marriage thing out of the way before selling up all his interests over here. Apparently they're going to start a radio station in Bermuda from the proceeds.'

'A radio station!' I said, intrigued. 'How quaint. But tell me, Tara, do you happen to have his number about you anywhere?'

'As a matter of fact I do,' she said. 'Do you have a paper and pen handy?'

'Oh, yes. I think you'd better give it to me before any-one else hears this latest piece of intelligence.' I wrote down the number and placed it beside the phone for use in a moment's time. 'You'll come in tomorrow and I'll have the contracts drawn up?' I asked her.

'Yes, not too early though. I'm planning on sleeping in for once.'

'Well, let's say mid-afternoon then. Now, can I trust you with something?'

'Of course. Haven't I just trusted you with that piece of P.W. gossip?'

'That's exactly why I'm going to ask your advice on something. It's about who's going to take over James's job when I go. Listen to this idea, but hear me out before saying anything. It's got a lot more going for it than you might initially think.'

The first meeting. Tommy arrived promptly in my office at 11 a.m. and I was pleased about that as I had a busy day ahead of me and wanted to get all these problems resolved before Christmas. For a moment, I didn't recognize him. I hadn't seen him in about a fortnight, since the afternoon that I had spoken to him in his apartment, and we had only enjoyed a couple of quick phone calls in the meantime. He'd taken a week's holiday, if that's the right word, at a health farm and had enrolled in a drug rehabilitation programme on an outpatient basis, which made me proud of him.

'Tommy,' I said, looking up at him as he strolled into the office, having seduced his way past my secretary without having to be announced. 'What have you done to yourself?' His hair was cut short into a dark, tufty French crop. His contact lenses were gone and he wore an elegant pair of circular glasses with a pale thin shell outer rim. He was dressed in a light, casual suit and he looked healthier than I had seen him in quite some time.

'I decided to make myself a little less obvious in the streets,' he said. 'Not that it'll be that long before I'm forgotten anyway.'

'Well, it's certainly made a difference,' I said, impressed by his new, mature look. 'You look a lot better. Is it for a part?'

'No, it's for me,' he said smiling. 'Like I could get a part right now. Do you have any idea what the insurance premiums on me would be like?'

'Well, not off hand, no,' I said, indicating the chair

508

opposite me. 'But I take your point. Sit down anyway. I'll order some coffee.'

'Tea for me,' he replied as I buzzed the intercom and asked for some refreshments. 'Well,' he continued looking around him casually, 'this place doesn't look very festive. What are you, some sort of Scrooge or something?'

'I'm the Ghost of Christmas Past,' I said. 'But I haven't had time for Christmas decorations. It hardly seems worthwhile to me. The years all go by so fast. They're blending into one.'

'And there are *so* many of them too, right?' he asked with a grin. I could tell that he was still sceptical about what I had told him, but I also knew that he vaguely believed me because he was maintaining a certain nervous distance from me which was unlike him.

'There've been a few,' I acknowledged. 'So how's Andrea?' I asked, changing the subject; I figured that having gone through the whole story once with him I didn't want a repetition of it. He had been the only person I had told in 256 years and I guessed that it would be a while before I spoke of it again. He could believe or not; it was his choice.

'She's enormous,' he said, laughing. 'But she's due any day. She's terrified it's going to come tomorrow.'

'Yes, she mentioned that to me before,' I said. 'Well, time will tell.'

'We're thinking of getting married, you know,' he said and I looked at him in some surprise.

'Really?'

'Just thinking about it. She's stood by me pretty well over these last couple of months. We've said that if we decide to get married we'll wait for one full year between making the decision and doing the deed.

509

Just in case. We don't want to do it just for the baby's sake.'

'That sounds sensible,' I said. I picked up a paper-weight off the desk and examined it carefully, hesitating slightly before getting down to business. It was one of those rare possessions that had travelled with me everywhere; I had stolen it in Dover around 1759 and it had been all around the world with me since then. 'Tommy,' I said, suddenly changing the subject. 'I wanted to talk to you about something.'

'I figured that,' he said. 'Your summons sounded pretty urgent.'

'Well, it's not *that* urgent,' I said. 'But it's something I want to sort out. First of all, what exactly are your plans for the future? Or have you yet to decide?'

He exhaled loudly and looked around as if I had just asked him for the meaning of life. 'I don't know,' he said after a long pause. 'I honestly don't know.'

'The show isn't going to take you back? Now that you're cleaning up your act?'

'No,' he said, shaking his head, 'definitely not. The public don't care any more so I'm out. I'm contracted to two further weeks of work within the next couple of months so they're giving me the testicular cancer after all. They're going to kill me off. It's going to be quick and painful.'

'Oh, I'm sorry,' I said, feeling a bizarre urge to comfort him and ask him whether there was anything I could do to make him more comfortable.

'Well, there was always a chance that it would come back,' he said sadly. 'We were prepared for that. So what can you do? It's going to strike quickly, so I'll be coming back from my three month holiday in America and straight into hospital where I'll linger just long enough to learn that Tina is going to have my baby and to have a quick affair with a hospital nurse who's going to get sacked a couple of weeks later and become a barmaid in the local pub, the way people do. They're hoping to groom her as the next Sandy Bradshaw.'

'That a fact?' I said, only barely listening. 'Well, there we are. End of a chapter I suppose.'

'Nine long years.'

'A novel then. Never mind. Every good novel has an epilogue and so will you. What does your agent say? Are there any parts for you? Can you surprise us all and rise from the ashes like a phoenix?'

He laughed and shook his head. 'There won't be any parts for me for a *long* time, Uncle Matt,' he said. 'I'm virtually unemployable. I'll be lucky if I can get a job in pantomime this year and anyone with a glove puppet can get one of those. Which is so fucking irritating because I'm *good* at what I do.'

'I'm sure you are,' I said.

'And I *know* that business like no one else does. You can't spend half your life doing something and not pick up on every aspect of it,' he said, shrugging his shoulders. 'I don't know what I'll do.'

'Well,' I replied, putting my cup down on the table and leaning across towards him, 'that's what I wanted to talk to you about. A job. I think *I* might have something for you.'

'I don't need charity, Uncle Matt,' he said and I couldn't help but laugh inside, considering the thousands of pounds I had already given him over the last few years, idiotically funding his drug habits. He hadn't known such high-minded principles then.

'It's not charity,' I said. 'I need someone and I think you might be the man for the job. I *think* so anyway.

I'm taking a bit of a risk but you're the one who's always saying how he knows the television industry inside out. Tell me this, Tommy. Do you really want to be a star, or do you just want to work?'

He shrugged. 'Like I said. I've been a star. It doesn't interest me or attract me at all.'

'Good,' I said, smiling and leaning back. 'Then it's time to get to work. How would you like to run this place?'

He blinked and looked around, as if he wasn't quite sure what I was referring to. 'What place?' he asked. 'You mean here? The station?'

'Yes.'

'You want me to work for you?'

I grimaced. 'In a manner of speaking. I'd still be the shareholder. The major shareholder now, in fact. I want you to manage the place. Day to day operations. Complete, operational hands-on management. James Hocknell's old job. The one I'm doing now. What do you say?'

He looked astonished, as well he might, for I was making him an exceptional offer. 'Are you serious?' he asked and I nodded. He burst out laughing. 'Do you really think I can do it?' he added in a quieter voice.

I wasn't sure, to be honest, but I wasn't about to tell him that. I trusted him. And I believed he meant it when he said that he knew the industry. 'Yes, I think you can,' I said. 'There's just one other thing that I should mention.'

'Yes?'

'Lee Hocknell.'

'Ah.' Tommy nodded and looked a little bit abashed. The mention of Lee brought back memories of his

512

overdose to him; to me it meant something a little more serious.

'I had a chat with him the other day,' I told him. 'He's not pursuing that other business any more, thank God. Your little brush with mortality bothered him a little I think. But I've offered him a staff writer's job here. How do you feel about that?'

'Why?' he asked in surprise. 'Don't you want rid of him?'

I shrugged. 'I don't know,' I said. 'His father was a good friend. I owe it to him. I told him, however, in no uncertain terms, that if he ever again mentioned the circumstances of his father's death, I'd . . . well, I told him that I'd have him killed.'

'You told him *what*?'

I laughed. 'Well, I didn't mean it, obviously. But he wasn't to know that. Anyway, he knows that we didn't do anything to his father so he's happy enough. Just a little scared. I suspect he'll use this place as a stepping stone to something else. Probably best if he does too. Just give him the evil eye whenever you see him around the building. He's just a boy. He frightens easily.' Tommy laughed and shook his head in bewilderment. 'So come on,' I said. 'About the job. What do you say?'

He looked at the ground and shook his head, smiling. 'You're a very unusual man, Uncle Matt,' he said after a moment. I laughed.

'I have my moments. Well? Yes or no? Or do you need time to think about it?'

'No,' he said, and for a moment I was amazed, and disappointed. 'I don't need any time to think about it. My answer is *yes*.'

*　　　*　　　*

513

The second meeting. I dropped in to Caroline's office around lunchtime and she was standing in the middle of the floor, looking around her in confusion as if she had lost something, but couldn't quite remember what it was.

'Are you all right?' I asked her and she spun around, a hand to her chest in surprise.

'I didn't see you there, sorry. No, I'm fine. I just wanted to make sure I hadn't forgotten anything, that's all.'

'Right,' I said. 'Why, are you going now?'

'I certainly am,' she said gleefully. 'A full week off as well.'

'Well for some,' I replied, pointing to the chairs. 'Let's sit down for a few minutes, shall we?' She stared at me for a moment, as if fearing the worst, and chose the side of her desk to relax against. 'What are you doing for Christmas?' I asked in an attempt at conversation. 'Visiting your father?'

'God, no,' she said with a scowl. 'You're not going to believe this but he's marrying some *child* in Bermuda. I mean *I'm* practically old enough to be her mother. She's obviously just after his money. I mean it's hardly his body, is it?'

'I wouldn't know,' I said, feeling there was nothing to be gained by telling her that this was not in fact news to me. 'Perhaps it's love,' I added, just to irritate her. Bad of me, I know, but there you are.

'I'm going to my mother's in fact,' she said. 'She'll probably drive me crazy after about fifteen minutes but if I don't go it's just her and the cats and she's likely to shove her head in the oven instead of the turkey.'

'Why would she want to stick her head in a turkey?' I asked, and Caroline gave me a withering glance. I coughed and continued. 'Right. Well, look, there was

514

something I wanted to talk to you about before you went.' I had questioned the sense of holding these two meetings on Christmas Eve, but I figured that one would have a positive outcome and the other probably wouldn't. And even this *could* go well, I thought, although it seemed unlikely. What was important was that *I* wanted to have the whole business settled by Christmas. 'You have spoken to your father then,' I continued.

'Yes, of course. Last week. Why?'

'Ah. Not since then, no?'

She looked at me suspiciously and came down from the desk, settling into a chair instead. 'No, why do you ask?'

'Well, firstly I wanted to talk to you about the job,' I said. 'James's old job.'

'You always call it *James's old job*, Matthieu, despite the fact that you've been doing it for the best part of six months. Why is that?'

'Has it really been that long?' I asked. 'Good Lord. It's no wonder I'm feeling tired.'

A smug smile crossed her face. 'You've made a decision then,' she said and I nodded.

'I'm making a few changes. Firstly, you'll be pleased to know that all is well with Tara Morrison. She'll be back from the first of January and will spend a couple of months researching the best type of news programme we can put on. We're hoping for perhaps a March first premier.'

'Excellent,' she said, nodding. 'That's a good decision,' she added firmly as if I was reporting to my superior officer.

'I've also made my decision about James's old job and I have to admit that you were right on one thing.

You don't have to work your way through every step of an industry ladder in order to reach the top of it. You just have to understand the way that the ladder is put together.'

'Thank you,' she said, grinning enthusiastically as if I had just offered her the job, 'I'd like to think that I've proved that with the way I—'

I held up a hand to silence her. 'For that reason I have decided that I should go with someone who has shown a great deal of enthusiasm, a real track record in the business and, moreover, an understanding of the television medium. Someone who understands what the public want and will give it to them. Someone I trust absolutely.'

A long silence. 'Yes?' she whispered.

'The new managing director is going to be Tommy DuMarqué,' I finally said. She blinked and, after a moment, burst into laughter.

'Tommy DuMarqué!' she roared, as if this was the most ridiculous idea ever. 'You've got to be kidding me. The soap star?'

'Not any more. He's got testicular cancer.' Her eyes and mouth opened wide like a fish and I quickly qualified that. 'His character has, I mean. He's being written out of the show. You know about this whole drug business that's been—'

'I know he's your *nephew* is what I know,' she shouted. 'You're giving the top job here to your nephew, a self-confessed drug addict who sleeps with his sister-in-law and has never even stepped outside of London in nine years? What kind of qualities are those? What kind of experience?'

I stared at her in amazement. 'I think you're mixing up the—'

516

She didn't care. 'What on earth are his qualifications, Matthieu? Can you tell me that?'

'Yes,' I said firmly. 'I can. I just did. He's passionate, he's capable, he's knowledgeable. He's also turned over a new leaf. And I think he can do the job. That's qualification enough.'

'And you think it'll stay turned, this new leaf of his. For God's sake, he'll probably just roll it and smoke it!'

I thought about saying something but didn't. She shook her head as if I had gone crazy.

'Well, I'm sorry,' she said eventually. 'But you'll just have to tell him that it's not on.'

'I can't do that, Caroline.'

'Well, then, you're going to have to find a way, all right? You and Alan might have a majority shareholding between you but I still control thirty per cent and I will not have that man as managing director.'

I sighed. 'Caroline, those shares were your father's to control, not yours. They're not there just to give you a good job.'

'Nor are they there to employ dubious members of your family. You can get on the phone to Tommy right now and cancel whatever ridiculous offer you made to him or I'll do it myself.'

'You're not a shareholder,' I insisted.

'*My father is!* And while he's in—'

'Your father *isn't*,' I said, over her shouting, and she stopped immediately.

'What are you talking about?' she asked. 'Of course he is. He owns thirty per—'

'Your father has sold his shares,' I informed her. 'I'm sorry to be the one to tell you this, he should have told you himself. He sold them, Caroline. You don't control them any more.'

She shook her head again and I could see tears spring into her eyes.

'You're lying,' she said, although she knew that was not the case.

'I'm afraid not. I'm sorry.'

'Who did he sell them to then?'

'To me,' I said. 'Obviously. So you see I do have control over these matters. I'm sorry if you're upset but I don't want to lose you from here. Honestly, Caroline, I don't. Tommy will, in time, make whatever changes he sees fit but I promise you, on my honour, that as long as I have controlling interest in this television station there will be a job here for you.'

She nodded and looked at the ground, having nothing more to say. I took this as my cue to leave and stood up and walked to the door.

'The thing is,' I said as I went, 'I've never had any children. And I've never really owned my own business before, oddly enough. Putting Tommy in charge . . . well, it turns it into a family business. And I like that idea. He's about to become a father himself. I'm sure you can understand.'

There didn't seem to be anything more to say so I returned to my office. A few minutes later I heard her own door shut and her high heels disappearing towards the elevators, and I sighed with relief. It was done. I was free. It was over.

I could go home now.

Chapter 26

An Ending

Eventually, all the stories and all the people blend into one.

My memory is good and my mind is alert but there have been times when I have struggled with names within this memoir and I must admit that there are one or two people along the way – some of the mothers of the Thomases for example – to whom I have either been forced to give pseudonyms or to ignore altogether. There are too many people to remember and 256 years is a long time.

Almost everyone is dead now anyway. Jack Holby and I escaped England without being captured and travelled to the continent, where we separated after a few short months. Jack travelled on to Scandinavia and I never heard from him again. I am pleased that I didn't betray him and have always had a curiously indeterminate feeling towards Dominique's death; sometimes one can realize that a person is unworthy of love and love them anyway; one can form an unexplainable attachment that cannot be broken even when the object of one's affection breaks the confidences with which you entrusted them. Sometimes the one you love is blind to your feelings and for all your conversation you cannot find the words to explain it.

Tomas, the younger brother whom I had left behind to live with Mr and Mrs Amberton, grew up and came to find me in my new home in Munich, where he began a brief career as a bank robber and was bludgeoned to death by a teller on his twenty-third birthday. Perhaps I should have taken him with me originally as planned.

I've made a lot of mistakes in my life but at least I got it right in the end. Because Tommy is alive. He started work the day after Christmas and has already come to me with a dozen good ideas for the future. I'm officially retired. He'll do fine.

My plans for the day were simple. The city was alive with preparations for the new year celebrations and the last thing I wanted to do was to make myself part of that insane conference of drunkards, prophets, terrorists and plebeians who felt a sudden urge to mark a moment in time with other members of their species. I could imagine the scene only too well, for I had been there before.

I've seen the century turn twice already and now another is upon me. I never grow tired of living. People today find it hard to believe what things could be like a hundred years from now, as if their level of advancement is as good as it gets. But when I was born you travelled on horses and in carts; now we travel to the moon. We wrote with pens, on paper, we sent letters in order to communicate; not any more. We have found a way to escape the very thing which our existence guaranteed us – life on this planet.

And so I went for a walk. I put on a coat and a scarf, for the winter had set in and I could feel the cold suddenly, and took a walking stick from a fine prop in my hallway, a wedding present from Bismarck's secretary on the occasion of my eighth marriage (to her, as it happens), and stepped out on to the streets of London. I walked for several hours until I grew tired. I felt an urge to wander the streets and set off through Charing Cross Road, across to Oxford Circus, up to Regent's Park and London Zoo which I hadn't visited in years. I turned for Kentish Town and had a sandwich and a beer in a pub which was decorated for the festivities. At three tables in a row were an old couple, concentrating on their food and happy in each other's silent company, a middle-aged husband and wife drumming their table irritably, looking stressed and exhausted already, and a teenage couple, both wearing what I took to be new clothes and new haircuts, laughing, joking, touching, feeling, kissing. During one such kiss, the boy's hand strayed gently to her breast and she slapped it away laughing, and he stuck his tongue out at her with a wide smile, balancing his thumb on the tip of his nose and waving his fingers dramatically before they both dissolved into giggles, and I laughed too.

I strolled through Camden Town, down towards St Pancras and around by Russell Square and Bloomsbury, where a small park opposite an enormous red-brick hotel had been covered over with a tarpaulin in preparation for the night-time celebrations. Eventually out on to the Tottenham Court Road, towards Whitehall and into St James's Park where the crowds were gathering already, my signal to return home and soon. To the front of the Queen Victoria Memorial, where I stood and stared at the palace for a few moments, briefly recalling my three visits, a dreadful romance, and the characters I had seen occupy the building which faced the millennium with a nervous swallow. And then back home, to Piccadilly, where I closed the twentieth century behind me, those two simple words which seemed to imply progress and revolution and hope and ambition more than any others, and prepared to see in its successor.

The phone rang in the evening around six p.m. I picked it up warily, ready to refuse any last minute invitations. However, it was Tommy on the line, calling from the same hospital where he had lain in a coma a few months earlier.

'Congratulations,' I said, smiling widely when he told me the news. 'And how's Andrea? Is she all right?'

'She's tired. But she'll be fine. It wasn't a difficult labour. Well, not for me anyway . . .'

I laughed. 'That's wonderful news,' I said. 'I'm very happy for you both.'

'Thanks, Uncle Matt,' he said. 'And listen, I want to thank you again for what you've done for me. This is a new start. I feel like my life is going to begin today. I'm off the show, I'm getting healthy again. I've got a family, a great job.' He paused and I didn't know what to say; he was truly grateful and it made me feel wonderful to have succeeded for once. 'Just . . . thanks,' he said.

I shrugged. 'Don't mention it,' I told him. 'What are uncles for? Now, tell me, what are you going to call him? You know we haven't had a plain old "Tom" in about eighty years. How about that? Or maybe "Thomas". Or is that too formal for a baby?'

Tommy laughed. 'I don't think we'll be using either,' he said and I blinked in surprise.

'But it's tradition,' I said. 'All your forefathers have always called their—'

'We're thinking of Eve,' he said quickly.

'*Eve?*'

'Yeah. It's a girl, Uncle Matt. Sorry to disappoint you, but we've had a baby girl. I'm afraid I've broken the cycle. You think you can deal with a niece for once?'

I laughed out loud and shook my head. 'Well, I'll be . . .' I said, truly amazed by the news. 'A girl. I don't know what to say.'

I hung up the phone and stood there for a few moments, lost in thought, finally running out of words. I'd never anticipated a baby girl before but somehow it seemed right. I was happy for him. And for her. It was a new start, a fresh line. Maybe there would be no more Tommys from now on. Eventually I shook myself out of my reverie and began to walk slowly back towards the living room. I stopped at the bathroom and stepped inside for a moment, switching on the light above the sink by the small string that controlled it. Turning on the tap, I bent forward and allowed the cold water to run through my fingers for a moment. It made me shiver but then, pausing for a moment with a towel in my hands, I caught sight of my face in the mirror. There was no doubt about it. I was in tremendous shape for a man my age. But, as I looked closer, I noticed some small lines beneath my eyes where no lines had been a few weeks earlier. And my hair, always an attractive shade of grey, looked as if it was beginning to turn white. And below my left ear a mark was spreading which looked dangerously like a liver spot. I stared at my reflection in surprise and held my breath.

I pulled the cord sharply and the light went out.

THE END

The House of Special Purpose
John Boyne

'An exciting, fast-paced story . . . absorbing and richly satisfying'
THE TIMES

RUSSIA, 1915: Sixteen-year-old farmer's son Georgy Jackmenev steps in front of an assassin's bullet intended for a senior member of the Russian Imperial Family and is instantly proclaimed a hero. Rewarded with the position of bodyguard to Alexei Romanov, the only son of Tsar Nicholas II, the course of his life is changed for ever.

Privy to the secrets of Nicholas and Alexandra, the machinations of Rasputin and the events which will lead to the final collapse of the autocracy, Georgy is both a witness and participant in a drama that will echo down the century.

Sixty-five years later, visiting his wife Zoya in a London hospital, memories of the life they have lived together flood his mind. And with them, the consequences of the brutal fate of the Romanovs which has hung like a shroud over their marriage . . .

'John Boyne brings a completely fresh eye to the most important stories. He is prepared to look at the dark, yet somehow manages to find whatever light was there in the first place. He guides us through the realm of history and makes the journey substantial, poignant, real. He is one of the great craftsmen in contemporary literature'
Colum McCann

'Boyne writes with consummate ease, and is particularly good at drawing the indecently rich world of the pre-revolutionary Romanovs'
INDEPENDENT

9780552775410

Mutiny on the Bounty
John Boyne

PICKPOCKET JOHN JACOB TURNSTILE is on his way to be detained at His Majesty's Pleasure when he is offered a lifeline, what seems like a freedom of sorts – the job of personal valet to a departing naval captain. Little does he realize that it is anything but – and by accepting the devil's bargain he will put his life in perilous danger. For the ship is HMS Bounty, his new captain William Bligh and their destination Tahiti.

From the moment the ship leaves port, Turnstile's life is turned upside down, for not only must he put his own demons to rest, but he must also confront the many adversaries he will encounter on the Bounty's extraordinary last voyage. Walking a dangerous line between an unhappy crew and a captain he comes to admire, he finds himself in no-man's land where the distinction between friend and foe is increasingly difficult to determine . . .

'An excellent story . . . written with a total command of naval expertise, without ever spilling into pedantry, Mutiny on the Bounty is storytelling at its most accomplished'
INDEPENDENT

'A mesmerising tour-de-force . . . this is a remarkable and compelling piece of storytelling'
IRISH TIMES

9780552773928

The Boy in the Striped Pyjamas
John Boyne

'A small wonder of a book . . . a particular historical moment,
one that cannot be told too often'
GUARDIAN

What happens when innocence is confronted by monstrous evil?

NINE YEAR OLD Bruno knows nothing of the Final Solution and the
Holocaust. He is oblivious to the appalling cruelties being inflicted
on the people of Europe by his country. All he knows is that he
has been moved from a comfortable home in Berlin to a house in
a desolate area where there is nothing to do and no-one to play
with. Until he meets Shmuel, a boy who lives a strange parallel
existence on the other side of the adjoining wire fence and who,
like the other people there, wears a uniform of striped pyjamas.

Bruno's friendship with Shmuel will take him from innocence to
revelation. And in exploring what he is unwittingly a part of, he
will inevitably become subsumed by the terrible process.

'The Holocaust as a subject insists on respect, precludes criticism,
prefers silence. One thing is clear: this book will not go
gently into any good night'
OBSERVER

'An extraordinary tale of friendship and the horrors of war . . . raw
literary talent at its best'
IRISH INDEPENDENT

'A book that lingers in the mind for quite some time . . . a subtle,
calculatedly simple and ultimately moving story'
IRISH TIMES

'Simply written and highly memorable. There are no monstrosities on the
page but the true horror is all the more potent for being implicit'
IRELAND ON SUNDAY

'Stays ahead of its readers before deliving its killer-punch final pages'
INDEPENDENT

NOW A MAJOR FILM

9780552774737